Books by Sarah Shankman

Impersonal Attractions
Keeping Secrets
Now Let's Talk of Graves

as Alice Storey

First Kill All the Lawyers
Then Hang All the Liars

NOW
LET'S TALK
of GRAVES

• *Sarah Shankman* •

POCKET BOOKS
New York London Toronto Sydney Tokyo Singapore

AUTHOR'S NOTE: This book is a work of fiction. Names, characters, places and incidents are the product of my imagination and are used fictitiously. Although Comus is the name of a real krewe in New Orleans, this story is not based on any real characters or events associated with Comus.

POCKET BOOKS, a division of Simon & Schuster Inc.
1230 Avenue of the Americas, New York, NY 10020

Quality Printing and Binding by:
BERRYVILLE GRAPHICS
P.O. Box 272
Berryville, VA 22611 U.S.A.

To Lynda Rodolitz
and to the memory of Allan Jaffe
of Preservation Hall—for the good times

Special thanks to Ann Culley in Raleigh and Joseph Epstein in New Orleans for reading, for many kindnesses, and for generous advice. Jane Chelius, a love, and the best of editors. Dana Isaacson, kiss kiss. Matthew Gee, computer wizard, you saved my life. Harvey Klinger, superb agent, prince, and shrink. Johanna Tani, copy editor extraordinaire. Luisah Teish's *Jambalaya* (Harper & Row, 1985) was an invaluable resource for voudou. And to Stanley Dry, best of all—for your heart, mine.

Let's talk of graves, of worms, and epitaphs;
Make dust our paper, and with rainy eyes
Write sorrow on the bosom of the earth;
Let's choose executors and talk of wills.
                                        —*Richard II*

•

One

•

They hit Sam with the Hurricane right at the gate.

Laissez les bons temps rouler. Let the good times roll.

The unofficial welcoming committee, a bunch of free-roaming drunks, left her holding a tall glass of the strawberry-colored kick-ass punch that had made Pat O'Brien's famous—that and the piano players' dirty songs. "Long John," the one about a hard-driving dentist, had been Sam's favorite when she was a teenager, used to pack six in a car, make the long trip down from Atlanta for Mardi Gras. Drunk as skunks Saturday through Fat Tuesday. Nobody'd ever heard of *underage* in the Big Easy of the sixties.

Now, on the day before Mardi Gras, half past noon, twenty-odd years later and ten years sober, Samantha Adams shifted the long black garment bag she was carrying over one shoulder and looked around the Delta gate for a place to put down the drink.

Over at the edge of the waiting area Harry Zack was watching Sam —though he didn't know her yet. He was watching her because she was a tall, very pretty brunette, a lot easier on the eyes than the pie-eating lady evangelist who'd caught his attention on the pay TV, courtesy of the chubby young blonde in the waiting area who'd been stuffing the TV meter with quarters. The evangelist was famous in New Orleans; her name was Sister Nadine. The pie Nadine had in one hand, the one that wasn't holding the tambourine, looked like lemon meringue to Harry. Looked pretty good, though the tall, very pretty brunette with the head full of soft dark curls looked sweeter. Trying not to be too obvious about it, Harry slid his eyes up Sam's legs. Up to her great chest. Elegant nose. He had a thing about women's ears, but hers were hidden behind the curls and silver hoop earrings. She had huge brown eyes, and a classically beautiful face that reminded him of some star he'd once seen in an old movie on TV.

Then his imagination skipped over the how-do-you-do-my-name-is-could-I-call-you-sometime-first-second-third-date business and he wondered—after all that—where would he take her? If, after a leisurely lunch at Galatoire's, making love to her from the very first minute with his mind, his eyes, little sighs, lots of good wine, she said yes? Where would they go, skipping hand in hand out of the restaurant together?

He closed his steel-gray eyes, the one on the left having less far to go —the lid drooped just a little. He could see the place in his mind. A cottage at the Maison de Ville in the Quarter. Jammed with antiques. Bathtub big enough for two. Bed even bigger—draped with old lace. The perfect love nest.

Now, wouldn't that be nice?

Take it to the Lord in prayer, the TV blared as Sister Nadine cut loose. Harry opened his eyes and the bedroom vanished. But the brunette, with a smart-alecky sort of grin on her pretty face, hadn't.

It's you she's staring at, Harry Zack. You, right there.

But it wasn't Harry she was seeing. Sam was grinning off into space, seeing her friend Kitty Lee in her mind. Kitty, who was supposed to meet her at the gate. Kitty, who was always, chronically, since they'd been roomies twenty years ago at Stanford, late. Kitty, yelling at her on the long distance every day for the past week: *Why don't you hurry up and get your butt over here, gonna miss the whole goddamn Mardi Gras. Don't make the Comus Ball your ass is grass might as well stay home.* Then, when Sam finally did get a breather, filed her story on the shooter picking off some of Atlanta's finest citizens like deer right through their picture windows, left the *Constitution* and its Byzantine problems behind her, grabbed the last seat on the flight—now, where was Kitty? Well, hell, hadn't everyone always said that woman would be late to her own funeral?

Sam's gaze focused. *Not bad,* she thought, zeroing in on Harry. Not bad at all. In fact, in the looks department, great. Wide brow. Nice nose. Couldn't see the color of his eyes from here. Blue, maybe. Or was that gray? High cheekbones with bright spots of color just beneath. Fair-skinned with a dark shadow of stubble. Wide mouth—a little pouty. That look was in, wasn't it, at least for models. Well, he could model. Broad-shouldered and lean, though not much taller than she. A ringer for Paul Newman's son. Grandson? Oh, Lord. He *was* pretty

young. Pretty *and* young. That wild tangle of black curls could use a
shearing. So is that what she'd say to him if she got the chance? *Young
man, you could do with a haircut.* Sound like his aunt. His mother.

Well, hell, why not? Younger men were in fashion these days,
weren't they? And she'd been considering, so far only in the abstract,
the possibility of grabbing up one for her own amusement. And, matter
of fact, it wasn't as if the handsome young man in the rumpled raincoat
wasn't staring back. Of course, he might just be thinking about stealing
her pearls. But more likely he was searching for an opening line. She
straightened her back, give him her good profile. Thirty-nine and a half
wasn't, by God, dead and nailed down. Not yet.

Harry caught Sam's look and flashed her a little smile. Then, suddenly shy, he looked away, his gaze searching for a place to light, land-
ing on the chubby young blonde whose rear was a real tight fit in the
TV chair. She seemed to be mesmerized by Sister Nadine and that
lemon meringue, licking her lips and fingering a little gold crucifix.
Another necklace spelled her name out in big gold letters: TERI.

He wondered what the pretty brunette's name was. Laura? Suzanne?
He sneaked a look back at her. Whoops. She was still staring. Waiting
for him to make the first move, maybe. Jesus! He stared down at the
floor, up at the ceiling. He'd *promised* himself next time he'd have one
ready. Well, sucker, this *was* next time. And what did he have to pull
out of his bag of tricks? Nothing more than a handkerchief. Thank God
for small favors—it was clean. But he needed it, he was sweating like a
pig. He blotted his forehead, swiveled his gaze back to the chubbette.

While he was waiting for the right side of his brain, the so-called
creative half, to kick in, come up with something clever to say to the
brunette, he'd practice his new trade on this lady. He was an insurance
investigator now, right? So investigate.

He'd start with age. How old was Teri? Nineteen? Twenty?

(How old was the brunette? Old enough to be interesting, that was
for sure. But not *too* old, and, when a woman was as attractive as that,
who was counting?)

Back, boy, back. Okay, Teri, her baby in a wet Pamper squalling on
the floor beside her. Well, that's what happened to them, girls from
Westwego, Mandeville, Slidell, maybe over the state line, Pass Chris-
tian, Biloxi. He was warming to it now. They got married, got pregnant, got fat, and the good times were over before they were old
enough to vote. Droves of them rolling carts out into the K Mart park-

ing lot. Disciples of Sister Nadine. Leading the good ol' dead-end fat-ass life.

The blonde turned her head, catching him staring. Wasn't that always the way? Well, he didn't want to say anything to *her,* which meant he could probably chat her up like crazy. But lookahere! What a nasty shiner she was wearing.

No mystery there for crack investigator Harry Zack. Miss Teri hadn't gotten the chuck on the table quick enough to suit ol' Billy Bob. Or hadn't properly chilled his Dixie beer.

But she'd hang around for a while yet—time for Billy Bob to break an arm, some teeth. Harry had seen more than he cared to of women like her. They made him sad, but you couldn't make them listen. She'd have to come to it in her own time, hang around until she got fed up lying about running into doorknobs. Then she'd take Junior there and split. After about two payments, Billy Bob'd get behind on his child support. The next thing you know, he'd decide she shouldn'a got custody of his only begotten son anyhow. He'd sneak over to the baby-sitter's, sweet-talk her in that way he had, grab that kid and—Harry peeked back at the brunette. Oh, hell. She had company now. What difference did it make if he were batting a thousand making up stories about the blonde, when all he wanted to do was sidle up to the brunette, give her the big slow smile he'd inherited from his daddy, say howdy?

Kitty Lee had no problem doing that: "Lord have mercy, Sam, if you ain't a sight."

Sam grinned at her. There she was, ladies and gents, redheaded, blue-eyed Miss Kitty Lee, still five foot two, hadn't grown an inch.

"Sorry," Kitty said, breathless. "Couldn't find a parking spot. Bastards wouldn't let me leave it at the curb, like I used to. *Nothing's* like it used to be. Jack-in-the-Boxes and Burger Kings. Not a single sign left of graciousness and gentility."

Sam snatched her into a big hug. "Thank God for Kitty Lee. Mouth going one hundred twenty-two miles per hour. State patrol ought to ticket that thing."

Kitty stood back, tiny feet wide apart. If Jimmy Cagney had been born a southern woman, he'd have been named Kitty. "You're right! But shut up and let me take a look at you. Damn!" All this out of the side of her mouth. "Still beautiful, goddamn *unnecessarily* tall, and abso-*lute*ly right. I am *so* glad to see you." Taking Sam's arm and pulling her along. "Come on, let's go get your luggage and blow this dump. Grab some lunch, go home and visit with Ma Elise. She's dying to see you."

"And me her. Let's git." Sam could feel her Southern shifting into third gear the second she laid eyes on Kitty. "What are we waiting for, three choruses of 'Dixie'?" She hefted her garment bag and a tote.

"That's your luggage? That's it? Oh, Jesus, spare me. I couldn't get my undies for a weekend in something like that. Are you sure you—"

Sam jiggled the bag. "Turquoise-blue silk to the floor. Caroline Herrera. Hideously expensive. Shameful décolletage displaying thirty-nine-year-old bosom intactus. Gonna knock 'em dead at that ball."

"Oh, Sammy! Most of 'em already are. Ancient and pickled."

"Well, what the hell? I'll dress for you. We'll kick up our heels. Swig us some *serious* root beer."

Harry'd give a lot to see Sam—wasn't that what Kitty Lee'd called her—in her ballgown. Maybe he could get ol' Kitty, one of his big sister Sudie's best friends, to introduce them later. But that very minute, the Delta flight from LaGuardia had arrived at the next gate, and he faded to invisible behind a column.

Here was the lady he'd been waiting for, the one he had business with —the one who swore she'd suffered severe whiplash, not to mention all kinds of emotional trauma, when her little tobacco-brown Mercedes coupe had been popped from behind.

She sure didn't look like she was feeling any pain right now, this redhead scooting right along in a too-tight white jumpsuit, big shoulders, with a red fox coat thrown over one arm. You'd think the gentleman of Italian descent in the dark, shiny suit who'd been waiting for her would carry the coat, what with the whiplash and all. But maybe the gentleman—whom Harry knew to be Joey the Horse, a famous, in some circles, man-about-town—was having a hard time remembering about the neck injury. The lady, whose name was Chéri, wasn't wearing her neck brace, or much of anything else, under that jumpsuit. Now she was tossing her red hair like a mane and twisting her neck this way and then that to kiss Joey on both cheeks. Not just once, but twice. Well, she was French, Chéri, right?

The camera Harry carried in the canvas duffel over his shoulder was clicking away like crazy.

Yes, indeedy, his uncle, his mama's brother, Tench Young, and, more important, sole proprietor of Young Preferred Reliance Insurance and Investment Company, was gonna be right proud of him.

Harry, he'd said not too long ago, now here's your chance to stop breaking your mama's heart, straighten up, and fly right. Come work for me and learn to be an insurance investigator, join the real world, give up that crazy songwriting dream, and get real. Son, 'fore you know it, you'll be a vice president. Take over old Preferred Reliance from me when I get ready to step down from this son of a gun.

Hell, why not? Harry had given Uncle Tench the slow smile. Why not bag the off-again-on-again jobs—cab driver, process server, oil-rig jockey, anything he could think of to maintain his reputation as a hell-raising bad bad Uptown boy pretending he was trash. After all, *boy* was losing some of its cute, especially since he'd awakened one morning a couple of months ago after a night of too many Dixie beers and too few women and realized he'd crossed over the line into thirty while asleep.

Harry clicked off another couple of shots of the sashaying Miss Chéri. Yep, Uncle Tench—who never paid a dime to anyone unless they could prove beyond a shadow of a doubt that their claim was purdee, absolute, no question about it, watertight, not even to a pretty woman, yeah—Uncle Tench was gonna be right proud of this boy. Correction, young man.

Out past the automatic sliding doors Sam and Kitty and Joey the Horse and Chéri all sort of banged together—everybody except Harry, who'd faded off to one side, not wanting to be seen.

"Excuse me," said Joey the Horse, bowing a little at the waist, always the Old World gentleman around the ladies.

Sam smiled.

Kitty smiled.

Harry smiled too—at the back of the cab dispatcher, who just then glided by where he was standing sort of hunkered down behind a luggage cart.

Which is why he didn't see what happened next. Sam did though. Eagle-eyed reporter never missed a trick.

What happened was this: A little guy—young, light hair, slight build, snub-nosed cute, the Michael J. Fox type, and about that size, smaller maybe, five-four or -five—started walking through the crosswalk over to the sidewalk where Sam *et al* were standing, when just about the same time a gigantic white stretch limo belonging to none other than Joey the Horse started to pull in curbside.

The little guy, still on the other side of the car from Sam, yelled something. She didn't quite catch it, but she could fill in the blanks.

Then the little guy slapped his hand up against the driver's window, which began to power down.

Slow.

Real slow.

Then the door whapped open. Hard. Knocked the little guy down. A huge black driver looking like a Sub-Zero refrigerator-freezer in a powder-blue suit was standing there, looking sub-zero cool behind his shades, staring down.

Then, as if in slo mo, Sam watched the little guy reach into his jacket. Uh-oh. She'd been witness to this kind of scenario several times in a professional capacity, but this was vacation, thank you very much. She grabbed Kitty's arm, jerked open the door of a cab waiting at the curb, pushed Kitty inside, and fell atop her, head down.

"Drive," she said.

"Lady, I have to wait till my dispatcher—"

There were popping sounds outside now, like a car back-firing. Three times.

"Drive, dammit! I'll make it worth your while."

He drove fast—just like in the movies—and for a good long time before he asked, Where to?

"Bourbon Street." Sam sat up off the grumbling Kitty when the coast looked clear, ran a hand through her curls, and said, "I didn't come all this way to spend my afternoon as a material witness to one goddamn more shooting when I could be eating oysters at Galatoire's."

Two

The tourists on Bourbon Street were waiting in a long line. Galatoire's takes no reservations—except the walk-to-the-front-of-the-line-if-they-know-you kind.

"Miss Lee," the man at the door had said, and, smiling, had passed them right on in. Sam had to admit she liked that.

It wasn't until they were at a table in the middle of the one bright, high-ceilinged dining room, waiting for a glass of white wine and Sam's Perrier, that Kitty came to.

"I left my car in the goddamn parking lot."

"Oh, my God!"

They laughed like young girls, heads back, mouths open wide. Well-tailored businessmen at neighboring tables smiled at them. *Bons temps rouler.* Why not? It was New Orleans. Carnival time. Anytime.

"So later we'll go back. Maybe we'll run into G.T., you remember her, Aunt Ida's granddaughter. Wait, *great*-granddaughter. She's over to the house a lot and maybe she'll give us a ride back out. Got herself a job as an ambulance driver." Then Kitty looked up at their waiter, who hadn't bothered them with a menu. "Gerard, I'll start with the shrimp remoulade, then the trout meunière."

Sam ordered oysters en brochette and trout Marguéry. She'd been dreaming for weeks about the battered and fried oysters with bacon and lemon on toast. And the Marguéry sauce: a thick yellow roux chock-full of shrimp and mushrooms.

"Soufflé potatoes and green salads," the waiter suggested. "And little dishes so you can share?"

Sam nodded. Here was a man after her own heart. She sipped her water and looked around. "Kitty, you remember that time we were here with—what *was* his name? Chauncey? Boisvert? Duplessy? Trey? One of your fancy New Orleans monikers, but I know it ended in a Jones."

"Well, I guaran-damn-tee you he's never forgotten *your* name, sugar pie. Not even after twenty years. Every once in a while at a party, real late, this dreamy look comes over Boley Jones's face and he says, 'Kitty, do you know that time in Galatoire's your friend Sam from Atlanta took all her clothes off and—' "

Sam was somewhere between flattered and embarrassed. "Well, hell, you can't let every little old thing that ever happened when you were on the booze keep you out of places. Hell, I'd have nowhere fun left to go. You either."

"Why, what on earth do you mean?"

As if she didn't know. Kitty had always been one to kick up her heels. Had even turned her high spirits, her way with people into her very own, very profitable public relations company.

Now Sam watched Kitty reach into a pocket of her sea-foam-green silk blazer and pull out a silver lighter and a pack of Picayunes, a local brand. She lit one of the forty-plus cigarettes she would smoke that day, sucked the smoke down, and exhaled hard.

The cigarette's funky aroma took Sam right back. She closed her eyes, remembering how the Quarter used to smell on steamy days when she was visiting Kitty from school, before the Jax Brewery over by the river became a bunch of boutiques. The smell of Picayunes was rich, yeasty, always bespoke New Orleans.

Kitty.

And Eddie Simms.

For it was that same smell which lingered in the still, quiet San Francisco bedrooms where Eddie, a southern boy who smoked Picayunes while he worked, had left the carved and cross-hatched bodies of women he'd come calling on with a Buck knife and a bouquet of snow-white roses. Sam's series about him on the front page of the *Chronicle* had earned her prizes as well as several job offers, including the one from the *Constitution* that had taken her home to Atlanta a couple of years before.

Now she was telling Kitty how that move was looking like a less than judicious one, as the then-newly-serious *Constitution* had run aground.

"So what's happening now? Sounds like you're up to your ass in rattlesnakes, that piece I read about the newspaper in *Vanity Fair.*"

"Just about. Pit vipers. We should have known Kovach, the editor, wouldn't last. It's been a mess since the suits with the calculators ran him off. Should have known they weren't going to let the man run the newspaper as if folks were literate. Wanted to read the *news,* for chris-sakes. *Graphics,* the suits say. Give 'em color pictures, like on TV."

"Doesn't sound good."

"Excuse me, ladies." Gerard was back with their food.

"It ain't, sweetcakes. But let's don't let it ruin a perfectly good shrimp remoulade." Sam reached over to Kitty's plate and speared a bite of the cold shrimp smothered in creole mustard sauce. "Ummmmm. Maybe I'll find work in New Orleans. Lunch here every day. The Bon Ton. The Bistro."

"Wait a minute, before you get me deep into lunch, I just want to know, you gonna fish or cut bait on the paper? Or do you have a choice?"

Sam shook her head, her mouth full of shrimp. Then: "They're not firing people, if that's what you mean. Folks are just disappearing. Going off on vacations that are really job interviews. Hell, we lost our Pulitzer-winning political cartoonist, turned around, and stole yours." She pointed with her fork. "The *Times-Picayune's*."

"*Et vous?*"

"*I*'ve had offers. It's that I feel like I only got back to Atlanta. I'm just getting used to it again, speaking Southern, getting the freeways down."

"Any other game in town if you want to stick around?"

"Certainly no other newspapering. And the great old days of magazining there are long gone."

"So?"

"Right now I'm planning on eating shrimp and oysters till I pop." She caught the waiter's eye and pointed for more of both. "Hoke— that's my managing editor—keeps trying to tell me things are gonna turn around. He's wrong. The only thing's gonna turn is me. Turn forty."

"Isn't that a shame?"

"You too, toots."

"Yeah, but you go first. You'll be sure and let me know how it feels?"

"Probably about like a swift kick in the tuckus."

"You know," Kitty said, leaning back in her chair a little. "I've been giving this matter a lot of serious consideration, and I've decided Perrier makes you mean."

Sam laughed. "You could be right. But the tradeoff with bourbon is that at least I have all my shoes now."

"Oh, yeah. You and your Ferragamos. Dropping 'em all over the Bay Area." She leaned back even farther in her bentwood chair.

"You know you look just like an old man chomping on a cigar when you do that?"

Ignoring her, Kitty continued. "Tossing your tennyrunners in the gutter 'cause they pinched."

Sam couldn't resist joining in, poking fun at her former self. "Spending half my days buying new ones and every night getting rid of them 'cause I never broke 'em in before I was wasted again. There must have been a trail over half of northern California of my eight and a half double A's."

"To the old days." Kitty raised her glass.

"And the new, improved ones." Sam paused. "The nineties an improvement? I can't believe I said that. Drunk or sober, I miss the hell out of the sixties, don't you?"

"You better know it." Then Kitty got serious. "The drinking here gonna bother you? You know what Carnival is."

Sam shook her head. "Amateur night. Give me some interesting folks, something worthwhile going on, the alcohol's no problem. Not that boozers are exactly the crowd I hang with these days."

"Except for me."

"Except for you." That was a joke. Kitty drank, but hardly kept pace with most New Orleanians. "So, listen, about Carnival, I didn't get a chance to ask you what's this business with the callouts—those things that came along with the invite? And just by the way, sending it registered mail was cute but unnecessary."

"Why, honey, we have to make sure invitations don't get in the mitts of the hoi polloi who are lying in wait for them. We're talking about the Mystick Krewe of Comus here. We're talking tradition back to 1851. We're not talking fly-by-night."

"What I really don't understand is how on earth do such fine folks put up with *your* mouth?"

"No choice. Whole thing's hereditary. 'Course, *I'm* not a member anyway. Comus is an old boys' club. Brother Church belongs. Daddy did. I get it from both sides, actually. My mama's daddy was Comus too." Kitty waved an imaginary fan. "We ladies just come along with our gent'men, like any other property—cattle, cotton. 'Course, I was a *Queen* of Comus. Third straight generation. My mama, Estelle, God rest her soul. Grandmama, Ma Elise. This year Church's Zoe makes it an uninterrupted fourth."

"I know you've explained all this rigamarole to me a million times. But—you know I've never been except when I was a kid."

Kitty nodded. "In the street with all the other riffraff. That's the *public* Carnival. Krewes put those on for everybody. The balls are another matter. 'Course, even some of them are public. But *not* Comus. God, taste this trout."

"Eat half and we'll swap plates."

"When did you turn into such a *gourmand?* Not that you weren't always a healthy eater, but—"

"*Gourmet,* my dear. You know how we recovering drunks are. Got to have something to obsess about. Food's my latest. I've even become a rather spectacular cook since Peaches is never in our kitchen at Uncle George's. She's too busy teaching all of Atlanta how to read with her literacy campaign."

"Well, you've definitely come to the right place. In this town we've always talked restaurants before sex or politics. Even beats football."

"You think I could get the recipe for this sauce?"

"We'll ask Gerard. Now, is there anything you want to know about the ball tomorrow night?"

Sam whispered, "Maybe we shouldn't even be talking about it here —it being so secretive and all."

"Secretive?" Kitty hooted. "Darlin', you don't even know the meaning of the word. *Exclusive* is what we're talking here. You've got your attitude on crooked. Why, there are still geezers grousing about having had the Duke and Duchess of Windsor as guests of honor forty years ago. What with *her* past. And poor old Huey Long never got an invite to anything. Made him so mad he tried to ban Carnival. Might as well have tried to close the river down."

"No wonder most people just drink in the street."

"Great. Great. That's the thanks I get for breaking my butt to get you in. I had to put your name in to the invitation committee months ago to get you certified."

"Come on." Sam laughed.

"I'm not kidding. You think the Piedmont Driving Club over in Atlanta is something? They are *nouveaux* upstarts compared to us. I want to tell you your pedigree *barely* got you in."

"Yeah, well, you know how seriously I take all that bull."

"Oh, my, yes. You always were so proud of trading in your debut for that little green Triumph you had at school. You're the biggest reverse snob I've ever known, *Miz* Adams. But your uncle George still flies the flag, doesn't he?"

"Belongs to the Driving Club? Sure, for business. But since his retirement he never goes. Now, lay off my grand egalitarianism, and quit changing the subject, and answer my question about this callout business. I didn't come all the way over here not to know what's going on, make a fool of myself."

"They don't call them reporters for nothing, do they?" Kitty rolled her eyes up at the ceiling. "Okay, okay, callouts are dance cards—of which I wangled you two. Your name gets called out loud when it's your turn to dance with the gentlemen who have sent you the callouts."

"And the rest of the time I boogie with whoever I want?"

"It's more like a waltz than the boogie, and the rest of the time you sit. There are only about six tunes, and the members first have to make sure they've taken care of their own women. So two puts you in the Ms. Popularity stakes. With none you'd sit up in the balcony and watch with the other biddies who'll be checking you out through their mother-of-pearl binocs. Who's *she?* they'll say."

"You think I'd come all the way from Atlanta to *watch?*"

Kitty sighed. "There are local women who have never done anything *but* watch. You don't understand how exclusive this all is. How *important* to us. Why, there have been *threats* over callouts not forthcoming. Acts of vengeance over queenships. *Suicides.*"

"Why don't those who are snubbed just move to another town?"

"Because—"

And then Kitty realized that Sam was putting her on. No matter that Sam had chosen to skip her debut in Atlanta, that she had lived for many years in California, or that she had a liberal education and an even more leftish turn of mind. Once a belle, always a belle with those Deep South sensibilities—even if they were well hidden most of the time.

"Quit wasting my breath with your bullshit, woman," Kitty said.

"You're absolutely right. We have more important things to worry about. Like does Galatoire's still make jelly crepes for dessert? And where's our coffee?"

Three

In the Crescent City, drinking in a neighborhood bar is a legitimate and time-honored avocation that has nothing to do with which side of the blanket a man was born on or the amount of cash in his pocket. Such bars are egalitarian clubs where Uptown and Downtown mingle, where one sees old and new friends and neighbors, exchanges gossip, bets on sporting events. The clientele is mostly male, though not exclusively, New Orleans being an equal opportunity drinking town.

The Pelican on Magazine was such a bar, a few blocks downtown and riverward from the house in the Garden District which Kitty Lee shared with her grandmother, Ma Elise. In fact, the Pelican was the very spot where Kitty's husband, Lester, the well-bred prize who had come her way after she was Comus queen as easily as if he popped out of a Cracker Jack box, had literally lost his mind. On the eve of their first wedding anniversary, Lester Lee, Kitty's second cousin as well as her husband, had pulled a .38 out of his jacket and splattered said mind all over the Pelican's well-oiled mahogany. Right now, at just about that very spot, sat the red-haired Chéri whom Harry Zack had followed.

It had been easy to tail the big white limo from the airport to Chéri's house on the very private Audubon Place—a location so private, in fact, Harry had had to park his car outside the gate and do an end run around the guard on foot. He'd strolled by Chéri's great cream-colored Victorian extravaganza just in time to see the lady jump out of the big car, pop in her front door. No sooner had the white limo pulled out of sight than she'd popped out again. While Harry watched from across the street, she backed out of her driveway in a blue Mercedes coupe, a twin, except for the color, to the one she'd cracked up. Probably a loaner—or, who knew, maybe the lady had a spare. Then she wheeled over to the Pelican, a place Harry knew but didn't frequent, tending to do his hanging out in the Quarter near where he lived.

As Harry had sauntered in, about ten beats after Chéri, the barman had stopped polishing glasses to greet her. She'd leaned across the bar for the big buss, working that pretty neck again, and kissed him on both cheeks.

Now, down at his end of the bar, Harry signaled for a Dixie draft. Chéri gave him a quick glance with nothing on it, then turned back to the barman, who was named Calvin. "You would not *believe* what happened at the airport. Here, at Moisant, I mean. My friend picked me up, and just as his car, his limo, pulled in, this little bitty guy who was crossing the road on foot, like, took offense. Thought the limo had cut him off. Beat his little tiny hand on the window. My friend's driver, who is this gigantic black dude, got out and I thought, Oh, Jesus, sucker's bought the farm now, driver's gonna turn him into *mah nez*. Then right next to us this car backfired, and that little dude, he—"

"Crapped his pants," said Calvin.

"No!" Chéri shrieked, getting high off the telling of it.

Harry looked around the room. The whole bar's attention was focused on her, which it would have been anyway considering that she was the only pretty woman there and certainly the only one in a too-tight white jumpsuit unbuttoned to East Jesus.

"No! Lissen! What he did was, he fainted. Fell out right there in the middle of the road. Thought he'd been shot, I guess. The driver just picked him up like he was a little old kitten and held him in his arms till this cop car made it on around the circle and they called an ambulance. I tell you, the traffic was a mess. We stayed there, couldn't get out till the ambulance came." Chéri flopped her red mane. "Hit me again, Calvin." She paused for a moment, downed the drink. "Did you know," she continued, "they have women ambulance drivers? I didn't know that. But this one was. Pretty black woman, young, about my age give or take a year or two."

"You thinking about getting yourself a job driving an ambulance, honey?" asked a portly, red-faced Uptown lawyer whom Harry knew to be Maynard Dupree.

"You think I ought to, Maynard?" Chéri dimpled.

"I don't know. You did, casualties might get up off their stretchers and walk on into the emergency. Healed by the sight of you." Maynard let his eyes drift down slow to her bosom, like he was being cool, forgetting that his wife, Marietta, sometimes played tennis with this woman, a fact that, when he thought about it, was a puzzlement indeed. "You know what I mean?"

"Oh, Maynard," laughed Chéri, twisting and posing on the barstool like a beauty queen, "can't you just *see* me racing through town with that siren blaring?"

Harry pushed his duffel bag with the hidden camera a little closer, getting what he hoped was a good shot of her long neck preening, with the front page of the *Times-Picayune* he'd dropped on the bar in the picture. With the date showing. Yep, Uncle Tench was gonna be proud of him all right, all the money Harry was saving him and Preferred Reliance Insurance on Chéri's claim.

Just about then a tall, lanky man in a pearl-buttoned shirt, sitting down the bar from Maynard piped up. "You say the woman driving that ambulance out at the airport was a skinny black bitch?"

"Now, watch your mouth in front of the lady," warned Calvin.

"Sorry, ma'am. No offense," he said.

Harry had seen this man—long, tall, looked like a cowboy in his jeans—where? Yes! When he was working rigs off Grand Isle. Pipe-handler. One of those nervy, macho bastards fitting new lengths of pipe onto old while the end was still drilling, whirling a couple hundred miles an hour.

"No offense taken." Chéri dimpled at the tall pipe-handler, proving she was a good ol' girl who could hang with the best of 'em. "You're right though. Driver was skinny. Skinny, light-skinned woman."

"Bet it was G.T."

Calvin nodded. "Bet it was, Jimbo."

Jimbo. Harry *knew* he'd seen him before. Jimbo King.

"That G.T.'s Jimbo's neighbor, lives in the other half of a duplex, double shotgun, over on General Pershing, right off St. Charles," Calvin was explaining. "Jimbo's always bellyaching about her. Messing in his bi'nis."

"Who's bellyaching?" Jimbo leaned into it. "And the street's General *Taylor.* Not General Pershing."

Calvin jumped back as if he realized a good bartender never would have stepped out that far anyway. "Hell, Jimbo, you know what I mean."

"Yeah, well, you'd be griping, too, some bi—some*body* wouldn't even let you have a fight with your wife without sticking her nose in."

"You ought not to be fighting with your wife in the first place," Chéri put in.

"Well, I'll tell you, pretty lady, you may know what you talking about when it comes to *your* life—fancy clothes, talking about limos and show*furs*—but not *my* life. Times ain't been this bad in the oil bi'nis since, shit, since things was powered with steam. That's why wim-menfolk is acting so uppity." He turned away from Chéri now, addressing the other men. "Wimmen'll do that when you got so much weighing on you you cain't hardly see over it. Just keep pushing and pushing. Trying to wear the pants."

"That's what you were saying before," said Maynard. "When you were talking earlier about your wife. What was it you said to her?"

"You mean after she got back up off the floor?" Jimbo grinned.

Harry looked away, stared out toward the door. Slimeballs like this made his flesh crawl.

Jimbo answered Maynard. "Said, 'Cain't you see I'm carrying a heavy load here, woman? Man out of work don't need none of your shit.'" Then he paused for a sip, following his shot of bourbon with a slug of diet Dr Pepper. He ignored the pout growing on Chéri's face like she'd been popped by a bee.

Harry didn't miss it though. Then he looked back at Jimbo. *Mean* sapsucker—sucking his *diet* soda through his crooked grin and his bad, white-trash teeth. Yeah, a man like Jimbo would think diet pop was just the thing when he was out of work. Laying up, his lean would turn to blubber when times were bad. But Harry could see Jimbo had lost neither lean nor mean.

"So what'd she do then?" asked Maynard.

"After she picked herself up off the floor? She commenced to screaming."

"And then?" Maynard asked, then looked around, hoping he didn't sound like he was getting off on this tale—which he was.

With that, Chéri pointed her pretty nose in the air, picked up her soft suede bag and said, "'Scuse me, *gentlemen,*" coming down hard on that last word, then wheeled back to the Ladies.

Jimbo didn't miss a beat. "Why, then, she got up on her high horse and started badmouthing my plans."

"What plans are those, Jimbo?" asked Calvin.

Maynard turned his big bright meaty face to look at Calvin, who sneaked him the tiniest of winks.

"The plans for my getting on the 'Tonight Show.'" Jimbo paused, then belched. "With the lawn chair."

"The lawn chair?" Maynard repeated, asking the question in that way lawyers do.

"Whyn't you tell our friend here about it?" Calvin poured Jimbo another shot. Gave Maynard another little wink.

"Well," said Jimbo, "I'm gonna fly out to my old rig in a lawn chair so's to show them dumbasses in Washington what a man can do iffen he's got some ingenuity. What *they* ought to be doing, they wasn't so busy jerking off."

"Ought to be flying in lawn chairs, you think?" said Maynard.

Harry could see the effort it was costing Maynard to keep a straight face.

And he was right. Maynard was wondering, what the hell was this redneck talking about? And, more important, was there any action in it for him? Maynard hadn't gotten to be where he was—senior partner of his law firm, chairman of the United Way, not to mention captain of Comus (a not-very-well-kept secret)—by just sitting around snapping at flies, not knowing how to figure the percentages. *That* was for damned straight.

"Yep. I read in this paper about a guy flew a whole long way out in California tying a bunch of helium weather balloons to a lawn chair. Got up to sixteen thousand feet. Got on Letterman, too. And he didn't even have anything to prove. But I do, see?"

Maynard said, "You think it'll make a statement to the gov'mint?"

"Yeah, that's my plan. That's her, all right."

Jimbo kind of hunched himself forward on the bar for a minute, then leaned back and looked Maynard up and down. Taking in his thousand-dollar gray wool suit with the little chalk stripe, fitting just great over his prosperous belly. The fat, well-barbered cheeks. The short, dark hair. The almost-handsome face, the muddy brown eyes a little too close together. The buffed black calf lace-ups. The gold cuff links. The serious watch.

"Well, fuck a duck, man." Maynard leaned over and slapped Jimbo on the back. "I think that's a damned great idea."

Jimbo's pale eyes shifted just a tad. "Whut is?"

"Your plan. It's fantastic."

Jimbo considered that for a minute. Harry could see it in his eyes: *Fantastic* was a word used by sissies who usually slugged their single-malt Scotch at the hoity-toity Bombay Club. "You do, huh?"

"Sure, I do. Might even be willing to get behind it with you."

"Whadd'ya mean?" Jimbo's eyes moved slowly, considering, the way country people do.

"Put some cash into it. Help you get some publicity."

"Why'd you wanta do that?"

" 'Cause I think the U.S. gov'mint sucks. Letting this city go down the tubes, that's for damn sure, selling our oil bi'nis out to the Ay-rabs."

"Damn straight," said Jimbo. He lowered his shot glass to a spot on the bar which Calvin had just wiped clean. Let it sit there for a minute. Empty.

Maynard didn't get to be chair of the United Way being stupid.

"Calvin." Maynard signaled with a forefinger. Two more. One for him. One for his buddy—the wife-beater. "I can't believe your wife doesn't think it's a fantastic idea too."

Ah, Harry thought. Now we're getting back to the part of the story that interests old Maynard.

"Hell, you know how they are. Women never appreciate a damn thing you do, are always trying to get things their way."

"So what happened?"

"Happened? I slapped her 'round some more. Didn't really hurt her. Tiny little ol' trickle of blood coming out of her mouth. *That's* what really set off that colored girl we wuz talking about. The ambulance driver, my next-door neighbor, that G.T."

"What'd *she* do?" asked Maynard.

"Banged on the door. Called up on the phone. Said she'd already called the cops. Said she was getting Teri out of there if I was gonna beat her bloody. Like it wuddn't Teri's house. Teri's bi'nis. *Our* bi'nis."

Teri. Harry's mind flicked back to the necklace on the chunky blonde he'd seen earlier in the airport. The gold letters spelling out TERI, her name. The shiner starting to come on, purple and blue. The wet baby squalling. Teri watching Sister Nadine. Waiting for a plane to get the hell out of Dodge or just waiting?

"The cops come?" Maynard asked.

"Yeah. They come. It was all over then. Nothing for 'em to see."

"Teri'd shaped up?"

"Nawh. She went on over to that bitch's. I let her go." Then Jimbo revised that. It didn't sound right. "I *told* her to go. I said, 'Get the hell out of here. And don't come back either.' "

"Unh-huh." Maynard shook his head.

"Hell, I had enough truck with the cops. Don't need no more. Besides, it's better that way. She'll be sorry soon. Come crawling, begging me to take her back in."

"I wouldn't count on it if she's staying with that G.T.," Calvin said. "Everybody knows she's a witch, practices that voodoo. Dyke too, prob'ly. She's gone have your Teri turned queer, Jimbo, you don't hurry up and get her back."

"Shee-it." Jimbo dragged the word out so long you could see it like a smudge of paint, then slapped his empty shot glass down on the bar again.

Maynard gave Calvin the nod.

"You know," Jimbo said, turning his glass this way and that, staring into the amber liquid as if it could tell him things. "I been thinking seriously about stringing up that little old voodoo queen."

Maynard laughed nervously. The way little boys do, Harry thought, when they realize they've wandered into a big boys' game.

"Nawh. I ain't kidding." Jimbo shook his long blond hair back out of his eyes, stared right at Maynard. "What you think about killing her?"

"What are we talking about here, Jimbo?" Maynard's voice climbed an octave.

"*We* ain't talking about nothing, man, 'less you decided you want a piece of this action too." Then he got real slow and real sly, giving it some. "Along with my flying-lawn-chair deal."

Calvin laughed. Harry allowed himself a little smile since nobody was paying him any attention anyway. Jimbo, he thought, wasn't as dumb as he seemed.

"I don't think you ought to talk about killing people," Maynard said, "Even joking. It's just not good bi'nis. You can't never tell what might happen. I mean, something *might* happen, and then people'd remember what you said."

Jimbo leaned across the bar and slapped Calvin on the shoulder. "You see, Calvin. That's why this man here's wearing the fancy suit and I'm busting my butt and wearing these raggedy jeans. Man knows how to *think*."

"That's right," said Calvin. "That's what lawyers get paid for is thinking."

"That's right," said Jimbo. "So what you're telling me you're thinking, see if I got this right, is that if *you* were fixing on killing somebody, you wouldn't say nothing about it? That right, Mr. Dupree?"

"That's right." Maynard grinned, comfortable again with words, terms, definitions.

Yeah, Old Maynard was feeling like a quarterback now, Harry thought. The stud hoss from University of Virginia. Calling the shots. Everybody looking at him. Not knowing they thought he was a fool. "I wouldn't breathe a word. I'd just *do* it." That's right. Maynard Dupree was a man of *action*. Sheeeeit.

Jimbo and Calvin slapped high-fives, a salute to Maynard Dupree and his way of doing things.

Slick.

Yep, yep, thought Harry. Slick bullshit.

Just about then Chéri made her way back down the bar, finished in the Ladies, a fresh coat of orange lipstick glistening.

"Well, don't you look pretty," Maynard said. "I sure hope we didn't say anything to offend you, Chéri."

"You couldn't offend me if you tried, Maynard Dupree." She smiled, but with something behind it. Harry thought she'd been cogitating on more than lipstick and hair spray during her trip to the Ladies. "But I was just wondering, seeing as how, you being the captain of Comus and all, running things, and that pretty little Zoe Lee getting to be Queen of Comus this year . . ."

Maynard gasped. Way to go, Chéri. Harry grinned. Got him. The identity of Queen of Comus was a *big* secret, the kind Uptown stiffs took more seriously than death or taxes.

Chéri went right on. "I was just wondering if that's why you were sitting around this bar tying one on like any other N'Awlins trash, if it stuck in your craw that Zoe's being queen . . ."

"How do you know that?" Maynard sputtered.

Chéri didn't even blink. "As I was saying, Zoe Lee's being Comus's queen makes her Miss Hot-Shit Society of N'Awlins this year. I mean, what with you being Comus's captain and seeing as how her daddy Church Lee is not exactly your best friend, it seems to me all you'd had to do was say *no,* blackballed her. But maybe balls *are* the question here. Am I right, Maynard honey?"

"Go fuck yourself," Maynard snapped.

"Now, wait a min—" Calvin started.

"Never mind, darlin'." Chéri grinned, picking up her orange fox and flinging it over one shoulder pad like *she* was the linebacker here.

Harry had to give it to her. Hell, if it wasn't his job to get in her way, he'd be glad to see her screw Uncle Tench out of a couple hundred thousand. She wasn't his type, but this past half hour he'd warmed considerably to her.

"Now that we know who's who and what's what, I think I'll just be moseying," Chéri said, then sashayed on out like she knew the whole room was watching her rear, which it was.

A few minutes later Harry drained his beer, threw some bills on the bar, and slid out. A couple of other men farther down the bar did the same now that the floor show was over.

As he passed behind Jimbo, who didn't even give him a glance, the pipe-handler was muttering, "We could do 'em both. That redhead and the nigger. Two-for-one deal."

"Throw in Maynard's buddy Church Lee," Calvin said, "and I bet you got yourself a taker."

And then they all three laughed. The pipe-handler, the Uptown lawyer, and the barkeep. Booze laughing. Booze talking. *Tough* guys, Harry thought. Jesus.

Four

•

Early the next afternoon, Mardi Gras, Fat Tuesday, in a big old house on Prytania Street in the Garden District, blue-eyed Zoe Lee was standing in her candy-striped bedroom, staring at her naked self in a full-length mirror.

She didn't like what she was seeing.

Of course, no woman ever does. Breasts too large, too small, cockeyed, too low, too long. Then you could move on to waist, bottom, thighs, knees, calves, upper arms. But why bother? It's always the same song—taught to them by their mothers, their grandmothers, all the way back to Eve, who got it from Adam that she was a little heavy in the keister and ought to try running a few laps around the Garden and laying off the pasta.

Who was Zoe to fight the tide?

Yet her story, like all stories when you look at them up close, was a little different.

Twenty-year-old Zoe Julianna Lee was five feet six inches tall and weighed an even one-twentieth of a ton.

At least that's how she always thought of her one hundred pounds.

"Gotta get the tons off," she said to herself, pulling her masses of dark curls atop her pretty head while she turned and squinted at a bulge on her backside.

To anyone else it would have been the beginnings of a cute behind.

She reached for the Ex-Lax. Chocolate. Radical. Yummy-yum.

Well, hell, what was a girl to do when she was, like, practically force-fed for an entire debutante season at one breakfast, brunch, luncheon, tea, cocktail party, dinner, supper, a grand total of five hundred disgusting party meals one right after another?

After all, this was New Orleans, where hostesses couldn't show their faces in public, not to mention *po*-lite society, if they didn't lay on buffets of oysters and shrimp and crawfish floating in béarnaise, béchamel, beurre blanc, cream, hollandaise, lemon-butter, mushroom, mustard, remoulade, and velouté sauces. And that was for starters.

Just the thought of the food she'd faced since the deb season began made Zoe want to puke, or, as her friend Chloe would say, talk to Ralph on the big white phone.

Zoe stepped into her pink and white bathroom and did that very thing, smartly.

Zoe was very good at praying to the porcelain goddess, or, as her father would say, vomiting.

It was one of her talents that Ma Elise, her great-grandmother, had failed to enumerate when catching Sam Adams up to speed on the family. No, Ma Elise hadn't talked to Sam, who was visiting Ma Elise and her aunt Kitty a couple of blocks away in the house where they lived together on Third Street, about Zoe's daily vomiting.

But, yes, Zoe actually did do a few things other than sleep, try on endless clothes (size three) which she wore to all those parties, and look at herself in the mirror—not that Ma Elise knew about them all.

For one thing, she was quite a little entrepreneur.

Her father, Church, was a doctor, right? Which meant he could write prescriptions, right? And left lots of those cute little 'script pads lying around, right?

Zoe had been able to fake his signature since she was eleven years old and began forging notes to her teachers down the street at Mc-Gehee so she could skip school and hang out smoking cigarettes in Lafayette Cemetery.

Actually, she got *very* good at signatures, so good, in fact, that it wasn't long before she was writing notes for anybody who had five bucks.

Another thing about Zoe—she was very careful with all that green. She didn't spend her earnings, but had it changed into silver dollars and built towers of gilt, castles, and silos of coins, all over her bedroom. They beat the hell out of dollhouses, except she had to dismantle them every day before the cook or housekeeper came sneaking around. No matter how many KEEP OUT—THIS MEANS YOU!!! signs she posted on her door, no one ever did. They had orders from her father to lurk— standing in for her mother, who had run off and left her long before the silver skyscrapers began.

It was very complicated, Zoe thought, this business in life of acquiring and losing. You could earn all the silver dollars you wanted to, and then, *poof!* someone could break in and steal them. Or you could have a mom one day, and then, *shazam!* she'd flown the old coop before her little biddy was even half grown. So much for all those stories about mother hens. And then there were pounds—as in fat. They were the opposite of money and mothers. Once you collected them, you couldn't *ever* get shut of them. They'd hang around for the rest of your life like glop on your waist and hips and thighs. *Disgusting.*

Some things you couldn't hold on to. Some things you couldn't lose. It was all very random. *Very* complicated.

But back to the 'script pads. By the time Zoe was twelve, she and her friends were serious devotees of uppers and downers. One of their all-time favorites was 'ludes. It was, like, *so* funny to watch people 'lude out and fall down, especially at those dumb dance parties their mothers (her father) made them go to, you could die laughing when people went *kaboom.*

Though after a while that got dangerous.

Oh, no, not the 'ludes. 'Ludes wouldn't hurt you. But getting caught writing 'scripts could. Like fry you. Like Big-Time Trauma. Like, puhleeze, who needed the grief?

Especially if you were a smart little girl like Zoe who could figure things out.

What Zoe had figured out a couple years ago, well, actually she hadn't figured it out—it was more like she fell into it, but that was a trick in itself, wasn't it? Like, some people could fall into a pot of gold and think it was just another pile of shit. Zoe kept her eyes open. She knew the diff.

It all started at her friend Chloe Biedenharn's first tea, the announcement party for her debut. Zoe was in the ground-floor bathroom behind the stairs in Chloe's grandmother's big old house over on St. Charles, honking up two or three stellar lines of coke by herself like a greedy porker, when Dr. Cecil Little came barging in.

"Why, excuse me, darlin'," he'd said, all flustered-like. He turned away, but she saw him sneak a peek. *That's* 'cause he thought she was taking a pee and thought he might *see* something. You'd think they'd get used to it, seeing something, since they were doctors, but they were *all* like that, all her father's friends and her friends' fathers—who were all the same people really. Trying to sneak peeks and cop feels and then pretend they weren't. It was enough to make you puke.

But *then* he caught her act, zeroed in on what she was doing.

"Why, Zoe darlin'," he'd said, easing back into the room with his long, skinny arms like a praying mantis and shutting the door.

Locking it. For a minute there Zoe thought she was going to have to yell *fire! fire!* which was what old Ida over to Ma Elise's house had told her to do when rape was in the air.

"You got some more of that sugar to share with your uncle Cecil?" he'd asked.

Boy, was she relieved. *That* was all he wanted. Why, sure, she'd said, reached in her little evening bag, hauled out her stash, and cut him two lines on the mirror of the solid gold compact her daddy'd given her for high school graduation.

Sure as shooting he'd dug out his wad of hundreds and peeled off one for tooting, then wiped off the damp end and tucked it down the front of her blue party dress.

"Don't guess you got any more where that come from, do you, sugah?"

"Why, Dr. Little"—and she truly was surprised—"I'd of thought you'd have plenty of access."

"Oh, no, Miss Blue Eyes. You ought to know doctors are *very* careful about that. Don't *ever* like to be holding."

"You don't say."

Zoe had turned back to the vanity by then, checking out her mess of curls, her lipstick, and brushing around her nose. There was nothing more embarrassing than coming back from the Ladies with coke all over your face. But all the time she was thinking.

"So what *do* you do for blow?" she asked.

"Grub. Like I did just now."

"That's not exactly grubbing, Dr. Little." She grinned, making her dimples real deep.

She knew that trick always caused a man like Dr. Little to want to stick his tongue in them. It was smart—to distract a man when you were doing business. 'Course, they just thought she was a dumb little twat they were chatting up, so they never figured that out. She'd learned the bit from watching old Bette Davis movies on the VCR. Girl didn't have a mama grabbed her role models wherever.

"I wouldn't call a C-note grubbing," she said.

"Well, hell!" He laughed his hearty there's-lots-more-where-that-came-from-little-girl laugh.

Then, like it was an egg she could hold in her hand, it came to her— oval and perfect and self-contained—her plan.

But right now, this very minute, the doorbell was ringing. They were here, the Mardi Gras army. Zoe threw on a pink silk robe and ran down the stairs.

Leading the troupe were her great-grandmother, Ma Elise, and Ida, who'd been with her a hundred years, the two little old ladies toddling in, leaning on each other, looking for all the world like a matched pair of salt and pepper shakers. Following them were Aunt Kitty and her friend Sam. They were all here to watch her get dressed and keep her company while drinking champagne and eating turkey sandwiches.

Close behind was the dressmaker she'd seen for a thousand fittings, who'd made the incredible white and silver gown she'd wear tonight with its mantle and a twenty-foot train. It was resting in a room of its own across the hall. The hairdresser was trailed by a makeup artist. Mr. Adler insisted on coming himself from his Canal Street store, carrying dark blue velvet boxes holding the diamonds and pearls her daddy had bought her. A lady from the newspaper asked a million stupid questions. She grinned for a photographer.

They would comb her and curry her and document her and then, for the last time this season, fold her into a limo. This time she'd be all by herself, she and The Dress (there would be room for no one else) and whisk her off to view the parade and on to the ball. And finally, except for the Queen's Breakfast, another *meal,* it would all be over.

Unless she stayed in New Orleans, of course, where no one would ever forget or let her forget she'd been Queen of Comus. Not for the rest of her life. Not for one red-hot moment.

Five

Sam stood transfixed at the edge of the glittering ballroom. And she'd spent no little time at fancy-dress affairs, having grown up in the white-gloved, I'm-so-charmed-to-meet-you Piedmont Driving Club, Sweet-Briar-or-Randolph-Macon-for-school, Smith-or-Vassar-if-you-were-smart set in Atlanta. She'd worn more than a few silver slippers and full-skirted ballgowns, but none of it held a candle to this Maskers Dance of the Mystick Krewe of Comus.

Just for starters, the security at New Orleans's Municipal Auditorium was drum-tight. Compared to this, the White House dinner she'd once attended with her uncle George was loosey-goosey.

The evening before, Kitty and Ma Elise had primed her with more details on the *enormity* of Carnival, the preparations for one beginning as soon as the previous year's was done.

"Every year each krewe—that's a carnival organization—" said Kitty.

"I *know,*" said Sam.

"—has to pick a theme. The newer, tackier ones choose things like TV shows or cartoon characters, pop stuff. The Old Guard sticks to the classics, mythology. Then, once you have a theme, there are the parade floats to be designed and built. Costumes to be made"—she ticked them off—"invitations, party favors, and doubloons to throw off floats for the crowds. And, *of course,* invitation lists to scrutinize."

"Courts to be chosen—and queens," piped up Ma Elise. The still-beautiful old lady was wearing a purple lace dressing gown, tucked into a wing chair, and sipping cognac half as old as she was. "Did Kitty tell you the one about the Queen of Rex whose pushy father insisted she be crowned? So that year's Queen of Comus, to whom she'd have to pay her respects when their balls ended, quietly resigned, and they replaced her with a shopgirl? So Miss Upstart Queen of Rex had to bow to a—

well, she was from a decent family—but to this Uptown crowd she was a nobody?"

Sam and Kitty laughed.

"What?" Ma Elise said.

"I think you just told her, Meems," said Kitty.

"Oh, well, anyway, where was I? Preparations—there are decorations for the balls, of course. Then scripts, sets, and costumes for the tableaux—those are where members of the krewes and their ladies pose like living dioramas, acting out stories. It's silly, really, you'll see. And, my goodness, music, food—lunches, dinners, post-ball breakfasts. All sorts of people to be seen to—float drivers, flambeaux carriers, cooks, waiters."

"It's like each krewe," said Kitty, "having at the most a couple hundred members, building the Rose Parade, a ballet, and an opera rolled into one every single year. And these are men with businesses to run, professions, families. Which is why the city's never moved out of the Stone Age."

"It's true." Ma Elise nodded. "But don't ever tell anybody we said so."

"Sure, it's a lot of fun," Kitty continued, "but it's also why everything's gone to pot. We can hardly compete with the state of Mississippi, for chrissakes, much less the Japanese, because all our energy goes into making parties, riding floats, fluffing up our ballgowns."

But now as Sam smoothed the skirt of her own deep turquoise gown and looked around this magnificent ballroom, she was glad these people had gone to all the trouble. The women were done up to a fare-thee-well in satins and ermines and bugle-beads, jet, and jasmine, and lace which had blinded more than one Belgian nun—puffed bouquets of ladies dressed by Lacroix, Saint Laurent, Chanel, and de la Renta—joyfully overdressed, overjeweled, and overperfumed. It was quite wonderful, this fantasyland of white and silver, Comus's theme this year being *The Winter's Tale.* Crystal chandeliers showered thousands of points of lights down on the costumed crowd. Masses of snowy lilies and roses, narcissi, and forced magnolias perfumed the waltz-filled air.

It was a spectacular explosion of diamonds and pearls, woodwinds and brass, a swirl of sound and illumination.

For the moment Sam put it out of her mind that Comus and this ball were a throwback to all that was snobbish, discriminatory, racist, and exclusionary.

Kitty and Ma Elise had talked about that last night too, explaining and bemoaning, yet in some ways justifying.

"The old-society, old-money version of Carnival has nothing whatsoever to do with what the public sees," Ma Elise explained. "Nothing to do with the hoi polloi, the *nouveaux,* and certainly nothing to do with blacks or Jews. I'm not saying that's right. I'm saying that's the way it's always been. Except that, you know, the very first Rex was a Jew named Louis Salomon, and, in fact, the organization of Rex has always had some Jewish members. But a Jew could never *be* Rex. Rex must *call* on Comus, don't you know, at the end of their two balls, and except for a very few spectators at the Comus ball recently, well, it's just not done—"

"That's—" Sam started.

"Ridiculous. I know. But that's how it is. Now, as for blacks, just like the gays, they have their own krewes, their own parades. In fact, Zulu is the first parade to roll Mardi Gras morning, throwing coconuts as favors. And did you see the black Indians?" Sam shook her head. "Oh, my dear, you must. Tribes like the Wild Tchopitoulas with the most fantastic costumes. Beading and feathers—and they dance. It's quite wonderful. And Comus still uses black flambeaux carriers to light the parade route. But that's all street business."

The *real* Carnival, Kitty explained, the one that counted, the one that the Lees knew, took place behind closed doors. The real Carnival traced its lineage back to the 1850s. It was controlled by private men's clubs like the Pickwick, the Boston, and the Louisiana, who in turn were the power behind the old-line Carnival organizations. Boston Club was mostly Rex. Pickwick numbered many of the Mystick Krewe of Comus. It was these clubmen's debutante daughters, like Zoe, who filled the courts of each year's balls. And those balls—which were conducted with all the formality and secrecy and protocol of the court of Louis XIV— were closed to everyone except that tiny, tight fistful of New Orleans's white elite who passed the torch from father to son. The *real* Carnival couldn't be broached, the keys not bought, begged, borrowed, or stolen.

And only occasionally was an outsider like Sam allowed a peep.

"Quick," said Kitty, a powder puff in pink and gold. "We'll grab those two seats." She pushed Sam right past the boutonniered committeeman who was trying to help them to chairs near the stage in the reserved callout section.

"She had first dibs." Sam nodded toward a titanic dowager upholstered in silver, who fixed them with a glacial glare.

"Tough titty," Kitty spat out.

So much for grace and gentility.

Kitty pointed toward the stage. "Here we go. Heads up. The processional's beginning." Trumpets blared. The masked king, a bowlegged old geezer in a short little doublet of white and silver, would have fared better in long pants than the obligatory tights. He took his seat beneath a huge sculptured crown of gold, looking for all the world like a bantam rooster. Then each of the six maids was individually presented with no less pomp than if it were her wedding day.

"Do they have to be blond?" Sam whispered.

"It helps. Blond and blueblooded."

"And rich."

"Not always. Some of them are born to the lace—good blood, no bucks. The organization passes the hat, but"—Kitty waggled a hand—"it's a hard way to go. Kissing ass for all those parties and clothes."

A riotous fanfare cut loose. The audience stood as one and applauded.

"Hip, hip! Hip, hip!"

"Elizabeth the Second, no doubt," said Sam.

Kitty shook her head. "No, it's Zoe. This is it—*the* moment. They say once you've been Queen of Comus you might as well die and go to heaven, 'cause it don't get no better."

The cheers swelled to a roar.

"And is that true?" Sam yelled above it.

"Sure was in my case. All the rest of it's been downhill. Forever after."

Sam turned back to Zoe, and memory transformed her into Kitty at that age. Kitty was a beautiful woman now, but Sam had known her then—unblemished red-gold and pink and cream. How dazzling she must have been in her diamonds and silk train. Like a dewy ripe peach about to be plucked—by Lester Lee. Gorgeous, dashing, aristocratic, crazy, weak Lester, who would blow his brains and Kitty's dreams to hell after 364 days and nights of love.

Sam shook her head, and the queen turned back into Zoe, who was in her own right quite heart-stoppingly splendid. When Sam had last seen her, Kitty's niece was fully made up and coiffed but had left her house in her underwear beneath a dressing gown so as not to wrinkle The Dress.

Here she was in full, glorious regalia. Though *far* too thin and pale, high spots of excitement colored her cheeks. And there was The Dress —that magnificent, low-necked gown of white satin embroidered with bows of silver sequins. Around her shoulders rose a high, plumed ruff of net and diamanté. Her diamonds and pearls were perfection, including a crown set atop her own glory of dark curls. Behind her flowed twenty feet of silver satin edged with ermine.

"Isn't she something?" said Sam. "Too bad she has to spend the evening chatting up the king. He looks like a real toad."

"He is. And older than Church. But his family's so grand, we don't talk about that."

"Her Majesty. His Majesty. Ladies. Lords." In a plummy voice the master of ceremonies tried to get everyone to settle down.

"Is that Bert Parks?"

"Nah. But he does have the same tan."

"And the same toupee."

Now the stage was aswirl with scores of masked lords and ladies pantomiming a scene from *The Winter's Tale.* Bowing. Scraping. Mincing. Posing.

"Isn't it a riot?" Kitty grinned.

"Sort of like the pageant in Mrs. Roussel's class—third grade."

"Exactly. And they're so *serious.* They've been practicing for months. It's the high point of their year."

"And yours?"

Kitty made a rude noise.

Sam laughed. "What's Zoe's take on all this?"

"Pretty sanguine. I get her out of here once in a while. To New York. Out to the Coast. She's got a fix on it, that outside of N.O. this means jack. You tell people you're going to be Queen of Comus and they say, Do whut? But these folks"—Kitty waved a hand—"they'd *die* if they suspected this wasn't the very epicenter of the universe."

So why do you stay here? Sam wanted to ask. Why do you do this year after year? But that was grist for a long sitdown. Not now. Not here.

The lords and ladies pranced for a while longer, then the tableau ended and the orchestra struck up. The king and queen took the floor.

"Let the dancing begin!"

"Miss Cynthia Butler!"

"Mrs. Archibald Ross! Mrs. Ross!"

"Miss Penelope Addison!"

Black-coated committeemen sporting yellow boutonnieres circled their section, calling out the names of the chosen ladies, who rose to take the arms of masked and costumed gentlemen.

"Did they forget us?" Sam poked Kitty, reminding her she hadn't come all the way from Atlanta to sit.

"Just wait. I told you, wives first, then mistresses and/or widowed mothers. They'll get to us after that."

Sam, hated cooling her heels. A dancing fool since she was big enough to bop, she wanted to be out there.

She closed her eyes for a minute, and Sean waltzed in on another wave of memory. Her sweet, redheaded Sean O'Reilly, San Francisco's hip-popping, slipping, and sliding chief of detectives, her own true love. They'd made lots of good moves together.

"Miss Samantha Adams."

They'd had a date to go dancing the night he'd flown up into the air above rain-slick Van Ness Avenue, tapping his way up into the sky, falling back dead. Stopped in the middle of his twirl through life by a drunk driver.

"Sam!"

Kitty was hissing in her ear. She snapped to. Easy does it. One ball-and-chain, one buck-and-wing at a time. She stood, ready to put her little foot right there.

"Miss Adams?"

A tall masked man in a golden costume was waiting. Giving her his arm. Leading her onto the dance floor. Now, this was more like it. Dancing with a stranger whose face you couldn't see was a hoot, the stuff of fairy tales.

"Mademoiselle." He bowed and brushed his mask above her hand in a kiss, took her in his arms, and whirled her out and about and around, her silk skirt swinging.

This was more like it.

Until he stumbled and almost fell.

Then she caught a whiff of whiskey from under his mask. Dragon breath.

Ditto her second partner.

Both drunk as skunks, having imbibed widely and deeply at the in crowd's bar behind the stage. Boys would be boys even if they were dressed up in fancy white tights and cloth of gold.

Fairy tales, indeed.

No Prince Charming for Miss Samantha in this bunch. Not tonight.

Nope, she was afraid that as in many things, her anticipation—shopping for the turquoise ballgown, flying over from Atlanta, primping and prettying—was the best part. The reality was a bunch of drunk snobs playing at court.

For fairy tales were just that, the stuff of young girls' and fools' dreams.

* * *

A couple of blocks away, General Taylor Johnson drove her great-grandmother, Ida, up to her house on St. Ann in the Quarter. They sat in the bright red ZZZ Service ambulance pulled up beside a NO PARKING ANYTIME sign at the curb.

"I don't know why you had to go to all this trouble, cutting your ambulance through police lines. I told you I could get home my ownself," Ida was saying.

"Maw Maw, if you don't beat all. First you think you're taking the bus, which isn't running downtown tonight anyway. You think you're gonna get yourself down here practically right in the front yard of the auditorium—which you couldn't get near tonight if you were God Almighty. 'Less He happened to know somebody in Rex or Comus. You'd think you gonna fly? You got that kind of gris-gris, old woman?"

Ida just sniffed and shot G.T. a look. Then she reached down somewhere inside her clothing and pulled out a little pouch, dipped some snuff behind her bottom lip, said, "Let me get on in my house, where ain't nobody fussing at me."

"In a minute. I want to finish telling you about what happened."

"Okay, go on. So the little skinny white boy you picked up fainted out at the airport is laying up in the back of the ambulance."

"And Arkadelphia and I—you know who Ark is?"

"The big fat white boy from up north Louisiana you drive with sometimes."

"Right, Ark and I are just cruising. You can tell there's nothing seriously wrong with the boy but the cops say haul him, we haul him. We're stopped at a red light right after we get onto Williams Boulevard headed toward St. Jude's. Next thing we know, people one car over start hollering.

"Ark, I said, we can't help those people no matter what their problem, we got a full house here, when finally I make out they're talking about our rear door." She turned around and pointed at the back of the ambulance.

"Lord have mercy, Ark said, we've done let him roll out in the middle of the road.

"But it wasn't that at all. The little dude had taken that opportunity, had flown."

"Just got up off that stretcher?"

"Like he had good sense. And I stood there in the street, the people in the next car pointing, and I see him, a little speck in the distance, making tracks like the devil's on his tail. I mean, moving."

"Tee-hee," Ida laughed in her high little-old-lady laugh. "I'd like to seen that. I bet it was cute."

"Well, it wasn't cute when we had to fill out the forms. There's eleventy-hundred forms on everything in this business. And the ZZZ folks don't take too kindly to our just *losing* a customer. We don't even know who to send the bill to."

"Well, won't you be glad, girl, when you in medical school. Don't have to be putting up with all this nonsense. Little white boys running away in the middle of Williams Boulevard."

"You don't think there's ever a place where there ain't crazy folks, Maw Maw, now, do you? Going to be the same folks I cart to that emergency room. Now, stop fumbling with that door. I'll come around and help you."

G.T. handed her great-grandmother out, feeling how frail she was, like a bird. She hated to think about that; besides, she'd been dreaming about weddings—a sign somebody close was going to die.

Then Ida—who had taught her her first chants and charms, how to light candles, build an altar—picked up on her vibes. "What you afraid of, girl?"

There was no use lying. Maw Maw saw right through her, easy as water-gazing. "Somebody passing."

"You been working the charm?"

"Twenty-third Psalm, morning and evening, three times each. Got my seven-day white candle going in a saucer atop my Bible open to it."

"Well. It'll work. Dark angel either pass us on by or the chosen'll go over peacefully."

"I hope so."

"Rest your mind, child, you think it's me. I'd tell you if it was, but it ain't my time."

G.T. relaxed. That was indeed what she'd been afraid of. "Well, I'm certainly glad to hear that, Miss Ida. Now, why don't I let you get on inside to take care of your company—how are Teri and the baby doing?"

"Just fine. I started her on the nine baths soon as you left her last night. Did the white bath to wash away the hurt her husband—what you say his name is?"

"Jimbo."

"That Jimbo laid on her. Let her know the goddess'll help look after her. The blue tonight'll calm her nerves. Need to get shut of that anger, put her at peace. Need to make her see she's got to protect herself."

"I apologize having to leave her with you. I couldn't rouse anybody else what with Carnival. All my altar sisters are out partying."

"What do you mean, child?" From the front porch she pointed at a sign on her building that read MARIE LAVEAU APARTMENTS. "Mam'zelle's here always was a safe house for women and children."

"Yeah. But Mam'zelle's been dead over a hundred years, and this house wasn't hers—just built on the same site."

"What makes you think she ain't here? Lord knows I talk to her every day, and not just when I'm working the mother either."

"What's Teri think about all this? I bet she thinks you're a crazy old black lady talking trash."

" 'Course she does. Least part of her does. But the other part sees her baby calming down. Precious little boy. And herself calming too. She get it together soon."

"Well, give her a big hug for me and tell her everything's gonna be okay. We'll find her another place to stay."

"That's what *I* be worried about—what happens that junkyard husband of hers finds her."

"We'll cross that bridge soon."

"You hexing him, child?"

"Well, I sure as hell ain't blessing him with white light. I've warned that sucker more than once."

"Like I taught you from you'se a little girl. First law of nature be—"

"Self-preservation."

"Thass right. Now, get on with you. Off my porch, wasting my time lollygagging. Shoo."

Six

•

As the bells of the St. Louis Cathedral tolled midnight, Sam watched the King and Queen of Rex ("The folks," said Kitty) troop over from their own party in the Municipal Auditorium and bow to Comus ("High society and tradition"). That bow was the coup de grâce. The madness, high and low, was ended.

But there was *one* more thing: the Queen's Breakfast at the Roosevelt, which is what the locals called the Fairmont though it had changed hands and names about fifteen years earlier.

After a short ride down Canal in a light rain, Sam and Kitty flew up the hotel steps, trailing the long black capes that Lee women had always worn to balls. Zoe had already arrived with Ma Elise.

"Miz Kitty," nodded the black-and-red-uniformed, brass-buttoned giant of a doorman. In the lobby, gold columns soared up, up to a gilded ceiling. A sea of plush red carpet rolled through to the next block.

Kitty tapped Sam's arm and pulled her into the Sazerac Bar.

"Let's go in here for a few minutes," Kitty said. "It'll take a little time for Zoe to get changed out of her gown before she and Ma Elise come down to the ballroom for the breakfast."

The Sazerac was a long room that would have been right at home in an old movie. It was paneled in African walnut and lighted in pink. Hopperesque murals showed Jackson Square, the riverfront, the French Market, a plantation scene.

It reminded Sam of the Tosca Café in San Francisco's North Beach, where she and Sean used to go for late night cappuccinos. Both rooms were frozen in time. You expected to see young Scott Fitzgerald or, in a flash of shimmery satin, his beautiful Zelda. Your old friends would wait for you there.

"Kitty!"

Sure enough.

The hail came from the depths of a long gray sofa.

"Y'all come keep a lonely man company."

"His name's Harry Zack." Kitty turned to Sam.

The man stood, and Sam looked into his face and saw the same wide brow, straight nose, and rosy cheeks that she'd admired at the airport.

"He's young," Kitty continued in her ear, "but kind of interesting. You'll see."

Indeed, thought Sam. Oh, yes indeedy.

The introductions done, Kitty asked Harry, "What are *you* doing here? I thought you were still in Nashville."

"I've been back a few months—keep meaning to call you for a drink. And I'm *here*"—Harry patted a cushion on the sofa beside him—"because I make it a practice to hang out in the Sazerac every Mardi Gras evening and buy pretty ladies drinks." He motioned a waiter over, then continued. "In commemoration of that Fat Tuesday in 1949 when a bevy of you all, pretty ladies that is, stormed this hidebound and, until then, exclusively male institution. Now, what's your pleasure?"

"Fat Tuesday, 1949, my foot," Kitty fluttered, having earlier had a glass or four of champagne. "You boys always do know the most arcane things." Then to the waiter: "The usual."

"One Sazerac." The waiter looked at Harry. "Two. And you, miss?"

"A Perrier. With lime," Sam said. Harry turned and gave her his slow smile.

Yep, she thought, it was him all right, the handsome young man from yesterday. Had he come up with an opening line yet?

"And to what do we owe the pleasure of your company, Miss Samantha? You over from Atlanta to observe our quaint customs and peculiarities?" he asked with that interesting accent of a cultured New Orleanian, East Coast urban, though the intonation and vocabulary were southern.

"Why, yes," she said. "Customs and peculiarities. That's exactly it."

"And our friend Kitty took you to Comus. What'd you think?"

Sam laughed. "Pretty quaint."

He laughed too, displaying some lovely white teeth with a little gap between the front two. She liked that. And she liked the wide shoulders beneath the tuxedo jacket. He still hadn't gotten a haircut, and his posture—he slouched into the sofa—could use some improvement. But the drooping right eyelid was *very* interesting—a little lazy, a lot sexy.

"Didn't I see you at the airport yesterday?" she asked.

He grinned. "Guilty as charged. Of course, I saw you too. I never forget a pretty face."

And I'm a sucker for one, thought Sam. Always have been. Probably always will be. A predeliction for male beauty passed down from my mama which makes me weak in the head. And in the knees.

"Well, hell, I was at the airport too," said Kitty. "Why didn't you say howdy?"

"I was"—Harry paused—"*meeting* somebody. Actually I was working."

"They hiring bands out at Moisant these days?" Kitty asked, then turned to Sam. "Harry writes and plays music."

Harry shook his head. "I've given it up. No money in my rock 'n' roll kind of C and W. I'm going straight."

"What do you play?" asked Sam, thinking of a drummer from back in her drinking days. She never could quite conjure up his face, but definitely remembered his hands—

"Keyboard. But as I said—hardly at all anymore. Weekends, maybe. Pickup bands here and there."

"So what do you mean, you were working at the airport?" Kitty insisted.

Harry laughed. "I'm working right now too." He cocked a crooked grin at Kitty. "What do you think?"

"You want me to guess?"

"Working the crowd. Jewel thief," Sam said.

Harry laughed, turned back to her. "No, but I like it."

"Hotel burglar. Cash. Credit cards. Assorted pretty things," Sam continued.

"I like that too. I can see you've definitely got me pegged as a criminal type."

"Maybe you've missed your calling."

Sam could see his chest puff a little, going along with it. He had a sense of humor. That was nice.

"Kitty said you're with the *Constitution*. What do *you* do?" he asked.

"Write. Crime beat."

"Ah-ha! So you definitely can recognize the type."

"Oh, yeah. It's all in the eyes."

"Really? Tell me what else you see."

"This isn't palm reading, Harry," Kitty said.

"You planted a bomb," said Sam, mock-serious.

"Nope."

"Kidnapping. Here to collect a *big* ransom. Run away to—"

"Bali," Harry said. "You ever been there?"

"No."

"Wanta go?"

"Why, Mr. Zack." She fluttered her eyelashes just a tad, though in her mind her bag was packed. Swimsuit. Black lace nightie—

Then: *"There* you are!" a voice boomed from the door, so loud they couldn't ignore it. "Kitty Lee, sister woman, I've been looking all over for you."

"Oh, shit," said Kitty. "It's Church, three sheets to the wind."

Sam looked up at Kitty's brother. It had been years since she'd met him, and that briefly. He was a very tall man with a bony, ugly-handsome face and deep circles beneath his eyes. He looked like Abe Lincoln on a bad day. There was a race-horse blaze of white in the thick, dark curly hair which he tried to pomade down in a long, old-fashioned style. But the most striking thing about him this particular evening was that he was drunk—absolutely reeling.

"So *this* is Samantha." He leaned into their table now, spraying them with spittle.

"Now, Church, you've met Sam before. Don't you remember?"

And suddenly it struck Sam that their most recent meeting had been this evening. "Did I dance with you earlier at the Comus ball? You were masked?" she asked.

"Well, darlin'!" His fumy laugh was booming, expansive. "I certainly couldn't tell you that. Though I certainly was at the ball. Did you see my baby girl? My Zoe?"

"I did indeed. She was absolutely beautiful." Sam paused. "But I could swear it was you."

He leaned over, whispered slyly, "Comus secrets always secret."

Now close behind Church followed a round, doll-faced man with wavy blond hair. He extended his hand. "Howdy, howdy. I'm Tench Young."

Church said to Kitty, "Haven't even brought Samantha around. You that ashamed of your brother?"

"Don't be silly, we were over earlier this evening, but you weren't home. Now, why don't you and Mr. Young sit down? You know Harry Zack?"

"Know him?" thundered Tench Young in that hearty manner of some southern men, as if he were about to hand you a check for a million dollars. "Harry here's my nephew!"

"Oh, I'm sorry, I'd for—"

"My right-hand man. He's working for me. Even as we speak!"

"You selling insurance, Harry?" Kitty grinned at him. "You here writing policies for wives think the old man won't make it through the night?"

"Chief bottle-washer," Harry muttered.

Sam watched the flush creep up his neck. His uncle was embarrassing him.

"Nose like a bloodhound," Young roared. "Nothing you can hide from that boy. Doing investigations for me. Saves me a shitload—'scuse me, ladies—of money. Kind of young man I want to have on my team. Bring him up in the company. Take over from me someday—when I get all those little fillies of mine married off. Sad, you know, man has no sons." Young reached across the table and slapped Harry on the back, in the process spilling Sam's drink. "Oh, I'm so sorry, my dear."

Sam dabbed at the water on her turquoise silk while politely brushing away his apologies. She ought to have known better than to get all dolled up for a bunch of drunks, she thought. Saran Wrap would have been more appropriate, or combat boots and a raincoat.

Harry was handing her his handkerchief. "Hope you didn't ruin your pretty dress."

"Thanks. It's just water. It'll be okay."

"Do you want me to—"

But she never heard what he was going to offer. Another wave of merrymakers crowded into the room, drawing everyone's attention.

Tench Young punched Church in the arm and pointed. "Hey, bubba. There's your friend, Maynard Dupree."

Church turned, frowning in the direction Tench pointed. "That son of a bitch," he growled. "Look at him. Too bad he didn't fall off that horse in the parade and break his neck. All dressed up in his captain costume, looked like a fool trying to be Roy Rogers. Did you see his horse rear up, bucking like a bastard in front of the reviewing stand? Zoe waving her little hand off. Thank God he didn't have the grit to block her being queen. I would have shot him."

"Now, watch yourself, son," Tench said, laughing up at his tall friend. Then he turned back to the table. "Every time Church sees that old boy Maynard Dupree, he gets all pushed out of shape. I've warned Church to stay away from him. Makes his blood pressure shoot right up and I cain't afford for this ol' hoss"—he squeezed Church's arm—"to be kicking the bucket. Not with all the insurance I'm carrying on him."

Church laughed, showing lots of pearly teeth. "Don't you worry about me," he said. Sam noticed the humor didn't extend above his mouth. His eyes were somewhere else. They looked like they were seeing something awful. Then he focused back into the room. "It's not my health I'm worried about. It's going to the po'house." He laughed his big empty laugh again.

"Well, I reckon this whole sheebang has cost you a sou or two, hadn't it, son?" Now Tench slapped Church on the back. He was one of those men who constantly touched, poked, prodded. "Little girl's debut and on top of it being queen. Ain't chicken feed, is it?"

That was Church's cue to laugh again, but instead, he looked away. Sam watched him stare at the mural of Jackson Square for a long count of five. His brow gnarled like a gathering storm. Then he blinked.

"Church?" Kitty frowned at her brother.

He shook his head and turned back with a big grin. "Think somebody just walked on my grave." He shivered, hamming it up for the effect. "You ever have that feeling?"

Sure, everyone nodded.

"Well, listen." Church rubbed his hands together. "We better get into the ballroom. Gonna miss my baby's breakfast." The man was used to getting the show on the road, Sam thought, a surgeon accustomed to giving orders. "Celebrate the last couple of hours of my baby's being queen. Come on, y'all." He hustled everyone out of their seats. "Let's *eat* us some breakfast. *Drink* us some champagne. *Make* us some merry." Now he was herding them out of the room. "Put it all on my tab," he called to the waiter, who nodded. "All of it, Charlie. Nobody's money is good here tonight. Nobody but Church Lee's."

It was two-thirty when they piled out of the hotel into waiting limousines, waking drivers who had grabbed the chance for a little snooze.

"Church!" Kitty called to her brother on the sidewalk. "You come on with me and Sam and Zoe. There's room for you with us. Ma Elise went home a long time ago."

"Nawh." He waved. "I left my car in the parking lot 'fore the parade. Here it is right now." Church slurred, bobbing and weaving. The attendant stepped out of the old black Mercedes, palmed Church's tip. "I'll drive it on home."

"We can't let him do it," Sam said. "He's way too drunk."

"He won't listen," said Zoe in the tired voice of one who's given up trying.

"Of course not," said Sam. "You can't reason with booze. But let me see what I can do. Since I'm not family, maybe he'll let me drive."

She was out of the limo and halfway to Church's car, running over in her mind what she was going to say to him, what she said to other drunks while doing Twelve Step work. She spoke his language, had been where he was more than once. With a lot of luck she might keep him from getting behind the wheel.

But he was too fast for her. There was not even a prayer of grabbing the keys. Bang. Slam. The dark car lumbered out into the street and picked up speed. Its tires squealed as he turned right onto Canal.

"Come on." Kitty had rolled down her window. "We'll follow him home."

Sam jumped in the front seat with the driver. "Do not lose that car."

"Yes, ma'am!" He accelerated, burning rubber.

Then began a rerun of the drive from the airport the day before. There had been too many movies filmed in this town, Sam thought. Everybody was cruising for a bit part.

"We have *got* to do something about Church's drinking," said Kitty. "He won't say, but I know a friend of his, a member of the State Licensing Board, has spoken to him unofficially, warned him he's risking a lot with his behavior. And his malpractice insurance—there's been a suit—"

Zoe stared out the window. Her reign as Queen of Comus was finally, finally over. And her daddy was drunk again. All that glitter and glory—and none of it was real. Well, maybe the diamonds around her neck were, she thought, fingering them. Nothing had changed. Here they were, rolling down old Canal Street. Next year another girl would sit on the reviewing stand at the Boston Club and watch the Comus parade pass by. Would *her* life change? Zoe stared out into the soft rain. The streetlights were ringed with yellow halos. She closed her eyes and could still see them behind her eyelids—like golden crowns. They'd be gone at first light.

No one in the long limo noticed the car that pulled in right behind, making them a little caravan. Church in the lead, the long black car full of women now the filling in the middle of a sandwich.

The limo crossed double yellow lines and ran red lights, following Church. Where were the cops, wondered Sam, when you needed them?

Up ahead the taillights of the Mercedes flashed and flashed again as Church fishtailed around Lee Circle, coming into where St. Charles became a boulevard. He was just easing through, sliding by. This drunk was lucky tonight, wasn't he? At least he had been this far, but he couldn't count on Lady Luck forever.

Sam remembered, it had been ten years since she'd driven like the man in front of her, her eyes struggling for focus but zeroing in on a little beam of light. She knew Church was holding on to a clear signal, a path that would lead him home. It had to, had to work, because the booze made him invincible. Nothing could stop him. Nothing could even touch him. With enough booze in him, like every other drunk, he was Superman. He was flying.

Of course, he might fly right over a pedestrian. Or through a stop sign. Or blow an exit, misreading it to mean *Come right on ahead, we like your kind.*

An incident like that had finally grabbed Sam's attention. She had gunned it at 105 mph past a STOP EXIT WRONG WAY sign south of San Francisco. She liked to drive fast when she was drunk. She liked to bad-mouth cops too—like the highway patrolman who had run her off the road.

"You could have killed me, you bastard." She'd lunged at him as he pulled her out of what was left of her Austin-Healy.

"I was trying to, you stupid bitch." He'd thrown her into the back of his black and white, not caring if she was hurt, snapping the cuffs on her. "Before you kill a real human being."

Nothing had grabbed her attention before. Shattered glasses, lost shoes, rolled cars, broken friendships and promises, hangovers, dry heaves, hallucinations, blackouts—none of it had jerked her up and made her face the fact that she was an alcoholic. She couldn't handle her booze, it was running her life, and *that* was a problem. But that next morning when she woke up in the women's drunk tank in San Mateo County with her license lifted and narrowly averted disaster staring her in the face, she hit bottom. She called her lawyer, then her doctor. Get me out of here, she said, and into a treatment program.

That had been her first step on the long road back.

In front of them, Church was weaving over into the street car tracks in the neutral ground, looking like he might not make it till tomorrow.

She wondered how many years he'd been drinking.

She thought about Zoe too. The apple never fell far from the tree. Sam remembered the look on the girl's face when she'd walked in on her earlier that evening in the ladies' room at the Fairmont. Zoe, wearing the simple white slip of a gown she'd changed into for the breakfast, was startled. She spilled her coke, looking like a little girl with her hand in the cookie jar. How long would it take for Zoe to hit bottom?

Then suddenly from behind them a car blinked its lights once, twice, and roared past.

It was a heavy car, a very old Buick, a make Sam could identify from the little holes down its side.

The Buick flew by, honking at Church, who swerved sharply to the right, missing another parked car by millimeters. Then the Buick kept going, squeezing past a cross street at the beginning of a red light, picking up even more speed and disappearing into the wet mist.

"Oh, my Lord!" said Kitty.

"Fool ain't gonna see dawn," said the driver.

"You're probably right," Sam agreed. "How much farther till we're home?"

"Six or seven more blocks," the driver guessed.

"Pray." Kitty punched Zoe. "Sit up and pray that your daddy makes it home in one piece."

Zoe, who had dozed off, groaned, "Oh, lordy."

G.T. didn't know what had come over her.

Usually she just followed the calls on the ambulance's radio. That's what she was supposed to do. But tonight, for the past half hour, she'd had this itchy feeling. A little voice inside kept whispering things.

"G.T., where the hell you think you're going?"

That wasn't the little voice. That was Arkadelphia Lolley, who was her partner tonight. The 300-pound white man from Tallulah bit down on his words real hard, the way people from north Louisiana did.

"We supposed to be sitting right here till we get a call to go. Covering our section. What exactly is it you have in mind? You hungry? Is it some oysters that you want? A po'boy?"

"That's what's on *your* mind, Ark. I can't even begin to explain what's on mine."

"Well, I just hope you tell 'em it was you who was driving when they call us in and chew us out for not being where we supposed to. What we gone do we get a call we can't get to in time 'cause you got some weird bug up your butt? 'Specially after we lost that little bitty sucker yesterday got up and ran? You think we ain't got enough trouble?"

"It's me who'll do the explaining," G.T. said, thinking that that was going to be awfully hard to do. She could just hear herself saying: Unh-huh, and then this voice in my head said: This here's the goddess speaking, said to get myself on over to Uptown. Right. Left. Left. Right. Now keep on heading toward St. Charles. *Good* girl. Like I was her baby child.

All of a sudden Church stopped. He gave no signal, no warning, just braked right in the middle of an intersection.

"Oh, my God," Kitty moaned as they pulled on around, double-parking a little way up in the next block of St. Charles. "Oh, Lord, what now?"

Kitty and Sam and the driver jumped out. Zoe stayed put.

Church stumbled from the Mercedes, leaned against its side.

"He's two blocks from home," Kitty muttered, lifting her pink silk which was already ruined in the quickening rain. "You'd think he could wait to take a leak."

"And that he could get out of the middle of the street," said the driver.

It was then that the Buick charged from out of nowhere. Or at least that's how it seemed in the wet, moonless night. The thirty-year-old car with the grille full of chrome teeth lunged from the river side of St. Charles like a charging dinosaur.

"Church!!!" Kitty screamed.

And then there was a loooong silence, the kind that goes hand in hand with disaster.

Sam had seen hideous things happen before. They were always in slow motion. They took forever. You could reach out and stop them.

If you could just make yourself move.

If you could only get there in time.

Sam ran.

She pulled up her skirt, kicked off her high-heeled silver sandals, and sprinted full out.

The face of her lover Sean, killed four years before by a drunk driver, flew through her mind.

She couldn't save Sean, but she could save Church. If she could just run faster. Faster. Faster.

But she wasn't Superwoman. She couldn't reach Church in time.

He was leaning over—maybe to throw up, maybe to tie his shoe. Whatever it was, it was the last thing Church Lee would ever do. The lumbering dinosaur of a Buick chewed right into him and took his head in one bite.

"Jehoshaphat!" said Arkadelphia as G.T. pulled up to the intersection. "Did you see that? Man popped up, his head squashed just like a watermelon. Holy Jehoshaphat!"

* * *

The driver of the dark Buick threw the car into reverse. Rubber fried. The big car swerved, just missed a royal palm. It grazed the rear of G.T.'s ambulance. There was the sound of tinkling glass.

"Oh, my Lord!" Arkadelphia groaned. "We're in for it now."

G.T. threw her door wide and jumped out.

The Buick straightened, tapped the ambulance again in a second pass, then roared across the grassy boulevard divider which locals called the neutral ground. The Buick crossed the streetcar tracks running down the middle of the neutral ground, turned, and headed back the other way, back downtown.

"Did you see him?" Sam yelled at G.T., who nodded. The two of them stood on the streetcar tracks with hands out empty, rain pouring down their faces.

They had both seen the driver for an instant, for a flash, inside the big, mothering Buick. Wearing a carnival mask.

Seven

•

Six weeks later Sam found herself once again on a plane about to land in New Orleans. They were almost in—the flat, timbered terrain giving way to the huge saucer of Lake Pontchartrain.

She hadn't thought she'd be back so soon, though her thoughts often turned to the city, to Kitty and her family, who'd been doubled over with grief when she'd left—and to Harry.

He'd called her a couple of times in Atlanta, had sent her flowers once—violets, which she thought was awfully sweet, as was he—but he was also far too young, even for a flirtation, and far too far away.

But now, as soon as she stepped off the plane, he was going to be right in her face. He'd called and said he'd meet her at the gate, and she'd said fine because there were a few things they needed to get squared away.

Kitty had called the week before, an absolute wreck. It seems as though in settling Church's estate they'd found he had a million dollars' worth of life insurance payable to his daughter Zoe—but Tench Young, his old friend who'd written the policy, said, unh-uh, no way. Tench would be happy to pay the quarter-million policy Church had carried for many years, but the additional three-quarters Church had bought six months before he met his Maker in the middle of St. Charles, forget it.

Tench said any policy held less than two years was subject to investigation.

Investigation of *what?* Sam demanded.

Church's death, Kitty answered.

Does he think he killed himself? Does he think Church was driving the Buick? What the hell do the police say?

Death by misadventure. They're working on it.

And until they catch the bastard who perpetrated the hit-and-run, Tench gets to keep his money?

He's sicked Harry Zack on us.

What?

Harry's running Preferred Reliance's investigation.

"It's a hell of a thing, Harry," she said to him, now walking down your standard gateway-to-hell airport passageway.

He tried to take her garment bag, but she shrugged him off. She didn't need someone who looked like JFK, Jr., in a beat-up old raincoat doing her favors, not if he was going to be on the other side. Because that's why she was here—to see what she could do to help Kitty get Tench (and Harry) off her back, settle this issue, get Zoe her money, let the Lees get on with their lives.

He kept walking, then finally shrugged.

"It's only business." Though inside he wasn't thrilled about Uncle Tench's assignment either, except it had brought Sam back.

"I thought you were an old friend of the Lees', of Kitty's. Wasn't your big sister in Kitty's court when she was—doo-dah—Queen of the May? Doesn't that make them like blood sisters?"

"Queen of Comus. That's right, we're all old friends."

"Guess I have a hard time seeing that, since Kitty says you're the one going around asking the rude questions, looking for dirt on Church."

"And getting precious few answers."

"So give it up."

He shot her a look. "Do me a favor, Sam. Don't bust my chops."

"You could have said no, thank you very much, Uncle Tench. You could have passed."

Harry thought about that for a minute, about that day Tench had called him into his big-as-a-battleship corner office. He'd been running his hands through his blond waves, saying: Son, ol' Church was a friend, but you understand, this is bi'nis. *Big* bi'nis. He was chewing on his five-buck cigar. His little eyes were pale and cold, reminding Harry that he'd never really liked his mother's brother much in the first place. Tench had said, Now, I don't begrudge his darling little girl that first quarter mil, that's the kind of bite we're set up for. But this other three-quarters? No way, son. Tench hitched up his pants, adjusted himself, went on. There's no way a man takes out that kind of monster new *in*surance right 'fore he dies, 'less he *knows* somethin'. Don't ever'thing show up in the preinsurance medical. He still *could* have had a preexisting condition would turn that claim to mush no matter what the cause of death. The postmortem don't say jack—you know that was a lick and a promise. Now, I *know* the man was killed by a hit-and-run. I *know* that. But there's somethin' here not on the up and up, either prior to—or in the doing. And you're gonna find that thing, save us the big bucks. Ain't you, son?

It had crossed Harry's mind to say at that juncture, Thass right, yes suh, boss, to do the Stepin Fetchit routine they'd taught him as the Only White Boy at Grambling. Yeah, Grambling had taught him a lot—which was a surprise, since he'd meant going there as a joke after he'd gotten himself thrown out of Choate, then flunked out of his first year at Harvard, bad, *bad*, boy, Grambling had been his answer to his father's plea to go to school *some*where, *any*where. But once the brothers had gotten over the fact that he was white, this boy who'd grabbed up a three-year track scholarship—Fastest White Boy in the South, they called him—they'd taught him moves and jive and street smarts. They'd taught him how to lay down a mean, driving rhythm. Taught him if a man keeps calling you out, get the first lick in, no matter what, and *make it count*. Yes, Grambling had been a triple-A educational experience. He learned he didn't know diddle about being *bad*. Learned a whole lot about being a decent human being. He also learned when to bob and when to weave and when to cut his losses.

That's what Harry had really thought, the day last week when Tench laid all that bull on him about Church Lee: He ought to cut his losses. Tell Tench to shove this job and stroll. He'd had his mouth open to do that when he thought, But wait!

Where'd it gotten him, that decision he'd made when he was a youngster, when he'd thrown over all that Uptown, Garden District, blue-blood bull that was his heritage? Got him fifteen years, three nickels, of driving cabs, working rigs, process serving—all to support his songwriting, music-making jones—what'd he have to show for it?

A handful of demo tapes, that's what he had, when everybody he knew was married, renovating double shotgun houses uptown in the Lower Garden, bitching about their 2.5 kids' tuition, going to tennis camp, working on their serves. Were they so wrong? Maybe *he*'d screwed up. Maybe he ought to try it, wear a suit and tie, work his way up some ladder, saying, *Yes suh, boss.*

Now he looked at Sam, questioning his motivation and thought, What the hell? But instead of saying that, he reached for her bag again, *Here, let me take that.*

No thanks, she answered, a pretty woman walking about two steps ahead of him, shouldering a carryon that looked like it weighed fifty pounds. She strutted like a dude in boot camp with something to prove.

"Are you sure?" he asked again.

"That's all right. I got this far."

"It's tough to be a gentleman these days."

That slowed her down. She laughed—she had a *great* laugh—and handed him the bag.

"It's been so long since I've seen a gentleman, I forgot what y'all look like."

Harry relaxed. Maybe she wasn't going to hold this business against him after all.

"You want to go by the Central Grocery, grab some lunch, sit down and talk about this thing?"

She nodded yes.

They were down the escalator now, across the lower level, passing the civilians at the luggage bays who hadn't learned yet how to pack.

The automatic doors slid open, and they stepped out into the warm Gulf air. Sam took a deep breath. The air felt like hot sheets and warm perfume.

Down, girl, down, she reminded herself. This was business.

But New Orleans air made you think like that. Whereas back in Atlanta, an hour earlier, it had been chilly. A piss-and-vinegar late-March morning, it was the perfect kind of day to fly over to New Orleans, take names, and kick a few asses. She'd help her friend Kitty get this insurance mess straightened out, chomp down some crawfish, and be back in her own bed the next night, night after at the outside.

She was still holding to that plan. And if the cute man who represented the guys in black hats wanted to take her to lunch, well, why not? There was no reason you couldn't get down to brass tacks at the same time you were getting on the outside of a muffuletta.

In the parking lot she learned that Harry drove a beat-up VW Rabbit convertible the color of a Campbell's soup label that had been lying in the sun for about ten years.

"They didn't have one with bullet holes?" she asked, giving him two southern gentleman points for handing her in, shutting her door.

There was litter on the floor, wires where the radio used to be, no inside handle on her side.

He grinned. "You have to hustle to get those. At the police auction, the baby drug dealers snap 'em right up."

The Rabbit became more compact as Harry jammed it into a parking spot right near the Central Grocery on Decatur, across the street from the French Market. A huge tanker loomed on the river just behind the market and the seawall.

A few minutes later they were sitting at the counter inside the old

Italian grocery store, sharing a thick, round Italian loaf stuffed with ham, Genoa salami, provolone, and garlicky olive salad—a muffuletta.

Halfway through the sandwich Sam sighed. "I think I'm gonna live." She took a long swig on her cream soda, then looked Harry straight in the eye: "So what's the deal?"

"The *deal* is I'm trying to dig up something to save Tench the $750,000."

"You paid the first quarter."

"Yeah, but Zoe can kiss the rest good-bye if I find *any*thing fishy. Preexisting medical condition. Suicide. Any kind of stink."

"You know, I *saw* Church get smacked by that Buick. Suicide would have been real hard to pull off, driving the car himself. Give it up, Harry. It's open and shut. Hit-and-run."

"Well, I know it looks that way. But as we say—it's my job. Considering all the possibilities. As *you* say, asking the rude questions. Snooping around."

Actually, it sounded like *her* job as an investigative reporter. "You know you're making the Lees very unhappy. Especially Ma Elise." She wasn't above beating him about the head with an eighty-three-year-old old lady.

"Look, this is no day at the races for me either. But I couldn't duck this. Tench dragged me in special."

"You should have stayed in rock 'n' roll. Country 'n' western."

"What's that supposed to mean?" he barked.

She jumped. Boy, he did have a temper! Tourists stared from their stools down the counter. Well, she was pushing a little hard. "I'm sorry. Calm down."

No sweat. He shrugged.

She filed away that sore spot. "Fine. So what've you got?"

"Whoa," he laughed. "Hold on. You think I'm just gonna lay my hand on the table?"

"Why not? You got something big, I'll check it out. It holds water, Kitty and I'll talk about it. See if it's worth giving a couple of lawyers new Mercedes for battling it out. I don't think she's in it for the money though."

"*You'll* check it out! Not in it for the money? What have *you* been smoking?"

"Really, Harry, she's not. You of all people should know this is about honor. Son, we're talking several generations of Lee pride you're stepping on."

She saw him flinch at the *son*. That was okay. After all, she was a woman with business to attend to, a grown-up who'd been sniffing out leads when he was still shagging flies in junior high.

He wasn't backing off. "Horse manure! We're talking green, lady. *Lots* of things change when you're talking green. People's eyes light right up, whirl around like pinballs."

"Just tell me what you got."

He leaned back on his stool and took a long swig on his Dixie beer, deciding how to play this.

"Church was a bad boy," he said finally. "We specialize in bad boys in New Orleans."

"How bad, and you're stalling."

"Stalling? I'm withholding."

He let his left eye droop down to match the right, like shades drawn. It was a cute trick.

"Why do you keep assuming I'm gonna lay down?" he said.

She stuffed the last bite of sandwich into her mouth and talked around it. "Look, if you had something really hot, you wouldn't be here, having lunch with me. You'd be down at your uncle's office, letting him put another gold star on your report card."

Harry flinched.

"I'd say you don't have diddly," she continued. "You think if you sniff around me, I'm gonna help you."

"What!" He reeled back on his stool so hard, she thought he'd fly. *"Help* me?"

"You've got a fair-to-middling record as a process server. Sure, I know you've found a couple of big ones, but that doesn't exactly make you a private dick. You know what I mean?"

He socked himself in the forehead. "I can't believe you checked up on me." When he got excited, he did nice falsetto. It was probably very effective in the right song. Too bad this wasn't it.

"Of *course* I did. You think I'm gonna fly over here empty-handed? Without doing my homework? This is not the minors, honey."

"Do you know your attitude stinks?"

Harry stood, stalked to the front counter, snagged himself another Dixie, and plopped back down.

"It could really get on a person's nerves."

"Really?"

She was smiling her good smile, which was about the equivalent of his slow one. She'd figured if things were going to be like this, she might as well use everything she had in her arsenal.

"So you're doing all the background, right?" she said. "Just poking around on a fishing expedition, hoping against hope something's gonna turn up?"

He didn't answer.

"You found out Church was a drunk. BFD."

That got him. "Well, it *is* a big deal. His drinking was getting him into some deep dooky."

"Such as?"

"Such as a friend from the State Licensing Board had been giving him some advice that he ought to try to quit the sauce."

"Yeah, well, that's not the same as his confessing to or being tried for an offense, is it? I mean, he was still innocent until proven guilty, wasn't he? Or has the AMA thrown out that little tenet of our system of jurisprudence?"

"You know damned well they haven't."

"So, it wasn't like he was subject to action by the AMA's review board?"

"No, he wasn't." And then Harry realized he was being snookered, that he was already well into the little card file he'd compiled on Church.

She could see it on his face, and then his shoulders collapsed a little. Good. Maybe he'd cooperate, drop this nonsense, or at least work with her on getting it settled. That would be great because she didn't have much time. She needed to get in, out, and back to Atlanta. She'd told her boss, Hoke, she'd be gone a couple of days at most.

Hoke had accused her of going on an interview. Said she was another rat deserting the paper. Said she had no loyalty. No grit. No stand-and-fight-the-good-fight.

Hell, now that she thought about it, why was she in such an all-fired hurry to get back to that? Skull and crossbones flying in the city room. She didn't know what she wanted to do. There were tough decisions ahead about her career, her brilliant career. No wonder she was over here in the Big Easy, playing at saving a damsel in distress.

"Yeah, probably," Harry said.

Sam gave him a blank look.

"Excuse me," he said. "Am I boring you here?"

"Church's drinking. Check. What else?"

"Well—"

The way he slid into it, she could tell he thought this was hot.

"—there's a doozy of a malpractice still hanging fire."

"Retinal surgeons have screwed up before. I'm sure it happens every day."

"And somebody ends up blind."

"I'm not being the heavy here, Harry. But what does the price of rice have to do with Church's life insurance?"

"Let's say a former patient he hadn't been so successful with held a grudge. Offed him."

"Okay, let's say. He's murdered, you still pay."

Harry waggled a hand.

"What do you mean *maybe?* Murder cancels the payoff? It makes him dead, doesn't it?"

"It gets pretty murky. Open to discussion."

"I see. Open to settlement is what you mean. If the circumstances make the dearly departed look like a big enough ass, maybe the family would settle for a little less, and you all wouldn't yell about it so loud. Like maybe you'd yell so softly, the papers wouldn't even hear of it?"

"Something like that."

"But you'd have to prove it. Get a conviction."

Again Harry's hand made like a sick fish.

"Oh, really? Speaking of conviction, what are the police doing? The call was hit-and-run, right?"

He nodded.

"They have any interest in finding out who, or they've got better things to do with their time than investigate the slaughter of a prominent citizen in the street?"

"Couple guys working on it."

"Which couple guys?"

"Blackstone and Shea are their names."

"That sounds like a magic act. Is one of them a short guy, never talks? Other one a big guy you can't shut up?"

"Very funny."

"So what do they say?"

"They say nothing so far. There's no trace of the car."

"It wasn't exactly your everyday Honda Civic. Shouldn't be that hard to find, thirty-year-old Buick big as a boat."

"Yeah, but if it's disappeared into a garage somewhere, the bottom of a bayou, what good is that?"

"What about the trace?"

"Found two that fit the ticket in the city limits. One up on blocks in a collector's garage. Cherry. No dents, no nothing. The other is missing in action. The last registered owner, a little old lady across the river in Algiers, died six months ago. Nobody knows what happened to her car."

"Well, that's very handy, isn't it? Now, what else on Church besides the drinking and the malpractice. Other possible enemies?"

"You heard the same thing I did."

"What thing?"

"In the Sazerac Bar, Mardi Gras night."

"That's *right.*" Sam's eyes lit up. "I'd forgotten about that. That guy your uncle was talking about with Church, he came in the Sazerac, hail-fellow-well-met, Church bristled up. Delacroix. Duchamps—" She snapped her fingers a couple of times. "Help me out here, Harry."

"Dupree. His name's Maynard Dupree."

"*Right.* Church got his back all up. Didn't he say something about wishing Dupree's horse had fallen on him? What was he talking about, a horse?"

"Dupree is the captain of Comus. He rides a horse in the Comus parade."

"So they're both in Comus, the same carnival—what do you call it?"

"Carnival organization. Krewe."

"And they hate each other? Or, at least, Church hated Maynard?"

"Yeah. I asked Sudie, my sister, about it."

"Don't *you* belong to Comus?"

"My dad does. I dropped all that stuff years ago."

Sam raised her eyebrows. A man after her own heart—at least when it came to the social razzle-dazzle. But that wasn't the point here, was it?

"So what's the scoop on their feud? What's Sudie say?"

"Nothing. She said I should ask Mama."

"And?"

"She gave me the big brush-off. Pretended she didn't remember. You know, the way people do when they don't want to talk about something. My folks are famous for that. They think I'm still six years old."

"So?"

"I'm asking. I'm asking. You hear one thing here, one thing there. I think it goes way back, to when Church and Maynard were kids, maybe."

"Well, Kitty will certainly know."

"Right. But she sure as hell ain't telling *me.*"

"Well, she ain't telling you diddle, is she, darlin'? That's why you want to team up with me, get the inside track."

"*Wait* a minute—"

But there was no slowing Sam down. "That Church-Maynard Dupree business is definitely worth seeing about. I mean, assuming that the thing to do here is to follow through on your plan of just stirring up every possible little old pot and see what comes of it."

"Thank you so very, very much. You make our work sound so scientific."

"*Our* work!" she snorted. "And this isn't exactly the FBI lab, in case you haven't noticed. Just two pore little old dumb Southerners doing what they can with their limited abilities. By the way, was Church into anything kinky? Do you know?"

"You mean like boys?"

"Yeah, yeah. Or little girls."

"Or collie dogs? Can't find anything. Probably a pretty clean liver on that score."

"So what *did* he do for sex? Man's been divorced—what?"

"About sixteen years."

"And? Did he take a vow of celibacy when the wife ran off? That is right, isn't it? She left him? I think that's what Kitty always said."

"I'm not sure, and don't give me that look. I told you I haven't hung with that crowd in years, and besides, Church is—was—a lot older than me."

"Yes, I know."

He answered her smile with narrowed eyes. "Okay, I'll check it out. I *do* know he's squired around several ladies. Widows and divorcées always making a play for him, eligible well-to-do man with the right color blood."

"As in blue."

"Right. But he stayed slippery."

"Seeing anybody recently?"

"Nobody of any consequence, unless he's got her well hidden."

"What does that mean?"

"Means nobody steady. Nobody he's knocked up. Nobody who thought he was gonna marry her. Church just kept it all real light and easy. A date here. A horse race there."

"He played the horses?"

"Just an example. He went every once in a while. So does Zoe."

"Now that you mention her—what if Church's death—*assuming* that there's something here other than your simple hit-and-run—had something to do with her? And, before I forget it, what about the ex-wife? Where is she?"

"Seems to have disappeared. Probably worth tracking."

"You bet. Woman could have been sitting on a big, festering grudge that finally came to a head. Now, about Zoe."

"What about Zoe? Queen of Comus, you know that. Deb. Junior at Newcomb. Too skinny. Looks anorexic. Bulimic, you think? One of those?"

"You can be both, though she's probably the latter. I checked out her medicine cabinet, and I suspect she binges and purges. She's got enough Ex-Lax to start her own drugstore. *And* speaking of drugs, has a very expensive little nose."

"When did you do this?"

"Do what?" She gave him big eyes. "The medicine cabinet? Mardi Gras, when we went over to her house to watch her get ready for the ball."

"Is that your SOP when you go over to somebody's house?"

What kind of snoop was he? The man had no natural curiosity. "Sure, don't you?"

"Not recently. Anyway, so she's a cokehead?"

"Yep. And I caught her snorting in the Ladies at the Fairmont."

"That night we met?" His voice dropped a tad.

"Yeah, Harry. On that momentous occasion. If you don't count your making eyes at me in the airport the day before."

"Jesus. You ever cut anybody any slack?"

"Sure. After I've had coffee."

"Well, why didn't you say so? We can have espresso here."

She shook her head. "I need to stretch my legs. Been sitting all day, on the plane—"

He stood. "Then let's go. Café du Monde's brewing tourist swill, but we could get a cup to go at Chez Madeleine, corner of the square. Go for a stroll."

"Just a minute. Let's finish this thought." She pointed a finger in his face. Her polish was bright red. "What does Zoe's being on coke give us? Anything?"

"Maybe nothing. Maybe a lot. I think it's worth taking a look-see."

"I think so too. Now, what else?"

Harry shook his head. "Nothing pops right up. We have enough for starters, don't you think?"

What he didn't tell her was about the conversation he'd overheard in the Pelican the afternoon before Church died: Maynard Dupree and Jimbo King, the pipe-handler, joking with the barkeep about a two-for-one deal. Offing the ambulance driver, G.T., and his redhead, Chéri. And what was it the barkeep had said? *Throw in Maynard's buddy, Church Lee, and I bet you got yourself a taker.*

Harry wasn't telling Sam about that. A man had to keep something in his trick bag, didn't he? *Son* would check it out. See where it went. Maybe pull it out at the last minute, *shazam,* dazzle the pretty lady with it. After that lunch at Galatoire's. After a couple of hours at the Maison de Ville or maybe a suite at the Royal O. Maybe then he'd give it to her, for dessert.

Sam stared at Harry's grin. What was that sucker hiding? Well, it didn't matter how many aces he was holding in his lap because he'd missed a most important point. He hadn't even mentioned Church's finances. The surgeon looked well-to-do on the outside, but who knew? People were more close-mouthed about money than sex. A man would rather tell you he was screwing a mongoose than he was on the skids. *Cherchez la femme* was a bunch of crap. In the nineties, *cherchez les* bank statements was more like it.

But there was no point, she thought, in telling Harry everything. After all, it was his investigation and *his* territory. Then after he'd done all the legwork, helped her clean up all this mess, well, he'd have learned something, wouldn't he?

And maybe then she'd teach him another trick or two.

Sam grinned back at Harry.

Eight

Kitty and her grandmother, Ma Elise, lived in one of those grand old houses Uptown, with an acre of grounds and gardens and ten bedrooms. It sported a full complement of white columns, lacy cast-iron balconies, a music room with a rosewood square grand piano, a sun room, banana trees surrounding a brick patio complete with dripping fountain—all built in the 1850s by Augustus Lee, who'd made his fortune as a sugar merchant.

In the dining room now, after a dinner of Ida's wondrous gumbo, Sam, Kitty, Zoe, and Ma Elise were pushed back from the long walnut dining table (it could seat twenty with all its leaves) enjoying their coffee.

"The Garden District has always worn a proud face, you know. Most of the houses staying right in the same families," Ma Elise was saying.

"Well, it sure feels solid—real safe," said Sam.

"Oh, Lord, no," said Ma Elise. "I didn't mean that at all. Things have gotten terrible."

"The whole city has," said Kitty. "The crime rate's just awful. Thefts. Burglaries. Purse snatchings. Muggings. Can't tell us from New York 'cept we have worse heat and humidity."

"And here," said Ida, who'd stepped out of the room for a minute, now reclaiming her seat, "the pirates knock people in the head right on their own doorsteps."

"They read the society columns," said Kitty, "check out the parties, probably jot them down in their datebooks, wait for folks to come home late with their jewels."

"Or *rob* the parties" said Zoe. "I was at two this season that were held up."

"You're kidding," said Sam.

"I wish. Both times guys marched in, wearing ski masks, carrying shotguns, got us down on the floor, took everything. And you know the story about Daddy."

Sam shook her head. "He was robbed?"

"Oh. Well—" Then Zoe looked around the table, for all the world like a little girl seeking permission, Sam thought. She was still quite shaken by her father's death. She looked like a ghost with her translucent white skin—blue veins showing through—against that riot of dark hair. And she was even thinner than before, if that was possible.

"Go ahead, Zoe," prompted Kitty. "That's why Sam's here—to listen. You never can tell what might be helpful in settling this business."

Zoe reached for the coffeepot, poured herself another cup. At dinner Sam had watched Zoe eat enough for three. She wondered how long she'd wait to throw it all up. "It was about—what—six or seven months ago," she began haltingly. "September? October? Sometime after the party season had started. Daddy was mugged coming home late one night."

"Getting out of his car?"

"No—walking. We'd been to a party over at Celia Maguire's, just a few blocks up from our house on Prytania—"

Sam nodded. Since Church's death, Zoe hadn't returned to that house, had moved in with Kitty and Ma Elise.

"—and I'd come home a lot earlier. I'd walked with some other girls and our dates. Daddy came along later by himself. And that's when he got mugged."

"Was he hurt?"

"A cut on his arm, but it wasn't bad. I almost lost it when I saw the blood."

"His attacker had a knife?"

Zoe nodded. "I was scared to death, but—it was funny—Daddy was, like, excited. I guess 'cause he'd gotten away—outrun him."

"I think it made Church feel like a young colt again," Kitty laughed. "Beating out a bad guy—especially a younger man."

"He took Church's wallet?"

"Daddy said he tried to. But he didn't let him get away with anything."

"Did the police ever catch him?" Sam knew how unlikely that was.

" 'Course not," said Ida. "Pirates like rabbits, jumping all around. Police know there's hardly any point, going in those projects to catch 'em. I don't know what it's gonna come to." She shook her head. "Drugs. No jobs for our young mens. End up bashing decent peoples in the head."

That was true. They all nodded. New Orleans, its inner city predominantly black and poor, was doing no better than any other metropolis in fighting poverty and illiteracy and their handmaidens, drugs and violence. The only difference here, perhaps, was that the haves and have-nots lived cheek-to-jowl, grand neighborhoods like this abutting slums. Riches were flaunted every day in the faces of the poor—and not just on TV.

Sam looked around the table, deciding what tack to take. It was always best to interview people one on one. Especially with Zoe here, there were things the older women probably wouldn't say. But a little dinner-table brainstorming *could* prime the pump for later.

"Now, let's assume this mugger didn't know Church," Sam said. "But was there anyone who did who might want to hurt him? Enemies? Old grudges?"

The question lay on the table. Finally Kitty said, "Did Harry tell you about Cole Leander?"

"I'm not sure."

Kitty and Ma Elise exchanged an even look, then Ma Elise nodded, and Kitty explained. "That's the malpractice suit."

"Oh, yes. He mentioned it. But I didn't have a name."

"Well, Leander's a real crazy person. *Not* that I'm not sorry about his condition, but he's caused us all a lot of grief." Kitty turned to her grandmother. "Ma Elise, did I tell you he called me the other day? I don't know what he wants now. I'm gonna have our lawyer get back to him. You'd think now that Church's gone, he'd have the decency to—"

"Is he crazy enough to do something?" Sam asked.

"Maybe. But he's blind, you know. After the surgery—"

"Which wouldn't keep him from hiring someone else to do his dirty work."

"*That's* up his alley for sure," said Ma Elise. "But I don't want to spoil Mr. Leander for you. You'll find him downtown at the Leander & Sons barn. He should be quite an entertainment for you. You'll see."

"Barn?"

"He builds carnival floats."

"Well, *that* should be interesting. Now, what's this business with Maynard Dupree I keep stumbling over?"

"Oh, that," said Ma Elise. "It's perfectly silly. I used to tell Church he needed to grow up and get over that. Their disagreement goes back to when they were boys in school together. You know, they're the same age."

Ma Elise paused. Sam could hear her thinking—*were* the same age.

The death of her only grandson had hit her hard. At Mardi Gras, Ma Elise had looked a pert sixty in her gold watered-silk ballgown. Now add back two decades.

"So what was the issue?"

"Well, now, I told you this was silly. When they were little, hardly into long pants, they had a fight over Peggy Patrick, a little girl in their class."

"And this went on for thirty, thirty-five years?" Sam's tone registered her disbelief.

"I know it sounds ridiculous. And it was. Words were exchanged, a few punches, as I remember, a couple of bloody noses, and then one thing led to another. They were both very bright boys, fierce achievers. Once the battle was joined, they never gave up."

"It must have been awkward since they traveled in the same circles."

Kitty hooted. "You're right about that. There *are* only about three hundred people in New Orleans, you know. In our crowd you see the same faces over and over, day after day."

"But they were very polite about it," Ma Elise protested. "When Estelle, my daughter, Church and Kitty's mother, was alive, she used to give Church holy hell about it. Said it upset everybody's seating plans at their dinner parties. But it didn't really. Their feud was just a given. You know, like somebody being allergic to tomatoes."

"We thought," said Zoe, "that Mr. Dupree might block my being Queen of Comus. Since he's the captain, the one who runs things. But he didn't."

"I thought the king was in charge."

"No, no, the king changes every year. Captains are like the president, and they go on forever," said Zoe.

"Well, I think Maynard knew what a stink that would have caused," said Ma Elise. "To have broken the succession, you being the fourth generation of Lee queens, well, you just don't let personal feelings get in the way of a thing like that."

Only in New Orleans, Sam thought, then asked, "Do you remember Maynard ever doing *anything* that would have been harmful to Church?"

"Well," said Kitty, "men who have known each other for years do join up together in business deals, and every once in a while Church would come storming in, say Maynard had done him out of some investment opportunity. But that sort of thing's so vague—" She waved her hand like a lace handkerchief. "I mean, nobody was really ever going to tell Church directly that something like that was Maynard's doing. It think it was just more a feeling he got."

"A little paranoia?"

"Well," said Ma Elise, "you know, if you're looking for Church's enemies, you have no further to go than himself and his drinking. His father drank too—" She glanced at Kitty. "And Estelle, Kitty and Church's mother, was known to have more than one sherry in the afternoon to pass the time. I tried to get Church to stop but—"

"*You* couldn't do it. You know that, don't you?" said Sam.

"I *know*, dear. But then, I look at people like you, who have found the strength—"

"Not strength. It's having no place to go but up or out—feetfirst—then finding something that keeps you straight. AA has positively *ruined* drinking for me."

Ma Elise laughed. "I wish they could have ruined it for Church too. Bless his heart, to have died drunk, *because* of being drunk."

Sam saw Ma Elise's tears gathering. She *had* been hit hard. Sam was afraid even to look at Zoe. It would be good to put an end to this, to shut the door so the family could pick up the pieces and go on. But what if, for some reason, the inquiry didn't fall out the way they planned? Poking around in a man's past—often it was better not to know.

"I wonder," Sam said, taking it slow, tiptoeing, "if you all have given any thought to dropping this insurance matter?"

"Well, *I* have," Zoe said with sudden fierceness. "I think we ought to just let Tench Young keep his damn money. I mean, it's not like I don't already have a whole bunch coming from the first policy, and I've got the house, and the cars, and the camp at Grand Isle and the condo in Florida."

Sam watched a look pass between the two older women, toting up the cost of school, the clothes, the baubles Zoe had always taken for granted. They would have calculated the upkeep of Church's house, now hers, over on Prytania, the housekeeper, the groundsmen, the gardener. Zoe *could* sell it, but no, on second thought, knowing the Lees, that probably wasn't an option.

"No way," Kitty said, "We'll fight Tench Young to the death on this one. That tightfisted son of a bitch, let him go screw somebody he doesn't know."

"He doesn't do business with people he doesn't know," Ma Elise reminded her.

"Well, isn't that more the pity?"

"I didn't mean to upset you all," said Sam, pushing back from the table. It was time to call it a night; she was a little tired, and there was enough in the pot to let things stew a little. She segued into a story about her old boyfriend, Beau Talbot, whom Kitty had always called the handsomest son of a bitch in the South, now chief medical examiner for the state of Georgia. They laughed at the tale of his recent wedding to a woman half his age, where the minister kept trying to get Beau to give the bride away to his best man, confusing the groom with the bride's father.

"Well, he ought to be ashamed of himself," said Ma Elise. "I never could abide these May-December affairs. I think it's disgraceful."

"You wouldn't say that if one of those cute little things you and Ida hang out with at the poolhall all the time wanted to hook up with you," said Kitty.

"I would so!" Ma Elise protested.

But Sam could tell from the twinkle in her eye that Ma Elise was lying. All it would take to change her mind was switching the players around.

A little while later, tucked into her four-poster in a big square corner guestroom on the second floor, Sam put down the book she wasn't reading and recalled that conversation—specifically the part about older women and younger men.

The women in her AA group in Atlanta joked about it: Get one you can train. *Love* those washboard tummies.

Marie, her old dearheart, her San Francisco sponsor, had married a man nine years her junior and said it was the smartest thing she'd ever done—other than getting sober.

Yeah. Well. But. Sam stared up at the brocade tester; the canopy above the bed was the same soft white as the bed curtains. The whole room was the color of heavy cream. A bride would be at home in here —or Miss Havisham.

Now, *that* was a creepy thought, poor old lady, old as Ma Elise, as Ida, forever pecking around the edges of her moldering wedding cake with her great expectations crumbling.

Yeah. Well. But. Sam had never had great luck with men. She kept losing them, misplacing them. Maybe she'd cure that with a change of vintage.

But wait a minute. She sat up. What was this self-flagellation? A luxury she couldn't afford. If she'd learned one thing in the program, it was that. Right, girl?

Fine. On the other hand, stand back and check the record. Granted, nobody had any luck in love these days, that seemingly having gone out about the days of King Arthur, but good Lord!

Item: Beau Talbot—the first love of her life. He'd jilted her when she was nineteen. Broken-hearted, crazy, she'd run off from Atlanta, from her uncle George, who'd become her father after her parents died. At Stanford, where she'd met Kitty, she'd discovered that she could drink, without even trying, in an afternoon, three-quarters of the way down a Jack Daniel's label. She met Jimmy Harris her senior year.

Item: James Covington Harris—tall, cute, bearded, ponytailed. Big-time draft resister. Scion of a fine Republican family in Rancho Santa Fe, richest community in the state. She and Jimmy burned flags and smoked dope and dropped acid and got arrested. Then they up and got married one wine-soaked afternoon in a public park complete with redwoods *and* a spectacular view of the ocean. Their gig, as they called it, lasted four years, only some of which Sam remembered through a scrim of various legal and illegal substances and to the accompaniment of the Grateful Dead, Joe Cocker, and Neil Young. Then Jimmy decided he'd had it with revolution and thought he'd take up law, as had three generations of Harris men before him. He also thought he'd put down his embarrassment of a spouse who, increasingly, was a bit too loud. The last she heard he was practicing law in southern California, living off the fat of the land with his blond, blue-eyed third wife.

Item: Faceless Men—a large number of them who she could not identify when she woke up the next morning, though she had a pretty good idea of what they'd been up to the night before. She ran through a lot of them for about six years.

Item: Sean O'Reilly—her hip-popping, bebopping, tall, lanky Irish setter of a SFPD loverman. Sean had appeared like a gift after the long, tough dry spell during which she regained control of her life. Lost, three years ago, to a drunk driver.

Item: Beau Talbot—a brief reentrapment due to a moment (okay, a one-night stand) of insanity. Thereafter, they were kind to each other in the manner of old friends, meeting most frequently on business in the Atlanta morgue.

Item: Occasional dates, no one special, i.e., a long dry spell, which, come to think of it, hadn't been all that uncomfortable. Actually, it was rather nice discovering the grown-up Sam all by herself.

Except that from time to time she could do with a spot of intimacy in her life. Or would you call that sex?

Was *that* why her mind was running around the edges of Harry Zack's collar, fingering open a couple of buttons? And wasn't she the one so flippantly asking Harry if Church had taken a vow of celibacy? What about herself? And if that were true, what was that package of condoms doing rattling around in the bottom of her purse?

Own it, Sam. You're a horny, about-to-be-middle-aged lady who's spotted a luscious mouthful of a young man.

And? The urges weren't exactly her fault. God made people that way.

"Sam?"

She almost jumped out of her skin.

Then the rat-a-tat-tap at her door sounded again.

"It's Ma Elise. May I come in and sit down?"

"Get back in bed," Ma Elise ordered. She settled into a slipcovered chair, tucked a quilt around herself. "My grandmother pieced this," she said, "from hair ribbons, her husband's ties, or maybe they called them cravats then, and scraps of her silk underwear." Ma Elise's white hair was plaited in a single long braid that reached halfway down the back of her pink flannel dressing gown. "We live with the past piled in with the present here. As if it were only yesterday—which it is in New Orleans time. Is it that way in Atlanta too?"

"Not so much." Sam was wondering what the old lady had come to tell her but letting her get to it her own way. "Some old families are still there, of course. But so many more of the new people."

"Yankees."

Sam smiled. "Yep. Took 'em more than a hundred years, but they've come back, and I'm afraid they've whupped us for good this time. Worse than kudzu. They've torn everything up, covered it in blacktop and shopping centers."

Ma Elise nodded. "The disappearance, as Kitty says, of grace and gentility. It's happening around the edges here too. There's an area out in Jefferson Parish, around the Lakeside Shopping Center, where there's row after row of discos, bars—New Bourbon Street they say. As if Bourbon Street weren't tacky enough. They call it Fat City. Can you imagine? Saying you live in Fat City?" She shook her head, and her braid flopped. She looked like a little girl dressed for bed. "Well, nobody cares what I think. That's why old people live in the past. Did you know that? Because the present stinks."

Sam laughed. "I really feel that way about lots of things."

"Well, you watch that." Ma Elise shook a knobby forefinger. "You'll be old before your time. *But,* that's not what I came in here for, disturbing your rest. Though it does have to do with the past, Church's past." She smiled at Sam's reaction. "I thought that would make you sit up straighter."

Then she went on about Church and his bride, Madeline. Madeline was the prettiest girl at McGehee—the same private girls' school, just around the corner, their daughter Zoe had attended. Sam scanned for what might be important, filing facts in imaginary folders.

Church: young and virile, fighting for the hand of the fair Madeline with his archenemy, Maynard Dupree. Ma Elise sketched out a Count of Monte Cristo duel in Audubon Park beneath a daddy-of-'em-all live oak tree. They'd stolen foils from the fencing salle at Tulane. Each would bear a prize from the field—a scar on the chin, above the brow— to be fondled, stroked, and kissed in the years to come. To the death! or so they said, except old Miz Tilletson walking her dog just past dawn called the cops on them.

In the end, Madeline chose Church.

Madeline: Sam imagined a small woman, not as thin as Zoe, but with that same wildness of black curls, in a gossamer white gown flowing down to the dewy grass, blowing a kiss to the triumphant Church from the tips of her shell-pink hand.

But what had gone wrong?

"I don't know," Ma Elise said. "They were very happy. This was before Church started drinking. Zoe came along and their lives were complete. Then, when Zoe was about six, Madeline packed a bag one day and left Zoe a note: *It's not you, darling. You're the best little girl in the world. I will love you forever.* Now, isn't that something to say to a six-year-old child—with not a word to Church. And off she ran."

Butter wouldn't melt in Ma Elise's mouth, thought Sam. But boy, oh, boy, was she lying, or at least not telling the whole truth.

"Where is she now?"

Ma Elise fiddled with the quilt. "I don't know. We never heard another word."

"Why do you think she left Zoe behind? That seems such an unlikely thing for a mother to do."

"I don't know. Of course she should have taken her."

"But then Church would have gone after her, wouldn't he? Or did he anyway?"

The old lady stared off into the past. "It's funny how things turn out. We used to be such a big family, but Estelle was my only child, and she's gone. She had Church and Kitty—and Kitty's had no children—which leaves only Zoe. So if Madeline *had* taken her, well, I don't know what I—"

Sam tried again. "And you don't know where Madeline is?"

Ma Elise was firm. "No, I don't."

"Her family must know."

"Oh, I suspect they do."

"Did you ever ask?"

"No. Why would I do that?"

"So you do see them?"

"Of course I do. We know all the same people. But, well, it would be rude—don't you see what I mean? None of the Villères would want to talk about that."

For the second time that night Sam thought, Oh, God, New Orleans. "What does Zoe know of the story?"

"She knows her mother deserted her. Of course, *we* think she ran away with another man."

That was certainly an interesting piece of news. "What makes you think that?"

Ma Elise shrugged—what else?

"And Zoe never wanted to know more?"

"I don't think so. We've never talked about it."

"But maybe she'd like to know?"

"Samantha, that's all there is to know. And if Church knows—knew —more, well, he never told me. Even if he did, I couldn't say anything about it, not even to Zoe. It would be disloyal."

"To whom?"

"Why, to Church, of course."

At that, Sam couldn't hold her tongue. "Ma Elise, I don't mean to be butting into your business, but are you aware that Zoe might have a few problems?"

"Like what, dear?"

"Like she's wasting away before your very eyes."

"Well, she *is* too thin. Yes, I can see that. But you know how girls are. I'm sure she wanted to look like Scarlett O'Hara for the Comus ball —you know, with an eighteen-and-a-half-inch waist. I was the same way when I was her age. Now that that's over, she'll put on some weight."

"But she's even thinner than she was back in February."

"Well, my dear," Ma Elise said, rising from the chair, throwing the quilt aside, "she's lost her father. Don't you imagine that's good reason for her to have lost her appetite?"

"Yes, but—"

But the interview was over. Ma Elise gave her her back, was out the door. But then she stuck her head back in. She was wearing the sweetest smile. "I'm so glad we had this little chat, dear. Sweet dreams. I feel so much better now that I've explained about Church and Madeline." The door was closing. "Good night, now. Nighty-night. Roses on your pillow—" Her little-old-lady voice faded down the hall.

Sam had barely finished jotting notes on what Ma Elise had told her, when there was another knock at the door.

This, she thought, is absurd.

"I know Ma Elise just left." Kitty poked her head in. "You can kick me out if you want."

"Hell, no. I'm here to talk, right? Come on in. Make yourself comfortable."

Kitty settled into Ma Elise's warm spot, snuggled under her great-great-grandmother's quilt.

"So, Kit, what've you got? Or are you just having trouble sleeping? Want to swap some what-ifs?"

Her old friend grinned. "What if I grow up and marry a rock star? What if I get pregnant? What if I run away—around the world for ten years—will you go with me?"

"Yeah. Like that."

"Actually, I heard Ma Elise creeping in and out of here, and I'm dying of curiosity. Did she tell you about Church and Madeline?"

"She told me Madeline ran away, not much more than that."

"Well, I don't know that there's any more to it. Church told me Madeline fell in love with somebody else. What is there to say?"

"Do you know who?"

"Nope."

"Did you like Madeline?"

Kitty played with the ends of her red ponytail. *"Like* her? Yeah, I *liked* Madeline. She was never my best friend; we sort of ran in different crowds. But I thought she was just fine—till she ditched Church and Zoe."

"Ma Elise said you've never talked with Zoe about it."

"That's right. Why would we want to pick at that old scab?" Now she was playing with the sash of her flowered robe. "I guess that means you think we ought to?"

Sam shrugged. "You know you're talking to a woman who lost her mama and daddy at twelve. And as much as Uncle George and Peaches and Horace have been family for me, I've always missed them. I'd imagine Zoe'd feel the same way. With Church gone—well, doesn't that open up the door to maybe finding Madeline? Surely there must have been some *terrible* thing that happened for her to leave her child that way."

"Well, there wasn't. What *she* did was terrible, and I don't know where she is. She could be *dead* for all we know, or care."

"Kitty, Kitty."

She was no better at lying than Ma Elise.

"What?"

Kitty always had had a short fuse.

"Even if she just knew the circumstances of her mother's leaving, don't you think it might help her with her problems?"

"Her food thing, you mean?"

"And her nose."

"What's wrong with her nose?"

This was going to be tougher than she'd thought. "Come on, Kitty. Your denial and Ma Elise's are only enabling her to keep sucking that stuff up."

Kitty leaned back into the chair, closed her eyes. "Okay. I know about the coke. Hell, I guess I just feel like she's got so much on her plate, and *now*, if I was afraid to approach her drugs before, can you imagine how I feel now?"

"Doesn't change a thing. She's still screwed up. She's still gonna end up killing herself if you don't try to help her do something about it. Her obvious eating disorder, doing coke. It all comes from the black hole, from the same place."

Kitty sat up. Back straight as a rifle barrel. "You make it sound like we've failed her."

"I didn't say that. I'm sure you've done a great job. But that doesn't change the fact that she's got some serious problems."

"Look." Kitty was standing now, the quilt in a tumble on the floor. "I didn't come in here in the middle of the night to talk about our failures in raising Zoe. I came to tell you something about Church, which is what I think I asked you over here for—to help us solve the insurance mess. You remember that?"

"I remember." Sam's tone was flat, nothing on it. One of the gifts she'd discovered she had when she got sober was that when the going got tough, she became quieter, calmer.

Certainly calmer than Kitty, who steamed ahead. "Well, put this in your bag of tricks when you set out on your hunt tomorrow. Church was seeing somebody, had been for a long time. Somebody he seemed to be real tight with. But it was a big-deal secret. This wasn't one of the Uptown ladies he squired around for show. It was serious enough for him not to tell anybody, not even his own family. Put that in your pipe and smoke it. By the way, did we talk about your fee?"

Whew! *That* hurt. "I'm here just because you asked me to come, Kit," Sam answered softly.

"Well, maybe we ought to have you on retainer. Or, let's say a percentage of the bounty. Fifteen percent of what we end up with? Would that be about right? An agent's fee, so to speak? So you can concentrate a little more on finding out the facts, getting this business settled, and less on giving advice?"

"Kitty, Kitty."

There was *some* sore nerve here. Something really eating at her. Or something that she was afraid of.

"Look—I didn't mean to—"

It was too late for apology. Kitty had already flounced out the door. Sam collapsed back on the drift of lace pillows behind her.

What was it Kitty and Ma Elise were hiding? Something about Madeline and Church. There was something there—she knew it. And maybe, just maybe— She closed her eyes and saw two young men dueling under a sprawling oak at sunrise while a young girl in a long white dress looked on, wringing her hands—just maybe it was something about Maynard.

Nine

In her dream, she and Kitty were on the beach at San Gregorio just over the hills from Stanford. Nineteen again, they'd polished off a jug of cheap red wine. Or, rather, Sam had. Kitty needed only a couple of glasses and she was flying, yelling about how she was not putting up with any more of this crap from Sam.

What crap?

It was right there, slipping, sliding, whoops, over the edge of the rocks like a dropped bottle, rolling, crashing, damn.

The thumping was in the hall outside. Sam jolted awake, rubbed her eyes, waiting for that old bastard, Mr. Hangover, with his retchy breath to come and sit on her face. Lots of mornings started like this. Then she remembered. Only a dream, my dear. She was safe, still had 3,650-plus sober days under her belt. One at a time.

She stretched long and tall under the embroidered bedcovers, rolled her neck. Aloud: God *Almighty* did I sleep!

She didn't know that before her arrival G.T. had helped her great-grandmother Ida turn the mattress in this room with the change of the moon and sprinkle it with crushed magnolia leaves, love oil, and talcum powder. Under the bed at the place where she rested her head they had placed a bowl of perfumed water.

All she knew was that she felt like getting up, getting out, and slaying a few dragons—as soon as she'd had breakfast.

It was one of her favorite meals, and if she was really lucky—and she had a feeling she was going to be because she could already smell Ida's chicory coffee—there'd be creole cream cheese with French bread. And beignets, Ida's about a thousand times better than the French Market's fried dough squares, white with powdered sugar.

She jumped out of bed, into the shower, and was reaching for her robe, toweling her hair, when she looked up to find Zoe sitting in a chair—the slipcovered one with the quilt. Zoe's great-great-great-grandmother's quilt. That quilt *had* to be magic.

"So?" said Sam, sitting down on the edge of her bed. "To what do I owe the pleasure?"

Zoe was wearing a pale yellow sweatshirt and pants, which were great with her coloring. But even though big and baggy, they didn't hide the fact that there was a skeleton inside. A zonked skeleton. Take a look at those eyes. First thing this morning, Zoe was already on a toot.

She chewed on a thumbnail. "You narc on me?"

" 'Bout what?"

" 'Bout the coke in the Ladies at the Roosevelt."

Sam liked that about youngsters. They might not tell you what *you* wanted to know, but they got right down to what was on *their* minds.

"Nope."

"Why not?"

"No need to. Kitty already knows."

One foot was jiggling now, a long, skinny foot in a white sneaker trimmed in the same pale yellow as the sweats.

"Does, huh? She never said anything to me about it."

"That's because she doesn't know how to approach you. She's scared."

"Of what?"

"Of losing you. She loves you a lot, you know."

"Yeah." Zoe was playing with a dark curl now, pulling it out, letting it pop back. "I know that. But why'd you say that about losing me? I'm not going anywhere."

"I wouldn't be so sure of that."

"Oh, yeah? Where do you think I'm going?"

"Into a hospital probably. You keep throwing up and snorting, I don't see where else you think you're headed. You're already losing a lot of the enamel on your pretty teeth from tossing your cookies. Have you noticed that?"

Zoe pulled her top lip down, then said, "Are you here to give me lectures? I thought you were here to help get my money."

"I can do two things at once."

Zoe was standing.

"Wait a minute. Let's talk." Sam knew sarcasm didn't work. So why was she popping off? She needed her coffee.

Zoe sat, waited.

"I'm not here to give you lectures. Actually, I probably wouldn't have mentioned it if you hadn't brought it up."

Zoe's foot was swinging again. "I just wanted to know."

"But I will tell you this."

Zoe leaned forward, ready to run right on out of there in those cute sneakers.

Sam knew what that felt like. "Wait, just listen to this part, and then we'll go on." She hit it fast, all in a rush, afraid of stopping. "I don't know if Kitty told you this, though you'd have picked it up last night at dinner if you were listening—I'm a recovering alcoholic. I was drunk for ten years, already well on my way when I was your age. No matter what you think, it's pretty much the same thing as your stuffing your face then puking your guts out and your tooting junk up your nose. Addiction all comes from the same place—the same hole in your middle that needs to be filled up. I've been where you are. I know you don't believe me. You think you're all alone. You're not. There are millions out there with the same problems, thinking they're dealing with them the same way you are, and failing. I can help you if you want to be helped, put you in touch with some people. That's the end of the lecture." Sam took a quick breath. "Now, one of the things I'm interested in is if there's any way in which your addiction could be related to your father's death."

"*What?*" Zoe shook her head as if a bullet had just sped past, which was more or less what Sam intended.

"Did your dad know you were a user?"

Zoe shook her curls. "No way."

"Are you sure? He was a doctor. He knew the signs, Zoe. He wasn't stupid."

"Yeah, but he wasn't around much either." Her answer was real quiet.

Sam could almost see her, a tiny girl in a big old house on a Sunday afternoon, playing alone in her room. She knew. She'd been there.

"He knew you were bingeing and purging."

"I guess so. Yeah, I mean he used to talk with me about my weight. Said I ought to put a little flesh on. But I think—" She held out a matchstick of an arm and her voice took on an edge. "I think I'm—"

"You think you're too fat. Now, I *don't* think your bulimia has anything to do with your dad's death—but drugs are a whole other matter. You *never* know what rabbit hole they're gonna lead you down."

Zoe stood and walked around the room as if she'd never seen it before. She ran her fingers along silver-framed pictures of relatives long dead, stared out the window for a while. Then she turned. "What do you want to know?"

"Just tell me how you got involved with coke. Tell me about your dealer."

That set her off again. Zoe paced, but this time she was moving her mouth too, starting back at the beginning, or least the beginning as she understood it. She told Sam about faking her dad's signature on notes to the teacher. Then doing it for other kids for cash. Changing the money into coins, the building blocks for the silver towers in her room. Then, because she thought that was off the subject, she jumped back to the 'ludes, faking prescriptions for them.

"And then, well, you know, one drug just leads to another. You can't keep doing 'ludes forever." She gave Sam a look, as if this were a quiz.

" 'Cause you keep falling down, is that what you mean?"

"Right." Zoe popped her a little grin.

It wasn't exactly cute, Sam thought, letting her feel smug, like knowledge about drugs was cool, but as all of the Lee women had let her know in one way or another, Zoe's problems weren't exactly why she'd been invited here today, were they?

"So coke became your drug of choice?" *For lots of good reasons,* Sam was tempted to add, the primary one being that it also suppresses your appetite, an extra added attraction for a bulimic. But she didn't.

"Right."

"And who's your dealer?"

Zoe gave her an even look, but her mouth stayed closed.

"Okay. I'll tell you why it's important. Let's say your dad *did* know you were using. Let's say he found out who you were buying the stuff from and he decided he was going to track down the son of a bitch, and I'm sure that's what he would have called him, and beat the doowaddy out of him. Do you think then maybe this person might have had reason to drive a Buick into your dad's head?"

"You bitch!"

Zoe was standing again, ready to roll.

"Sit down," Sam barked.

Zoe didn't budge.

There were times to be cool—and times not to. "I said sit the fuck down."

Zoe sat down with a big pout on her face. Her very very pale face.

"Call me what you want, but I'm also a realist. And though what I've painted for you is a highly unlikely scenario, it might also be the truth. And the truth is what I came over here from Atlanta for. Not to waste my time or yours. Not to be jerked around. Do you know what I mean?"

Zoe nodded.

"So let's get to it. Just tell me the name of your dealer, and I'll check him out. I won't tell him that you told me—"

"You promise?"

"—unless I absolutely have to. Like I said, there's probably nothing there. But I'd just like to close that door for myself. Okay?"

Sam was trembling a little inside. Playing the heavy wasn't her favorite game.

"Okay."

"So?"

"Billy Jack."

"Jack's his last name?"

"I guess so. That's all I ever heard anybody call him."

"Where do I find him?"

"He's a waiter at Patrissy's on Royal."

"Good. Thanks."

"Can I go now?"

"You may."

Sam thought it was the better part of wisdom not to remind Zoe that she'd invited herself in. She hadn't called this meeting in the first place.

Ten

Marietta Duchamps Dupree, wife of Maynard Dupree, Esq., mother of his three sons, former Queen of Comus, and president-elect of the Orleans Club, an Uptown ladies' social organization whose members met in its lovely mansion on St. Charles to lunch and talk about needlepoint, Audubon prints, Paris boutiques, and good works, had watched Maynard struggle into his clothes early that morning—forbearing to tell him that he needed to either get a new suit or lay off the cream sauces. Then Maynard heaved himself into his brand-new Lincoln and peeled out of their driveway.

The minute he was gone, she dialed her lover's number. "He's off to the wars. Wanta come over?"

"I'd love to, darlin', but I can't. Got business to tend to this morning."

"I remember when I used to be your only business."

"Now, sugar, don't be that way."

"Now, sugar," Marietta growled deep in her throat, and they both laughed. Then, "I sure do wish I knew what he was up to."

"What do you care?"

"You know I don't really. Except, if I get the goods on him—well, I could use another trip to somewhere nice. Like Barbados."

"Aren't you bad?"

"You loved Barbados. Especially knowing that Maynard was paying for it."

"I did. Ain't I bad too?"

"You are *terrible.*"

"So what you think?"

"I don't know. But he's been busting a gut to get out of here every Wednesday morning for about the past six weeks. Up at the crack of dawn. I *know* he's meeting whoever it is over in Lafayette Cemetery."

"You're kidding."

"I'm not. I followed him one morning. But I can't exactly trail him into there. He'd see me in a minute."

"You think that's where they're screwing?"

"Honey, I don't know. We *know* Maynard's weird, married me only 'cause my family's even better'n his, but, like I told you, after the three boys, bang, bang, bang, I zipped it up. Said no way, son. I'm off to Spa Land, staying six months if that's what it takes. You hire a nanny and nursemaid for those chi'rren. I am getting *svelte*. And *staying* that way."

"I *love* your knobby little knees."

"Get on with you." Then her laugh erupted. "Can you see Maynard huffing and puffing up against one of those old tombs?"

"Or *inside*. Maybe they got into one of those giant economy-sized numbers—the ones that look like a little temple—they're in there doing the dirty deed."

"Oooooh. That's *disgusting*. Gives me the shivers."

"You wouldn't think so if it were the two of us. You want to try it sometime? Don't you have the key to your family's mausoleum?"

"Oh." Marietta gave a little sigh. "I'm fanning myself. You have the nastiest mind in Orleans Parish. Chéri, you old sugar tit, you."

Maynard was humping all right, but not in the way Marietta envisioned.

He was busting a gut, trying to figure a way out of this mess. He was a lawyer, for chrissakes. How could he have let this dumb peckerwood get him into this can of worms? It was a disaster.

And it wasn't like he could go to somebody and *talk* about it.

What the hell was he going to say?

He looked down at his gold Rolex. As usual, he was late. He didn't know why the son of a bitch insisted on these crack-of-dawn meetings. Except *he* didn't want anyone seeing them either. But wouldn't you think they could meet somewhere *normal?* Up ahead, he could see one of the bastard's boots sticking out. He was always doing that, hiding behind one of the tombs and then jumping out. Boo! He was gonna kill his golden goose with a heart attack, he wasn't careful.

Maynard could just see himself sitting down with his father. Saying, Dad, there's something I need to talk to you about. The bulldog-faced bastard'd throw him right out of his study. Ever since his dad had gone head to head with Huey Long—Dad, being one of the Old Guard, tried to teach that country boy about city ways—he's never had a moment's patience for what he called pantywaists.

You wuddn't such a pantywaist, you'd have run that bastard Church Lee through, he'd always said. You never should have let him get away that day out under the oak in Audubon Park. Let yourself get stopped by an old bitch with a dog and a couple of cops who were on my goddamn payroll, for chrissakes.

Well, he should have. He should have had it over with some honor when he was young. His father would have fixed it for him then. But not now. No way.

And now, finally, Church Lee *was* dead. He'd got his wish at last. But boy oh boy was there the piper to pay.

"Counselor, oh, Counselor."

Goddammit to hell. The trash was playing with him, calling him from behind that tomb with the flying angel on top, like he was some kind of fish on a line.

If only he hadn't been so drunk. He couldn't remember much at all of that afternoon in the Pelican that led to this day.

Oh, sure, there were some things that stuck with him. He'd already had a few shots, he remembered that, crying in his beer and trying not to show it, pissed at himself that he hadn't stopped Church's kid, Zoe, from being queen the next day. He remembered how he was trying to think of something to embarrass her with, some stunt to pull in front of the reviewing stand or at the ball, when he'd gotten into that conversation with Jimbo. They were talking about Jimbo's beating up his wife. *That* was it—the part that suckered him in, that he liked, that dirty little secret down inside himself that he would never tell anyone—what *really* turned him on. Not that he'd ever slugged a woman—but it was the idea of it. . . . And then there were a whole lot more drinks. He was buying, he remembered that part, and that semitrashy redhead, Chéri, the one who played tennis with Marietta sometime, *anyway,* Chéri came in, twitching her butt all over the place, and then there was some joking about Jimbo killing somebody.

Killing that nigger ambulance driver, that's what it was. Lots of joking. Everybody knew they were joking, right? And then they threw Chéri in the pot. He'd said something about just doing it, not talking about it. It gave him a headache to think of that now.

And then Church.

Calvin was the one who said that. Something like—throw Church Lee into it and you got yourself a deal.

Well, it was a joke. Everybody knew about the feud between him and Church, how they'd been jacking each other around for years. Actually, they'd grown kind of comfortable with it, kind of affectionate toward each other, in a grudging sort of way, the way you do with a toothache you just keep chewing on. Something almost *pleasurable* about it.

The next thing he knew, Church was dead, squashed like a bug on St. Charles Avenue, a couple of blocks from his house.

How did that look?

Well, it didn't look good, he could tell you that, even if he could prove that he'd been sitting with a couple of boys in a suite upstairs in the Roosevelt after the Queen's Breakfast, having a nightcap. At least that's where he *thought* he was.

It was true that lately his drinking had been scaring him a little. He needed to cut back. Boy, he and Church had had that in common, all right. Blood boozers. Ha! But recently, every once in a while, it had gotten to where he just couldn't remember things. He'd have these little bitty blips of blackout, and then, a big one. The truth was, he wasn't really sure how he'd gotten home that evening. He remembered going into that hotel suite. But he couldn't form a picture of himself coming out. However, he was *damned* sure he hadn't stolen an antique car, that's what the papers had said, an antique car, and run over Church. Nope. He'd been having a nightcap upstairs with—well, he couldn't exactly remember who. But if anyone asked him, that was his story and he was sticking to it. So far nobody'd asked him. Oh, people gave him some funny looks, knowing about him and Church and their history. But nobody'd come sniffing around. The cops had kept a pretty low profile and a pretty tight lid on this thing.

The cowboy boot jiggled again and Maynard jumped, sick of it. He hadn't lost all the speed he'd had at the University of Virginia. He landed on that sucker with all fours.

Came up empty.

Nothing in the boot.

And then the son of a bitch jumped *him.*

Grabbed him around the neck.

Wrestled him back and forth on the ground.

Crook of an elbow holding him, choking him.

Jimbo saying, "You give? You give?"

Getting grass stains all over his good gray suit.

Goddammit.

"I give!"

"Say it again."

"Give!"

"Like you mean it."

"I mean it, you son of a bitch!"

"Now, now." Jimbo turned him loose. "There's the old Maynard."

Maynard sat up, a fat boy hunkering up out of the grass, humiliated.

Jimbo was laughing fit to bust a gut. He leaned back on his heels in his stocking feet, a hole in one sock. He rested his hands on the thighs of his jeans.

"You bring me something?" he asked.

That's what he'd said at the end of that first conversation he and Maynard had had after Church had got himself squashed like a bug.

Now, Mr. Dupree, us knowing what we know, what you gonna bring me?

Eleven

Harry was waiting for Sam in the Esplanade Lounge of the Royal Orleans, a wide, sunny atrium with windows onto the old Wildlife and Fisheries Building. On the St. Louis side paraded four little tables and comfy wing chairs, where anybody who looked halfway presentable could rest awhile.

For the past decade this part of the Esplanade had been Harry's unofficial office when he was in town.

There were a couple of pay phones tucked back beside the checkroom which some people knew to call, ring twice, hang up, call back, and if Harry was there, he'd answer.

More than once when he was with a date he wanted to impress he'd taken her into the lounge, slipped out, called the bell captain from one of those phones, and had himself paged.

Harry liked to think he'd grown out of that.

But with a woman like Sam, who knew? He might try anything.

Look at her there, swinging up the steps from the Royal Street side. Her short curls bopping, she was wearing a red silk top that stopped right at her waist above a short black-and-white polka-dot pleated skirt that showed off her legs. She had great legs. If he could write a song about the way that woman made him feel, he'd have Nashville eating out of his hand.

How would it begin?

I thought I knew how angels flew till you stepped off the plane.

Not bad.

She was striding toward him, hipbones first, shoulders back, head last, like a model.

"Hey, sport." Sam was snapping her fingers in his face. "You look like you're off on a slow boat to Tsingtao."

* * *

Harry ordered another cup of coffee. Sam was drinking iced tea.

"Shoot," she said.

Harry gave his watch a long look, as if to say it had been only about eighteen hours since they'd last spoken, and he'd had a few other things to do, including sleeping.

Sam registered the look. It meant he didn't have jack. That was too bad. He was awfully cute, and it would have been fun, working with him.

Then he said, "I checked with the cops, Blackstone and Shea. Nothing new. Not a peep on the car. You know, Sam, this town, family like the Lees, they give the impression they'd just as soon let it lie, the cops aren't gonna do a lot with it."

See? In her head she went over the list of people she wanted to talk with, wondered how long it would take her to get loose from Harry, get on with it.

He was still talking. "But I did find Madeline Lee. Zoe's mom, Church's ex, Madeline Lee Hebert."

Well, now. She sat up.

Harry was giving her his slow smile, like he'd been reading her mind, holding his ace.

"So she's remarried to somebody named Hebert?"

"Seems that way."

"How'd you do it?"

"Just checked with the DMV." He shrugged. "I had 'em run her name Madeline Lee, nothing. Then I looked up their marriage license, hers and Church's. Her maiden name was Villère. I had the DMV try it that way, Madeline, middle name Villère, and it popped."

"Aren't you the clever one?"

"*You* ought to know finding folks is mostly knowing how to use the public records."

"I do, but you get a gold star anyway."

He grinned, then flashed a notebook in front of her. The address on Madeline's driver's license, recently renewed, was in a town called St. Martinville.

"Where's that?"

"Couple of hours drive from here. It's a pretty little town in Cajun country." He stirred his coffee for a minute. "So, you wanta take a ride over there?"

"I might."

Clearing his throat a bit, he said, "I thought *we* might. It's a nice trip."

She nodded, thinking it might be fun, but who had time for fun? "A couple of other matters might have a higher priority."

"Like what, the malpractice case?"

"Cole Leander. That's the man's name."

"I *know*. I was going to tell you that."

She watched Harry's shoulders sag. Damn. One of these days she was going to learn that being faster and smarter than the next guy was not necessarily the way to go. If she were even remotely interested in the next guy.

"The ladies told me," she said, as if getting it from the horse's mouth weren't as big an effort as his sniffing it out. She was trying to give him back his points.

It *sort* of worked. "His warehouse is on the river end of Julia, if you want to talk with him," he went on gamely. "What else did they tell you?"

She filled him in on what she'd learned about the feud between Church and Maynard Dupree, their dueling over Madeline, Church winning her. Harry shook his head.

"So you never heard this story?" she asked.

"Like I said before, I just didn't hang out with that crowd once I started to shave. I wasn't interested in their internecine spats."

"I keep wondering why, after Madeline and Church got married, the trouble between Church and Maynard didn't stop there."

"Beats me." And then, as if seized—which he was—with a compulsion to prove to her that he had some other cards in his hand, Harry was spinning out that afternoon he'd followed Chéri to the Pelican.

"Wait a minute," she said when he finished. "So yesterday, when we talked about Maynard Dupree, and you said remember the conversation Tench and Church had about Maynard at the Sazerac, you had this in your back pocket. You knew that Maynard had been joking around about *killing* Church, for chrissakes."

"Maynard wasn't doing the joking. Calvin was."

"Who the hell's Calvin?"

"The bartender."

"So why was *he* joking about it? Did he just pull it out of thin air?"

"Look, all I'm doing is giving you further substantiation that there was bad blood between Maynard and Church."

"I already knew that." She could hear herself. Oh, God. "You've been holding out on me, Harry."

He grinned. "But honest, that's all I've got."

"Sure, sure. Like I can believe you now." She pushed her advantage. "Who else was there?"

"I told you. Jimbo King, a dude I used to see out on the rigs—"

Oil rigs? *That* was sort of sexy. "You worked on a rig?"

Harry nodded. "A while ago."

"You'll have to tell me about that sometime."

Why, he'd be proud to. He'd heard that little dingdong note of curiosity in the voices of smart women before, real smart women who carried tan briefcases and wore navy blue suits and lusted in their hearts after guys riding Harleys.

"It's not likely Jimbo and Maynard would be friends, is it?" Sam asked.

"Hardly. But that doesn't mean they wouldn't stand around shooting the breeze."

"Who else was there in the bar?"

"Some strangers, guys who were listening a little, but mostly minding their business. And Chéri, of course. She was there for part of the conversation. That's why *I* was there, following her." Then he told her about Chéri's tobacco-brown Mercedes and her make-believe neck injury.

"What day was this?"

"The same day, that Monday, right after I saw you at the airport."

"Is Chéri a redhead? Bright red hair, brighter than Kitty's?"

"That's *right*. You probably saw her at the gate. She came in on the flight from New York just after yours."

"She's a pretty woman; I remember her."

"Not bad." A little flashy for me, he wanted to say. My taste in women runs more toward classy brunettes—like you, for example.

Sam was running the redhead around in her mind. "Actually, I saw her later, outside. In fact"—she was warming to it now—"*she* was the one who was getting into a long white limo with this slick-looking man, probably mob—"

"Joey the Horse."

She gave him a look. "Joey the Horse, when that crazy little blond guy who was in the crosswalk got cut off and he started banging on the limo. The driver opened the door and knocked him down. Then the little guy reached into his jacket and—" She paused, realizing she'd gone too far.

"And what?"

The best defense was an offense. "Where were *you*?"

"Hiding behind a luggage cart. I told you I was tailing Chéri, snapping pictures of her without the neck brace. But have I missed something here? What does any of this have to do with Church or Maynard?"

"I don't know. Now I found out you're holding out this whole thing on me, where Maynard's joking about killing people—"

"I told you it wasn't really May—"

"I figure we might as well go back over the whole thing. You might have missed something."

"Thanks."

"Another viewpoint couldn't hurt. You know what I mean."

"Your call, lady." His hands were out flat, fanning sideways. "Whatever you say. Okay, so we're at the airport. The guy reaches in his jacket—"

She hadn't meant for him to go back *that* far.

"I'm waiting," he said. "What happened next?"

She might as well go for it. He said he hadn't seen what went down anyway. "The little guy got shot."

"Good God! Really?"

"Yeah, we just barely got out of there in time, would have been held up by the cops as witnesses the rest of the day. We decided to let some other citizens do their civic duty."

"In time for what?"

"To make lunch at Galatoire's." Then Sam was laughing, remembering herself and Kitty hightailing it, heads down in the taxi.

"Some reporter *you* are."

"I was on vacation. I didn't have time." Then she caught the look on his face, the sly smile. Uh-oh, he knew something she didn't.

"Well, Ms. Bigtime," he was saying, "for your information, the blond guy didn't get shot."

"*No?* Did you see it?" she wasn't giving in *that* easily.

"Not exactly. Chéri was talking about it at the Pelican."

"And—?"

He told her: What sounded like a car backfiring *was* a car backfiring. The little guy fainted. Then Chéri and Joey waited for the ambulance.

Then he said, "That was how they got to the killing part, I mean, the joking-about-killing part in the Pelican—talking about that incident and the ambulance. Chéri said something about the ambulance driver being a black woman."

"Was it G.T.? G. T. Johnson?"

"Yeah, that's right. A real piece of work, G.T. You know her?"

"Her great-grandmother Ida works for the Lees. Or used to work for them; she's as old as Ma Elise, has been with her forever. Mostly the two old ladies just hang out together. Kitty says they shoot pool. Anyway, *what* did they say about G.T.?"

"Jimbo was complaining about her. It seems as though G.T. is his next-door neighbor over on General Taylor."

"That's her name."

"What?"

"That's G.T.'s name, General Taylor."

"She's named General Taylor and she lives on General Taylor?" Harry asked.

"Listen. It's your city. I'm just visiting."

"*Anyway.* Jimbo was pissed off because G.T. had stepped in when he was beating up on his wife."

"I like him a whole lot already. He sounds like my kind of guy."

"You know—" Harry stopped and stared off.

"What?"

"When I was waiting for Chéri at the airport, when you were waiting for Kitty, there was this blonde wearing a necklace that spelled out her name. You know what I mean?"

"Tacky gold necklace with the big letters."

"Right, T-e-r-i. I can see it clear as day, which is the name of Jimbo's wife, that's what he said, and this blonde I saw had a baby and a shiner."

"And?"

"Well, that could have been Jimbo's wife running away. You know, I think I put it together when I heard him talk about her in the bar, and then it just fell out of my mind."

"Harry, we've lost our way here. We're way off track. What difference would it make if it was his wife?"

"Maybe it doesn't mean anything, but wouldn't that be weird?" He couldn't seem to let the thought go.

"It would be a coincidence. I'm very big on coincidences. That's why I'm such a good reporter. Things just fall in my lap. But let's go back here. You said this guy Jimbo was talking about killing G.T. Is that where we were?"

Harry explained how Jimbo had said he was thinking of killing G.T. because she kept butting in when he was beating up his wife and somebody, Maynard, he thought, no, maybe it was Jimbo again, said to throw Chéri in, too, kill Chéri too. Make it a two-for-one deal.

"Why Chéri?"

"Because she'd pissed Maynard off, hocking him about his hating

Church and being captain of Comus but not having the guts to stop Zoe from being queen. Then Calvin threw Church into it too. Said they'd kill all three."

"*Who* would?"

"Well." Harry scratched his head. "Nobody, exactly. It was all bull anyway. At least it *sounded* theoretical. You know, drunks talking, being stupid. Macho. But I can tell you this. The conversation made Maynard awfully nervous. He was *squirming,* saying they ought not to be talking like that. But the other guys, Calvin and Jimbo, they were just pulling his chain. Fat Uptown lawyer, you know, he was fair game."

Sam was thinking. She pointed a finger. "You know, G.T. was at the accident when Church was killed."

"She *was?* You mean she was driving the ambulance that picked Church up? I don't know, maybe the name of the service was in the police report, I didn't notice."

"Wait." She closed her eyes, thinking. "Yes, she *did* eventually drive Church to the hospital. His body. He was DOA."

"I know that."

"Okay, but she was already there. She happened on the scene just as it went down."

"Like a—coincidence."

"Yes, but I—well, I never got a chance to talk with her about it. Except we both saw the driver's face—the mask, rather. We both gave statements, but I had to get back to Atlanta. They certainly didn't need a houseguest in the middle of the funeral and all—anyway, the point is she was there. *In fact,* the Buick hit the ambulance too. At least once. Maybe twice. Are you thinking what I'm thinking? Is it possible?"

"You mean that *this* was supposed to be a two-for-one, kill Church, then G.T.?"

"Well?"

"How'd he get them both to the same place at the same time, by ESP?"

"Arranged it."

"He made a date with them? He said, Church, no matter how drunk you are, you be on the corner of St. Charles and First Street at quarter of three, Ash Wednesday morning, and G.T., you be there too. That's your theory?"

"Or maybe Church just got in the way. *G.T.* was really the target, but the driver missed. You know, Harry, you're never gonna amount to spit if you don't learn to consider all the possibilities."

"Amount to spit? *Spit?*"

"Shhhh. People are staring."

Actually, he was even cuter when he was mad, sort of like a kid with a busted train. And he'd be even madder if she told him that.

"So exactly where does this line of thinking lead us, *Miz* Adams?"

She spread her hands as if she'd delivered him a fait accompli.

"To Maynard, that's what you're saying?" Harry asked.

"To Maynard or Jimbo. Or Calvin."

"Not Calvin. No way."

"Why?"

"He's not the type."

"I beg your pardon."

"Just trust me. I'll humor you with Maynard or Jimbo, but forget Calvin."

"Humor me?"

"Humor you. As a guest, on foreign territory. I'll give you the benefit of my *considerable* doubt. Now, do you want to go grab a bite at Galatoire's?"

"It's only eleven-thirty. I just had breakfast."

"Forget I ever mentioned it. Now, would it interest you to spend a few minutes speculating about motivation here?"

"We know Maynard's motivation. He had a hate-on for Church for about a zillion years."

"I'll grant you that. Now, what about Jimbo?"

"I don't know about Jimbo. Maybe Maynard paid him. That's why we've got to talk with him."

"Okay. Now, as I, in my poor, benighted way understand it—"

"You're leaning on that awfully hard."

"—we need to talk with a bunch of people. Madeline, Church's exwife, who might have suddenly decided after all these years to kill him. Cole Leander, whom Church blinded, who's pressing the malpractice suit. Maynard Dupree, of course. Jimbo King—"

"Yes, even if it was drunk talk. And I want to talk with G.T."

"You don't suspect her?!"

"No, of course not. But she *was* at the crime scene, her ambulance did get hit, and Jimbo had been talking about killing her. But I'm leaning real heavily toward Maynard right now, because their thing goes back so far."

"I can see that. You want to talk with anybody around him? His wife?"

"Maybe. Who's she?"

"Marietta Duchamps Dupree. Former Comus queen."

"Of course she is. Why didn't I think of that? Yeah, probably. How do you feel about it being Maynard?"

"Seems most likely. Him or Cole Leander. But we've got ourselves quite a list here of people to interview. Anybody else leaps to mind we ought to check out? Chéri? Joey the Horse? The little blond dude trying to cross the street at the airport? Joey's driver? Teri?"

"Don't be ridiculous. Just because I wanted to *explore* all the possibilities. God, and I thought I was going home tonight."

Harry grinned. "Looks like you're gonna be here for a while."

Sam ignored that. "Though, you know, if Jimbo makes any sense in this—like maybe Maynard hired Jimbo to do his dirty work—Teri just might know something—"

"Right. And what about Zoe?"

"Oh, I almost forgot. There's her supplier, if we take that angle." She checked her notebook. "You know somebody named Billy Jack?" Then to herself: "I wonder if that's *really* his last name."

"Billy Jack? Doesn't mean a thing. Any idea where we can find him?"

"Zoe said he's a waiter at Patrissy's on Royal."

"Good. Anything else related to the family? What about Ma Elise or Kitty?"

"Nooo. . . . Though I don't think either of them's telling me anywhere near the truth about what happened between Church and Madeline. I *think* Kitty would have leveled with me if there were anyone trying to get at *her* for some reason through Church. And let's don't forget what I told you Kitty said about Church's seeing someone, someone he kept secret. I want to know who that is. And Ma Elise? I can't imagine. Zoe? We've got Billy Jack. Oh! They were telling me this story about Church getting mugged."

"When?"

"Back in the fall sometime. Zoe said the beginning of the deb season."

"That's six months ago." Harry sounded skeptical.

"That long ago. You're right, it's probably nothing. Zoe said Church got a burst of testosterone, outran the mugger, who came up empty. Didn't even get his wallet."

"Too bad Church couldn't outrun a Buick."

Sam gave him a look.

"I know. Bad joke." He pushed back from the table. "Okay, so where do you want to start? There's a *lot* of talking to be done here.

You want to split it up?" Of course, he wanted to hang out with her. He was hoping she'd say no.

"Sure. I don't want to start with Maynard, though."

"Fine, I'll take him."

"No way. Maynard's mine."

"Did I miss something? Didn't you just say—"

"I meant, I want to work up to him. I want to know more before I go barging in on the most likely suspect."

"Excuse me. How far back would you like me to start?"

"Why don't you see if you can nose out who Church was seeing?"

"You're a pain in the butt, you know that?"

She gave him a level look.

"Okay, okay. Ladies' choice."

She made a face like she had gas, then, "Or you could start with Billy Jack."

He raised an eyebrow. "What about Jimbo?"

Noooo. She wanted Jimbo too. Oh, God, this was stupid, her trying to work with Harry. She'd never been good at sharing with anyone. It wasn't her fault; she was an only child.

She tried a counteroffer. "If you do Billy Jack, you could have lunch at Patrissy's. You could do it right now. Weren't you hungry?"

He considered that for a minute. "Actually"—he threw money on the table, stood, taking her elbow—"you follow me. I'll point you at Cole Leander's on Julia. And we could stop by Mother's. It's on the way."

They were down the steps in a flash.

Hell, why not? she thought. "Killer oyster po'boy at Mother's, as I remember."

On the sidewalk now he smiled the slow smile. Food was food. Foreplay was foreplay. It didn't *have* to be Galatoire's before he took her by the hand and they played out the rest of his daydream.

Twelve

Sam was drunk on food, on a Ferdie Debris from Mother's. Harry'd convinced her she had to try the combo: juice and gravy and bits of browned roast from the bottom of the pan over ham and roast beef on a French loaf with creole mustard, lettuce, and tomato.

She was staggering—an easy mark for the two little kids outside Cole Leander's barns, which were not red, as she had imagined, but a series of enormous pale green Quonset huts.

"Hey, lady, gimme a quarter, we'll watch your car."

"Yeah, where's it going?"

"Goin' bye-bye, you don't get some 'nsurance."

She was already reaching in her purse for change.

"Neighborhood's that tough?" She looked up and down the industrial street. Except for a couple of big trucks, nothing moved.

"Neighb's *bad.* Thanks, lady. We watch your car good."

"How come you're not in school?"

"We waiting for lunch."

Sam scanned the street again. "Doesn't look like any cafeteria to me."

"Yeah. Uh-uh, well, you just wait till the truck come. San'wich truck be here, Mr. Leander he turn the sidewalk into a *restaurant.*"

The taller boy thought he'd gotten off a good one, shoving the shorter, probably his brother, almost knocking him down. They exchanged high fives.

"Mr. Leander buys you lunch?"

"*Two* lunches. Sometimes three."

Just then a truck painted with red and yellow stripes toodled around the corner and stopped. Its music reminded Sam of long-ago county fairs, the oom-pah-pah of a calliope.

"*Old* Mr. Leander?" she said.

"That the one."

"*Blind* Mr. Leander?"

"One used to chase us with dogs. Go blind, my mama say, he got humble. Watch out now, lady. Out of the way. Here Mr. Leander come."

With that a side entrance of one of the Quonset huts opened, Cole Leander exited behind a German shepherd guide dog. He filled the whole door frame, a giant in a bright orange jumpsuit. He was silver-haired, egg-shaped with a bay window of a belly—in his handmade alligator cowboy boots about six and a half feet tall.

His voice was thick and rich. "Delilah, you smell any boys out here?"

The dog barked, the signal for a well-practiced routine—the two little boys assuming four, or was it six, voices, running in circles, shaking Mr. Leander's hand from different heights, now squatting, now on tiptoe, then the shorter perched atop the taller's shoulders. They included the man who sold the sandwiches in the joke—*Buster*'s what he called all the boys, real and imaginary—shoveling out franks as long as the old man and the boys kept ordering.

When they'd stuffed down their fill, "This here lady's looking for you," the older child said, the one who'd taken her quarter.

"She is?" said Cole Leander. The blind blue eyes turned toward her. "You want a hot dog, darlin'?"

"No thank you, sir. I just ate over at Mother's."

"Well, well. Idn't that wonderful? You know, I'd like to take these boys"—he waved in their direction—"over there sometime. Think they'd like some of those *big* ol' po'boys, but we, my driver and I, couldn't fit 'em all in the car. This many boys. Idn't that a shame?"

"It is, indeed." Sam grinned at the two miniature extortionists. The smaller one stuck his tongue out.

"Well, now, boys, y'all get on back to school," he said, shooing them like biddies, "me and this lady's gonna go on inside, see what she wants with a pore old blind bastard."

The interior of the dimly lit barn was a freak show, a surreal world of giant cowboys and coiling serpents, pirates and showboats. Toothy crocodiles yawned. Skulls gaped. Bogey stared into the face of Miss Liberty. Bay after bay of plaster and plastic and papier-mâché phantasmagorica reached as far as Sam could see.

Mr. Leander, who knew his inventory by heart, was giving her the tour.

"You use them more than once?" Sam asked.

"The figures? Oh, sure. Some krewes do the same thing year after year, though most don't. Now and again they'll swap or buy from one another. Your less affluent krewes will rent floats that rolled earlier in the season and we'll rebuild for them. But the units they sit on—now, there's where you got your history." Leander patted the side of an green and purple Greco-Roman extravaganza. "Yep. Like this baby right here. What you've got under this here Comus float is an old, and I mean *old,* farm wagon. Pull that skirting up, darlin'."

Sam was looking at an iron-rimmed wheel with wooden spokes.

"You see what I mean?"

Cole Leander was one of those men who was passionate about his business, who couldn't tell her enough—once he'd rearranged her introduction of herself to his own liking. By him, she was doing a feature story on the art of float-building.

"Oh, yeah, we're a Pic'N'Pac store of the bi'nis," he was saying. "Got everything here you'd need. The tractors to pull the floats once we build 'em. Kings' and queens' crowns, masks, we got your doubloons and your tossing favors, your gift items. We even do you the insurance."

"You do?"

"Well, through our old friend Tench Young."

"Sort of keeps it all close to home."

"That's the idee. Just a little cottage industry—Mardi Gras."

He laughed at that, and Sam could see he was taken with the notion. Carnival was the kind of "cottage" industry that afforded him alligator boots worth a couple thousand and a diamond ring on every finger. Some of them were dazzlers. Though it was possible they were fakes, like the cache of rubies and emeralds spilling out of a treasure chest behind her. But she doubted it.

Sam and Leander were sitting in his little glass-enclosed office now. His secretary, a motherly type, had brought them each a cup of good chicory coffee. Leander was reared back in his chair. Delilah rested her muzzle on one boot.

"I met your insurance man, Mr. Young, during Carnival. In the Sazerac Bar," Sam said. "I was over here then. Guest of Kitty Lee." She watched his face carefully. But all she saw was a big grin which stretched the waxed ends of his handlebar mustache out wide.

"Kitty Lee," he said. "Idn't she a darlin'? You known her long?"

"Since college."

"Well, idn't that wonderful? I always think that's grand when friends stay in touch over the years. 'Course, if you're an old hound like me, don't ever leave your home grounds in the first place, it's not like you ever lose track of *any*body. Though you might want to sometime." He laughed at that, showing his good humor. "Well, I reckon you heard about the hard time old Tench is giving Miss Kitty. And Ma Elise. Zoe. God Almighty, those Lee women, ain't they something?"

"They are indeed. And they are having their problems with Mr. Young."

"*Problems!*" Leander Cole hooted so loudly, Delilah scrambled to her feet. "Whoa, girl. Daddy didn't mean to scare you." Then to Sam, "Honey, Tench Young got hold of a nickel belongs to you, you got more than problems. You got yourself a hell of an ordeal. Now." He leaned forward as if he could read her face. And she wasn't so sure he couldn't. Then his voice sharpened a little, though it was still sweet—like a well-made piquant sauce. "I been wondering when somebody was gonna come around wanting to talk with me about Church."

Sam didn't say a word, just kept breathing.

"Idn't that really why you're here?" Suddenly he'd given up his fiction that she was there on assignment.

"It does interest me."

Leander roared at that, laughed till he had to wipe the tears. "*Interests* you. I bet it does, missy. Seems to me, ought to interest *somebody,* man gets run down in the middle of St. Charles Avenue, prominent citizen, insurance worth a million, you'd think *some*body'd be asking some questions, wouldn't you—especially of an old friend sued him for ten times that."

"Ten million?" She hadn't known Leander's suit was for that much.

"That's it, missy. That's what I asked for after old Church showed up his snout a little too deep in the ether, happened to be *my* morning I was having him do a little patch job on a retina. I'd already lost the other eye a couple of years earlier, let the same problem go too far 'fore I went for help. So when old Church made that little slip with the laser, well—"

"And you're still pursuing it with his estate?"

Cole Leander let the question sit for a nice long time. The man hadn't worked in this rolling stock form of theater all his life to have no sense of timing.

"Nawh," he drawled finally with a big grin. "I'm gone drop the suit."

"You're settling?"

"Honey, you don't hear so good for a reporter. I said I'm dropping it."

"Why'd you want to do that?"

"Because I decided to forgive him. Man's dead. What's the point? And all the money in the world idn't gonna bring back my sight, is it?"

"Nooooo. But—"

"Seems strange, don't it? Makes you wonder."

"It does."

"Seem strange to you a man could be the orneriest son of a bitch in the city for nigh onto seventy years, then suddenly turn into an old sweetie?"

Sam laughed.

"Well, I was that. You ask anybody. I did great work; me and my boys could build you a float that would make their eyes pop out there on Canal Street. But do you think I would give you the time of day?" He didn't wait for her to answer. "Nawh. I was *mean*. I was a nasty man with nasty ambitions. Mammon was my god. I wanted to roll"—he shifted his great shoulders and belly back and forth—*"wallow* in greenbacks. In greed. In emeralds and diamonds and rubies."

He paused and took a long swig of coffee.

"Though"—and then he laughed—"you might notice I'm still partial to the diamonds." He rubbed his belly, rocks on his fingers flashing. "But you got to allow a pore old blind man a few indulgences—even after he has found the Lord."

Sam had had a feeling they might be headed in this direction.

"Oh, yes." And even with those two words she could see the tent, smell the sawdust and the sweat of a revival preacher. "Yes, I found my salvation in the Lord not too long ago, and just in time, praise the Lord. He wrenched me away from my life of selfishness, money-gorging, and sin."

Leander stood and began to pace around the small office. Delilah, who'd caught this act before, lay her nose on her front paws and watched, moving only her eyes.

"I was lost. Oh, yes, Miss Samantha Adams of Atlanta, Georgia, I was lost. But now, praise the Lord, now I'm found."

The voice was a roller coaster locked into that good-old-time-religion groove. Voice of velvet. Yes, indeedy, Jimmy Swaggart, homeboy from upriver Baton Rouge, had nothing on Cole Leander.

"Have you taken to preaching, Mr. Leander?"

"Oh, no, sugah. Though I thank you for thinking so. That's a compliment. No, I've taken to listening. I'd never listened before in my life."

"And after you started listening, you decided to forgive Church Lee for—"

"Go on. Say it. For blinding me. Yes, but also for giving me vision."

"I beg your pardon."

Cole Leander threw his head back and shook it. He looked like George Schultz doing Bert Lahr doing the Cowardly Lion. He even roared on cue.

Then the voice dropped back down, making a loop-de-loop into a satiny whisper. "Because you see, I am blind but *now* I see. It was Church who introduced me to that blessed angel. That blessed angel of mercy, *praise* her name, Sister Nadine."

Thirteen

"Well, I made an ass of myself last evening, didn't I, but it wasn't the first time, and I suspect it won't be the last, will it?" Kitty was apologizing to Sam over the phone.

"Probably not. But there is one thing I want to talk with you about."

"Yeah."

"About my fee. I really don't think fifteen per—"

"Take a hike, Adams."

"That's what I thought you would say."

"We aim never to disappoint here at Lee & Associates Public Relations. Now, what the heck you been doing since I kicked the poop out of you last night?"

Sam told her about the meetings with Harry and Leander—saving for dessert what Leander said about dropping the lawsuit.

"You think he's trying to get you into bed?"

"Nawh. He's too old—and too holy."

"They're never too old, and you know that's not who I mean."

"Harry? He's too young."

"Ha! And you're keeping your fingers crossed on that one, ain't you, girl?"

"Am not."

"Ah, Sammy, Sammy. This is old Kit you talking to. Now, what you waiting for? 'Fraid he's gonna run you to ground?" Three beats passed. "You know, think about it, Harry might have the stuff to do that very thing."

What stuff was Kitty talking about? "You want to sit around all afternoon talking trash or you want to get on with business here?"

"Well, pardon me, Miss In-a-Big-Hurry. You lived in California too long, girl. They've turned you into a Yankee."

Sam laughed. "That's for sure the first time the Left Coast has ever been accused of lighting a fire under somebody's fanny. Most folks think you go out there for the big snooze."

"Not N'Awlins folk, honey. You know we got the national monopoly on relaxation. Cain't get no work done before lunch—too busy drinking coffee, and then *afterward*—well, you need a little nap, then it's cocktail time and—"

"Kitty, you'd tell me if there was somebody you thought had it in for you, wouldn't you? Wanted to hurt you through Church, I mean—"

"Why, of course I would. Why? Did you run up on somebody said something different?"

"Nope. Just checking. What about Ma Elise?"

"You kidding? She's already outlived all those what were jealous of her beauty, or our family, or our old house."

"That pretty much leaves Zoe, doesn't it?"

"So, what you got?"

Sam took a deep breath. She didn't want to raise Kitty's ire again, harping on the same sore spots.

"Two things. One, Harry's found Madeline."

There was a long silence. Finally Kitty said, "Good. You'll take care of your business with her, and then we'll see where that leaves us. Vis-à-vis Zoe, I mean."

That was a step forward. One more. "And Zoe told me the name of her supplier."

"Yes?"

"His name's Billy Jack. That mean anything to you?"

"Not really. Though this is the second time I've heard it today. Harry called and said something about the same man, left you a message."

"Gee thanks, Kitty. You're a hell of an answering service."

"I was getting to it. He said, just a minute, let me find my glasses here. She read off the words: Billy Jack's no longer at the restaurant. No forwarding. I'll go at him another direction."

Whatever that meant, Sam murmured.

"Wait," said Kitty. "There were two more calls. G.T. said she wanted to talk to you. She left her work number."

"I was going to call her. Woman has great ESP."

"Honey, ESP ain't the half of G.T., once you get to know her. And Hoke Tolliver called. Your boss, he said to remind you, in case you'd forgotten."

"Such a card, that Hoke."

"He said he would appreciate it to hell and gone if you would give him a jingle." Sam could hear her lighting a cigarette. "He sounded kind of cute."

"He is, if you like a man who looks like a hound dog with a crew cut. And you'd have to beat his wife, Lois, off with a stick first."

"Girl, why you bothering me with these little details?"

"Before you go back to earning a living, tell me about this Sister Nadine that Cole was talking about, said Church led him to her."

"Cole Leander's lost his mind is what. Church wouldn't ever have anything to do with that preacher woman. My brother may have had a whole slew of vices, but proselytizing folks, even a slimebag like Cole Leander, into the clutches of TV evangelists wasn't one of them."

"TV?"

"You haven't caught Sister Nadine's act? Oh, that's right. I forget she's on the local cable. But I tell you, she ought to be national. International. Hell of a lot better than Joan Rivers."

"That's not saying much. She's funny, you mean?"

"Hysterical. Ask Ma Elise or Ida. They catch her every afternoon—when they're not over at the poolhall shooting snooker with the boys in tight jeans. But Church—?" And then there was the slighest, the tiniest of pauses. Sam knew something had dawned on Kitty, something she wasn't telling. Then Kitty raced on. "Never Church. If you wanta see her yourself, she's on at three. When ladies get tired of watching Oprah parade herself around, they flip over to Nadine."

"But Leander talked like he *knew* her. Not on the TV, but in *person.*"

"Anybody 'round here can reach right out and touch her, they want to go over to her church. I think she calls it a tabernacle. It's right on the edge of the Quarter, over on North Rampart almost to Esplanade."

"She preaches every day?"

"They broadcast her show live, from right there, every afternoon people got money in their pockets think it's gonna buy 'em a seat in God's balcony. Ma Elise and Ida have been. They said it was some show."

"I guess it's a hell of a lot easier than getting a chair upstairs at the Comus ball."

"See? You've already figured out the appeal of a lady like Nadine in a city snobby as this one. Preaching about an equal-opportunity Jesus. That and the pies—well, you'll see."

"Did you say pies?"

"Listen, I got to get back to work here. Get out there on the street, girl. *Earn* that fee."

"Sit on it, Kitty."

"Thank you ever so much, sweetheart." An imaginary cigar waggled in her voice.

Kitty's Groucho routine had always made Sam laugh. "By the way, Kit," she said, signing off. "It's impolite to keep an old man waiting. Even if he is a slimebag. You ought to return old Cole Leander's call. He's got something real interesting to say."

Talking to G.T. on the phone, Sam could hear the *blap blap blap* of the ambulance's siren in the background.

G.T. was dropping somebody off at Charity. She said it ought to be the last run of her shift. Then she'd have Ark drop her at the St. Louis Street police station, on the rear boundary of the Quarter. It was the safest place in the neighborhood, she said, and there was something near there she wanted to show Sam.

Did Sam think she could find it? She'd meet her out front. Oh, and bring seven dimes, said G.T.

"Man couldn't find his own butt with both hands UPS delivered it to him," Detective Blackstone was saying to his partner, Shea, standing out on the steps of the St. Louis station at shift change. They were talking about their captain, Perkins, who they both thought was a fool. On a good day.

"Uh-oh," said Shea, watching the ambulance pull into the parking lot. Then back up, turn around. "They done come for you, 'Stone. I thought I been smelling something the past three or four days. Reckon you been brain dead at least that long, that Black Jack got ahold of you."

"Yeah," his partner answered. "You gone think something else got ahold of you in a minute here. You see who that is? General Taylor Johnson, what hauled Church Lee to the emergency. Gonna want a full report, wanta know how come we been dragging ass on that thing."

"Yeah. Well, just tell her the truth, 'Stone. A, that it ain't none of her cute little business. And B, we're stupid, no count, don't know what a whole lot of nines is."

"Don't have to tell her nothing. That woman, she just closes her eyes, she *sees* it."

"Yeah. Well, let's give her our whole caseload and see if she can whomp it. Then you and me can tie up the loose ends, haul our fat asses into Earline's old man's boat, head on out to Grand Isle do some fishing. Weather's too nice us to be hanging around this city busting heads."

"I hear that."

Just about then G.T. popped up to the bottom step with her neat little feet laced into a pair of black Reeboks. She was already out of her whites, back into her workshirt and jeans, her regulation street clothes. In her left hand she was carrying a couple of white carnations. She said, "How y'all doin'?"

"Fine. Fine," answered Shea. "You come over here to give us those flowers or bust our chops?"

"Just using your steps to meet the lady's gonna do that little thing for me."

"Uh-huh." Blackstone gave Shea the big wink. "And who's that gonna be? Superwoman?"

"Marie LaVeau, more likely." Shea laughed. "Ain't that the name of that old voodoo queen? One y'all conjure up in your meetings?" He punched Blackstone in the arm. "When y'all stabbing chickens?"

"That's your business." G.T. smiled a pretty smile at them. "Stabbings. Beatings. Killings."

"You get the feeling Miz Johnson here ain't impressed with us?" said Blackstone, giving Shea a wide-eyed look.

"I think she—" Then something else caught Shea's attention. "Lordy, would you look at that? Who you think that is, son?"

"I don't know, but I have the feeling she's headed over here. Probably needs our help in the worst way." Blackstone was tugging on his belt, hoisting his trousers up.

G.T. was already down the steps. Bye-bye, she waved. Then she turned and flipped the words back over her shoulder. "Pretty woman's name is Sam Adams. She's gonna show you boys up something terrible on this Church Lee business. You better get moving, you planning on saving face."

Shea looked at Blackstone. Blackstone looked at Shea. They shook their heads and laughed. "No way, lady. No way."

Fourteen

●

Sam and G.T. were walking uptown on North Rampart toward Our Lady of St. Guadeloupe. Just beyond the church were the Iberville projects, built on the ruins of the legendary Storyville. That once-infamous red-light district had worn a gay, grinning face above a pestilential underbelly. In the present-day grim and deadly projects, what you saw was what you got. This was a neighborhood the guidebooks warned visitors away from.

Sam knew that. "Wait, where are we going?"

G.T. answered. "For a consult."

Sam put her hand on G.T.'s arm. "Whoa, let's stop right here." She didn't even know this young woman. Sure, there was her reputation as a voodoo queen, but did magic make her impervious to mugging, rape? And would whatever Invisible Protective Shield enveloped her work for Sam too? "A consult with whom? Where? About what?"

As they stopped on the front steps of Our Lady, Sam took a closer look at G.T. She had seen her only that one time, the night Church was killed, and that was in the rain and the dark.

General Taylor Johnson was in her early twenties, of medium height, lean, lithe, and light-skinned. Her brown eyes were almost golden. Her long, reddish-brown hair was plaited in little braids laced with bright beads that clicked when she walked. All in all, she looked more like a cute college student with a pert nose and an easy smile than a voodoo queen—though Sam wasn't really sure what one of those looked like.

"What do you mean, a consult?" Sam asked.

"I thought we'd go talk with Mam'zelle." Then G.T. pointed behind the church to the gates of St. Louis Cemetery No. 1. Behind it rose a city of white marble tombs.

"Mam'zelle's here? Mam'zelle who?"

"Mam'zelle Marie LaVeau."

The famous voodoo queen. But wasn't she dead? Of course she was. Otherwise they wouldn't be calling on her here.

"Now, why would we want to do that?" Sam asked. "Listen, I was going to call *you* to talk about Church Lee. We can do that in a coffeeshop."

"Yes. But it might help a lot if we visited Mam'zelle first." G.T. smiled; her strong white teeth looked like little tombstones themselves. "Look, I knew why you wanted to talk with me. Ida told me; besides, why wouldn't you? I was there when it happened, right beside you. I know all about the insurance business, and I'm happy to help you any way I can. But you have to respect where *I'm* coming from." She waved a hand toward the cemetery.

Sam nodded. Maybe. "Go on."

"You probably think I'm nuts, wanting to do this before we start, but that's 'cause you're not from New Orleans. Most people 'round here have no problem with folks practicing the ancient arts. It's part of our religion. Natural as breathing. It helps us get what we need and what we want."

Sam smiled skeptically. She'd lived in California. She'd known people who bayed at the moon, called themselves witches, did all manner of the bizarre. But none of them had ever practiced voodoo. Besides, this young woman looked so normal. She told G.T. that.

G.T. laughed. "I *am* normal. What d'you think—I'm gonna cut your gizzard out? Set you on fire? Listen, I'm a college student—straight as they come."

Well, Sam had called *that* right.

"*And* a trained emergency medical technician. In a couple of years I'm going to medical school. Nothing crazy about that, right? All I'm asking you to do here is step inside the cemetery with me and ask Mam'zelle for a blessing to help us with this thing with Church. She's closer to him than we are, you know, since he's passed over."

Well, she did have a point there, *if* you believed in the hereafter. "Let's sit down on the steps here," Sam said, "and you tell me all about Mam'zelle."

They sat, and G.T. started: "She was a powerful woman in the same way women, especially black women, have always been powerful." Her smile was wry. "Manipulating, hiding, slipping, and sliding."

Then she leaned back and spun out the tale. Marie LaVeau was a free mulatto born in New Orleans around 1800. A hairdresser, and a surrogate mother for many quadroon (one-quarter black) women, she arranged for their common-law (for there was no other kind) marriages to white men through *le plaçage*, a tradition in which a woman of color was courted by a wealthy white suitor, usually after having met at a quadroon ball. Through a surrogate such as Marie LaVeau, the white paramour would meet the woman's parents, agree to buy her a house and to settle a certain amount of money on each of their issue.

Thus Mam'zelle had entree to the rich and powerful white men of the city whom she manipulated with gossip collected from their servants —and from her own psychic abilities. The house she owned on St. Ann was given to her by the father of a young white man whom she saved from the law with a gris-gris—a charm.

The location of the house—where Ida lived now—right at the foot of Congo Square, now Beauregard Square, part of Louis Armstrong Park, and directly in front of the Municipal Auditorium where the Carnival balls were held—was convenient for a voudou queen.

V-o-u-d-o-u, said G.T., was the proper spelling of that word. Then she pointed down the street. They could see the auditorium, the square, the places she was talking about.

To placate whites who were suspicious of voudou, Marie ordered public dances performed in the square every week. Whites thought them magic, but actually they were pleasure dances, Dahomey mating dances, handkerchief dances, conducted to the drumming of a donkey's shinbone.

Mam'zelle invited the police to these bogus entertainments. When the curfew cannon was fired at nine o'clock, the slaves returned to their quarters behind their masters' houses, but the free woman Mam'zelle took her wealthy white clients home to serve them drinks and take their money for powerful charms.

Her compassion was legendary. She tended victims of the yellow fever which plagued the city in the 1850s. Her house became a refuge for orphans and women in distress. And, through her contacts with the rich and powerful, she frequently intervened between the courts and the black community.

"Marie the Sainted" they called her for her work with prisoners. She visited those condemned to death, building an altar, praying with them, giving them gumbo laced with painkilling hallucinogens.

Legend has it that when Mam'zelle grew old and tired, she stepped into a cabin on Bayou St. John and emerged the next morning as a young woman who was known as Marie II, her daughter. After her there may have been a Marie III.

"What is for sure," said G.T., "is that her practices have been handed down through generations of women and are still alive and well."

"In you?"

"And in others."

Sam considered. Maybe it was mumbo jumbo. Maybe it wasn't. But what could it hurt to go pay their respects, unless muggers got them in the cemetery— "Okay, but everybody's told me to stay out of these places."

"When you're *alone,* that's for sure." G.T. pointed a warning finger in her face. "But with me you're safe." Then apparently judging that her audience was warmed up, she handed Sam one of the flowers she'd been carrying. "Ready?"

Sam nodded.

"Now just watch me and do what I do, and stay close beside me."

So Sam followed G.T. the few steps to the cemetery gate, where the young woman kissed her white carnation, gave it a long look, and tucked it inside her bra. She motioned to Sam to do the same. Then G.T. knocked three times on the gate with her left hand, scraped the soles of her sneakers on the sidewalk, and called in a low voice: "St. Peter, St. Peter, please let me in."

Sam repeated the words. She was starting to get into this thing. Besides, if she ever wrote a piece on New Orleans, she'd be hell on local color.

G.T. paused and seemed to sniff the air, then smiled. "I feel a tingling in my spine, a glowing in my belly. That means it's okay."

"Great," said Sam. "What next?"

G.T., motioning her to follow, stepped over the threshold. She stopped on the other side and then turned left, walking loose-hipped down the aisle to the first right turning.

There she stopped. "This is it." She pointed. "Mam'zelle's tomb."

The mass of dirty white marble looked no different from its neighbors except for the hundreds of X's inscribed on every surface.

"Lots of people been here before," said G.T., then reached inside her shirt, pulled out the carnation, kissed it again, and dropped it on the ground in front of the grave.

Sam played Follow the Leader.

"Mam'zelle, it's General Taylor Johnson," said G.T. in a loud voice, then gave Sam the nod.

"And Samantha Adams." Sam felt only a *little* foolish, talking to a grave.

"We're here because we need your help and your guidance. We want to know what happened to Church Lee. We want to know who ran him down." Then G.T. stepped back a bit and motioned to Sam to speak.

She didn't know what else to add. "What should I tell her?" she whispered.

G.T. gave her a sharp look. "Why *you're* here."

To humor you, sweetie, she thought. Then—okay. Why not? You get one wish from the voudou queen. Make it good. Then to her surprise she heard her mouth saying, "I need your help with Zoe Lee."

G.T. nodded approvingly. "Follow me." She began walking around the tomb, stopping every few feet. "It's called Making the Four Corners." Then, with her back to the tomb, she raised her arms to the sky, lowered them back to the earth. Her lips were moving. "Say a prayer," she ordered.

Sam wasn't real big on religion, but one petition *was* familiar to her: God grant me the serenity to accept the things I cannot change, the courage to change the things I can, and the wisdom to know the difference.

That said, she followed G.T. back to the front of the tomb, where they pressed their foreheads against it. G.T. reached into her jeans pocket, fished out her seven dimes, and dropped them in the basket hooked to the front of the tomb. Sam did the same with the coins G.T. had asked her to bring. Then G.T. picked up a piece of red brick lying on the ground and used it to add her *X* to the thousands on the tomb. A *big X*. Sam's was even bigger.

"Thank you," G.T. said to Mam'zelle.

"Thank you," echoed Sam.

"Now wait. Shhhhh. Listen."

Sam didn't hear a thing.

"Listen harder."

She closed her eyes again. And then the message came. It was the one she'd heard a thousand times before. One word, the hardest one for her.

Patience.

When she opened her eyes, G.T. was reaching out to her. They left the cemetery hand in hand, pausing to knock again at the gate with their right hands, scrape their feet once more. "Please let us out, St. Peter," they chorused. Then they stepped up over the threshold, stepped *big,* like little girls playing a game.

Out on the sidewalk G.T. asked, "Do you feel sad?"

"No."

"Scared?"

"Not anymore."

"Good, then we don't have to back up and do this again. Let's go have ourselves a drink over at the Napoleon House instead and start figuring this thing out."

Pavarotti was belting out an aria from *Madame Butterfly* over the speakers above the ancient bar at the corner of Chartres and Toulouse. The Napoleon House was the kind of place where they replastered every hundred years whether they needed to or not. It sported bare light bulbs, opera posters, checkerboard tile floors, and had been one of Sam's favorites when she was drinking. Sober, she still liked it.

They sat at a dark wooden table beside an open arched door. G.T. sipped a beer in the late afternoon light. For a while the music was enough, and they were quiet.

Sam gazed out at the tourists draped with cameras out on Toulouse. She'd bet none of them had been taken to St. Louis Cemetery No. 1 for a blessing from Mam'zelle by a New Age voudou queen.

Ah, New Orleans, New Orleans, she sighed to herself. She truly loved this city, one that casual visitors never got to see, though they thought they did. They flew back home with their Mardi Gras beads, T-shirts, Hurricane glasses, a little smug about their hangovers, proud that they'd let it all hang out on Bourbon Street, done a little too much partying in the town that care forgot.

That time forgot was more like it. That's what the city was all about. Time. Blistering heat. Water.

The oil companies could come and build all the bronze glass towers they wanted to on Poydras Street, pretending that progress had come to town in a big way.

But progress had already failed. The bottom had fallen out of the oil market, and the Poydras towers were mostly empty like many other buildings in the city. Empty except for ghosts.

No, New Orleans wasn't what the tourists thought, nor was it about business. New Orleans was a state of mind—slow, Mediterranean, indolent, easy. It was stuck in the fifties. The 1850s Uptown in the Garden District. The 1950s Downtown.

It was a living museum of its proprietors—Indians, French, Spanish, then the French again before Napoleon sold the whole territory to Jefferson for a few bucks.

The very bar where they were sitting was so named because a group of loyalists bought the building for the little emperor in case he needed a safe place. Most certainly he would have preferred it to the island of Saint Helena, where he spent his last miserable days constipated from the English gruel.

Then, too, New Orleans was a swamp, a yellow-fever-ridden bog perched on the edge of Lake Pontchartrain, a favored destination of Caribbean hurricanes, and at the bottom of the muddy Mississip, the drain for the continent.

It was a lazy city that would rather preserve itself and its ways than fight. The Confederate flag had flown less than a year when David "Damn the Torpedoes" Farragut asked the mayor nicely to lower it please, and Reconstruction started.

New Orleanians had always relished good food, good music, and they loved to dance. They adored political intrigue and still talked about redneck Huey Long as if he were a present-day threat to gentility and the Old Guard and their way of life. It was home to a state comptroller who—just before they hauled him off to jail for being more greedy than was seemly even in a climate of consummate corruption—said that when he took the oath of office he hadn't also taken a vow of poverty. Over long lunches in the city, the line still got a big laugh.

But mostly, and forever, it was a flat place of water and light. Here the sky was a huge bowl that on hot days filled with mile-high clouds, and, just when you thought you couldn't stand the heat one more minute, it dumped down afternoon rains with a violence that was both sudden and magical. New Orleans grew and thrived in the midst of swamp and lake and bog. It smelled of heat and rot and boundless vegetation. It was bayous and thick, clipped lawns, bearded live oaks and fuchsia crepe myrtle, banana trees, pink azaleas, bamboo, roses, camellias, bougainvillea, hibiscus, oleander, and jacaranda blooming trumpets of blue. Its outskirts were populated with alligators and musk-rat and water moccasins waiting for a chance to creep in and settle on your patio just when you thought yourself safe behind thick, cool walls that bespoke civilization.

And then there was the black/white thing. Look at General Taylor sipping her beer. Kitty had told Sam the young black woman was named after the street on which she was born when her mother's taxi didn't make it to the hospital on time. She lived on that Garden District street still, a street dubbed for a slave-holding general, Old Rough and Ready, who later became president of the United States. Now, wasn't that New Orleans?

Fabulously wealthy landowners like Kitty's ancestor, Augustus Lee, had brought blacks from Africa to New Orleans to work their plantations, grow their rice, raise their children, build their houses in the Garden District. Now those slaves' descendants, like General Taylor Johnson, were in the majority, a majority that elected light-skinned mayors with names like Morial and Barthelemy, who were part of the black aristocracy.

So on the surface, at least, those slaves' descendants ran the Big Easy. In truth, however, that old dictum still held: In the North, whites said to blacks, Get as big as you want, but don't get too close. In the South, get as close as you want, but not too big. So New Orleans's black mayors *looked* big, but the real power was where it had always been, in the hands of their close, Uptown, white neighbors.

Now in the Napoleon House, Sam awoke from her reverie. Pavarotti had long finished his aria, and the mournful thrumming of Beethoven's Waldstein Sonata filled the air.

It was time to get down to it.

So she asked the young voudou priestess, pre-med student, ambulance driver about *her* neighbor: "G.T., tell me about Jimbo King."

G.T.'s eyebrows rose. "Now who've you been talking to?"

"What can you tell me about him?"

"Nothing good—but what does he have to do with Church?"

"Maybe nothing. I'm feeling my way here."

G.T.'s eyes focused somewhere deep inside. "You know, I think about Church Lee every day—and dream about him too. *Something* led me to be there when he was killed."

"What do you mean?" Sam made a mental note to come back later to Jimbo.

G.T. recounted how something had compelled her to drive the ambulance over to St. Charles that evening.

"A feeling, you mean?" When G.T. nodded, Sam went on. "And do you think the Buick hit you on purpose?"

"You know, I've been running that over and over in my mind. I *think* it was an accident."

"Even though he got you twice?"

"The man was just all over the place, wasn't he? Bouncing out of control."

"Are we sure it was a man driving, not a woman?"

"I don't know. We *think* it's a man, don't we? But that's in part because of the mask."

"Explain."

"It was a man's face, wasn't it, on the mask."

"You're right! But whose face? Anybody special? Mickey Mouse or—"

"No, it was just cheap goods you can buy in any store, 'specially in the Quarter. Just a plain old creepy man's face."

G.T. was smart, paid attention, and had good instincts, the kind of good woman who'd always been dangerous for the bad guys to have around.

"So let's go back. The car hits your ambulance twice, and you think it was an accident. So there's nobody you know who wants to hurt you?"

"Nobody just springs to mind. Except Jimbo King when he's tanked up, maybe, if you want to talk about him. He's not so bad when he's sober."

"And he has it in for you because of his wife?"

"Umm-hum. He doesn't like it that I've stopped him from killing her a couple of times."

"*Killing* her?"

"He probably doesn't see it that way. But it's all the same if she ends up dead, isn't it? The way I figure it, anytime a man starts beating up on a woman, there's murder on his mind."

"I couldn't agree with you more. But let me fill you in on something here—" And then Sam told G.T. about the conversation Harry had overheard in the Pelican. "So you think Jimbo was kidding or not, talking about killing you?"

"That makes it look pretty bad for him, doesn't it? But I don't think he's got it in him to do something that *active,* if you know what I mean. He's the type who would sort of *slide* into something. If it were easy. If it were sitting right there."

"So, let's try this. He's hired by someone, let's say Maynard, to kill Church. And you just happen along, led there by a hunch, whatever, and he pops you a couple of times after he gets Church, once he sees you, hoping for a twofer."

"It's an interesting idea. Except I don't think the driver behind that mask was Jimbo King."

"Why not?"

"Jimbo's over six feet tall. Didn't the driver look a lot shorter than that to you?"

"I'm not sure. Especially in that old car—in the rain and the dark."

"It *did* happen real fast. But he seemed short to me."

And that was a very important point. Sam had been focused on

Church. What a good idea to talk with G.T., whose attention, it turned out, had been on the driver.

"Now, back to Jimbo, even if he is too tall. Maybe he was scrunched down."

"Maybe."

"He was particularly angry with you on that afternoon in the Pelican because the night before you'd helped his wife?"

"Teri. That's right. I took her and the little boy away from the house."

"Where did you go?"

"To a safe place. I'd rather not say exactly where."

She was right. The address of a women's shelter was a secret best kept. "Has she gone back to him?"

"No."

"You know where she is now?"

"I know where she's staying. I know she and the baby are okay."

"Has Jimbo talked with you since then?"

"No, he glares at me if we run into each other coming out of the house. But I wouldn't say on his best day Jimbo's the world's greatest conversationalist."

"Has he asked you where she is?"

She shook her head. "He knows better than that. I will tell you something, though. What you said about somebody hiring Jimbo to kill Church? Well, he's been hired to do *something*. Or he's discovered a pot of gold. He has himself a new shiny black car. New clothes. Jimbo King looks like he's hit the mother lode."

"What do you think? Drugs?"

"Looks like that kind of money. But, unh-huh, I don't think so. Or if it is, he's pretty high up on the hog. There's not been the usual signs, folks coming and going, doorbells ringing day and night."

"Great. That's great. Now, do you know Maynard Dupree, the man Jimbo was talking with in the Pelican?"

"You think he's put Jimbo up to something? 'Fraid I can't help you, nope. I know the name, of course, from listening to Ida talk about the Lees all my life. I know that he and Church had a running feud, I never knew about what, and I don't know him personally."

"So you wouldn't know him if you saw him with Jimbo?"

G.T.'s forehead furrowed as she tried to put Maynard and Jimbo in the same picture. "No, so I guess I *could* have seen him and not known him. What does he look like?"

"Big man. Heavy. Red-faced. About forty-five. Your standard prosperous Carondelet Street lawyer. I'll see if I can rustle you up a photo."

"Great."

"Now let's talk about Zoe."

G.T.'s mouth turned down, and she shook her head. "What do you want to know? I guess it's no news she's got a whole mess of problems."

"You know about the drugs?"

"Uh-huh."

"Harry's tracking down her dealer, thinking there might be something there if Church had gotten wind of who he was. Zoe says his name's Billy Jack."

"Never heard of him. But if he's supplying Zoe, he must be one heavyweight dude."

"What do you mean?"

"Oh, I see. You've not got very far with Zoe, if you think she's just using."

"She's *dealing?*"

"Wheeling and—. Ida told me about her habit, says nobody else in the house wants to know about it. I didn't believe it at first, so I kept my eye on Zoe. Did a little asking around. Found out it was more than just a habit. Girl's big time."

"Why on earth? It's not like she needs the money—unless she's got a *very* serious habit—"

"Blow can get expensive. Then, on the other hand, who knows why people do what they do? Lots of hungry to be filled up in her, Ida says."

This presented a whole other scenario. If Zoe were dealing, God only knows what she'd gotten herself into—who might want to get their licks in. Church's death could have been a warning.

G.T. leaned back in her chair. "Did it ever occur to you we could chase ourselves around in circles on this from now till Christmas and it could turn out we're dealing with your basic hit-and-run? Nothing more to it?"

"Just as likely as not. What do your instincts say?"

"I think whatever spirits sent me over to St. Charles to watch Church Lee get killed didn't do it to waste my precious time. I think you've got yourself a serious row to hoe here. And"—she looked out the big arched windows, checking the darkening sky—"I think I've got to get going."

Sam paid the check, and they stepped out into the early evening. The air smelled of flowers in hanging baskets. Of the brown and muddy river. Of hot sidewalks now cooling in front of restaurants, hosed down by white-jacketed busboys.

They strolled toward the bus stop. "What about Cole Leander?" asked Sam. "You know him?"

"Oh, Lord, yes. One of my uncles works for him at his barn."

"I was just out there visiting."

"Uncle Rich says he used to be the meanest man on earth. Then, when he went blind, all of a sudden he got religion."

"That's what he told me. He said Church—whose surgery blinded him, and he was suing Church, did you know that—?" G.T. nodded. "—Church introduced him to Sister Nadine, who changed his life. Now he's dropping the suit. Does that make sense to you? Or that Church would even know Sister Nadine?"

"I've never been one to predict what rich white men might do."

They walked by Harry's hangout in the Royal Orleans. Sam looked up at the windows, but he was nowhere in sight.

Now they were standing at the corner of St. Louis and Royal. "Zoe's dealer Billy Jack used to work at Patrissy's on Royal," Sam said. "Is that near here?"

"Up that way." G.T. pointed uptown on Royal toward Canal. "Across from the Monteleone."

Across the street from Sam and G.T., leaning against the illegally parked white stretch limo belonging to Joe the Horse, was his man, Lavert Washington.

That's what Joey and Horse, Joseph Cangiano to his sainted mother, always called Lavert. My man. He'd gotten the idea from watching *My Man Godfrey,* the original 1936 version with William Powell and Carole Lombard—not the remake with David Niven and June Allyson which he'd ripped out of his VCR and asked Lavert to throw down the toilet.

Lavert, who'd been making *tête de veau* at the time in Joey's state-of-the-art kitchen, dropped it down the garbage compactor instead.

Having a man, Joey had thought, some kind of majordomo, would tone up his act as the heaviest of the heavy hitters in the organization—which he had become since his uncle Carlos was spending what looked like would be the rest of his life on a long vacation with the feds. Uncle Carlos, who may or may not have been instrumental in wiring Lee Harvey Oswald to do the dirty deed, had left him Lavert—who at the time had just been a kid of twenty, juking around doing odd jobs, numbers running, moving heavy things, some of them full of cement, etc.—along with his empire and the keys to the house in the Quarter on Governor Nicholls.

Joey had seen Lavert's potential. A, he wasn't stupid, having done a couple of years at Grambling reading the likes of Hemingway and F. Scott Fitzgerald in addition to playing football—before he busted up his knee and lost his scholarship. B, his size *was* impressive, which meant that he was handy to have around, just in case, and he looked great in a cutaway. Joey liked that a lot—watching people's faces when Lavert answered the door. C, and this was the best, which Joey explained when goombas who didn't have better sense asked why he'd taken an *uomo nero* into his organization, the man had a natural talent for the culinary arts, which had developed into something spectacular when Joey sent him to cooking school with Marcella Hazan in Bologna, which was in Italy, and to La Varenne, which was in France.

Now Lavert looked up Royal Street in the direction G.T. was pointing, up toward the Monteleone.

The good old Monteleone.

He never drove past it unless he had to.

Joey kidded him about that a lot.

"My man drives all the way around the block avoiding that hotel. Thinks it's a jinx."

Let Joey think what he wanted to. Joey knew Lavert had earned his bones, spent his time chopping cotton up in Angola. Lavert knew all about good time, bad time, humongous *bad* mothers who would stare you down in the yard, give you the knee-walking creeps, make even a man the size of Lavert look like a little toad.

But Joey didn't know Lavert had spent time in 'Gola because of the Monteleone.

Sweet stuff in the Monteleone.

Well, indirectly sweet stuff.

He'd had the hots for this little girl named Sharleen who was working there as a maid while she was saving up enough to go to beauty school, and she'd call him over at his mama's house when there was something special in one of her rooms.

He'd go over and check it out—jewelry, cash—whatever it was they left lying around. But he wouldn't take it then. Hotel security would be pointing the finger at Sharleen in about five seconds, it happened more than once.

He'd just bide his time. Lavert was born with the gift of patience. He'd wait and follow them. Tourists sure were fools. Getting drunk, falling down, walking into dark alleys.

It wasn't hard.

Things were going pretty good.

But then hotel security figured it out anyway and put the screws to Sharleen, who never had been a particularly loyal little girl. Though she was sure something in the sack. And Lavert always had been a fool for little bitty girls who liked to sit on top of him and scream.

Sharleen was a screamer all right. She was screaming at the top of her lungs when she snookered him into that last hotel room, had clean sheets already on the California king-size bed, said didn't he want to take a little jump. She was screaming her head off: *He's the one, the one made me do it, said he'd beat me up, big old boy like him, little thing like me scared to death.*

His mama was wearing some pearls he'd given her, belonged to a fat white lady from Grosse Pointe, when they came to his house. She wouldn't look Lavert in the face for the longest time even when she came to see him on visiting days, like to have died of the shame of it.

That little incident cost him three years peeling potatoes in the 'Gola kitchen, the beginning of his culinary skills.

But he hadn't been past the Monteleone since.

Now he was wondering what it was General Taylor Johnson was interested in up there. Pointing it out to that tall brunette he'd noticed that day, a month, couple of months ago, nawh, around Mardi Gras time, that was right, he and Joey were picking up Chéri at the airport. This brunette and her friend, a strawberry-blond kind of redhead, had been standing right there when that little bitty old white boy had pulled that stupid trick, fainted right there in the middle of the road.

He remembered because they had jumped into a cab like they were making a getaway. Like something out of a movie. He'd liked that.

Now, what was that brunette doing with G. T. Johnson, who he'd been in love with since that day—since she'd pulled up in her red ZZZ ambulance and carried that little white boy away.

He'd been trying to figure how to make a move on G.T. ever since.

He'd mentioned her to his mama, who knew her people, used to live around the corner from them in Slidell.

Everybody knew everybody else's kids then. Kid'd do wrong he'd get five or six whippings before he ever even landed on his own front porch, where his own mama'd be waiting for him with a belt already warmed up. His mama said she used to go to heaven 'n' hell parties with G.T.'s mama at the church. Both of them saints, buying a plate of chicken and a cold drink and going on in the church to read the Bible and sing gospel songs while the sinners sat outside with their plates,

drinking beer and dancing to music on the record player. She said
G.T.'s mama got to be a witch, did sand dancing, cured nosebleeds for
chi'rren with a wet brown paper bag and a key on a shoestring. Her
grandmama and her great-grandmama, that Ida, witches too. Said stay
away from that girl. A witch and got high-falutin' ways. Talking about
going to medical school. Ain't gonna have no use for the likes of you.
Woman like that make you crazy. Carve you up for one of her cadavers,
use your manhood in one of her voudous. No telling what she likely to
do.

Well. That was all the inspiration he needed—besides having been
struck by lightning the instant he'd first spied her. 'Specially now that
he'd discovered that he could do more things than anybody thought a
black boy, albeit ex-English major and ex-football player, and okay, ex-
con, could do—cook in French and Italian, not to mention Cajun, creole, and soul, a thing that didn't depend on his size and strength, well,
Lavert had some plans of his own. Of course, he had to get away from
Joey the Horse first. But once he did that, he could sure use a little
woman by his side.

Wouldn't hurt a man wanted to go into the restaurant business—
where, he'd read in a magazine, seventy-eight percent of them folded in
the first two years—to have a woman could work a little magic.

Now, looking at G.T. across the street with this woman he'd also
seen *almost* at the same time, the same place certainly, he took it for a
sign.

A man dealing with a magic woman ought to start paying attention to
signs.

He strolled toward them, slow, easy, man his size had to be careful
not to rush up on people.

"Ms. Johnson," he said in his nicest voice, holding out his hand. "It's
good to see you again."

Both women turned and looked at the towering black man.

She'd seen him somewhere before, Sam thought, then noticed the
white limo in the background.

At the airport.

Then, in her mind, she ran out the rest of the story that Harry told
her, Chéri talking, this giant waiting with the little guy in his arms till
G.T. came in her ambulance and picked him up.

"You two know each other," she said.

"We've met." Lavert smiled.

He had a great smile, Sam thought. Easily as good as Harry's. Now
he was introducing himself, reminding G.T. of the airport incident.

"Oh, yes," G.T. said.

"I trust you got the little man to the hospital safely," Lavert said.

"Well, as a matter of fact, we didn't," G.T. said. Then she started telling him about the little man's hauling ass, though she didn't say it that way, not knowing why she thought she ought to talk like a lady in front of this gangster man—'cause that's what he was, everybody knew about Joey the Horse, his reputation, *and* about his man. "You should have seen him running like a chicken with his head cut off right up the middle of the sidewalk." Then G.T. laughed.

"Well, maybe that was good riddance," Lavert said. "The boy was crazy, acting like that. Maybe he had rabies or something. You wouldn't want to get too close to that."

"I've been up against worse than that," said G.T., bragging a little. "But, you know, that little man got me in trouble. I'm still getting grief at the office about that file. There is nothing they hate more at ZZZ than a file that's not closed out. They'd rather see somebody die, zip that file right up 'long with the body bag than leave one hanging."

And there it was, Lavert thought. Just like that. He smiled. "Why don't you let me take care of that?"

"I beg your pardon," said G.T.

"I'll find out who that boy was and his"—Lavert searched for a word he thought she'd like—"disposition. Let me help you out." It wouldn't even be that hard. He *knew* he'd seen that little dude before. Man in his position, he'd just do some asking around.

"Now, why on earth would you want to do that?" G.T. gave him a look from up under her lashes. Not so much that you could call her a flirt. Just a tad. Just enough.

There, thought Sam, was a girl who knew how to play a man like a fish. Though she wasn't even sure that G.T. knew she was doing it. It came to some women naturally, even some women who didn't know *anything* about magic.

And it was sure working a mojo on this big one, who was stumbling all over himself, reduced to a puddle of jelly.

"Well, I—I just thought it would be nice. Our folks knowing each other and all," Lavert said.

"Our folks? What on earth are you talking about?" G.T. asked.

Then Sam listened with only half an ear. Lavert was talking about old times somewhere else, running his rap. G.T. was smiling, laughing. Oh yeah, I remember that.

Sam turned toward the Royal Orleans and saw the back of Harry, no mistaking that trench coat he thought made him look like a P.I., walking in the door, now up the steps. She watched a minute longer. Yep, now he was sitting at a table in the Esplanade Lounge, checking into his unofficial office.

"You ever have the beans and rice over to Eddie's," Lavert was asking.

"Once, but it's too hard to find. I get lost every time I try to go over there." G.T. shook her head like the very thought made her impatient. The beads in her braids made a clicking sound.

"What you do is"—now Lavert was the professional talking shop to a fellow driver—"you gotta remember Law don't cross no major streets, goes under 'em. You head toward the lake on Elysian Fields, make a U-turn under the bridge at I-10, double back, and turn right on Law. Eddie's 'bout four blocks, right-hand side. Ought to let me drive you sometime. Or even better, I'll make you some beans and rice—"

Nope, G.T. and Lavert didn't need Sam. They were doing just fine their ownselves.

Fifteen

About three blocks away on Decatur, in a less than genteel bar called The Abbey, Billy Jack Joyner was floating Dixie beer on top of some primo toot, trying to concentrate on *The Racing Form*. But today nothing was working. He had a case of the mean reds.

He'd just gotten off the phone talking with Willie, the maître d' over at Patrissy's, who'd said somebody had come by looking for him.

Now, wuddn't that the pits? Like he didn't have enough on his mind. Like bi'nis wouldn't just flow like water if they wouldn't mess with him.

That was the one thing that still amazed Billy Jack about bi'nis. He'd always thought it was something hard. Something mysterious. Something that only people went to college knew how to do. Till he started his own little candy store. That's what he liked to call his coke bi'nis. Mobsters in New York worked out of candy stores. He read about that at LTI, the reform school in North Louisiana where he'd spent some time when he was a kid.

Billy Jack had never wanted anything in his life as bad as he wanted to be a mobster.

That was why he hadn't minded so much when his mama wanted to leave Ruston, that little dump in North Louisiana where he was born in 1965. Even if New Orleans was lousy with niggers, he was thrilled to pieces to move there 'cause it was the home of the big man, Carlos Marcello. He didn't know then that the feds were about to fuck Carlos up and send him away.

Of course, Billy Jack was just a kid then, sixteen when he got out of LTI.

It was right after that his mama said let's go to New Orleans. She just knew she'd make the big time there. And sure 'nuf she had. There were no flies on his mama.

But then, there was *nothing* on his mama when she floated into his daydreams. He'd think about how she looked when he was a little bitty boy, was bad, and she used to chase him around the house in her altogether, swinging a switch, a flyswatter, a rolled-up newspaper, anything that came to hand. Once she'd jumped right out of the tub and came after him and his smartmouth with a wet washcloth. That's how he liked to think of her. Running. Wet. Bouncing up and down.

He'd told Frankie Zito about doing that Dr. Freiberg, called him Dr. Frisbee, shrink at LTI, what had said them terrible things about him and his mom. He told Frankie he could show him the newspaper clippings, of course they didn't have his *name* in them, but he did old Frisbee good, right before he blew Rustontown. Frankie said, History, do it again.

Black or white? Billy Jack asked. What they'd wanted had been nothing—taking a guy out, dropping him off the Pontchartrain Causeway.

So, he'd said, to Frankie. Now I'm a made guy.

Billy Jack hadn't liked it when Frankie laughed. Said you ain't got the blood, stupid. We'll let you do scum, we don't want to get our hands dirty. Make a few bucks. But you never be family. Don't ever make that mistake.

Make a few bucks, what a joke. He was making it hand over fist with his candy store. Not with scum, either. His business was strictly Uptown. You lived downtown of Lee Circle, call somebody else.

Business. Bi'nis. The thing that was truly so astounding about it was that it was so easy—just like selling Hershey's Kisses or ice cream sodas. The money flowed.

In fact, that was the problem.

The coke bi'nis was so much like just being your ordinary insurance salesman that Billy Jack had been getting a little bored.

He needed more excitement to keep him from getting antsy, so he did a few things on the side from time to time. Scared a few citizens. Hit a couple 7-Elevens, Pic'N'Pacs.

He'd also fallen into the habit of going out to the track.

Before he knew it, he was hooked.

A couple of times he took along Zoe Lee, one of his best customers. But he stopped doing that. It pissed him off that she'd always win. And she didn't even use a system.

Billy Jack had a system. It was all about numbers. He had it all figured out on his computer, had designed a special program in D-base. You could *buy* programs, sure, but they weren't for him. He entered in post positions, horses' birth dates, jockeys' birth dates, the odds, of course. And the date of the race. It was bound to work out.

Lots of times it didn't, though. That was the funny thing.

So now, for example, he was coming up a little short. Which is probably why Frankie was looking for him.

Things had been just a little slow lately. But that was to be expected, regular ebb and flow of bi'nis always slow during Lent, Uptown folks got holier than thou, cut down on their fun, and Zoe, who moved a lot of stuff, had punked out on him. She said she wasn't buying somewhere else, but he knew she was lying. She was on his list of things to do something about.

And he didn't like Frankie bugging him either, saying if he couldn't deal with the weight, they'd find somebody who could.

Couldn't Frankie tell he ought to lay off a little? Show some respect.

Respect? Christ! Think the wop would know about respect.

And here it was almost Easter.

Billy Jack needed all the cash he had on hand to pay for his mom's Easter present. She was gonna love it. A diamond cross. Eleven diamonds. Half a carat each. The absolute best. Set in genuine platinum. The man at Coleman E. Adler on Canal—he'd asked Zoe, who knew where to go—said it was the finest of its kind he'd ever seen. Perfect stones. Came from Russia, time of the czars. Billy Jack wasn't exactly sure when that was, but he knew his mom would be impressed.

And here it was Wednesday; Sunday was right around the corner, and he didn't have the cash for Adler's yet. It wasn't a problem, really. He could always get more bread. If nothing else, this town was lousy with 7-Elevens. He would tell Frankie Zito that.

And then, like out of nowhere, something cold grabbed him in the gut like a Tastee-Freez cone had slipped down his throat, straight into his belly without passing Go.

What if it wasn't Frankie Zito who was looking for him? Actually, Willie hadn't said. What if it was those fucking cops with some other beef? Something his mom would hear about?

He signaled to Buster for the tab. He had to get out of there. Had to get out in the street, over to Patrissy's, check this thing out.

He stepped out onto the sidewalk. Skinny black cat almost ran under his feet. Billy Jack kicked at it. He hated cats.

And there, look, see, right across the street, was a nigger meter maid putting a parking ticket on his black Lincoln Town Car.

Billy Jack went berserk.

Motherfucker! he screamed.

Charged across the street, breathing hard through his mouth, big snatches of air, almost hyperventilating.

He was gonna kill her. That's all.

Then, zap, like a big old rubber band from the sky snapped him back, he got ahold of himself. Stopped dead in the middle of the street.

Horns honking. Tourists from Iowa freaked, almost ran him down.

That was okay. It was all tit for tat in the big numbers game—the one up in the sky, where everything was ones and zeroes.

Nigger got him. He'd get one back.

Billy Jack could always make the numbers come out.

Sixteen

●

"What'cha been up to, lady?" asked Harry, rising from his seat in the Esplanade Lounge. He probably looked like a fool, but he couldn't do anything about his grin. He couldn't help it that he was always so happy to see Sam. "Got this thing whupped?" He glanced at his watch. "You've been in town more than twenty-four hours. Already on overtime."

She plopped down, checked him out out of the corner of her eye. God, he looked so *fresh*. He had wonderful skin—like a baby's. "No, son, it is not *whupped*. Of course, if you'd done right in the first place, passed on this case when your uncle Tench handed it out, I'd be home in Atlanta with my little dog, doing what I get paid to do, instead of charity work for my friends."

"Listen, I been meaning to ask you. How the hell old are you, anyway? Fifty? Fifty-five?"

Sam's head jerked like she'd been slapped. What the—?

"I'll tell you, reason I asked, now I'd put you at thirty-four, thirty-five, tops."

Still, she winced. There'd been the time they'd been light by *ten* years.

"But the way you talk to me, like I'm a little idjit child, calling me *son*, I figure you must be at least old enough to be my ma. Am I right?"

She relaxed. *That's* all he meant. "Shut up, Harry, and order me a drink."

He grinned. He had her where he wanted her for a change. Said to a passing waitress, "Perrier with lime," out of the side of his mouth.

"You doing Bogey imitations now?"

He winked. "Call 'em as you see 'em, sweetheart."

"Puhleeze." But she couldn't stifle her smile. "Wanta hear the scoop on Mr. Leander?"

"He bought the Hope diamond."

Sam laughed. "Aren't his sparklers something? I thought Atlanta was full of weirdos, but, boy, y'all do have the types. Anyway, he says he's dropping the suit against the Lee estate."

"Well—how do you like that? What do you think that means?"

"Don't know, was hoping you'd tell me."

"Let's look at it. One, he doesn't need the money. *Never* needed the money."

"Right. So the suit was brought because he was so pissed."

"Perfectly natural, considering we're talking about his sight."

"Absolutely. So why's he dropping it?"

"Church is dead. He's got nothing against his heirs."

"Which gets us no closer to knowing if he might have engineered Church's exit."

"What was your gut feeling when you saw him?" Harry asked.

Sam shrugged. "You know, he's that type. Old, rich men—hell, Harry, they've been playing games so long, *they* don't even know which way's up. Couldn't deal a straight hand if they had to. Except—well, the crazy thing about him was he told me he'd forgiven Church because of Sister Nadine. The TV evangelist."

"*What?*"

"He said Church had introduced him to her and she'd changed his life. He talks like a Born Again."

"You've *got* to be kidding."

"Would I make this up?"

Harry scratched his head. "Hell, I guess it could happen to anyone. But it seems hard to figure. Plus that gives us Church being hooked up with Sister Nadine somehow. I'll tell you, this town is getting crazier every day. No wonder everybody drinks."

"So I thought I'd go and make a call on Sister Nadine later this evening. See if there's anything there."

"Prob'ly worth the time. Besides"—he grinned—"can't wait to see your take on her."

"She's something, right?"

"Listen, could you get me her autograph, for my sister Sudie. She collects freaks. So, what else you been up to?"

"Well, if you really want to know, I've been with G.T. Johnson over at St. Louis Cemetery No. 1 getting the blessings of Mam'zelle Marie LaVeau."

"Hey. Never said there were any flies on you, woman. She give you some gris-gris, you'll have this thing wrapped up by suppertime. Which reminds me"—whenever he was around her, Harry just couldn't get the great food—great loving doubleheader out of his mind—"you wanta go grab a bite somewhere?"

"Thanks, no. I'm going home to spend some more time with the ladies." Not that she wouldn't have liked to while away the evening with him, but first things first. And now it was his turn to do some show-and-tell. "So, Kitty said you struck out on Billy Jack."

"I love the way you put that. I did not strike out. I just didn't find him waiting for me with open arms at Patrissy's. I ran him through Motor Vehicles. No such cat. And trying first name Billy or William, middle name Jack is going to get us about five thousand possibilities across the state. I can guarantee you that."

"Pretty common, right?"

" 'Specially in North Louisiana."

"How come you all say it like that?"

"North Louisiana? Just snobby, I guess. It really is like another state. More like the rest of the Deep South—Mississippi, Alabama—dare I say, Georgia."

"And South Louisiana is—?"

"New Orleans and Cajun country, up through Lafayette, is more European than southern. We think those folks up in North Louisiana—Baptists eating white bread and frowning on dancing and anything else that's fun—well, it runs contrary to our hedonistic nature."

"And they think you're all going to hell."

"That's pretty much the size of it."

"Speaking of going to hell, the word from G.T. is that there's more to Zoe's involvement with drugs than Billy Jack. G.T. said she's dealing."

"Oh, crap!"

"Precisely my sentiments."

Harry leaned his head into his hands. "There's no telling what's gonna be in *that* ball of wax, depending on her contacts. Put her in dutch with the Italian faction, she could be history right before our eyes."

"Don't I know it. I'll push Zoe, see if I can get her to tell me about her dealing. Girl may have the answer right in her hand, not even know it. *Or* know it and not want to cop to it."

"Great—*if* you can get her to talk. By the way, I've been asking a few questions about Maynard Dupree. Now I know he's on *your* list, but I thought it couldn't hurt."

Boy couldn't be trusted to stick to the game plan. "You're gonna scare him off."

"I never said I was going to do exactly what you wanted. Besides, does it make any sense, when our families run in the same circles, not to use what I've got?"

Maybe she *was* being too stiff-necked. "Okay. I see your point. So?"

"So."

"So?"

"So—" He pushed his coffee spoon around on the little table. "So nobody knows nothing about the feud, except that it goes way back."

Sam couldn't help but laugh. "You talked with a bunch of old friends and you got zip?"

He could feel himself flush. He was 0 for 2 in this meeting and fading fast. "You're so smart, you try. I'm telling you, Sam, you don't know anything about Old New Orleans. Even if you're on the inside, if they think it's none of your business, they'll cover for each other until death. *After* death. There's no telling what you'd find in those mausoleums uptown in Lafayette No. 1 if you pried them open."

"No thanks, I'll pass." Then she made him an offer. "Listen, if I promise you we'll go see Maynard together when the time feels right, will you leave it alone?"

She could tell from his expression, he wasn't at all happy about the way she put that.

"Maybe." He shrugged.

"I beg your pardon?"

She sounded like his third-grade teacher, the one he and some other kids had once locked in the basement. "Get off my back, Sam."

"Okay. Okay." He was right. She was pushing him too hard. She needed to watch that. "Listen, G.T. told me a couple of interesting things about Jimbo. Said, one, he's too tall to have been driving the Buick."

"The driver was short? Is that the way you remember it?"

"I'm not sure. But shorter than Jimbo, according to her."

"Jimbo is pretty tall."

"*And* that Jimbo seems to have a new source of serious income."

He hated to have to say it, another point on her scorecard. But he did. "Great. That looks like something, huh?"

"Worth checking out, I'd say."

"I'll get right on it."

Silence hung in the air.

He leaned back in his chair. "You're saying you'd rather do it yourself."

"Well—" This was very hard for her. One of the lessons of the program was that it served no one to insist on shouldering things all by yourself. It was a lesson she had to learn again and again.

"You think I'm a total fuckup," Harry said.

"I didn't *say* that. I just have some trouble with—" Letting you have the good parts. Letting go of the reins.

"You didn't have to. Listen, now *you* listen." His chair hit the floor loud and hard. He couldn't help it. His ego was on the line, his young man's ego. "I never asked you to come here. I never asked you to poke your nose, pretty though it may be, into my business."

He was standing, reaching for his wallet.

She felt terrible about this. "I'll get it," she said.

"Goddammit! Do not tell me that you will pick up the check when I am telling you to go screw yourself. When I am telling you that I have had it up to here with your bossiness and your pushiness and your talking to me like I'm a five-year-old."

He pulled a wad of money out of his wallet without looking and tossed it on the table.

"And do *not* tell me I'm leaving too big a tip. This is *my* table in *my* favorite hangout in *my* town. And from now on I'm working on *my* case. By *my*self. *Capice?*"

He grabbed the worn backpack that served as his briefcase and flung it over his shoulder.

"Do you understand what I'm saying, Ms. Adams?"

She did.

"Good."

He stomped off in the direction of Royal Street, then pivoted and came back. He pointed a forefinger in her face. "You are the most infuriating woman I've ever met."

He wasn't the first man who'd ever said that.

"I said I understood."

"You are driving me absolutely crazy."

"I'm sure that's what all these nice people wanted to know."

"Why can't you just cut me some slack? Why do you insist on having everything your own way, calling all the shots?"

"I don't."

She knew she did. Or she *almost* did. But it was *her* case. Well, his case too. She knew that.

"You most certainly do."

"I do *not.*" Two beats passed. "You're right, I do. It's a serious character flaw."

Harry smiled a very wintry smile.

"Thank you, Miz Adams. Thank you so very much. Call me if you need me. *If* it's a matter of life and death. But otherwise, from now on, we'll pursue this matter, all matters, separately."

"Right." If that was the way he wanted it, good riddance.

"And good night."

He strode away for real this time.

Good, indeed. She watched the top of Harry's handsome head disappear down the Royal Street steps. Why *couldn't* she cut him a little slack? Why was this lesson so hard for her to learn?

Dammit.

Seventeen

"Mr. Dupree, I'm sorry, sir, but you're going to have to stand still."

The little tailor sounded like he had a mouth full of mush, but it was just straight pins.

Maynard was trying, but how *could* he stand still?

He stared at himself in the pier glass the tailor had brought into his office along with the fabric samples, the chalk, the tape measure, the pins. He stared at a fat man looking like a fool in his undershirt and baggy Brooks Brothers shorts, black knee-high socks, with blue and white seersucker for a summer suit draped all over him, wondering where the years had gone—along with the beautiful boy he'd once been.

How could he stand still when his life was crumbling around him? And he sure as hell didn't mean what Irv Goldblatt, the best Jew internist in the whole South, had told him about his cholesterol. It was the call this morning from Cole Leander that was about to give him a heart attack.

"Now, what do we think about vents?" the tailor asked.

"*We* don't," Maynard snapped.

Saaaaaaay, ol' hoss. That's how Cole had begun. Bastard hadn't sounded that pleased with himself since he'd fixed the Sugar Bowl. Saaaaaay, Maynard, you know there's a pretty—or so they tell me—girl reporter over from Atlanta asking questions 'bout you snuffing old Church. Maynard had protested, of course, Cole going on like they were talking about a golf game, for chrissakes, like it was nothing. Said he heard that that boy Harry Zack had his nose in it too. Of course it was bi'nis with him, Tench Young's bi'nis. Couldn't blame Tench, said Cole, wanting to save himself the gold. 'Course it'd be too bad if he did it at your expense, wouldn't it, ol' hoss? Maynard could hear himself sputtering the whole time like a sprinkler out in the St. Augustine grass gone wacko. Saying he didn't know what the hell Cole was talking about. Cole laughing, like to bust a gut. The old man was vicious as a rattlesnake; he didn't care what people said 'bout a pore blind man getting religion. Miserable old cuss, prob'ly killed Church himself. 'Cept, of course, he couldn't of been driving the car, but he could of paid somebody to. Could of paid 'em a lot. Could of paid 'em in gold, in diamonds. That's what Maynard bet had happened, God, if he *only* could remember, oldest scam in the debutante's book—Honey, I was so drunk I don't remember, what did we do after we—but he *couldn't* remember, he really *couldn't,* but now he bet it wasn't him at all, wasn't that fool Jimbo either, it was Cole all along—

"Mr. Dupree, are we going to want real buttonholes on the sleeves as usual?"

"What? Oh, yeah. Uh-huh. Whatever—"

Maynard looked down at the top of the tailor's head. He could reach right over and grab the old silver Comus stirrup cup off the corner of his desk, or better yet, that paperweight, favor from the ball of '78, '79, somewhere around in there, bash his head right in. Man wouldn't ever know what hit him.

Then Maynard caught his own eyes in the oval mirror. What the hell was he *thinking* about?

It was Marietta's fault. Last night she'd been nagging at him, wearing that smug little look he couldn't stand. It got all over him, her acting like she knew something. Something he didn't know and would wish he did. Or something that was going to cost him. Sometimes Marietta got on his nerves so bad he wished she were dead.

Jesus! What was wrong with him? Some men couldn't get their minds out of the gutter. He couldn't get his out of the grave.

"Mr. Dupree, I *told* him you were—" Sally Jean Simpson, his secretary, bustled in, her silver wig all in a twitter, turned about halfway around on her head.

"Well, Sally Jean, honey, I don't mind if you don't mind seeing me in my und—"

"Mr. *Du*pree! How you doin', son?"

And then Maynard realized why Sally Jean was bent all out of shape. It was Jimbo King stiff-arming her as he pushed past.

"Mr. Dupree—I—"

"It's okay, Sally Jean. Just go on out and shut the door."

Jimbo flopped, his long legs sprawling into one of two red leather wing chairs. He faced the antique partners' desk Marietta's father had given Maynard the day after their engagement announcement.

"So this is how the rich boys do it," Jimbo drawled. "New custom-made suit, never even have to leave the office."

"Mr. Dupree," the tailor said, "would you like for me to—"

"I'd like for you to just keep on keeping on, Herbert." Then to Jimbo, hoping to edge him out with some class, after all this was *his* home territory: "You know, most of my callers try to make appointments."

"I did that," said Jimbo. "Yes, sir. I shore did. I called up that old lady out there and she told me you were out. Said that the last time I called and the time before that. I started to get the feeling that you were avoiding me, and, now, well, we couldn't have that."

Behind Maynard's back, Herbert, who was measuring for jacket length, gave a little laugh.

Jimbo stood and started circling very slowly around to the side of Maynard.

"Did you say something, Jack?" He was talking to Herbert.

"Sir? No, sir. And my name's Herbert. Herbert Stanley. Would you like my card?"

"Nope. Don't think so."

And with that, Jimbo swooped down like a great bird on the little man and jerked him up. He held Herbert with one arm across the man's chest and carried him like a calf he'd wrestled in the rodeo.

"Now, Maynard, as I was saying, it just doesn't seem friendlylike to me that after the conversation we had this very morning, and after you promised me you'd get right back to me with an answer, you wouldn't be taking my calls. Do you know what I mean?" Jimbo threw open one of the office's tall windows, which opened onto Carondelet, with the other arm, the one that wasn't holding the kicking and screaming Herbert Stanley.

"Mr. Dupree, make him put me down!"

"King, for chrissakes, you're scaring the man."

"That's what I intend to do." Jimbo spit out the toothpick that had been sitting in a corner of his mouth and watched its downward progress. "Lord, that thing took a long time to fall. How far is that?"

"We're on the fifteenth floor," said Maynard. "Now, look, King—"

"Mr. Dupree! Help me! Help me! Oh, my God!" Herbert was more out than in the window now.

Jimbo went right on as if they were sitting at a lunch counter sharing an order of onion rings. "As I recall, what I said to you this morning was that I really don't need any more clothes, not even fancy ones like this little dude makes for you—" And then he jiggled Herbert a bit.

"I'll make you a suit," Herbert cried. "A coat. A vest. Anything you want. Oh, sweet Jesus!"

"That's right neighborly of you," Jimbo said. "But as I was saying, Maynard, I don't need clothes or cars or any of them other things I might be buying with your money. What's on my mind is I'm getting kind of anxious to get on with the flying-chair business."

What the hell, Maynard wondered, was he was going to do now? It wasn't like he could just pick up the phone and call the police. Jimbo was crazy. He'd probably just drop Herbert. *That* was all he needed. First Church, his lifelong enemy, getting squashed like a pumpkin, and then his tailor taking the big dive out of his office window. After a while, if it got to be just one thing after another, even *he* couldn't keep it out of the *Times-Picayune*.

"Help!" Herbert was yelling. "Help! Please, somebody help me."

"Now, Herbert, you hush!" Maynard ordered him. "You're going to draw a crowd."

The little tailor's eyes got *that* big as he realized the true nature of the fix he was in. He began whimpering and sniveling.

"Look, Jimbo, I told you I'd do what I could and get back to you," Maynard said. "These things take a while."

"I want TV."

"I'll get you TV."

"Guaranteed coverage. The news at six and ten."

"Now, that may be—"

Jimbo started jiggling Herbert up and down.

"Oh, Jesus. Bless Jesus. Help! Help!" The tailor was hysterical now. Spittle was flying everywhere. "God! Jesus! Mary! Help meeeeeeeeee!"

"Would you *stop* that!" Maynard said.

"I think you ought to know I cain't hold him out here all day. Any minute now I'm liable to let go. My arm's getting tired."

"Okay, okay," Maynard said.

Then Jimbo returned to his plan. "We'll need some announcements ahead of time on the TV. Like coming attractions. Make sure they'll be a bunch of folks watching. And maybe we could have the mayor, the chief of police. Hey! The governor could come down from Baton Rouge."

"The governor?" Jesus! The cracker's ambitions knew no bounds.

Jimbo frowned. "By helicopter it's only 'bout fifteen minutes. Not such a big trip. 'Course, on the other hand, we could just let this little old fellow drop. We could tell people about what happened to your other friend. We could—"

"Stop!" Maynard yelled. That's all Jimbo had to say, and he was wet all the way through his drawers, through his undershirt. He was sweating like a pig. His heart was beating about two hundred times a minute. He just knew he was about to have a coronary, if not a stroke.

"Mr. Dupree?" It was Sally Jean on the intercom. "Are y'all all right in there? I heard—"

"Get off the box, Sally Jean. We're fine!"

"As I was saying," Jimbo drawled, "tell everybody 'bout what happened to your friend Church."

Maynard's mind was reeling. What *had* happened to Church? Jesus! Jimbo kept playing him like the fool he was. Fool to ever let this thing go this far. Here he was, about to get in the middle of another mess, Herbert splattered all over his sidewalk, he still didn't have a fucking clue if he'd killed Church or if Jimbo had done it because he'd paid him to.

"Mr. Dupree?" It was Sally Jean again on the intercom. "Your wife is on the phone. She wants to know—"

"Shut up, Sally Jean!"

On the other end there was a squawk, and then the line went dead.

"You know," said Jimbo, "I been thinking maybe we ought to have official launching ceremonies out at the lake. What do you think, Herbert?"

Herbert was sobbing now. "I don't know what you're talking about."

"Jimbo, good God, have mercy!" Maynard said. *"Yes!* The mayor. The police. The president. Whoever you want."

"The president?" Jimbo turned, pulling Herbert back in a little bit, and gave Maynard a big grin. "I never even thought of that."

Eighteen

•

BEULAH LAND TABERNACLE, the big sign said outside, but Sam didn't think Sister Nadine's church looked like any she'd ever seen. From the scruffy street it resembled a block-square four-story warehouse except for the first-level colonnade trailing blue tile. On top sat a golden onion dome that the neighbors hadn't peeled, yet.

Sam stepped through the open front doors into a Moorish lobby that soared three stories high, lighted by two over-wrought iron chandeliers. Old movie theater was the style of decor—and a clue to what the tabernacle must have once been. But the usual Greco-Roman-Egyptian-Chinese statuary had been replaced with figures of the Christ Child and the Virgin Mary. There was something strange about these Marys, though. They were either pregnant or obese.

Sam took a closer look. Funny Thing Number Two: all the Marys had the same face, the same pretty smile, the same fat cheeks. This had to be Nadine.

"Help you?"

Sam jumped a foot high as a tiny old man dawdled through a side door with a broom. "I'm looking for Sister Nadine."

"Well, go on back that way." He flapped a hand like it was a dust rag over toward the right of the lobby. "Through those doors, up one flight of stairs. I reckon she's up there, all right."

Sam thanked him, and at the top of the stairs found another set of double doors. When she pushed them open, all her preconceptions went bye-bye.

It was by now edging onto seven P.M., yet this office, a study in black and soft gray modern Italian design, was humming like the coffee had just perked and it was rise-and-shine time.

"May I help you?" asked an officious little number in an expensive black suit that looked nice with the furniture.

Sam gave her her name and her *Constitution* business card.

"I don't think you have an appointment." The suit frowned.

No, she didn't. And she hated to intrude. But she was in town for only a little while. Would it be too much trouble to ask—?

The suit's neatly coiffed head bobbed up and down. Nothing else moved, not even the heavy gold ear clips. Sam could take a seat, she said. The pile of magazines and papers was neat too. *U.S. News & World Report. Forbes. Money. Barron's.* The *Journal.* Not a single *Broadman Hymnal* to be found.

All around her, business bustled on well-shod feet. Women, mostly young, came and went across an ocean of pale gray pile, pausing at intersections with sheafs of papers, reports, ledgers, giving her little polite smiles.

It was all cool, calm, efficient, and serene—the women as well-tuned as a bunch of Stepford wives.

Against a back wall Sam spotted a mainframe computer about the size of a large car. An old Buick, say. Her mind slipped into reverse. She replayed that night—the rain, the dark, the crash of heavy steel.

"Ms. Adams?" The suit was back. "Sister Nadine will see you now."

Just went to show you how wrong a person could be. TV evangelist? Female? Rubenesque statuary downstairs? Kitty had said something about pies? A cross between Julia Child and Tammy Bakker was sort of what she had in mind.

Not this rotund, to be sure, but suavely beautiful woman in her mid-forties, her gold and platinum hair twisted into a chignon, silver at ears and throat, her bulk artfully camouflaged head to toe in floating drifts of black. Roseanne's body beneath Kathleen Turner's face.

"Ms. Adams." The voice was Turner's, too, husky, sexy. The grip firm. "What can I do for you this evening?" In Nadine's sleek office they sat facing each other on black leather club chairs to the right of her desk—a cool white marble slab.

Sam was nonplussed. In her line of work she'd happened upon corpses that gave her less pause than this living woman's persona.

Sister Nadine smiled. "You've seen me on TV."

"Nooo."

"They told you I play the tambourine, speak in tongues, and wail."

"Something like that."

"They tell you I don't wear shoes too?"

Sam couldn't help looking down. Beneath trim ankles Nadine wore beautiful black calf pumps.

Nadine laughed. "Look, I give them what they want. Remember what H. L. Mencken said."

" 'No one ever went broke underestimating—"

" '—the taste of the American people.' It's the secret of my success." Nadine smiled. "And what do *you* want, Samantha?"

"Sam." She laid out for Nadine her mission for the Lee family.

"Oh." Nadine's pretty face clouded. "Dear Church. I do miss him so."

"So he *was* a—"

"A believer?" A rueful smile. "Church was a good Uptown Catholic. He wasn't one of my followers, though he believed in my work and sometimes recommended that people like Mr. Leander come and talk with me. And we were friends."

As in lovers?

"Special friends?"

"You might say that."

Sam didn't want to let it go.

"How special?"

"Now, Sam. I could never answer a question like that for a member of the press, could I?"

So be it. But she thought romance was the right track. Nadine *could* have been Church's secret girlfriend, the one Kitty had hinted at. Her public image would be ample reason for the secrecy.

"I'm curious. Do *you* think his death was accidental?" She watched Nadine's face carefully.

"I do." The evangelist answered without a quiver.

"So you don't know why anyone would have wanted him dead?"

"I didn't say that. I do. Or, rather, I *did."*

"That's a *yes?"*

"You've met Cole Leander?"

"I have."

"Cole wanted to do terrible things to Church."

"And do you think he did?"

"No. I *know* he didn't."

"How?"

"Because we talked about that, and he came to see that the right thing to do was to forgive Church. To pray for his salvation, to pray that he would never make such a terrible and careless mistake again."

"So you do believe—?"

"In the power of prayer? In the power of salvation? I'm not a total shuck-and-jive artist, Sam."

Sam would blush when embarrassed till the day she died. Now the blood spread up her neck and face. "I meant—do you believe what Leander said? That he wouldn't"—she stammered—"I didn't mean that I thought you—"

"Of course you did. You see me on TV, you see a fat woman with long blond hair streaming down her back, dressed in a white robe, singing and dancing and telling you how Jesus loves you just the way you are. For your ownself. How Jesus wants you to make a *joyful* noise. Wants you to *love* yourself. *All* of yourself. *Be* yourself. Even your *fat* self. Sister Nadine even gives you recipes for pies. *Of course* you think I'm a shuck. But that's because you don't come from what I come from. Don't know what I know. Don't know the mingy tight pinched little lives people like me grow up with. Don't know how much we'd love to *love* the Lord."

Nadine's voice had been growing bigger and deeper and wider. Now its cellolike resonance filled the room. In one graceful movement she was out of her chair, whirling around the room on nimble feet.

"Rednecks want to love the Lord same as other folks, looser folks, do. Want to *sing* the praises of the Lord. *Dance* the jubilation of the Lord. Raise Him up while they're partying down.

"Folks don't want to spend their whole lives feeling bad. Feeling guilty. Sad. Eating saltine crackers and drinking Welch's grape juice, pretending it's the Body and the Blood."

Nadine was swaying now.

"Folks want to *feel* jubilation. *Feel* joy that they don't need booze for. Don't need drugs for. Don't need anything but the power of their own hearts, telling 'em to do what comes natural."

Then Nadine took a deep breath and seemed to catch herself in midflight. She floated for a moment, slowed, then stopped. Reached inside her sleeve and pulled out a white square of linen edged in lace and wiped her brow.

"I ain't one of those southern women what *glow*," she said, putting on the accent. "How about you?"

Sam laughed. "Me either. I *sweat*."

Sam could see why Church would be drawn to her. *She* was drawn to her. Nadine had that thing, that magic, that all stars possess.

Nadine settled herself back down. "Well, well, now, now. You must forgive me. I get carried away. Now, we've talked about Church. Cole Leander. Is there anything else you want to know?"

"Yes. Do you know Church's daughter, Zoe?"

Once again a cloud crossed Nadine's smooth brow. "I've never met her, but I pray for her."

"You do? Why?"

Nadine stared at her with amazed blue eyes. "Why, because of all her problems. She's such a *sad* child. I hope somehow we can save her."

"Church talked about her?"

"Of course. He was worried sick about her."

"He knew about the drugs?"

"The cocaine? Yes."

"Did he know she was dealing?"

"Oh, dear." Nadine took a long deep breath, then sighed. "No, I don't think so. He never said so to me."

"Do you think he would if he'd known?"

Sam waited. Finally, softly, Nadine said, "I don't know. I think so, but I can't be sure. Oh, it makes me so sad to hear you say that about Zoe. Our *young* people. Our poor children. They've inherited a hard world, haven't they?"

"Indeed they have. I wouldn't want to be in their shoes, have to start over now."

"Nor I. *However.*" She was up on her feet again, but not because she was moved with the spirit. Sam could see that Nadine was moving on to something else in her mind. Some other agenda was pressing. The interview was done. "We do what we can."

"And what's that?" Sam was gathering her things together, but she wanted to know what Nadine meant.

Nadine waved her hand at the offices out through her open door. "Is this where you think the money stops? I make millions with my ministry, you know."

"I have no idea what you do."

"We invest it. Half the young ladies you see out there are financial planners. The money grows like Topsy." She grinned. "That's the nice thing about money, you know. Now, I'm not saying that I don't live very nicely, I'd be the first to tell you that I do, but the bulk of what I raise goes into shelters for women and children and for rehab centers. We have three centers in the state and we're building more."

"Rehab for whom?"

"Youngsters with drug problems. They come to us, at no charge, for a minimum of eighteen months. They learn real-life skills, build projects, I mean buildings as well as their self-esteem. We have construction contracts all over the state—though right now we have to work harder because the economy's so slow. That's how Church and I met. He'd heard about my work and came to talk with me about Zoe." They were at the door now. "He loved her so."

"But she wasn't ready to enroll in your program?"

"No, she wasn't."

"She hasn't bottomed-out yet." Sam thought, it takes the Lees a while. Sometimes, like Church, they don't live long enough to begin the long climb back.

"No," said Nadine. "She's not ready to help herself."

Then Sam heard herself saying, "I know something about it. I've had my own problems with alcohol."

Nadine's sweet smile was like the Marys' downstairs. Patient. Understanding. Compassionate. "That doesn't surprise me."

There were spooky ladies in this town. G.T. and her voudou and now this.

"Did you read my mind?"

"Just a feeling. The Lord sends us those we need. He works in mysterious way." Nadine was still smiling the Mary smile.

But it faded the moment Sam left. As the door clicked closed behind Sam, Nadine picked up a silver picture frame she'd earlier turned facedown on her cold marble desk. Now she ran her fingers across the features beneath the glass and whispered, "Oh, sweet Jesus. What have you gone and done now, sweet baby mine?"

Nineteen

•

Lavert, dressed in chef's whites, was standing over his six-burner Garland, making sauce for Joey, who called it gravy. He and the boys were lounging at the other end of the kitchen around a big round table.

That same table had been the site of many a meeting. There, over ziti with rapini, the decision had been made to do Mickey Boy Gambino. Over braciola, Ralphie "the Ear" Zambolini's fate had been sealed. And it had been a first course of bruschetta the boys were enjoying on that night when Joey's uncle Carlos decided it would be just the ticket to help D.A. Jim Garrison implicate Clay Shaw, the director of the Trade Mart who'd renovated the apartments next door, in the Kennedy imbroglio.

But that was all way before Lavert's time, and even before that the oak table had sat in Carlos's mother's kitchen, and her mother's before her in Messina.

It wasn't just fancy Uptown citizens who furnished their houses with antiques, who knew about keeping things in the family.

"Hey, Gino, you tasted my man's gravy?" Joey was saying now.

"Sure, I tasted his fucking gravy. Lotsa times."

Joey's heavy glass tumbler of Valpolicella hit the table with a thud. Gino's shirtfront looked like Ralphie the Ear's when they'd finished with him.

"Hey!"

"Hey your fucking self, talking 'bout my man's fucking gravy. It's my *mother's* gravy. You treat it with respect."

Gino knew when to stand up for himself and when to sit down. Speaking about Joey's mother, even inadvertently, it was best to do the latter.

"Sorry, Joey. I didn't mean nothing."

"Okay, you apologized to me, now apologize to my man."

Lavert looked up across the top of the counter, steady gaze, nothing on it. He knew how hard this was for Gino, didn't want to have to pay the price for it sometime down the road, when Gino, with a fresh round in his Uzi, might mistake him for some other nigger, as he'd later explain.

"Sorry," Gino muttered.

"Right." Lavert gave him a little smile. No teeth.

"That's more like it." Joey was in good spirits again, rubbing his hands together, pouring more wine, grinning like somebody'd just given him a G-man for Christmas. Happier than when Lavert had figured out the recipe for the spaghetti sauce from tasting Joey's mom's. Pretending that the penciled scribbles she'd sent along would do the trick, when they both knew she wouldn't give him ice in hell. Presuming to cook for *her* Joey. She'd show him.

She'd left out half the ingredients. *All* the secrets.

But she didn't know what a palate she was up against with Lavert.

Joey was telling the story now. Of course, it was *his* mama. He was allowed.

"And she couldn't believe it. He'd even got the cloves."

"Stuck in the onion." Lavert nodded.

"Right!" boomed Joey. "He figured out you don't chop up the onion. Let it sit whole stuck with cloves in the gravy while it's cooking, then take it out. She liked to have, Holy Mother of Jesus"—Joey crossed himself—"died."

"But after that—" Lavert added.

"After that"—Joey was pounding on the table with his fist now, jostling glasses—"she made him an honorary member of the family. She comes over and sits right here"—he pointed at a stool near the range—"and tells my man secrets."

"We trade," Lavert said. "Together we are one mean team."

The boys knew what they were supposed to do.

They howled.

Then wine flowed all around.

"So, Joey," said his little brother, Pasquale, "you pleased with the way things going down?"

"I hate to say it." Joey knocked on the wood table. "I'm happy. We moving more product than ever, squashed those fucking gamooshes over in Miami, showed 'em how to *do* business."

"He's happy," said Frankie Zito.

"Happy," echoed Jilly Mirra.

Lavert, chopping garlic with a swift motion of his chef's knife against the cutting board, whap, whap, whap, thought, everybody's so damned happy, this was the perfect time to run his little blond guy from the airport up the flagpole. See if any of them could ID him.

"We got another load coming in from La Guajira tonight," said Jilly.

"Here's to the spics." Pasquale raised his glass.

"God love 'em." Joey laughed.

"Listen," Lavert began, "any of you know—"

"There is one thing, though," Frankie said.

Lavert went back to chopping.

"What?" Joey turned to Frankie. Fast.

"It's nothing, really. I mean, nothing I can't take care of. Nothing."

"What?" Joey asked again.

"Really, I shouldn't have brought it up."

"Fucking what? You brought it up, you brought it up. Now what?"

"Somebody's asking questions about one of my troops."

"One of *us?*"

"Naaah. One of my punks. Little asshole name of Joyner. Billy Jack Joyner."

"So? Who's doing the asking? Heat?"

"Not unless he's under. Guy asking's a local. Used to do some process work. Now he's dicking around for some insurance company."

"And?"

"He's just been asking around about this Joyner is all I'm saying."

"But you don't think guy asking's working for nobody else?"

"What do I know, Joey? Joyner kid could have a shitload of parking tickets. Smashed his car up on the I-10. I'm just telling you what I know."

"Sounds to me like you don't know dick."

"I know I'm about up to here with this Joyner anyhow. He's not moving what he used to move, whining about the Carnival season—"

That got a big laugh.

"He wanta be queen didn't make it?" Pasquale asked. "Probably what you stuck us with, Frankie. Some twinkie small-time punk street dealer wants to wear a dress."

"Shit, I'm sorry I brought it up."

"Well, I'm not," said Joey. "I don't like it somebody's asking something about somebody we do business with." He thumped the table for emphasis. "You know what I mean?"

Everybody nodded, even Lavert, who was chopping meat with a cleaver now.

"What you say this guy's name is?"

"Billy Jack Joyner."

"No, asshole. The gamoosh is asking the questions."

"Harry Zack."

Lavert dropped his cleaver. *Whap!*

•

Twenty

•

Sam was sitting with Zoe in the candy-striped bedroom the young girl had claimed at Ma Elise and Kitty's house after her daddy died. Peeking from under the bed's flouncy dust ruffle was an empty package of pork rinds. Sam wondered how many of those Zoe had stuffed down before she'd made her pilgrimage into the bathroom to the Great God Ralph.

But Sam wasn't there to talk with Zoe about that. "Cocaine," she was saying to the young girl with the big dark circles under her eyes.

Zoe shrugged, Yeah?

"Talk to me about your dealing. How'd that come about?"

If you insist, Zoe's eyebrows signaled. Then she spread her thin hands and took Sam back to that primo important conversation she'd had with Dr. Cecil Little when he'd walked in on her in the bathroom at Chloe Biedenharn's grandmother's house the afternoon of Chloe's first tea. His trying to sneak a peek, then realizing she was doing something even more interesting than lifting the skirt of her blue party dress, slipping her a C-note for a little toot. Laughing his there's-lots-more-where-that-came-from-little-girl laugh.

"So I said," she continued, " 'Most of the time, you must go to parties, Dr. Cecil, and not luck out. You can't always count on finding someone like me in the ladies' room. So it would be convenient for you if there was someone else holding for you. I mean, someone you could count on seeing, say, maybe once or twice a week. Someone who knew all the same people. Who went to the same parties.'

" 'Why, Miss Zoe Lee!' "

"I had to give myself a pat on the back for that one," she said to Sam, "for my plan. It was a natural, a simple, brilliant natural. But then, the best things are."

She and Dr. Cecil Little did see each other at *least* once a week. Because, as she explained, in New Orleans society you had your country clubs, New Orleans and Metairie, your Southern Yacht Club, your men's lunch clubs, Boston and Pickwick, your ladies' Orleans Club, your old-line carnival organizations, Comus, Rex, Momus, your members of the board over at the Ochsner Foundation and Tulane, your United Way, your kids in McGehee and Sacred Heart, your Little Lakes Duck Club when you felt like doing some shooting.

But it was all the same people, numbered about two-fifty, three hundred all told, that you saw over and over. Never anybody new, at least not socially. You either had Old New Orleans blood or you didn't.

There was nothing more pathetic, Zoe had heard her daddy say more than once, than to watch a big-deal corporate executive move into New Orleans and buy his huge house and furnish it all new and shiny and settle down with his little wife to wait for the creamy engraved invitations which would never come except from other miserable parvenus.

Whereas if you were born into it, New Orleans was one long party—starting with the Twelfth Night, Carnival, Easter, followed by the Jazz and Heritage Festival, then Spring Fiesta, and Halloween. November 1 was All Saints Day, when you visited your dead and made a picnic on the grass between the graves. It was only a hop, skip, and a jump to Turkey Day and Christmas and then, count your fingers and two toes, you were back at Twelfth Night again. Life was one Big Easy round of slapping the same backs and brushing the same cheeks and shaking the same hands your whole life over.

Now, why couldn't one of those little hands pass a small package, a prettily wrapped present, a *petit cadeau* in the never-ending crush of kissy-face? It could. No problem.

So Dr. Cecil Little fronted Zoe a couple grand to make the first buy for him from Billy Jack, whom she'd met hanging out at Patrissy's. Zoe doled out the stash like a school-mistress giving stars for good behavior.

And it was awfully good blow.

It was so good, in fact, that Dr. Cecil couldn't keep it to himself.

Zoe knew he wouldn't be able to. That's what she was counting on, expansion.

Before long, Dr. Cecil had provided her with a whole network of august customers, pillars of the medical profession with very greedy noses, who didn't want to be caught holding.

Pretty soon, there wasn't a social gathering in town where you didn't hear the cry, "Where's Zoe? Is Zoe here yet? Where is that sweet thing?"

It made her feel like a star, she said to Sam. A princess. It didn't even matter to her anymore that she was as big as the side of a house—even if everybody said different—that her mother had run off and left her, that her father was a lush whose personal habits were getting sloppier and sloppier.

It didn't matter, because everywhere she went people were calling her name. She was like a light at the tippytop of one of those towers of silver she used to build in her room.

And if they missed connections at a party, Zoe made house calls.

Which was more than she could say for her clients, the last home visit by a New Orleans physician having been made in 1963, right after JFK was shot over in Dallas. Which was before Zoe was born, of course.

She teased her docs about that, about how lazy they were, how they couldn't get off their duffs even if someone was dying. Yes, they all said Zoe was a great tease. Laughter was good for business.

And business had been super supremo excelente until—here Zoe blinked back tears—until that awful night on St. Charles.

She took a deep breath. Stiff upper lip. On with it.

In fact, business was so good that through a broker/client she'd developed a fairly high-risk portfolio.

No flies on this child, thought Sam.

She held a mix of precious metals, moderately leveraged real estate partnerships, developmental oil and gas, aggressive growth stocks, and long-term high-grade bonds. All doing very well, thank you.

In addition, she was no piker at the Fairgrounds, betting on winners more often than not. She chose them by their jockeys' colors and the horses' names.

All *very* interesting, Sam nodded. "But let's get back to your supplier, this Billy Jack. What I really want to know is if he might have any connection with your father's death. Did he have any reason to hurt you? Had you—double-crossed him in some way? Done something—I don't know—"

"I can't think what. I've made him lots of money. But, on the other hand, he's nuts. Crazy. A psycho."

"Great, Zoe."

"But nothing I can't handle," she rushed to reassure Sam. "He has an awful temper, but I know how to stay on his good side—except at the track. When I win and he loses, it weirds him out."

"Is *that* enough to make him want to hurt you—or your dad?"

"I don't think so. Would be pretty stupid, wouldn't it? Well, except he is kinda stupid. No, not stupid, exactly. He's great with numbers, has a thing about them. But he's trash." Zoe gestured, one hand palm out, as if that explained it all.

"Most drug dealers are not exactly aristocrats."

Zoe laughed. "I am."

Sam had to give her that.

"But I would suppose you haven't seen much of Billy Jack since your dad—"

Two beats. "No. I haven't. I haven't been doing any business at all."

"Have you heard from him?"

"He's called a couple times, left messages on my machine over at the house. I left word for him that I was shut down."

"Does he know why?"

"I can't remember exactly what I said. Probably just that I wasn't dealing now."

"Do you have his phone number?"

"Yes, but it's a machine too—somewhere. No one ever answers except the machine. I don't even know if he lives there."

Right outside Zoe's room at Ma Elise and Kitty's house, Billy Jack was sitting in a tree staring in at them.

He could make out only a word now and again, but then, he hadn't come to listen. He'd come to watch the little show he'd planned for Zoe.

He'd gotten the idea for the show after he'd gone to Patrissy's and talked to Willie, the maître d' who'd said nuh-unh, it wasn't Frankie Zito was doing the asking after him, was some good-looking young guy in a trench coat, didn't look like anybody in the organization. That weirded him out, so he'd stomped out of Patrissy's and jumped in his car. When in doubt, it was best to get moving.

As he drove, he came to some conclusions pretty fast. It was a cop who was asking after him. Or the DEA. He knew it. And he didn't have time for that crap right now. He needed to do *more* bi'nis, not less. No time to be laying low, Easter Sunday right around the corner and the man at Adler's still holding his mama's diamond cross in his fat little hands.

With that, Billy Jack's suspicion had coiled tight around itself. Okay, who'd ratted him out?

Well, take a look.

Who'd been acting funny?

He'd sat dead still in his Lincoln Town Car at a green light, horns honking all around him. Fuck 'em. Hold on a minute. He wanted to get this right.

His mind had flipped through his customers.

A–Z.

Bingo.

Zoe Lee.

It didn't take him but a few minutes to formulate a plan, throw the Town Car into gear, start rolling again.

He loved it—a natural.

Now, sitting in his ringside seat waiting for it to happen, Billy Jack rubbed his hands in anticipation. He couldn't wait to see the expression on Zoe Lee's face.

The phone rang just then and Zoe jumped.

Like *that.*

Like when she was six years old and Chloe's big brother, Malcolm, had caught the two of them, her and Chloe, playing doctor and said if they didn't do a rerun for him—that's it, little girl—he was gonna call her father. Like *she* had done something bad. Just a little kid, she'd believed him, had jumped *that high* for years every time the phone rang, thinking it was Malcolm gonna narc on *her.*

Like that.

But then, somebody *had* been calling off and on and hanging up. But she didn't tell Sam that.

"Hello?" she said. "Hello? Hello?"

The caller on the other end hung up.

Out in the tree, Billy Jack grinned. That call was the signal. All systems were go. Now.

Within minutes Zoe's phone rang again. Sam reached for it, but Zoe was too fast.

Billy Jack, with a handkerchief over the mouthpiece of the portable phone he had up the tree with him, said, "You rat."

"Who is this?"

Sam was shaking her head. Hang up, she whispered.

Zoe mouthed: Billy Jack.

That was different. Sam looked around for an extension, but Zoe shook her head, then turned the receiver out. They listened cheek to cheek.

"You shouldn't rat on your friends," he said.

"I know that's you, Billy Jack," said Zoe. "Don't try to be so creepy."

Silence. Then: "You rat!"

"I didn't rat. I don't know what you're talking about."

"Cross your heart and hope to die?"

"What?"

"Cross your heart and hope to die?"

Zoe thought, what was this hope-to-die crap? He'd said it twice. Zoe'd never said it even when she was a little kid, just like she'd never prayed *if I should die before I wake.* People who said stuff like that were nuts.

And then she got it.

"Are you threatening me?"

Billy Jack laughed really loud—like thunder out over the lake on a summer afternoon. "Why, what makes you think that?"

"Then why did you say it?"

Before he could answer, the downstairs doorbell rang.

Sam signaled to Zoe to get the door, she'd hold the phone.

"I have to go. Doorbell's ringing."

"Let somebody else get it."

"Nobody else is home."

"Are you sure?" The bell rang again. "Oh, yeah. I can hear that. Listen, why don't I stay on the phone while you see who it is? These days you never can tell."

"Like *you're* gonna protect me," Zoe laughed.

"Go get it."

"Oh, all right."

Zoe threw a quilted satin robe over her nightclothes and ran barefooted down the stairs.

Sam could hear Billy Jack's excited breath on the line.

Downstairs Zoe stood behind the locked door. "Who is it?"

"Delivery, ma'am."

"From where?"

"Commander's."

"Commander's Palace? I didn't order anything."

And she didn't know they did takeout. Though, of course, Ella Brennan would do *anything* to make you happy if you gave her enough lead time.

"I think your grandma did. I think that's what they said. It's getting cold, ma'am."

That was weird; it didn't sound like something Ma Elise, her *great-*grandma to be precise, would do. Through the peephole she stared at a tall young man with sandy curls who was wearing black pants and a white waiter's jacket. He was holding a white cardboard box in his hands. What the hell? She opened the door.

"Maybe your grandma felt guilty about not making you any supper," he smiled.

His front teeth were a little crooked. He was sort of a wonk.

"How do you know she didn't?"

"I just guessed."

Zoe signed the receipt which he slipped into his pocket.

The guy was still standing there. "So, Miss Lee, you better go eat this 'fore it gets cold."

And then she remembered her manners. "Oh, let me get you a little something." She started back into the house to find him a tip.

"No, ma'am. That's all right."

Quick as that, he was back down the brick walk. She didn't see a car. Well, Commander's was right around the corner. He probably walked.

Zoe ran back upstairs with the box, waving it at Sam, who handed her the receiver.

"So what was that?" said Billy Jack.

"Listen, thanks for baby-sitting me, but it was just a delivery boy."

Billy Jack smiled. *His* delivery boy, but she didn't know that. Yet. "What'd you get?"

"Somebody sent over something from Commander's."

"That's nice. What is it? Shrimp?"

"Oh, I don't know."

She eyed the box resting on her dressing table. If Sam didn't want a snack, she'd bury it deep in the kitchen garbage, where Ma Elise and Ida would never see it. She didn't want to hear any more lectures about her eating habits.

"Whyn't you open it up?"

"Look, Billy Jack," she said, "thanks a hell of a lot for calling and trying to weird me out, but I've got to go."

"Open it."

"You like surprises? If it'll make you happy, I'll open it."

She reached past Sam, who was staring at her with raised eyebrows, snagged scissors out of a drawer, and cut the red and white string.

Inside, in a little basket like fried chicken came in was—Jesus, she didn't know what it was. But it sure didn't look like something from Commander's.

"What is it?" Billy Jack asked.

"I don't know. Something fried. Something fried whole. Yuk," she said, backing away from it now. She'd gorged so much today that food in general was disgusting. Fried food was especially disgusting. And this, it looked like a little squirrel or something, was revolting. What could Ma Elise have been thinking about?

"It's Willard," offered Billy Jack.

"No, it's not Will—who the hell's Willard?" What was he talking about? "It doesn't have a *name* I told you, it's something fried."

"Don't you remember that movie? *Willard?*" he repeated.

"No, I don't. I don't have time to go to—" And then, click, she did. She remembered. Willard was a rat.

Zoe screamed. She screamed and screamed and screamed and screamed and grabbed the box and tossed it out the window. She was so freaked out, she didn't even see Billy Jack sitting in the tree right there. She was about to throw the phone out, too, when she heard the Billy Jack's voice, low and slow, come slithering out of the phone like a snake.

"No more ratting. Billy Jack don't like ratting. Okay, darlin'?"

Darlin' was what Uptown bitches like Zoe called everybody. Billy Jack smiled. He liked that.

Twenty-one

Harry's slave quarter cottage behind a big house fronting on St. Peter was minuscule, but it sported its own courtyard and a few other sweet advantages.

He'd rented it ten years earlier from Allan Jaffe of Preservation Hall, and it abutted the hall, so if he was early to bed, he could drift off to Percy Humphrey's "Lord, Lord, Lord." Also, because Jaffe had had a soft spot in his gigantic heart for musicians of whatever stripe, the rent was less than the square footage.

Now it was after midnight, and Humphrey's band across the way had already packed it in. Harry was sitting in a canvas chair out in his courtyard dressed in a faded T-shirt and his shorts, staring at a half-empty bottle of gin. Harry was royally pissed. He strummed his old Gibson and tried it again.

> *I thought I knew how angels flew till you stepped off the plane.*
> *Smilin'.*
> *Oh, baby, I ain't lying.*
> *Said, Lord, this is heaven, let me lay my head right now front of that*
>   *moaning train.*

Moaning? Moving? Morning?

Harry banged the flat of his hand across the strings, which made a sound like a glass smashing if you throw it up against the wall hard enough. It was sort of like the sound of a man's breaking heart.

Sheeeeit, Harry, come off it, he said to himself. You ain't known the goddamn woman long enough she could inflict that kind of pain. You've seen her three times? Four? Maybe five you count that first time at the airport.

Yeah, well, how did you factor in those five/six weeks in between she'd come and gone and come again? All that time he was lying in his bed every night imagining her face right over his. Flying. Same thing every morning, waking up to her name.

He'd even found his feet out of control, walking him into a shop out on Magazine called Divine Light, where he'd asked the man behind the counter for a gris-gris to bring your lover back. Wait, wait, he'd explained. I *want* her to be my lover. *Then* come back to me.

The Divine Light man didn't even blink, just drew pictures and arrows with colored pens on a piece of parchment, rubbed it with sweet-smelling oil, tied it in a little red bag with a drawstring, then said, Five dollars, please.

Harry had been sleeping with it under his pillow ever since. God Almighty! The things he'd been dreaming. Now he reached for the gin bottle and topped up his drink.

So he was going to feel like shit tomorrow. He flashed back to Sam at the Royal O this afternoon, talking to him like he was a kid. The blood had rushed to his head. He'd felt like shit then. He felt like shit now.

He tried the verse again.

I thought I knew how angels flew till you stepped off the plane.
Smilin'.
Babe, I'm ready for dying.
Said, Lord, take me up, lay my head front of that moaning train.

Suddenly from out of the dark, a voice called, "You sure 'nuff gone feel like you been run over by a train you don't put that bottle down stop moaning them blues. Sound like a dog done treed a possum."

What?

Harry struggled up out of the canvas sling, his guitar rattling on the patio bricks. His legs, beneath his boxers, spread like he knew some mean moves. Watch it! He grabbed his bottle by the neck, just in case. "Who the fuck—?"

"Who the fuck you think?"

Harry shook his head. The voice was real familiar, but from somewhere far off in memory.

"I said who is it?"

"Open this goddamn door I'll show you who is it, unless you want me to cave it in."

"Lavert? Man, is that you?"

The gate swung open as the huge black man tapped it with his shoulder. "What it is, Harry Zack."

* * *

Two hours later, they hadn't budged. The gin bottle was long ago a dead soldier, and they'd wrung out a six-pack trying to get a handle on the fact that their paths hadn't crossed again until now.

Harry was shaking his head. "I bet if you were God, or if you were a bird—"

"Now, which you talking about?" Lavert grinned. He'd always loved listening to this boy talk, from the very first day they'd met at Grambling. "God ain't no bird."

"Now, you don't know that. God could be a buzzard for all you know."

"I *know* God ain't no buzzard. God's gone be a bird, he'd be an eagle."

"How come you so sure? Might be a pelican."

"Louisiana pelican." Lavert threw his massive head back and laughed. "Sheeeeit. Kind of thing you'd say, Zack."

"So like you're a bird up there, is what I'm saying, and you can see you and me. Like we had little lights on us all the time."

"What color lights?"

Harry narrowed his eyes. "You're just being difficult, man. Okay. I have a red light. You have a green light."

Lavert grinned. He could see it now. Like little figures on a game board.

"Okay."

"And here I am, with my red light"—Harry made a little hopping journey with the screw cap of the gin bottle across the low table—"going about my life. And here you are"—he fingered the guitar pick he was using for Lavert's marker—"with your green light, doing the same."

"Yeah, but for a while my light got kind of dim, sitting up there under a bushel in Angola."

"Okay, okay. But nonetheless"—Harry waggled the two markers—"it's got to be, if you could see it from up above like God, I bet lots of times, I'm just going out this door while you coming in the other." The guitar pick chased the bottle cap. "I paid my bill and left while you getting dressed to come hear the same tunes, same place."

Lavert picked it up. "Like I done slipped my dick out of some sweet thing you just wondering if you ever gone get hard again."

"Shit."

They slapped hands across the table.

"Can you believe this?" Harry said. "Tell me again, now, you were just talking with some guys, and my name came up?"

So Lavert told him a version of the truth, putting in that he was cooking for someone—leaving out that it was Joey the Horse.

"I like to lost it," Lavert said. "Almost cut my foot off when I dropped that cleaver."

"And then you just looked me up in the phone book, came over here. Hop, skip, and a jump away." Harry shook his head. "Unbelievable."

Lavert laughed. "Always been one of your favorite words. You 'member that time—?"

"You gon' tell that again? Jesus!"

"And then," Lavert said, spreading his hands in an expansive gesture as if he were speaking to a crowd, drawing them in, "little old white boy done fainted dead away in the middle of registration."

"Fuck. That gym was hot. About eleven hundred degrees."

"White boys don't know nothing about no heat. Ain't never worked in no fields."

"Yeah, yeah, yeah."

"Little old white boy, *famous* little old white boy, first one ever come to Grambling, got himself a track scholarship, we figure you done *run* all the way up from New Orleans, little old white boy lying there, looking like a ghost on the gym floor."

"You gonna take all night to tell this thing?"

"Comes to. Looks up at this circle of black faces peering down at him. "Says—"

" 'God, I didn't know angels were black.' "

And then they laughed, pounded each other on the back. It felt great to laugh like that.

"And nobody ever let me forget it," Harry said.

"Awh, it wuddn't that bad, was it?"

Harry shook his head, then tilted it back, staring up at where the stars were, except with the city glare you couldn't see them.

"Best years of my life," he finally said.

"Go on."

"I'm not kidding."

"All the shit we gave you?"

Then they both settled in their chairs a bit. Lavert chuckled low in his throat. "Me too. That's for damn sure."

"We had some good times, didn't we? You remember that time I won that big race?"

"Night of the football game that that one other white boy we had, come a year after you, scored the winning touchdown. Then two seconds later y'all's race, one of them what ended in the stadium, you come flying in in the lead, ahead of the pack, your pore little face red as a beet."

"Six weeks after that, people still congratulating me on that touchdown."

Lavert laughed. "How you expect us to tell y'all apart?" He stretched long. "Yeah, lordy, them was the good times. Listen, you want me to go over to the A&P on Royal get some more beer? Now that you got over your mean reds."

"I didn't have the mean reds, man."

"Yeah? Then why you sitting out there in your underpants moaning about some lady?"

Harry gave him a look.

"Don't hardcase me, sucker. Tell Papa L all about it."

"Awh, it's nothing." But the next thing Harry knew, he was telling Lavert about Sam—starting with that very afternoon.

"So she thinks you're stupid."

"That's what it feels like."

"She treat you that way from the git-go, you stupid to be messing around with her in the first place."

"Unh-uh. The first time I saw her she pretended I was invisible—not stupid."

"Where was that?"

"Day before Mardi Gras. Out at the airport."

"Oh yeah? What you doing out there?"

"Following a lady lied about a neck injury. For, you know, the insurance company I told you I'm working for."

"Oh, yeah? Lady white?"

"Yeah, Lavert. See, Tench Young is your equal opportunity—"

"Redheaded? Built like a brick shithouse?"

That made Harry sit up.

"Right! Chéri. You know Chéri?"

"Who the hell do you think was driving the limo, son, picked her up?"

"Jesus H. Christ! You work for Joey Cangiano, Lavert?"

"God, you white boys swear something awful."

"I can't fucking believe it. You're hooked up with Joey—we were *that* close to one another."

"You and your little old red and green light theory you'se talking about earlier, we been closer than that hundreds of times, bopping around the Quarter."

"Yeah, but see, that's exactly what I'm talking about. I was right there, but I didn't see you."

Then an idea occurred to Lavert. "So, you didn't see that little old white boy fell out in the street on me?"

Harry laughed. "No, but I know exactly what you're talking about."

And then he told Lavert about his hiding behind the pile of luggage and a taxi dispatcher that day so Chéri wouldn't see him. How he missed the big event, but overheard Chéri later in the Pelican telling about it.

"So you don't know who that sucker is," said Lavert.

"Who?"

"The little sucker fell out in the street, thought he'd been shot?"

"No, why?"

"I want to find him for G.T."

"G.T. Johnson?"

"That very lady. That girl makes my heart sing."

Harry clapped his hands to his head. "Unfriggingbelievable. You know she's sort of a friend of Sam's?"

"Sam a tall, good-looking black-headed woman? Curly hair? Chest?"

"Yep."

"I don't know her."

"Shit!" Harry punched Lavert in the arm. "Where'd you see her?"

"Standing out on Royal this afternoon talking with G.T."

"In front of the Royal O?"

"That must have been right before she told me I was ignorant."

"Because you didn't find this drug dealer?"

"I don't know. I guess that's part of it. Christ, I'd just told her I'd tracked down this woman Madeline Villère, used to—"

"What's his name?"

"Who?"

"The drug dealer, asshole."

"Billy Jack."

Lavert sat there like a big stone deciding whether or not to come clean with Harry.

Harry stared at him for a while, remembering Sam's legs beneath that polka-dot skirt. Then he added, "Billy Jack's what Sam said. I'm not sure if Jack's his last name."

"I heard you."

"So why are you sitting there looking stupid?"

"Cause I'd rather do that than listen to you say *unbelievable* again."

"What the hell are you talking about?"

"*That's* how your name came up, asshole. This evening when I was cooking dinner for Joey and the boys, Billy Jack is the creep Frankie Zito started talking about. Zito said somebody was asking about Billy Jack—who's one of their dealers, sort of a tenth cousin twice removed from the organization, you know what I mean. Boy's *way* down the line. But that's what got Joey all worked up, somebody was asking about a man even remotely connected to him. That somebody asking was *you*, son. That's where I heared your name."

A hand grabbed Harry's bowels. Did this mean he was dead? He was too young to be dead. "Joey gonna have me fed to the fishes?"

"Nah. I don't think so. Frankie Zito seemed a hell of a lot more pissed off at this Billy Jack—shit, what'd they say his last name was—than you."

"Jack's not his last name? You *know* his last name?"

"If I could remember it, I'd tell you right now, wouldn't I? I just wasn't paying that much attention, till they mentioned you."

"Shit."

"Listen. You want me to leave? I got better places I could spend my time, middle of the night, 'stead of sitting around with you. People who wear lots prettier undies. You know what I mean?"

"Fuck you, Lavert. You were in the frigging room when they said the guy's name, and you don't know know who it is."

"Yeah? Well, you're out at the airport, and you don't see me. Don't see the little guy who thought I'd shot him, the one G.T. picked up and ran out on her. Now, if I can find *him*, make me a whole lot of points with G.T. Whereas *you*, you got no problem. I can find you your goddamn Billy Jack Whazzits, Zack. All I got to do is ask Frankie Zito."

"For real?"

"What do you think this is, son? The comics? This is the friggin' organization."

"So you'll do that?"

"Give me one good reason I should."

" 'Cause I'll beat the shit out of you if you don't." Harry stood, the top of his head way beneath Lavert's chin, and slugged his old friend in the chest.

Lavert picked him up and held him straight-armed out, level, then drew him in and kissed him dead on the lips.

"Jesus H. Christ!" Harry sputtered. "The Jolly Black Giant's turned queer."

"No, I ain't." Lavert laughed. "I'm just so happy to see my best little old white boy again. I tell you what, sport."

"Put me down and tell me."

Lavert did. "We'll do a Batman and Robin. I get to be Batman. We'll find both those suckers and win those ladies. How's that, Zack?"

"Say *shazam*, man!"

Harry and Lavert slapped hands. Then the giant man lowered himself down, and they bumped knees, hips, and elbows. Just the way Lavert had showed Harry, trying to teach him to be a brother, back at Grambling in the good old days.

Twenty-two

The next morning Sam and Kitty were drinking coffee outside on the patio under a banana tree.

"How long did it take you to get Zoe to sleep?" asked Kitty.

"About an hour and a half. It took a while just to get her to stop screaming. I thought about pouring a bunch of Ma Elise's good cognac down her, but, well, you know that's against my religion."

"So what'd you use?"

"A little wormwood oil, pinch of wallbreaker powder."

Kitty laughed. "You called G.T."

"Hell, I figured, when in Rome—I got her on her beeper. She was over here in a flash."

"She brought her traveling voudou kit with her?"

"Guess she carries it in her ambulance. She was out here sprinkling oil in a circle around that tree"—Sam pointed to a flowering pink mimosa—"muttering about sending hexes back to their maker."

"Oh, Lord."

"Then she was up with Zoe, who was still carrying on like a banshee, dusting her and the room with—she said it was wallbreaker powder, would make Zoe peaceful."

"Did it?"

"Well, at least she stopped screaming. Then G.T. got us all three sitting in the middle of the floor, rubbing a couple of candles with oil. A dragon-blood candle to ward off Billy Jack's evil. And a double-cross candle to throw a hex back on him—to be precise."

"Precision is real important in voudou, God knows." Kitty lit another Picayune.

"Go ahead, smirk. But I'll tell you what. You'd been sitting here with Zoe, having a screaming hissy fit after that son of a gun ordered her up a deep-fried rat, you'd have been grateful for some magic."

"And I am. I am." Kitty reached over and patted Sam on the knee.

"But the idea of you and G.T. doing all that—" Then her tone grew grim. "But you are right about that bastard. I'd like to deep-fry *him*. Why would anyone *do* such a thing?"

"Darlin', I'm afraid he could have done lots worse. In any case, he kept talking about her ratting on him. It could be something totally unrelated or could be he got wind of Harry looking for him." Then she added under her breath, "Not that Harry found him."

"How *is* Harry working out? Or have you got him so nervous he can't hunt?"

Sam studied her manicure for a long count. "I don't know about that. But I have succeeded in making him so mad, he told me to go screw myself."

"Lordy, lordy, you always have had such a way with men."

"I think it's my Betty Boop routine."

"Well, hell. But wait." Kitty sat up straighter. "Let's look at it another way. If you've made him that mad, maybe he'll throw in the towel. Call off the chase. Tench Young'll give Zoe the insurance money."

Sam's mouth turned down. "I wouldn't count on that. If anything, Harry's probably working overtime to prove something, *anything*, to save Tench's money."

Kitty slumped back into the deep yellow cushion of the wrought iron chair. "Way to go, friend. I knew asking you to come help was the right thing."

"Don't get cute with me. I've been up to a trick or two myself." Then she told Kitty about the visit with the amazing Nadine.

"So you think she's the one? That she and Church were lovers?"

"I'm sure leaning in that direction. Though, still, if they were, what does that prove? Nothing."

"I can't imagine the preacher woman *killing* anyone. I mean, let's say Church had dumped her."

"I can't either. Though I can see why Church wouldn't want to bring her home to Ma Elise."

"Are you kidding? Ma Elise's one of her biggest fans."

"But would she want her for a daughter-in-law? Granddaughter-in-law?"

"I don't know that Ma Elise would have cared."

"What about Church's friends?"

"Now, that's another matter. They'd have cut him dead for sure. I mean, can you see Sister Nadine twirling around the floor of the Comus ball with her tambourine?"

"I'm telling you, Kit, that's all for show. The woman may have some humble roots, but you'd fall over dead at her sophistication. And I told you about her drug centers, and what she said about Zoe—about Church coming to her, looking for help for Zoe?"

Kitty shook her head. "Weird. It's all so weird."

"I know." They sat quietly for a bit, sipping, smoking. Then Sam said, "Listen, something else I've been meaning to ask you. Tell me about Church's money."

"What about it?"

"Do you know how much he had?"

"Not exactly. His lawyer's still working that out. Plus, with this business about the insurance—"

"Was Church in some kind of financial difficulty? I seem to remember, that night in the Sazerac, Tench Young teasing him about the cost of Zoe's coming out, of Carnival—"

"That's all it was, a joke. Church—well, one of the things he liked best about being an eye surgeon was it meant that he didn't have to depend on family money to be comfortable. Which is just as well, considering that the Lee fortune is sort of petering out."

Sam gazed out at three gardeners puttering on the immaculate grounds. Then she looked back at Kitty. Oh yeah?

"Don't judge by them. You know we still pay slave wages down here. Ain't nothing ever what it seems."

Sam smiled. In her business, she had reason to know that more than most. "And how about his practice? Must have been a slowdown after the business with Mr. Leander."

"I don't think so. But then, Church would never say if there was."

"Do you mind if I talk to his lawyer about this?"

"Be my guest. Though I doubt you'll get very far with him. Preston Peacock's about as closemouthed a member of that particular species as I've ever seen."

"Peacocks?"

"No. Lawyers."

Then another notion bubbled to the surface. "Kit, do Nadine and Church's ex, Madeline, have anything in common?"

"What do you mean?"

"I don't know. It just occurred to me to ask."

Kitty shook her head slowly, then reached for another cigarette. "No, I can't think that they would."

Kitty had hesitated just a tad too long—like she always did when she was lying. Or avoiding the truth. But it would do Sam no good to call her hand. She'd simply have to be more creative. Then she remembered that Kitty had still said nothing about Leander's canceling the malpractice suit against Church's estate. She asked if Kitty had returned Leander's call.

"I haven't. I *hate* that old bastard."

"Better talk to him, girl. He's got something mighty interesting to say to you."

"I could learn to hate you too."

"Not a chance. Listen, now, before I forget about it, I think you ought to have some kind of surveillance put on the house and a tail on Zoe."

"Are you kidding?"

"I'm not. She said this Billy Jack is a wacko. I'd believe it after what I saw last night. I'd hate for us to be sorry we didn't later."

"Jesus. Do you really think it's that serious?"

"I'm telling you yes. Listen, I'll call Harry—no, I guess I won't. You know anybody does this sort of thing?"

Kitty blinked her big blue eyes.

"Okay. Don't worry. I'll call around. I'll handle it."

"What am I going to tell Ma Elise?"

"Tell her the truth," said the old lady as she stepped onto the brick patio with her cane.

Twenty-three

Marietta Duchamps Dupree leaned back in her chair under a yellow-and-white umbrella, signaled to Howard for another couple of glasses of iced tea, ran her tongue across her top lip, tasting the sweat, and grinned across the table at Chéri.

Lordy, lordy, her life was good.

And here she was scandalizing the Club—one of her very favorite things to do.

Just a couple of minutes ago Bunny Crabtree and Sugar Rockwell had strolled by on their way out to the courts, where Marietta and Chéri had just finished a ferocious match—with protracted volleys so long and low and carefully placed that when one of them finally came to the net, the other moaned softly.

Now, damp and exhausted, they sprawled in chairs at the side of the pool. Bunny and Sugar had stopped for a minute.

"I see you've brought your guest again, Marietta," Bunny had purred, then turned to Chéri. "I'm sorry, darlin', I don't remember your name."

"Nor I yours." Chéri grinned, taking that opportunity to reach for a towel and blot beads of perspiration on her chest—her beautiful, freckle-strewn chest, the sight of which made Bunny feel like a boy.

Chéri knew that.

Chéri knew everything there was to know about both female and male psychology and any combination you could imagine thereof. Chéri may not have darkened the door of a classroom after she'd finished high school over in Thibodeaux, where her father, when he wasn't shrimping, was a volunteer fireman, but where human nature was concerned, she had a Ph.D.

"Now, I think you hurt that girl's feelings," Marietta said after Bunny and Sugar flounced off. "She's not gonna speak to me at the Orleans Club luncheon next week."

Chéri grinned again. Fiddled with the straw in her iced tea. Made her mouth a pretty pout around it. She knew Marietta loved her little pout, especially when she was just playing.

"Now tell me what it was you were so excited about on the phone when I couldn't talk," Chéri said.

Marietta sat up straight, took a quick peek around. This goddamn club had such ears, it might as well be wired for sound. "Sally Jean called me, she was just all to pieces. She said this gangster had come into Maynard's office, *threatening* him."

"Gangster? Honey, what you think she meant, gangster? That Sally Jean, she's an old lady, she don't know what the word means."

"She does too. Sally Jean is very smart. She's a little flighty, but you would be, too, if you had to put up with what she—"

"Yeah? Then how come half the time she's got her wig on sideways like it was a doily she just stuck up there on top of her head?"

"Chéri, you're making me mad, honey."

"Good. I like it when you're mad. You wanta go home, get in bed, talk about it?"

Marietta paused for a minute, as if she were considering it. But she wasn't really—not till after they'd spent some time in the steam bath. Watching the ladies slide glances at Chéri naked and glistening like a freshly washed nectarine was her all-time favorite brand of foreplay, and she wouldn't be rushed.

"Now, you want to hear what Sally Jean said or not?"

"Of course I do. Thank you, Howard." Chéri smiled.

Howard nodded as he dropped off another couple of glasses of iced tea. He shook his head, kept his grin to himself. That Miz Dupree knew how to tell a whole club Go fuck yourself without saying a word. Wuddn't she something?

"What I really want to know, May-retta"—which was how Chéri said her girlfriend's name when she was being silly, which was the way most people pronounced it anyway—"is if you're saying Joey went and hit on Maynard?"

"Honey baby, that is *not* what I'm saying. I know it wasn't Joey, not unless he's taken to wearing cowboy boots."

Chéri hooted. And once she got started, she couldn't stop, peals of laughter bursting out of her like Marietta had goosed her. "Can you see Joey in cowboy boots?"

"Not hardly. Not less Gucci's doing 'em."

"Oh, God." Wiping her eyes. "So what did this cowboy gangster want?"

"Sally Jean said it sounded like he was torturing Maynard's tailor. The little man was screaming to beat the band. Said he was a real redneck."

"The gangster."

"Yes, darlin'. Not the tailor. Said his name was Jimbo."

"Well, I'll be damned."

"You know this boy?" Marietta's eyes narrowed. "Honey, what you holding out on me?"

"Not a damn thing. Is he tall? Got long legs?"

"Sounds right. Sally Jean was so hysterical—"

"I bet it's that sucker I saw in the Pelican that afternoon with Maynard—he was flirting with me. You 'member me telling you about that?"

"Mardi Gras afternoon?"

"Day before, I think. That's it. This Jimbo and Maynard were real palsy-walsy. Maynard buying him drinks."

"Honey, Maynard would buy a golf cart a drink, once he's got going."

"You know what I mean. They were cozied up to each other. Could that have anything to do with what you think Maynard's up to? His little Wednesday meetings over to the cemetery?"

"Lordy, honey, I don't know. Wouldn't it just be the living end if Maynard had turned queer too?"

Chéri shook her head. "I don't think Maynard's the type."

"Why not? He gave up screwing me long time ago—must be screwing something."

"Maynard's not cute enough to be queer."

"Not all gayboys are cute, Chéri. Child, where have you *been?*"

"Not cute as you, that's for sure."

Marietta squinched up her shoulders, pushing out her own pretty chest. "I'm no homosexual, darlin'."

"Unh-uh, girl. You sure ain't. You just like to—"

Howard couldn't help himself, leaned over to catch the rest of that as he was passing by with a club sandwich heavy on the mayo for fat ol' Miss Boudrant, who couldn't even wait till lunch.

"—be with me." Chéri fluttered her eyelashes at Howard, then winked.

"Well, whatever it is, I think we ought to check up on it," Marietta said. "I think the time to divorce that silly son of a bitch is drawing nigh. And God knows, I want to do it to him. Put it to him. He's gonna have every divorce lawyer in the state of Louisiana on his side."

"Yeah, that's right. But like I told you, Joey's got lawyers'll make them little boy attorneys cry out in the night. Scream for their mamas."

"I know you keep saying that, darlin'. But I can't believe mob lawyers do divorces. Nobody Italian ever *gets* a divorce. Especially your type of Italian. They just make people disappear."

Chéri's eyes were as clear and blue as the sky out over the Gulf right after a big blow. She looked dead at Marietta. Smiled. Blinked once. Twice.

Twenty-four

Sam, wearing her new Reeboks, turned smartly out of Ma Elise's gate onto the sidewalk. That's what her body needed—to clear her brain—a good shaking up. Eight glasses of water a day, seven hours' sleep, forty-five minutes of sweat.

What she'd had here in the past few days had been more like coffee, coffee, and more coffee. Last night she'd tossed and turned, dreaming about Harry holding out a french-fried rat, saying, You're so smart, Ms. Know-It-All, howsabout *this?* Rich sauces and fat, fat, fat were marshaling forces to set up camp in her thighs, not to mention her brain.

Exercise. Exercise. Watch me do my exercise.

And a meeting wouldn't hurt a-tall. She'd call AA and find one.

Picking up speed, she swung her arms race-walking fashion as she headed toward St. Charles.

Who the hell did Church's ridiculous attorney Preston Peacock think he was? It truly was a wonder more lawyers weren't assassinated.

Oh, no, Miss Adams, darlin', *darlin',* he'd said on the phone, there was no point in her comin' in. He was far too busy, goin' to spend the whole week in court, she'd just caught him by his coattails runnin' out the door, but he couldn't tell her a thing about Church, his finances? Oh, no, that was privileged info, but his client was dead, well, that made it even more privileged, didn't it? And questions were, well out of the question, didn't matter that she was a friend of the Lees, no, no, no, no, no.

She wanted to rip out Mr. Peacock's tailfeathers.

She hit St. Charles at a fast clip, turned left, heading Uptown.

She waved at an ancient lady all in violet who had just stepped out on the front porch of a particularly splendiferous mansion. The woman stonily stared down her salute.

Quite likely she was one of those *grandes dames* Ma Elise had been telling her about—who never shopped, had everything sent. After all, it was *common* to go out in the street. You'd run into people you didn't know.

Like, she thought, picking up speed, heading toward General Taylor Street, Jimbo King.

The streets flew by: Washington Avenue, Sixth, Seventh, Eighth, Pleasant, Toledano, Louisiana, Delachaise, Aline, Foucher, Antonine, Amelia, Peniston. General Taylor was next.

And Jimbo King—who lived next door to G.T. on that very street.

Jimbo's name had popped to the top of her list of must-sees after she'd slammed down the phone on Preston Peacock. Now she remembered that she'd made that list of people to see talking with Harry in the Royal O.

Harry. She shoved him right out of her mind.

But then his pretty face popped right back up. She ran faster, working up a sweat now. Harry would go away. But wouldn't it be great to have him around now—to follow up on Billy Jack while she went after Maynard Dupree? Maynard was next, right after Jimbo King.

She and Harry could have danced through this investigation together, if only Harry hadn't wanted to lead.

Who wanted to lead, Samantha? a little voice inside asked her.

Okay, okay, so I *was* a little controlling, I'll give you—*kersplat.*

Sam sprawled on the sidewalk, done in by a live oak tree whose roots had made cookie crumbs of the concrete.

"Owh!" she cried, afraid to touch her scraped knees.

"Help you, ma'am?" A yardman was coming toward her, holding a bunch of red-hearted caladium in one hand. He turned off his Walkman and said, "You best come with me up on the porch."

"No, I'm fine really." Except her knees hadn't hurt this much since she was five and bounced off her bike in the middle of Peachtree.

The old man paid no attention to her, taking her arm, pulling her up, leading her to the porch. He settled her into one of a pair of rocking chairs.

"You stay." He pointed a finger, talking to her just like she did to her Shih Tzu, Harpo, who was back in Atlanta pouting right this minute.

"Here you be." The yardman was back, handing her a wet washcloth. "You dab that off good. Then we put some peroxide on it." He pulled a brown bottle out of his khaki pants pocket.

"Thanks." Sam smiled. "You make me feel like a little girl again."

"What you look like, too, running around in your bitty shorts." The old man laughed, his face crinkling up—the same color as a pecan pie.

"Ought to be staying out of the sun, anyway. Or carry you a parasol like Miz Villère." He jerked a thumb toward the mansion's front door.

Sam couldn't believe her luck. Church's wife had been a Villère before she'd married.

"*Madeline* Villère live here once?"

"Nun-unh. She be gone a long time."

"But she lived here?"

He pointed his chin downtown. "No, ma'am. She growed up down the street. Other side. This here's her cousin's house."

"But you remember Madeline?"

"Shore do. Pretty girl."

"You know what happened to her?"

The old man scratched his head. "Nawh. I shore don't."

"Didn't she marry Church Lee?"

"Unh-huh. She liked shoes."

"What?"

"Lots of shoes, I 'member that. Like that Imelder. Imelder Marcos. You know her?"

"Sure, I know who you're talking about."

"She made a record album. You know that?"

"Imelda Marcos made a record album?"

"Shore did. My grandbaby played it for me. I tole him ought not to - spend money on trash like that. Woman ought to be strung up."

"Imelda Marcos, you mean?"

He gave her a look. " 'Course. You think I mean Miz Madeline? Nawh." He shifted what looked like a wad of chewing tobacco. "Miz Madeline be an angel."

"What else do you remember about her?"

"Liked black brassieres. 'Course, I always did think those was kind of nice myself." The old man tee-heed.

He couldn't fool her with that one. "Imelda, you mean."

"Shore. You know, there's another woman on that album named Imelder too. Guess that's a popular name over in the Philippines. My son was over there in the war. Shore was. Left a hand. Guess it's buried there somewheres. Mine blew it clean off."

"I'm sorry to hear that. Do you know if Mad—"

"That Johnny Cash and Bob Dylan did that too, you know."

"What?"

"Made an album together. My grandbaby played that one for me. He shore keeps up on white folks' music." The old man laughed, showing a full set of brilliantly white teeth. "Excuse me." He spit off the porch into the camellias. It was chewing tobacco all right. "I saw him last night. He tole me he was moving up to Virginia. I said, sweet baby, I don't unnerstan' why you want to be moving out of the South. He said it still was."

"Said Virginia's the South?" Sam laughed. "Well, we know it's not."

"Where you from?"

"Atlanta."

"Yep." The old man nodded. "That's the South."

She couldn't resist. "Where do you think it stops?"

Old man scratched his head under his straw hat. "Well, Texas ain't the South. On the left side."

"Right."

"And Arkansas is. 'Cept that part up there in the left-hand corner got mountains. I been up there onct. Visited a cousin in Little Rock. We drove up in them mountains. That ain't the South. People's different in the mountains. And there ain't no black peoples, so how could it be the South?"

"Mississippi?"

"Shore. 'Bama, Georgia, South Carolina."

"Florida?"

"Well, I ain't ever been there, but they tell me it's a lot like New York."

"The southern part is, around Miami. What about Tennessee?"

The old man shrugged. "Yeah. Mostly. But—" He shook his head. "You know they got mountains too, I hear. I ain't never been there either. 'Cept to Memphis."

"And that was sure southern."

"Graceland." The old man spread his hands, pale palms up. Need he say more?

"What about North Carolina? Kentucky? West Virginia?"

"Prob'ly North Carolina, but not them others. I think you stop at South Carolina, you got it. What you think?"

"I think you ought to go on TV in New York. On the 'Today Show.' Explain it to folks."

That tickled the old man. He bent over, raised a knee like a little old flamingo, slapped himself on the rear right near the white handkerchief hanging out of his pocket. "Wouldn't that be something? Shore would."

"Would." It was hard not to copy his style.

He thought about that for a few minutes. "New York," he said under his breath. Staring out into the yard, he seemed to focus on something that needed doing, then said, "You want another glass of water?"

"Don't mind if I do." The longer she stayed, she figured, the better chance she had of getting him to talk about Madeline.

"Well, hold on. I'll—" But as Luther turned, a shadow appeared at the door.

"Luther?" The voice was a tremulous soprano.

"Yes'm, Tante Marie."

"I'll be needing you to help me soon on the east gallery."

"Yes'm."

Sam caught a shadowy glimpse of a tiny little old lady in a long black dress that came to the tips of her shiny black patent shoes. A cameo caught the ruffle at her neck. Her white hair was a coronet of braids. A pale hand fluttered. Then she disappeared.

"Who's that?"

"Tante Marie."

"Villère?"

Luther shrugged, of course.

"She looks so old—old-fashioned."

Luther laughed. "You can say that again. Tante Marie's kind of a throwback even for the Villères. Old-maid aunts like her used to live forever with the Creole fam'bly."

"Creole. That means her family's—?"

"Don't mean what you think." Luther shifted his chewing tobacco, then sat down on the edge of a step. "Don't mean no café au lait. Ain't none of us. Means descended from the French and, no, make that *or* Spanish settled here before the Americans."

"When Louisiana was a colony."

"You got that right. Creoles the best people. The finest. The *old* blood. My fam'bly, we always worked for Creoles. For Villères, that matter, since before the war."

"The war?"

"The War Between the States." Then Luther laughed at the look on her face.

"You think that's crazy, don't you? Keep working, generation after generation, for folks had you slaves?"

"I guess I do."

"That's 'cause you from Atlanta. Don't understand 'bout the way we do things here—these old fam'blies. See, we Fourniers descended from Prosper Fournier." He shook his head when he could see the name meant nothing to her. "Prosper one of the most famous servants of all time. He my great-great-great-great-uncle. Apprenticed in France when he was a boy, still a slave then, to a famous chef. Was a wonderful cook. Expert on the opera. The French opera being very big in those days. Prosper spoke French and Creole. Never did speak English, didn't have to. Rode to the opera with the Villères in their carriage. Sat front row center upstairs in the balcony for the colored. White people came up to him after, he such a expert, ask him what he thought of the voices. He tell 'em too. Shore 'nuff. Expert on wine too."

"Luther, you out here talking trash again?" And around the corner of the house walked a hulking white man. He seemed familiar to Sam, but she couldn't place him.

He tipped his big straw hat raveling at the edges. Then, squinting at her, he wiped the sweat off his forehead with a red bandanna from his overalls pocket. "Howdy, ma'am. Ain't I seen you somewhere?" He rocked back on his heels, considering, then pointed a pudgy finger. "G.T. You a friend of G.T. Johnson's."

"I *know* G.T."

"I'm Arkadelphia Lolley. I drive with her sometimes."

"Of course! Sam Adams." Sam extended her hand. "You were with G.T. the night of Church Lee's death."

"Pore old Mr. Church," said Luther, shaking his head. "Wuddn't that something? Turrible."

"I live over to Baronne," Arkadelphia said, jerking a thumb in that direction. "Run my machine"—and then he pointed at a giant mower which Sam hadn't noticed before parked to the side of the yard—"for folks when they need it. My extra job."

"Sure was unlucky for Church Lee that evening, wasn't it?" said Sam.

"Sure was." Ark settled his three hundred pounds on the steps beside Luther. "Luther, you reckon anywhere in that house there might be a glass of iced tea?"

"Might be." The old man nodded. " 'Specially if I go talk some sweet-talk to Ophelia." He stood. "I'll be right back. Then we'll sit out here have ourselves a little party."

That was fine with Sam.

"So you know the Lees?" she asked Ark.

"Nawh. I wouldn't say that. G.T. knows 'em though. Knowed 'em her whole life—through her family." He pushed his hat back and peered at her with pale blue eyes behind smudged glasses that made his eyes look huge. "Didn't she say something to me 'bout you staying with them? Looking 'round for clues?"

"You might say that."

"I used to have an aunt did that. Sure did."

"Looked for clues to things?"

"Unh-huh. She did it on her own, though. I mean, she wuddn't no police."

"I'm not either."

"Didn't mean to imply you wuz." One beat passed. Two. Three. "What *are* you, ma'am? You don't mind my asking?"

"I write for a newspaper over in Atlanta. But I'm here trying to find out what happened to Church so the Lees can settle the insurance."

"Uh-huh. Well, he got his head smashed like it was a watermelon wuz what happened looked like to me. By some crazy person wearing a Carnival mask driving a big old car."

"But who?"

"Oh. I see. You want to know *who* was driving the car?"

"Well, don't you think that'd be a good thing to know?" asked Luther, creeping out the screen door, carrying a tray of iced tea, little sandwiches on a plate, and a pile of sugar cookies.

"Lord! Would you look what this man's done!" Ark's fat face lit up like a Christmas tree. He reached for the sandwiches and downed two.

Sam watched him chew. Sheer delight was etched on his face. Arkadelphia was one of those people who was fat because he truly loved to eat.

"It's the sort of thing your aunt who looked for clues might want to know," she said eventually.

"What?"

"Who was driving the car."

"Oh, yeah. Kind of thing Aunt Stella would want track to earth all right." He washed down the sandwiches with a gulp of tea. "She tracked down all kinds of people. Was always good at finding things. Tracked that robbing preacherman, Otis Dew. Find him, could find anything."

"Could she find water?" asked Luther.

"Hell, anybody couldn't find water in the state of Louisiana ought to be put in the Home for the Bewildered," said Ark. "All you gotta do's look."

"Get smart with me," grumbled Luther. "Go on. Tell Miss Sam here 'bout that crazy Otis Dew now that you mentioned him."

"I don't see how's any of us got time," said Ark.

"I do." Sam nodded her head, southern girl recognizing the signs of a story coming on when she saw one. "I sure do."

Ark reached for another couple of sandwiches. "You never heard of him, you say?"

"Nope."

"That's hard to believe. He made some big news 'round here about ten years ago. Wouldn't you say ten, Luther?"

" 'Bout that. But I 'magine we knowed about it 'cause we live in the state. Might not be the kind of news that travels. Kind they put on the 'Today Show.' " He gave Sam a knowing wink. "And 'course you knew 'cause of your Aunt Stella."

"Whatever you say. Anyway, this Otis Dew, he was born around Peck."

"We going *way* back," said Luther.

"That's Catahoula Parish, up in my part of the state. Not too far from Ferriday, where Jerry Lee Lewis was from."

"And that Jimmy Swaggart," said Luther.

"Well, hell, throw in Mickey Gilley too," said Ark. "Everybody knows they all cousins." Then he scratched under his hat. "Now, Jimmy's cousin to Jerry Lee and to Mickey, but I'm not so sure if those two's kin to each other, but, now, you don't mind, Uncle Luther, I'll get on with this."

Luther threw both hands up in the air, said, Take it, son.

"Actually," Ark said, "Otis was a friend to all them boys. And was better'n all of 'em, in some ways."

"You'd have to prove that to me," said Sam.

"Well, he was." Arkadelphia started counting off the ways on fingers big as sausages. "He could sing like Jerry Lee. *Actually* he sounded an *awful* lot like Elvis."

"Humph," said Luther.

"Now, wait. Preach like Jimmy. And had the business sense of Mickey. And he was the handsomest man you'd ever hope to see. Kind of had the body of Dennis Quaid in that movie's made here, without his shirt. Big grin like Dennis too. But a softer face. Looked like that Patrick Swayze. Both of them's Texas boys, you know that?"

"I did." Sam made it a point to keep abreast of the best in cinematic male flesh. "Anything like Mel Gibson?"

"That's that *Lethal Weapon? Tequila Sunrise?"*

Sam nodded.

"Eyes. Eyes like that Gibson boy."

"Sweet Jesus," she sighed.

"Lord don't like you taking his name in vain," said Ark.

"Sorry," she said around a mouthful of sand tart, one of her all-time favorite cookies. "Go on."

"And when Otis got up to the front of the church, started singing and preaching, tears running down his handsome face, arms and legs in those fancy Eye-talian suits waving around like he was doing the hootchy-kootch, I tell you, those woman would stream up to the front and throw their bodies down. Just throw 'em down on the floor. Men too. Writhing. And then if he sang to 'em, well, you'd think he was Elvis come to life again the way they carried on."

"So why's your aunt Stella tracking him down? What'd he do?" she asked.

Arkadelphia sighed a big sigh, then stared off down the street like he was looking for the streetcar to come and take him somewhere people knew how to listen to a story. Didn't keep interrupting. Let a man tell it in his own time. Not like a passle of Yankees, kept cutting you off before you got to the point, tell you some silliness they thought was related to what you were saying, about their *own* lives, when you hadn't even warmed up. Hadn't even got started good yet. Sam and Luther could see that in Ark's staring off. They exchanged a look. Time to settle down, it said.

Ark waited. He drank another whole glass of iced tea. When he finished it he said, "Y'all through?"

Uh-huh, yes, indeedy, they nodded.

"Well, anyhow, as I was saying, Otis was from this family of Baptist preachers. His daddy was a preacher. His daddy before him. And Otis was smart. Went off to Baylor, the Baptist college in Texas, on a scholarship. Got himself a doctor of divinity."

Luther couldn't help but giggle.

"Ain't the candy, old man, that's what you're thinking. Then got himself a little church over in Shreveport. Worked that into a bigger church, and the next thing you know, he was preaching in the biggest church you ever saw in Houston."

"Back in the oil days?" asked Sam.

"You bet. Black gold pumping up out of the ground, forty bucks a barrel, and most of them old boys got lucky in the fields was Baptists. And they just couldn't do enough for the church—once they got through buying diamond rings and watches and stickpins and such, building houses and breeding race horses, fencing in ranches big as some Yankee states. Just dying to help Otis's church. So him and Mary Sue, that was his wife he met in the church choir in Shreveport, was from a real good family in the pipeline bi'nis, was living like a king and queen.

"Otis driving a white Cadillac. Mary Sue had her a matching white Mercedes. They lived in the biggest house you ever saw out in the River Oaks section."

"Tall cotton," said Sam.

"Well, that's what lots of folks said. Said it wuddn't seemly for a man of the cloth to be living so high on the hog. But then there's those that look at it another way. Say you wouldn't want the man who talks with the Man be driving around town in a raggedy little old Chevy, his wife wearing a Pat Nixon cloth coat looking like something the cats drug in. Especially with this crowd. Them boys wear their initials blazing in diamonds on their belt buckles, cattle brands clamped on their alligator boots in solid gold, new young second wives dressed up like something right out of the pages of *Vogue,* well, they don't want to be reminded that it wuddn't too long ago they didn't have a pot to piss in. 'Scuse my French. Don't want to be within five miles of anything don't reek of eau de cologne."

"So things were going great guns for Otis."

"Absolutely rooty-tooty, till they caught him."

"With his hand in the collection plate," said Sam.

"Naw. Otis wuddn't that stupid. Besides, they'd already give him so much, to want more he'd have to be just a plain greedy pig."

"Philandering," said Luther, throwing his guess in.

"Wait a minute," said Sam. "I thought you knew this story."

The old man laughed. "I do. Just got carried away, I reckon."

"Philandering?" Sam echoed.

"Well, sort of," Ark allowed. "You 'member how we started off talking about Jerry Lee?"

"Right."

"And did I mention Elvis?"

"Wait a minute. You said he affected women like Elvis when he preached. Is Elvis in this too? Elvis has been dead more than ten years."

"I *know* that. August 15, 1977. But what did Elvis and Jerry Lee have in common?"

"You mean besides singing?"

"Yeah."

"And being southern?"

"Yeah."

"And growing up near the Mississippi?"

"You're stretching it. Ferriday's real close, but Tupelo's nowhere near the Mississippi."

"It's *in* Mississippi."

"You meant the river, and you know it."

Sam had to back down. "I give."

"White cotton underpants," Uncle Luther giggled.

"What?" said Sam.

"They did," said Ark. "Luther's right. Both had a thing for young girls' undies."

"Both *married* young girls," said Sam. "Elvis had his Priscilla, and we all know about Jerry Lee's thirteen-year-old cousin."

"Ruined his career, didn't it? But you remember what they said about Elvis after he died? Grown women he was with, well, maybe a little on the young side, but legal—all with the same panties."

"I don't remember this, Ark."

"He made 'em all wear white cotton panties. *That* was what he liked. Well, Otis had the same problem. There he was, at the pinnacle of his career, couldn't stop chasing white cotton panties."

"That's disgraceful," said Sam, sounding like her aunt Lona.

"Well, now, before we get all high and mighty," said Ark, "I think we ought to think about what's on the TV these days, not to mention the movies and videos anybody can rent, walk in off the street. *Furthermore,* take a look at what's running around. Women, young and old, dressed up in high heels and short skirts and makeup? Wearing black fishnet stockings, dozens of rings in their ears, not to mention some in their noses? Tattoos on their behinds?"

"Arkadelphia! Where you been hanging out?"

"They're all over town. You just ain't been paying attention. You watch these Sacred Heart girls what they put on when they get home, out of them little plaid skirts and into their play clothes. Play! In a pig's you know what. Their mamas too. Some of them grandmamas."

"What are you saying, Ark?"

"I'm saying old Otis had plenty of temptation. It was everywhere. And just 'cause he's a man of the cloth don't mean he was blind."

"So what'd they catch him doing?"

"Pair of twenty-year-old twins had him tied down to a bed in a Holiday Inn with their cotton panties. Took Polaroid pictures. Sent 'em to the board of deacons."

"And the business hit the fan."

"Honey, they took back that Mercedes and that Cadillac and that house in River Oaks so fast it'd make your head spin."

"Where's Aunt Stella, Ark?"

"We getting there. So anyway, that's the last of poor old Otis as a preacherman. Mary Sue divorced him on the spot. Got herself on the next plane to the Dominican Republic, paper in her hand she'd made Otis sign, saying the divorce was okay with him, giving her what little they had left. Otis dropped clear out of sight. And nobody much cared. First Corinthians Baptist Church of Houston got itself a new preacher. Old man. No flash. Just did the Old Testament fire-and-brimstone thing. Everybody's happy."

"So?"

"So a couple years later, anybody'd who'd ever known about old Otis had done forgotten him, when these weird things started happening at Mardi Gras."

Taking it on faith that somehow he'd bridge the gap from one part of this story to the other, Sam said, "I thought that was the *definition* of Mardi Gras."

"Nawh. I mean *weird*. What it was was this man started appearing at fancy Carnival balls. Not like Comus, you understand, where it dudn't matter if you give 'em your right tit, pardon my French, they still won't let you in, but still real fancy ones. Like Osiris, which is especially rich. Athenians. Rex. Caliphs of Cairo—with a lot of new money."

"Do I hear that the tinkle of coins is important here?"

"You got it. And here's the trick. This man, in the right formal attire, top hat, cane, cape, the whole ball of wax, would get in without a wrinkle—finagled, forged invitations, nobody knew. But, anyway, there he'd be, tall and good-looking in his penguin suit, which meant he wasn't a member of the krewe—or at least he wasn't dressed for a parade or the tableaux—the best dancer on the floor, with callouts for the richest ladies."

"Callouts? How'd he manage that?"

"Nobody knew. But these ladies, some of them fat old battleships, maiden aunts like Tante Marie, would suddenly hear their names called when they'd be least expecting it, some of them sitting around in the balcony for years without a whirl, and there on the floor waiting for them would be Prince Charming."

Sam remembered her own expectations at the Comus ball and blushed, her tummy doing a little flip. P. C. Rich Right. Isn't that who every woman waited for—sometimes her whole life long?

"Wearing an Elvis mask."

"I beg your pardon?"

"That's right. Looking like Elvis—which wuddn't so unusual, people wearing all kinds of things and Elvis is always popular—and crooning in their ears while they waltzed. Sounded *exactly* like The King. Or so said the one or two who finally talked."

"After—"

"So, see, he danced them and romanced them, and then—he waltzed them right off the dance floor."

"To—"

"Their houses. Where, of course, these ladies being who they were, members of these fancy families who were all at the ball, nobody was home."

"Whereupon—"

"He'd make love to them like they'd never been made love to before."

"I like it so far."

"When they woke up, he have hogtied them to the bedposts."

"Oh, no!"

"Nothing ugly, just tied up. Everything worth hauling off would be gone."

"Ah. Jewels."

"Jewels, especially, but paintings, too, silver—and believe me, a lot of these folks think nothing of having service for a hundred—Persian, Chinese carpets, antiques of all sort—"

"My God, did he have a truck?"

"Sure did. Would load it right up."

"And in the midst of Carnival madness, nobody would notice."

"Nope. And the beauty part was—"

"Nobody would tell. It was too embarrassing."

"Absolutely! Seems like by the time Carnival was over, he'd have scored enough hits, there's *lots* of balls, to have retired for the season."

"Spend the rest of the year on the Riviera."

"Wherever. Oh, did I say the part about the underpants?"

"I was waiting for that little article of clothing to drop."

"If the lady in question was more partial to nylon or silk or rayon, he'd oblige her with a pair of his favorites before the festivities began."

"Came prepared?"

"All seemed to be a part of his seduction kit. Burglar's tools. Or if she had her own cotton, he'd help himself to a few pairs of those as he was leaving. Part of the booty."

"This gonna lead us to Otis Dew?"

"I bet you read the last page of mysteries first."

No, she didn't. But she was still impatient, her plea to Mam'zelle for help on that issue notwithstanding. "Sorry."

"Well, eventually a couple of ladies 'fessed up to the little parties, and a committee was formed—"

"They didn't go to the police."

"Child, don't be silly," said Uncle Luther, who'd been so quiet Sam had almost forgotten he was there. "Uptown folks don't go to the *po* - lice. No more than Tante Marie goes shopping. Why wash your dirty laundry—?" And then Uncle Luther got to thinking about what that laundry might be and was carried away again by a fit of giggling.

"As I was saying," said Ark, "a committee was formed by male relatives of the aggrieved, and they found them an investigator."

"Aunt Stella."

"That's right."

"Why her, might I ask?"

"Well, she's homefolks, specializes in being discreet, and her particular attraction in this case was that she was female. For talking to the ladies, don't you know?"

"I see. And what did Stella do?"

"Well, she came and talked to those who was talking, and that number grew, let me tell you, once the ball got rolling. It got to be sort of *the thing,* don't you know, to have been kissed and robbed by Elvis—"

"Kissed?" asked Sam.

"That being the local circumlocution." Ark sat back with his arms folded and a big grin. Proud as punch of his vocabulary and the impression it had made on Sam, whose major failing as an investigator was that she'd never managed to keep her feelings off her face.

"Anyway. She talked with all the ladies, and then, as was her way, locked herself in a room for the evening. The penthouse, I might mention, of the Pontchartrain, the committee sponsoring her being no slouch, and when she came out the next morning, which, by the way, was during Carnival season, said, I know who it is. Who? they all asked. But Stella wasn't saying."

"Otis Dew, of course. But how'd she know?"

"Stella has her ways."

"Come on, Ark. Don't con a con man."

"Why, Ms. Adams"—and then Ark batted his eyes behind the thick lenses—"whatever do you mean?"

"I mean spill the beans."

"*Well.* She had suspected him all along, I mean from the time the committee had first called on her and outlined the case."

"Why?"

"The Elvis business. The pretty ways. The build. And, then, Stella had the additional advantage of having caught Otis's preaching routine. Besides, the boy always did love nice things. After those Texas Baptists had given him a taste for the genuine article, you don't think he was gonna go back to no Dodge Colt, no Thunderbird wine, do you? Not our Otis, with his champagne tastes. Plus—"

"Don't forget the dog," said Uncle Luther.

"I was just getting to that, if you please."

"The dog?"

"Aunt Stella's hound Sweetpea. She got hold of some things used to belong to Otis, then ran Sweetpea around one of them houses he robbed."

"Wait a minute, Arkadelphia. You trying to tell me this Sweetpea could pick up a scent that was *years* old."

"You don't know Sweetpea."

"Yeah, but I do know a shaggy hound story when I hear one."

Ark held up his hands. "You want me to stop, I'm willing. I got three more lawns to mow before I go pick up the bleeding and the wounded with G.T."

Sam shook her head. "Go on."

"You sure?"

"Arkadelphia—" There was a knife in her voice. Poised at his throat. Which was exactly the response he was craving.

He took a deep breath. "So what Stella did was, she bought herself a fancy dress and went to every ball that seemed the least bit likely after that. Looking for Elvis."

"But you said lots of people went as Elvis."

"That's right. So, to avoid embarrassing folks who might wear the same mask or costume, she took along Sweetpea."

"Took the dog to the balls?"

"Listen, there are balls where elephants, gorillas, camels are real popular. Nobody's gonna pay much attention to one hound bitch."

"If you say so, Ark. So she found Elvis."

"Sort of."

Sam sighed. "Just tell me."

"That's what I'm trying to do. I guess it was the tenth or twelfth ball. And there'd been plenty of Elvises. But Sweetpea didn't even give any of them a sniff. Then, just about the time the committee was losing its patience, because they suspected he was at it again—none of this latest batch of ladies talking, but some houses a good deal emptier and a few *grandes dames* wearing some very suspicious grins—and believe me, neither the penthouse at the Pontchartrain nor Aunt Stella come cheap, when bingo! There in the midst of the dancing at Osiris, Sweetpea starts whining.

"Stella is holding her tight by her leash, and Sweetpea is pointing like crazy, but Stella can't find any Elvis anywhere.

"She's all over the place, her and Sweetpea, bobbing and weaving, afraid Elvis/Otis is gonna cut out with another prize before she gets to him when, lo and behold. She sees him."

"Elvis." Sam couldn't help herself.

"Nope. Jerry Lee."

"He's wearing a Jerry Lee mask?"

"Well, that's what she thought."

"Ark, I have been very patient."

Uncle Luther laughed. "You ain't been nothing of the kind, missy. I've seen banty roosters more patient than you, and if you've ever seen a banty—"

"What do you mean, Ark?"

"So she sights him, and she lets go of the leash. Sweetpea takes out across the dance floor, and before you know it, the man is up with the orchestra. Stumbling in and out of the saxophones and the clarinets. Put his foot through a snare drum. But not slowed down a bit. Gets up there on the stage, all mixed in with the scenery for the tableaux, and I'll be damned if Sweetpea didn't tree him."

"There was a tree on the stage, of course."

"A live oak tree. The theme of the ball was Tara. There were these—"

"That's okay. We can dispense with the scenery. So Sweetpea chased him up this tree."

"That's right. And Stella's right there, with her little pearl-handled revolver and lots of security, all in evening wear, of course, toting heavier firepower, guns whipped out all over the place, ladies screaming, some of them delighted to be able to use the smelling salts they been carrying in their little evening bags for years, just hoping against hope there'd be an exciting enough occasion to go all limp, somebody could whip out the salts, prove they're still frail flowers, and Stella's shouting above the whole thing, Otis Dew, you son of a bitch, freeze!

"He did, of course, Otis not being entirely stupid.

"And Aunt Stella marched right up to him. Get down out of that tree, she said. Come down here and face the music like a man.

"Dew did. Jumped right down, looking like a prize athelete.

Brushed his evening clothes off, like he'd mussed himself performing an act of galantry for some lady. I tell you, Aunt Stella's fingers were itching. She couldn't wait. She said, I know you're under there. You can't fool me with that Jerry Lee business. Then, timing it just right, everybody in the place stock-still, of course, band had long since stopped playing. Everybody having heard one of a thousand versions of the Elvis/lover story, what was supposed to have been happening, tales of ravishment too shameful to repeat, them old Creole ladies put their gossiping tongues together, do their gumbo ya ya, then Aunt Stella reached the tips of her fingers under that mask and ripped off the Jerry Lee Lewis face."

"And there was Otis Dew!" crowed Sam, knowing it all the while, of course, but the joy of southern storytelling was in the telling and the hearing, not the punch line. Except, in this case.

"No. There was Elvis."

"What?!"

"The face behind the mask was the spittin' image of The King himself."

"What are you telling me, Arkadelphia? Beneath the Jerry Lee mask he was wearing another mask? The Elvis mask?"

"No, he was wearing his face."

"Need I remind you again that Elvis is dead. And *was* dead at the time we're talking about?"

"Yeah. Yeah. Yeah," laughed Uncle Luther. "But not that boy's brother."

Sam just stared at the two of them. Little old black man. Great big fat white man. Both laughing.

"*Whose* brother? What are you talking about? I'm going to smack both of you, if you don't tell me."

"Don't get your bowels in an uproar, girl," Arkadelphia finally said when he got the use of himself again. "Now, did I tell you at the beginning that Otis Dew had a brother, Lamar who had gone to medical school?"

"You did not."

"Studied plastic surgery. Did real well, mostly over in Sweden, mostly doing sex change operations."

"And as a favor to his bubba, he turned him into Elvis."

"Sure did. Isn't that rich?"

"But why?"

"Why anything, sugar pie? Why blue skies? Why boys and girls? Why sex, drugs, rock and roll, greed?"

"I think you hit it on the button with that last one."

"Well, I 'spect so too. Think Otis Dew was greedy. Greedy for the riches of the earth those Houstonians had spoiled him with. Greedy for the roar of the crowd. Did I tell you the rest of the year he was on the Riviera, you got that right, there and lots of other places, doing Elvis impersonations? Had been on the TV lots of times."

"No, Ark. No, you didn't. But what do you think made him come back to Louisiana? Do this weird thing?"

"Don't know, sugar pie. Maybe there's more ladies wear white cotton panties in this climate than any other place Otis Dew had ever been."

And with that, Arkadelphia stood, shoved his straw hat back on his head, and lumbered off toward his mowing machine without giving her a backward look. Cranked the mower up and started doing whirlies in the Villères' grass.

Sam sat, feeling like she'd been run over by a particularly large truck, staring at Uncle Luther.

Who said, "Yep, well, listen, you feeling better, I guess I ought to be getting back to work."

"Easy for you to say."

"Hey, hey." Luther grinned, chewed a little, spat. "You ought not to let boys like Ark get under your skin. Just passing the time, you know. Telling you 'bout Old New Orleans."

"You telling me you think I ought to believe any of that?"

Luther scratched his head. Then from behind him, she saw the shadowy figure of Tante Marie flutter again. She thought she heard the softest giggle. Then the figure disappeared.

Luther saw her looking, grinned a slow grin, and gave her a big wink. He said, "There's one would tell you yes. You ought to believe every word."

"Luther, are you telling me Tante Marie was one of Otis Dew's victims?"

"Or beneficiaries? Depending on how you look at it?"

"Are you?"

"Honey, I ain't telling you nothing. Far as I'm concerned, we just been sitting here shooting the breeze, sipping a little tea."

He was right. And it had all been so pleasant, she'd forgotten not only her manners, but what she'd set out for in the first place.

She stood. "Listen, Uncle Luther. I really do appreciate the refreshments and your first aid. Thanks so much." She folded the washcloth and gingerly tried out her knees. Then she attempted an end run around Luther once more. "You wouldn't happen to know if Madeline Villère's over in St. Martinville, would you?"

He shook his head. "You know somebody else they ought to string up? Like that Imelder we was talking about 'fore Ark came along? Thinks she's a princess too? That Leona Helmsley. 'Course they did get her up on trial. Cheating on her taxes. I read 'bout that woman in a story in the *Picayune*. Thinks she's a queen. Ain't that something? She's an *American*. At least that Imelder's a foreigner. Could be a queen. You know what I mean?"

"Uh-huh."

"Well. Now, listen, anytime you come running by here in yo' bitty shorts, you want to stop and get a glass of ice water, some tea, you just holler, you hear? Old Luther, he get you some."

Then he took her by the elbow and led her off the porch. Her knees hurt like hell. Luther flipped the switch on his Walkman. Did a little cakewalk ahead of her down the pavement, listening to somebody good.

"Who's that, Imelda?" she asked.

The old man grinned, looking like a jack-o'-lantern. "Wynton. He my man, that Wynton. Homeboy." Executing a little slow drag. "That Imelder? Naw. She cain't sing worth spit. Ought to stuck to brassieres. High heels."

And you ought to stick to pumping people dumber than you, Sam told herself as she gimped off down the sidewalk. Which means not messing with the help. Lord knows, growing up with Peaches and Horace ought to have taught her that.

Yes indeedy, both Ark and Uncle Luther had done a number on her. Sam turned onto General Taylor Street, laughing at herself out loud.

Twenty-five

Sam didn't have to limp her way up the steps of the double shotgun on General Taylor to see who she'd come to see.

The left side of the house was G.T.'s, the right side Jimbo's. The two halves mirror images, named for their one-room-right-after-another-shoot-a-gun-straight-through-from-the-front-to-the-back construction.

Somebody who looked awfully like what Jimbo was supposed to was lying sprawled out in the side yard on his back.

"Hey!" he said, poking his head out from under what appeared to be a lawn chair he had propped up on short sawhorses. A very weird lawn chair. Above were your basic interwoven strips of green and white, but attached under the bottom was what looked like an inflatable rubber life raft. The raft was bright orange.

Running all around the edges of the chair and on its arms was a series of little metal anchors.

"Hi!" said Sam.

"Well, hi there yourself, good-looking."

Uh-oh. Maybe she should have put a little more thought into this—like not wearing running shorts for starters.

"What'cha doing here?" she asked.

"Building me a flying lawn chair." He grinned, showing lots of big white horsey teeth. "Wanta come on over here and see it?" He was lying propped up on his elbows now.

Not hardly, bubba. She shook her head. "What's gonna make it fly?"

He stood up. He *was* a tall sucker. He wiped the grass off the seat of his jeans with huge hands and reached for a big cardboard box. "These here weather balloons."

"You fill 'em with helium?"

"You got that right. You wanta go up for a spin sometime?"

"Thanks. I don't think so."

"Well, then, you wanta fuck?"

It was that kind of thing that made it real difficult to talk with some men. Once they'd said something like that, well, you could shoot 'em, but otherwise it was hard to keep on. Like look at this sucker, standing there, grinning.

"Thanks a lot, but I think I'll pass," she said with a little smile, like he'd offered her a cold drink.

"You sure?"

"Yeah. Listen, I'm looking into some business for the Lee family. You know Church Lee?"

"So that's what you doing here. Thought you was just strolling by."

"Killing two birds with one stone."

"What if we just fool around a little bit and see if you like it?"

"Maybe you had a conversation about him with a man named Maynard Dupree in the Pelican Bar some weeks ago."

Jimbo straightened up a little bit, like he was thinking of getting serious. "Honey, I get to talking in the Pelican, it could be 'bout anybody. Any little old thing. You wanta go on over there and have a few drinks? Maybe reconsider my offer?"

"Thanks, I don't drink. I understand you and Maynard were saying some pretty audacious things about General Taylor Johnson, your neighbor here"—Sam crooked a thumb up at the house—"and Church Lee. Maybe a lady named Chéri too."

"Now there's a pretty piece. Got a mouth on her, though. Just like you. That's okay. I like sassy women."

"Did you know Church Lee died that next night? After you and Maynard Dupree were standing around in the Pelican talking about killing him?"

"Is that the truth?" Jimbo scratched his head. "That's a purrdee shame. I sure do hate to hear that."

"Kind of makes it look bad for you, don't you think?"

"Naw." Jimbo reached over to a Styrofoam cooler, knocked the lid aside, and reached out a cold Dixie. "You sure you don't want a beer?"

She shook her head. "Thanks."

He drained it in one long swig. Belched. Grinned. Wiped his mouth with the back of his hand. " 'Scuse me."

"You mind my asking where you were that next night?"

"When was that? I don't remember exactly. Don't remember the conversation you talking about, for that matter. Though it coulda happened. I ain't saying it didn't."

"You mean you *could* have stood around the Pelican talking about killing somebody."

"Sure. Mean son of a bitch like me could talk about most anything. Don't you think?" Giving her a hard look.

"I wouldn't know." What she did know was that he was trying to scare her a little, but somehow she didn't think Jimbo was going to bump her off standing right there in his side yard before lunch.

"When was this?" he asked, giving up the tough approach, reaching for another beer, waggling it at her. "You sure I can't tempt you now?"

"Church was killed late Mardi Gras night. Almost three o'clock Ash Wednesday morning, actually."

"Well, I'm afraid I can't help you. I don't know where I was then."

"You don't remember?"

"Hell, no."

"Maybe you were asleep?"

"I'm saying I was drunk as a skunk, as any self-respecting person would be on Mardi Gras, and I coulda been passed out, or I coulda been still standing. I surely don't know, myself."

"Anybody with you who might?"

Jimbo grinned. "Oh, yeah. There's a whole lot of people with me."

"You were at a party?"

"Naw. I don't like parties. Least not the usual kind."

She knew she was walking into it, but what the hell? "What kind do you like?"

"Kind I put together myself." He really did look exactly like the Big Bad Wolf, standing there, grinning. "Lots of girls, not many clothes. You know what I mean."

"I think I get the drift. Any of these girls have names?"

"What'd you say you did for a living? Say you are a cop?"

"Nope. Actually, I'm a newspaper reporter."

"You *are?* Well, hell. Why didn't you say so in the first place?" Jimbo was looking awfully excited, smoothing down his hair, and shifting into another gear. "Listen, I didn't mean nothing, what I said earlier. I was just playing. You know how us stupid old boys are."

"I sure do." She grinned. What was this? Jimbo *liked* reporters?

"Listen. You here to do a story on my flying lawn chair?"

"No—I told—" Wait a minute. "Well—actually—it does sound kind of interesting." She reached in her little belly pouch, pulled out one of the small notebooks she always carried. "You want to tell me about it?" She settled right down on top of the beer cooler.

* * *

Who the hell was *that?* Teri wondered, driving by real slow. She knew she oughten to, but she couldn't help herself. Just like when she was in junior high, high school, her and her friends, cruising their boyfriends' houses. Curly-headed brunette getting up off the Styrofoam cooler *she'd* bought at Walmart, sashaying out of the yard in running shorts. Well, she might have known, no sooner was she out the door'n Jimbo'd be bringing 'em in. Hot and cold running whores.

And here she'd got up this morning full of fresh resolve. That's the one thing her grandma'd taught her—brought her up after Daddy died and Mama ran off to deal blackjack in Vegas. Mamaw said, Teri Lynn, you get up every morning, it's a whole new world, honey. Whole new slate. You just greet it with fresh resolve to make the best of it. Same thing Sister Nadine preached on TV. You try hard enough, you can be anything you want to be. Even if you are fat.

Not that that was the precise truth. Teri knew *that.* She wuddn't exactly a fool. Knew she wuddn't gonna be *Madonna.* She wuddn't Italian, for one thing. And she couldn't sing.

But. She could be that cute if she tried. She had naturally blond— almost white—hair. Didn't have to bleach the bejesus—'scuse me Lord —out of it like Madonna.

All she had to do was lose about sixty-five pounds. 'Course, Sister Nadine would say you didn't have to, but she didn't agree with her on that. 'Cause if she did, lose the weight, that is, Jimbo would love her again, wouldn't be so quick to get mad, knock her around. Actually, it was only sixty now. She'd already lost five this week. Not that Aunt Ida wuddn't feeding her, she was. She was the sweetest old black lady, taking her in like that, her and Doctor.

That's what her little baby boy was called. It had been her mamaw's idea. Doctor King. It had a nice ring to it.

And Aunt Ida giving her all those nice baths too. Made her feel so good. She didn't know if that was what had done it, or if it was staying home in the afternoons and watching Sister Nadine live 'stead of watching her later taped. She truly did believe that if you watched things live, you could get those people's vibrations, if you put your hand on the top of the TV. That was why some of them evangelists, they had you put your money on top of the TV right before you sent it to them. Then it was doubly blessed. So every afternoon that's what she'd been doing. Put her belly right up to the tube too. If you got those vibes, your reducing diet would work twice as fast, better than Optifast. She didn't care what Oprah said. She didn't like Oprah so much anyway. She was with Aunt Ida on that one, said there was something about that Oprah was shuck and jive.

That curly-headed brunette was gone now, had traipsed off down the sidewalk with kind of a limp. Teri went over it in her head again, what she'd been practicing to say.

Jimbo, honey, I do love you. And I know you love me, and you love Doctor. But I just cain't put up with the way you been treating me. First, I know you want me to lose weight. I'm already doing that. Second, I want you to come to the tabernacle with me, pray about it. See if you can find it in your heart to give yourself to the Lord, let Him help me with my diet, *even though Sister Nadine says it's okay if you're fat,* she said real fast under her breath. He'll make a new man out of you.

She *missed* Jimbo, got a hot flush all over her body looking at him across the street. She was squinched way down low in the car she'd borrowed from her friend Nouvelle—a girl she and Jimbo had met dancing to the jukebox over at the Mayfair Bar on Amelia Street one night. It was a brand new Trans Am.

Speaking of which, what was that shiny new black thing pulled up in their driveway? G.T. done bought herself a new wagon? Not hardly, saving all her medical school cash.

Teri sighed. You turn your back on a man half a second, and just look at that.

Now, look at *that!*

Little brown Mercedes pulling right past her, then wheeling into the driveway, brakes pumping, redhead waving both arms over her head at Jimbo, he jumping up, her tits nodding this way and that, could see 'em over to Algiers. Christ!

'Scuse me, Lord, but, now, would you look at that? Jimbo leaning over the side of that little convertible like he was a teenager over to the Clematis Bar, hanging out. Smoothing back an imaginary ducktail. Next thing you know he'd be singing "Don't Be Cruel."

What was he and that redhead talking about?

Leaning their heads real close together, then Jimbo looking real serious. Shaking his head no. No. Unh-uh. No way, Jack. Redhead gabbing away eleventy-hundred miles a minute. Waving her hands around like she was Italian. She didn't look Italian, though. Those great big sunglasses, she looked like a movie star.

Teri ran a finger under the gold necklace Jimbo'd given her when they first started going out. It had hung lower then, covered that little mole he liked to kiss right above where her cleavage started. The necklace was higher now, what with all her baby fat.

Now the redhead was starting up her motor, but not faster than Teri Lynn. Teri Lynn King. A tear slipped down her cheek, landed right above the little mole on her chest. *Still* Mrs. Jimbo King, thank you very kindly.

Twenty-six

Marietta was just walking out of the Pic'N'Pac store on Coliseum close by her house when Billy Jack was coming in the door.

She didn't even notice him, not that she would anyway. Marietta was the kind of Uptown woman could tell with her peripheral vision if a boy was Tulane or just trash.

On the other hand, he gave her a long look. Checked out the diamonds on her left hand, big enough to blind you. Thought how pretty they'd look on his mama. Thought about asking her, just for confirmation, you get those at Coleman E. Adler?

Heavy gold bracelet full of charms. Good watch too. Yep, yep. Middle-aged lady, not too bad-looking, she'd be worth taking down for her pretties if it wasn't broad daylight, middle of the afternoon.

You couldn't do individuals then. It was too dangerous. But, boy, was it exciting.

Well, she was gone now anyway. Billy Jack started cruising around the store. Seeing what was what.

Who was where.

Running his fingers across the candy wrappers. Milky Ways. Peppermint Patties. Almond Joys. Baby Ruths.

Picking 'em up and putting 'em down. Wrinkling up his forehead like he was concentrating. Trying to get his mind to decide what his mouth wanted to do.

Two kids behind the counter. Manager out to lunch.

Billy Jack knew that. He knew everything there was to know about Pic'N'Pacs and 7-Elevens. The work schedules. When they went to the bank. These hadn't been yet. That that little sign—said the cash register had only a hundred dollars and the clerk couldn't open the safe—was bullshit. He knew it all now. That once he'd got busted was because he was so young. Hadn't figured out you had to have a system. Had to know what was what.

Billy Jack pulled the brim of his red Peterbilt gimme hat down a little farther. He was starting to get pumped up now.

That was what people didn't understand.

Robbing things was *fun.*

As far as Billy Jack was concerned, it was better than almost anything. Better than a good meal. Better than Dixie beer. Better than coke. Hell, better than sex. Though it was kind of like sex.

It was being right on the edge. Walking a tightrope. No net. Only you calling the shots. But *anything* could happen. There was always the possibility of the wild card. That was what was so exciting about it. And then you had to use all you got.

Sure, he needed the money. *This* time. But lots of times he'd hit stores, hit individuals, just for the *fun.* Watching 'em go white—if they *was* white. Start to shake. Try to run.

He popped a look back at the clerks. Neither of them paying any attention to him. They never did till you gave them something to look *at.* Yep. They were both white, all right. But don't think he'd forgotten about that black bitch yesterday. One slapped that parking ticket—he tore it right up and stomped on it—on his Town Car. He'd find one later. Just drive around. Find one by himself. Herself. Pow. Even things up.

'Course you never could tell what might come cruising in here before it was all over.

Oh, boy. Billy Jack could feel himself starting to get a little hard.

The clerks—one *boy,* redheaded, lots of freckles with acne mixed in, one girl, blonde, kind of soft and blurry, like you could erase her nose or her mouth if you rubbed hard—they were laughing now. Still one customer. Big old fat guy, North Louisiana accent, sounded like home, buying a half-gallon of ice cream.

"You sure you don't want to come home with me and help me finish this butter brickle up?" he was saying to the blonde.

Ought to be ashamed of himself. Old enough to be her daddy. The girl was giggling, punching the redheaded boy.

"Naw. I sure don't."

Get on out of here, blubber butt. Haul it. Move it.

"Well, I reckon I better get on home. Louise gone wonder I didn't get run over by a truck."

"Well, thank you. We'll see you tomorrow," the boy was saying.

"If not sooner." The fat ass was laughing like he'd said something funny. Started shuffling toward the door.

Billy Jack picked up a Moon Pie, pretending he was gonna buy it.

Same time started pulling up the stocking. He'd cut the foot part off so he could slip it down around his neck, then jerk it up. Made him look like a monster, nose and mouth pulled everywhichway. Peterbilt gimme hat stuck back on top. Nobody'd ever recognize him. But it was kinda hard to talk. The fat man was gone. Careful that door don't hit you in the butt, son.

Then, *whap,* just like that, Billy Jack was at the counter. He pulled the shiny .38 Smith & Wesson he'd bought off a guy over in Slidell out of his belt.

There went their faces snow-white. The redheaded boy's freckles were standing out like little flecks of dirt. Like a truck had gone by real fast, him standing too close to the curb, and splattered him good.

The girl was crying right on cue, ought to be in the movies, great big old tears pouring down her face, blurring her nose and mouth even worse, except her mouth now was like it was turned upside down.

Wuddn't it funny, you had time to see all that? When you were doing something gets you on the edge like this, time just came to a dead stop.

"Empty the cash register and the safe," Billy Jack said through the tight stocking, his mouth a little dry, lips really having to work.

"Whut?" said the girl.

The boy's eyes were so big, you could see white all around the edges. He wasn't even breathing.

"Gimme all the cash!"

The girl looked at the boy like he was gonna say something. "What's he saying?"

Jesus Christ! Even if she was having trouble understanding him through the stocking, wouldn't you think she could just like figure it out?

"He wants the money," the redhead finally said in a rusty voice.

"*Well!*" she said.

Billy Jack thought he was gonna bust a gut. He truly could not believe the way she'd said the word. It was like every little pissant girl he'd ever grown up with. *Well!* Like the word had its hands on its hips. Like I'll have to think about that, let you know. Like you're a little old country boy and I'm a cheerleader and popular and my mama said I don't have to—

"Now!" Billy Jack screamed at the top of his lungs.

And right then the front door slapped.

The unexpected. The you-can't-figure. Here it was.

Billy Jack whirled.

* * *

Lavert stopped, one foot in the air. Held it there for a long second before he put it down, real slow.

He didn't even have to be told.

It just goes to show you, he thought, what a wonderful place the world is.

Not that *this* was wonderful. This little bitty honky motherfucker throwing down on him with that shiny little gun he must have bought yesterday in the Woolworth's, it looked that new, but prob'ly wasn't a cap gun. Lavert wasn't willing to lose a bet on that one. But what was wonderful was here he was, driving along, still half in the bag from his get-together with Harry Zack last night, thinking about old times, little glimpses of G.T. creeping around the edges, like a treat he was saving for himself, a treat so sweet he didn't even want to taste it yet with his tongue, knew it would make his shoulders squish together like ummmmmh, say, little tiny skate wings quickly sautéed and finished with a red wine caper sauce, knowing that she was gonna give him the time of day, knowing that she was just a little bit interested, feeling like he was sixteen years old, goddamned springtime in his soul, didn't even matter if it had been December outside, inside he had that feeling like he was just gonna bust, wanted to snatch up little kids on the street, drag 'em off and buy 'em ice cream cones, throw about two dozen of 'em in the back of Joey's limo, take 'em out to the zoo, buy 'em cotton candy, hot dogs, find a carnival, buy strings of tickets, loop 'em around their skinny little necks about three times, and let 'em ride. Let 'em twirl. Let 'em hang upside down in the Tilt-A-Whirl till they puked their little guts out. Who cared? He'd clean 'em up and take 'em home and plop 'em all around Joey's round table and make 'em spaghetti with Joey's mama's secret sauce. Then take them all home to their mamas before they got worried. Tell each mama how much he'd enjoyed the day with her perfect little angel child.

Now, *that* was love.

And that was what was so wonderful about the world.

That you could be so gone in your own mind, your own reality, your own little bit of space and time when *whap!* there was a whole other world.

Now, which was real and which wasn't? He looked at the little white boy. Was he for real? Standing there, legs spread like John Wayne with his six-shooter. And then he looked again.

Son of a bitch! Lavert leaned back his head and laughed and laughed and laughed like a man gone nuts.

"Freeze!" Billy Jack snapped.

What was so goddamned funny to this jigaboo?

Big jigaboo.

And then he knew.

Oh, fuck. He was screwed.

"Son," Lavert said, "I been looking all over for you."

"Well, okay"—dancing around a little now—"so you found me. But you better step back." Billy Jack waggled his gun.

"I got a pretty little woman wants to talk with you bad." One step forward.

"Hold it right there. I got nothing to say to no woman."

Another step. "I think you do. You owe her an explanation why you jumped out of her ambulance. Left her holding a bunch of paperwork."

"I give a shit."

"Now, is that any way to talk?"

"Listen." Gun was pointing up at the ceiling, then down at the floor. "You better get out of here. You've done stepped into something bigger than you."

Lavert laughed. "Ain't hardly nothing bigger than me."

With that, Billy Jack fired at Lavert's left foot. Missed.

Lavert didn't even jump. But it did give him pause. He said, "Now, what exactly would you like me to do?"

Billy Jack thought about that for a minute. He wasn't real sure. If he let this jig—who he now realized was Joey the Horse's driver, though he didn't think the jig knew who *he* was—back out the door, then when he left, what was there to guarantee the jig wouldn't just be waiting there for him?

"Move on around." He signaled to his right with the gun. "Get on over there with them."

"With who?"

Billy Jack swiveled his head quick to the right. To the left. Christ Almighty. The clerks was both gone.

He swiveled back.

The nigger had feinted the other way. Just like he was playing ball.

"Hold it!" Billy Jack screamed, and fired again.

Three jars of apple juice smashed and started puddling on the tile.

Then the doors slap-slapped again and Blubber Butt was here again, saying, "Hey, Dee Ann, Louise sent me back for the chocolate sauce."

The doors slap-slapped again and a whole passle of Sacred Heart girls came in in their shorts and big floppy shirts—it was a vacation week and they didn't have to wear those dumb uniforms—one of them named Berkeley, yelling, "Bubba, you better get your red head out here and give me a big smooch."

She'd just learned that last word from her mother, who grew up in the sixties, and had saved all her old clothes along with her old vocabulary. Berkeley was wearing a tie-dyed shirt so radical it would make time stand still, and she thought it had for a minute.

They all did. The girls and Blubber Butt, whose real name was Cleve, and Billy Jack and Lavert stood like a bunch of wooden Indians cluttering up the Pic'N'Pac on Coliseum. Billy Jack stood there, everybody staring at him, center stage, holding that .38, when suddenly Dee Ann and Bubba, the two clerks, jumped up from the floor where they'd been hiding behind the canned goods and the cosmetics and started chucking things. Canned tomatoes. Garbanzos. Alka-Seltzer. Midol. Spaghetti-Os. Not even looking. Just whatever they could grab up.

Didn't take the Sacred Heart girls but a minute to get into it too. Picking up movie magazines and the *Times-Picayune,* diet Pepsi, whatever else was close to the door.

Cleve threw a half gallon of fudge ripple.

Lavert was about ready to do his famous Grambling around-the-end sweep, when Billy Jack fired twice into the ceiling, which was just enough to make everybody freeze for the second and a half it took him to slide out the door.

Disappeared before you could say Jack Robinson.

Vanished into thin air in the middle of the afternoon in the middle of the Garden District.

Damn! Lavert said, standing out in the parking lot with his hands on his hips and a big swipe of fudge ripple on his face.

You'd think it'd be harder'n that for a little bitty old white boy to dematerialize.

Wouldn't you?

Twenty-seven

●

"Now I know"—Cissy Anderson was already talking ninety miles a minute when she opened the door—"you're gonna take a look around this place and think I'm dealing drugs."

She was right on the money. Sam was already wondering, as her shoes disappeared into the snowdrifts of white pile, if Church's pretty young blond office manager was in cahoots with Zoe. Your full-service, one blonde, one brunette, one-stop.

"Ha! You did, didn't you?" Cissy squealed, grabbing Sam's hand as if they were sorority sisters, dragging her through the living and dining areas of her miles-long loft in the down-by-the-river warehouse district of the Central Business District. Everything was new, huge, calfskin, and shiny.

"Or maybe I stole all Dr. Lee's money? That what you think? Listen, I hope you don't mind coming in here with me." She continued back through a wide hallway into a master bedroom with a mirrored ceiling and a wall-length dressing table littered with every product Chanel, Lancôme, and Alexandra de Markoff had ever made. The furnishings were Norma Kamali Home—black velvet chaise, chairs, and bed, everything draped with leopard and cloth of gold.

"But I'm meeting somebody"—heavy on the *somebody*—"for a late lunch, and I'm not nearly ready," Cissy went on.

She was wearing hot curlers in her dark blond hair, and a short black satin kimono. Her legs, in ash-gray stockings, were curvy and long—for a girl not much over five feet even in her spike heels. Her figure, that of a Barbie doll. Her twenty-five-year-old button of a nose turned up beneath a heavy coat of Honey Glow.

"Kitty called. I told her I would tell you the truth, the whole truth, and nothing but the truth, so help me God." Cissy held up a little hand with a French manicure. The gesture was real cute.

"I'm not the police," Sam said, looking around for a place to sit.

Cissy grabbed up a handful of bright silk dresses, sales tags still attached, from a black and gold tufted satin chair, and tossed them on the bed.

"I know you're not." Cissy dimpled. "But just the same, being questioned, it's just like TV. Like 'Murder, She Wrote.' Do you watch that show?"

Sam shook her head.

"Oh, you ought to. It's great. That skirt's a Kamali, right? Don't you just love her?"

What? Have to play a mean game of hopscotch to keep up with Cissy. Then Sam looked down at her lap and nodded.

"I almost bought the same one when I was shopping in Houston. It folds up to the size of a hanky. Must be great for traveling. Do you travel a lot?"

"Quite a bit."

"I bet your life is so exciting. I always wanted to travel. Actually, I wanted to be a flight attendant. Lots of my friends are. But my daddy said uh-uh, no way. He wanted me to be a doctor. He's a doctor. A plastic surgeon. But, hell, I didn't even pass high school chemistry, so then I was going to be an interior decorator, but I was up there in *New* York at decorator school, and this terrible thing happened to me. Somebody broke into my apartment and took every single thing I had, my color TV, VCR, microwave, my cute little computer, and *all* my jewelry, including the charm bracelet I'd had since I was a little girl with my teddy bear charm, my cheerleader charm, the one from Cindy Lou's wedding, and you know what the funny thing was?"

"What?" Sam had long ago learned that no matter what you wanted to know, people wanted to roll, you let 'em roll. Eventually you could work the conversation around, and in the meantime, they'd give you gold.

"That man, I guess it was a man. I don't think women go around breaking into people's apartments yet, even with women's lib, even in *New* York, he went into my kitchen cabinets and took a couple of cans of peaches—I like to eat canned peaches with cottage cheese—and punched little holes in them and sucked out the juice." Cissy gave a little shiver. "Don't you think that's weird?"

"I do."

"I did too. So when Daddy came up there on the very next plane after I called him and I told him about that, the *burglary*, not a *robbery* 'cause I wasn't home, you know, if I had been, that sucker would've been dead, they teach us how to shoot in Texas"—she hooked a thumb over her shoulder, as if Texas were in the next room rather than all the way across the state and the Sabine River—"he said to me, Come on, Cissy, throw what you got left in a suitcase—which was a joke, 'cause I've always been crazy about clothes, and I had about five trunks full of 'em still hanging there—and we're going home. So we did. I thought it was too cold in New York anyway, and there weren't any decent decorating programs in Houston, so I went to secretarial school. I found out I can word-process like a son of a bitch, pardon my French, and next thing I knew I was running my daddy's best friend's office. He was an ENT man. But then things got kind of funny"—Cissy rolled her eyes and laughed—"and Daddy and I decided maybe a change of scenery would be good, besides, you know, Houston's kind of depressing these days, what with the oil business being so bad. 'Course, New Orleans idn't all that much better, but I always do think it's best to broaden one's horizons. Don't you?"

Sam nodded, wondering if Cissy ever stopped for breath. She was a regular little whirling dervish, not only talking ninety miles a minute, but simultaneously picking up one colored pencil, brush, blusher, liner, concealer, mascara after another, and painting herself a right pretty little face.

Now she was applying a lash glosser over her second coat of mascara, watching herself in the mirror with her mouth agape.

"So when did you go to work for Church Lee?"

"Wait a minute." Cissy was outlining her lips now with a dark pencil. "There." She gave herself a kiss in the mirror, then giggled. "About a year ago."

"And did you like it—working for him?"

"Ummm-hummm." Cissy was applying a melon-orange lipstick, two coats. "I loved it. I have to let this dry a minute, then I'll do the lip gloss. He was great."

"You liked him personally?"

"Yeah. He was the nicest man to work for. Never raised his voice. Didn't flirt. Just explained what he wanted me to do and kept out of my way." Cissy giggled again.

"And he was a great physician?"

"Well." She stared off into the distance for a minute, then took a deep breath, turned, and looked Sam right in the face. "Nope. I told Kitty I'd tell the whole truth, and I ought to. Even if it means speaking evil of the dead. Don't you think?"

"I do."

"Well, you know he drank."

"Right."

"Growing up a doctor's daughter, I'll tell you, you just can't do that. It's gonna catch up with you." She cocked a warning finger. "Just like it caught up with Dr. Lee."

"The malpractice, you mean?"

Cissy nodded, the hot curlers bobbing in her head. Remembering them, she reached up and started pulling out big fat blond curls, which gave her an even stronger resemblance to Barbie.

"But that wasn't the first time he was in trouble because of booze. People know, you know. You may think they don't, but they do. And people knew Dr. Lee was drinking. Other doctors, that is. 'Cause his is a referral business."

"All his business came from other physicians."

"That's right. You just don't walk in off the street and say, Doc, I think I've got a little detached retina here I'd like you to fix." There was her giggle again. She was *awfully* cute. Especially when she said things like detached retina.

"And other physicians stopped referring to him?"

"Not entirely. But it was getting real slow."

"Do you think he was having financial problems?"

"Oh, yes. I know he was."

"*Really?*"

"Oh, yeah. I was right there. I saw what came in. What went out. I saw that he asked me to be patient about the raise that I was due. I took the calls from creditors on the phone. And you know, raising Miss Zoe wasn't cheap."

"Her coming-out?"

"That, and the Carnival business. Do you know how many dresses a girl has to have to *really* do a deb season in this town?"

Sam guessed a hundred.

The fingers on Cissy's right hand flashed in and out five times.

"Five hundred? You're kidding."

"I'm not. Well, maybe not quite that many, but you know, there are breakfasts, brunches, luncheons, teas, dinners, dances, balls, they go on for six solid months. That's a *lot* of clothes."

"Plus her gown for the Comus ball."

"Ten thousand—with the train."

"Nooooooo."

"I saw the bills. Designer in New York. Woman makes gowns for the opera stars."

"Ouch!"

"That's what I said. I told my daddy, I said, you think I spend money on clothes, you ain't see nothing. 'Course, they never even look that great on Zoe, bless her heart, poor thing's so skinny. You'd think somebody would do something about that." Cissy lowered her voice. "You know she has that problem, don't you?"

"What do you think it is?"

Cissy rolled her eyes again. "That anorexia. Don't you know?" She paused a minute, finished teasing her hair now, picked up a can of hair spray. "Cover your eyes you don't want this stuff in 'em." Sam did. "Okay. I'm through now. Though, actually, Cecil says he thinks it's something else—what Zoe's got. Starts with a B. Means she throws up. I never can remember it."

"Bulimia. Who's Cecil?"

"My fiancé. Dr. Cecil Little. Do you know him?"

"No. I don't think so." Though she sure remembered the story Zoe had told her, his walking in on her in the ladies' room at a tea, then giving her the idea for her cocaine business.

"Cecil's a friend of the Lees. Was a good friend of Church's. I never did call him that to his face, you know. Church. Always Dr. Lee. My daddy taught me that a long time ago. Doctors go to school all that time, they like to be called Doctor. It burns them too, did you know, when other kinds of doctors call themselves that. You know, like Ph.D.s. But they have a point, I mean, when somebody says *Is there a doctor in the house?* they don't mean some guy's got his degree in English, now, do they? Not gonna save your life, if you see what I mean."

"I do."

Cissy turned from the mirror now. All done. She gave Sam a dazzler of a smile. "Hold on. Just let me slip my clothes on. I've got to get going if I'm going to meet Cecil." She struggled across the thick pile in her catch-me fuck-me high heels, the spikes sinking in, and threw open the door to a closet larger than many people's living rooms. "I'll just be a minute."

She was gone long enough for Sam to reach over to her dressing table and sample a couple of bottles of perfume. Cissy stepped back out, buttoning a blouse of black Charmeuse above a black and gray skirt. A jacket was draped over her arm. Very plain. Very understated. Very Giorgio Armani. Very two thousand bucks.

"Do you like it?"

"It's beautiful."

"You know, my daddy always told me that he had raised me in a style that meant I'd *have* to marry in the profession. The medical profession, I mean. And he was right."

Sam laughed. "I think he was."

"Oh, I know. Believe me. I was in love with this cowboy once over in Houston. My daddy said, Honey, you just go right on ahead, you want to marry that boy, you can move out there on the edge of town with him and his mama and papa and put you a mobile home out behind their house, string you up some line for the diapers."

"Made his point?"

"He might have raised me vain, but he didn't raise me stupid." Cissy smiled. She turned this way and that so Sam could inspect the product.

"Absolutely stunning."

"Thanks. So listen." She sat down neatly on the bench to her dressing table, facing Sam now, her cute little knees together, careful not to wrinkle her skirt. "What else did you want to know?"

"I think I've got it. Church's finances are what I'm really after here."

"Well"—Cissy ticked off the items on fingers ringed by Tiffany—"that malpractice, the drinking, then the debut and the balls, their house uptown, plus Comus, the way he was used to living—" Cissy shook her head, pursing her glossy melon lips. "Not too long, he would of been broke."

"You're sure about that?"

"Why would I make it up?"

"No, I don't mean that. It just seems—"

"Seems don't mean jack. I'm telling you what's what." Cissy said the words with the precision of a little girl who would have a man's credit rating checked and rechecked before she'd give him a good-night kiss, never mind raising her skirts.

"Well, that's what I came for." Sam stood. "I thank you for your time, and I guess I'd better let you get going before you're late for lunch."

They were halfway across the living room when Sam thought Why not? "By the way, do you know Church's girlfriend?"

"Sister Nadine? Sure."

"*Really? That's* who he was seeing?"

Cissy laughed, showing lots of catlike white teeth. "Yeah. Idn't that a hoot? I thought you knew. Idn't that *great?*"

"Everybody else know that?"

Cissy double-bolted her door. Shook her head. "Naw. Nobody."

"So how did you?"

Cissy turned, gave Sam a big wink. "Secretary misses something like that ought to be shot."

Billy Jack was pumped now. Sitting in his Town Car, engine idling, knees jiggling, doing a hundred miles an hour standing still. Fingers drumming on the steering wheel.

God Almighty! Shit! He couldn't believe that big nigger walking in the Pic'N'Pac like that.

Whoowhee!

Wuddn't that the living end?

Those kids chunking things at 'im. He'd like to go back, do it all over again. Show 'em what was what. Pump a few rounds in 'em.

But that was okay. For now. He had better things to do. Like following this tall, curly-haired woman driving a rental car. She was a DEA agent. He was sure of it. After all, hadn't he seen her last night up in Zoe's room in that house where she was staying now. Holding a meeting, had to be about him. He'd take care of Miss Zoe Lee later. But first things first.

He wanted to know more about this bitch. He wouldn't be a bit surprised if she wuddn't in cahoots with the Big Man's nigger—it wasn't no coincidence *he'd* stopped in the Pic'N'Pac. Nigger was in with the feds too. He could *smell* it, them hot on his trail, just like a hound dog with scent in the wind.

So he went right back to where Zoe was staying. His instincts hitting one hundred percent, that black-haired bitch, there she was again, pulling out of the driveway.

This kind of mess was driving him crazy. He had to get back to the money-raising business. Maybe he'd tell the Big Man, Joey, about his nigger, like after the fact, get himself a reward. That'd come in handy in this temporary bind.

He took a look at the Rolex he'd nabbed off one of his fancy clients, needed a little extension. Wondered maybe the man from Adler's would take it. Naw. Jew jeweler wuddn't gonna do no trade-ins. Solid gold Rolex prob'ly wuddn't jack shit to him. Jew wanted cash. Well, he'd get rid of this—

Oops. There she was, heading back to her car. Now, who was *that?* Cute little blonde with the buns? He knew he'd seen her too. Somewhere. Goddammit. How many girls was in on this? Another little agent he was gonna have to do something about?

But wait. The little blonde in black and gray was talking to the doorman. The curly-headed bitch heading for her car.

Eeny. Meeny. Miny. Moe.

Which one? Which one?

Billy Jack shook his head. He'd been doing too much blow. It was like he was seeing double. He had to get focused.

"Excuse me, sir."

"What?"

Billy Jack turning now. Nose to nose with a *huge* motorcycle cop.

"You gonna have to move along."

"What?"

"In a No Standing, sir."

"I'm not standing, I'm sitting here. What's this standing shit?"

"You wanta step out of the car, please, sir? Careful with the hands now—"

Twenty-eight

●

Harry grabbed a twelve-seater commuter flight over to Lafayette, then rented a car for the short drive to St. Martinville.

It would've been nice to take a couple of days to do the trip. Fun to stop for lunch in Houma, where you can go see a Cajun woman who feeds you off her stove just like you were one of her many children. To show Sam the bayous, the oil towns of Morgan City, Raceland, and Lafayette, where Mercedes used to be thick on the ground. Now bust, they were receding back to the old days, the slower days. They danced once again to a Cajun tune. Fishing, hunting, trapping out of hollowed-out logs, pirogues, setting tables full of great lusty food, whole families swirling to zydeco in halls like Mulate's in Breaux Bridge.

Harry could just see Sam in a pretty dress, laughing, color in her cheeks, skirts swinging.

Not this time. Not this trip. *Damn* that woman!

He passed the city limits sign of St. Martinville, for sure one of this country's prettiest little towns. Live oaks draped with Spanish moss surrounded a center square. Church. Museum. Statue to the ever-faithful Evangeline. There was a park named after her a little ways out. On that same road lived Madeline Villère.

Madeline Villère Lee Hebert, now wife of Jack Hebert, once a waiter at Galatoire's—so she'd told Harry on the phone when he'd called to set up the visit—now proprietor of Hebert's, a spectacularly successful seafood emporium.

Harry drove past the restaurant. He could smell the good cooking out on the road. About a mile past was a sprawling modern two-story house of cream-colored brick with curlicued cast iron balconies and green shutters. A discreet sign in front read HEBERT'S GREAT DANES. Kennels stretched out behind.

Madeline answered her own door.

At first Harry couldn't get over the bulk of the woman—three hundred pounds if an ounce beneath a float of flowered gauze.

Then he zeroed in on her pretty smile, her beautiful face, her gracious manner.

They settled in a sitting room at the back of the house that overlooked the dog runs.

"That's the nursery." Madeline gestured with a bediamonded hand. "Those pups are five weeks old."

Harry nodded. "Beautiful." Then he hesitated, not sure exactly how to begin.

Madeline made it easy: "How'd you find me?"

Harry explained about the DMV.

Her laugh came from deep inside. "So it wasn't very hard."

"Not at all."

"Or you could have just asked Ma Elise."

"She *knows* where you are?"

"She's always known. But then—" Madeline stared off at something in the yard that Harry couldn't see. "No, of course not. No one would tell you. Or—what did you say was the name of Kitty's friend who's looking into what happened to Church?"

"Samantha. Sam. Sam Adams."

"Yes, well, I guess Ma Elise wouldn't tell her either. No point, really. Lord knows *I* wouldn't have anything to do with Church's death. That was all over a long time ago. Would you like some more coffee?"

Harry would. Madeline poured from a fine old silver service.

"Can you tell me about it?"

"About Church? Sure. I haven't felt anything about him in *so* long—but"—she looked off again—"Zoe."

She said the word as if it never passed her lips, except maybe in her sleep, or her prayers.

She turned big violet eyes toward Harry. Elizabeth Taylor eyes. Actually, she looked a little like Liz before she gave herself over to Betty Ford. And she was obviously the source of Zoe's mane of dark curls.

"She's fine."

"Queen of Comus."

"Yes."

"Is she beautiful? Ma Elise sends me pictures, but—well, it's not the same."

"Very beautiful."

"But too skinny."

Harry looked down into his coffee. It was a great cup of coffee. He nodded yes. Zoe was certainly too skinny.

"You gonna tell me about it, Harry?"

He didn't know what to say. Drive up in the yard of a woman who hasn't seen her daughter, as far as he knew, for fifteen years, tell her the girl's a bulimic with a drug problem. Throw in the dealing as an afterthought. No way, José.

Remember, they used to *kill* the bearer of bad tidings.

This neck of the woods, throw him in the swamp, 'gators destroy all trace in three chomps. Forget it.

"Trade you even-steven." He looked up. Madeline stared him dead in the eye, said, "I'll show you mine, you show me yours. No matter what. Deal?"

She was tougher than he thought. Besides, she had the right, didn't she?

"Deal."

Madeline stood, walked over to an intercom panel, pushed a button. "Kim, another pot of coffee, please." She settled back down in an extra-wide easy chair. "Now tell me what you know."

Well, he knew about the duel between Church and Maynard. That Church had won her. That she'd left when Zoe was six.

"Ran away with Jack." She pointed at a brass-framed photograph of a smiling, jolly-looking dark-haired man. "Did they tell you that?"

Harry nodded his head.

"Well." And then she spread her hands, about to begin the story-telling. "Did you know that Peggy Patrick was fat too?"

"Peggy Patrick?"

"The first little girl Church and Maynard fought over when they were in grade school, the one over whom they began their lifelong feud."

Ahh. And then the face of a third fat lady floated past a corner of Harry's mind's eye. Sister Nadine. He was beginning to see the pattern.

Madeline continued. "I don't know that either of them initially had a preference for big girls, big women, but that's the way it started, and that's the way it went. After Peggy there was a whole series, each larger than the next. The wags among their friends began to joke that pretty soon they'd be tracking down fat ladies in the circus. Now, I wasn't in that league, but I was a pretty hefty girl."

Harry couldn't hold her gaze.

She caught him. "No, wait. Don't be embarrassed. *I'm* not. I've always been this way. *Fat* is not necessarily a dirty word, you know, *unless* you suffer from fatism."

Harry winced. "I'm sorry."

"Don't be. You're a man. You can't help it."

"What?" Harry laughed.

Madeline just smiled. "Where was I, oh, then they both found me. Actually, Church found me first. Our families moved in the same circles."

Harry remembered she was an heir to the Standard Fruit fortune.

"And Maynard's didn't?"

"Not *quite*," she sniffed. "And then there was the duel. The famous duel. I'll tell you, it's the kind of thing will turn any girl's head. Can you imagine?"

Harry couldn't.

"Foils at dawn under the oaks. Pretty sexy stuff. Besides, I loved Church." Her voice melted on the words, then stiffened again as she added, "And I thought he loved me. Anyway, we had the most fabulous wedding. I mean, it stopped traffic in New Orleans. Even made *The New York Times*."

"Big time."

"Oh, yes, we definitely were. Though those same friends, the wags, tittered at the reception that it was as if Church were the highest bidder on a head of prime livestock. Of course, the simple fact of a wedding didn't make Maynard give up. We were no sooner back from our European honeymoon than Maynard started his campaign. All sub rosa, of course. But the flowers and the poems and tears caught in little crystal bottles and endless threats of suicide were enough. Especially since I was beginning to get the drift, not long after we'd sailed off on the *QE2*, that my young husband didn't really adore me at all but had just won a point in an incredibly long tennis volley—love not being the name of the game.

"So eventually I capitulated. Maynard made sure we got caught, of course. Otherwise, what was the point? Though it took me several years of to-ing and fro-ing between the two of them before I realized the true deep sadness of the contest. I thought there for a long while that love aside, I must be the most desirable woman who'd ever been born in the state of Louisiana, though a quick look at my backside in a mirror would have to raise the hard question: Who was I kidding?

"By the time I woke up and smelled the coffee, Zoe had come along —definitely Church's, I made damn sure of that—and was about six years old.

"Then, like a bolt of lightning, I finally found true love in the person of one Jack Hebert. My barrel-chested dark-eyed Cajun was light on his feet. Jack could and would twirl me around a dance floor as easily as he carried six full orders of crawfish étouffée, iced tea, and coffee into the dining room. And he truly loved me.

"It was as simple as that. He loved my fat cheeks, my smile (which neither Church nor Maynard had seen for years), he loved to watch me eat. Jack loved everything about Madeline Villère Lee, though he didn't think he, a New Iberia Cajun and a waiter, had a chance in hell of ever winning me away from that big house on Prytania. In fact, that's what he told himself when he'd get off work late at night and drive his old car uptown, circling our block again and again like a teenager, saying to himself, looking up at that grand house, son, what the hell you thinking about, you stand a chance against that?

"Which shows how much he knew. One day I happened to be passing by the Pickwick Club on Canal, where both Church and Maynard lunched every day, at separate tables, of course—my husband and my off-again on-again lover—both three sheets to the wind, standing out on the sidewalk like two male dogs, feet braced, spit flying, yelling things like—well, whad'dyu think the fat bitch meant when she—I didn't wait around to hear more.

"I called Jack and said, If you want me, come and get me.

"He was there in ten minutes flat.

"We never looked back.

"Except, of course, for Zoe."

Now it was Harry's turn to look off into the yard at someone Madeline couldn't see. Hadn't seen for years.

"Leaving her was such agony. But I couldn't stay. I just couldn't. And I knew if I took her, Church would track me down with bloodhounds. He'd *never* leave us alone. But if I left her . . ." Madeline trailed off.

"He'd let you go."

"He did. He did do that."

"And you kept in touch through Ma Elise."

"She writes me once a month. Sends me pictures. I have six albums of—" She looked over to a bookcase, shook her head. "And that's my story. Now you tell me."

So Harry did. He told her all he knew, everything that Sam had seen and learned from the Lees about Church's death—but mostly about Zoe.

Madeline didn't flinch until it was all over, and she moaned, "Oh,

God!" The tears brimmed over and ran down her round cheeks. "What can I do?"

"Well, Church is dead now, isn't he?"

"What do you mean?"

"Get in touch with her. She sure as hell needs all the help she can get right now."

"But don't you think she hates me?"

"Zoe? Why would she?"

"I left her, deserted her." Her voice was anguished.

"The good part is you're not too late. You're both still alive and kicking. Just because you left doesn't mean you have to stay gone forever. Hell, you know New Orleans. You from there, never any problem going home."

Twenty-nine

Well, it was time, wasn't it, thought Sam, to go to see Maynard Dupree. Unless she wanted to spend some more time tiptoeing around him. She *could* go see his wife.

What had Harry said her name was?

Stopped at a red light, she flipped open her notebook. There were coffee stains on the page from her last meeting with Harry.

Marietta Duchamps Dupree.

Harry.

Maynard's office was on Carondelet. She could drop in and beard him in his den *if* he were home. Otherwise, she was great at pumping secretaries.

Of course, some of them, like Cissy, were so primed you hardly had to lay a finger on.

She'd bet that wouldn't be the case with Mr. Dupree's.

She threw her mind back to Maynard, to the piggy-red face she'd seen that night in the Sazerac bar. The one who'd stirred up Church so.

That night she'd first met Harry.

Goddammit! Goddamn his eyes! Bedroom eyes. Get you a young one with bedroom eyes. That's what her friend Marie always said.

For what?

For fun.

She didn't have time for fun.

Balls.

On that note, Sam pulled over to the curb.

Billy Jack, having bargained himself away from the traffic cop with a little gift of nose candy, almost hit a truck trying to catch up with the curly-headed DEA bitch.

But then, maybe he ought to let her go. It looked like he was going to have to anyway; he'd lost sight of her ahead. But what if this was a trick, the traffic cop just pulling him over till another fed could get on *his* tail. Maybe there was somebody closing in behind *him* now. Somebody in a big heavy car like that big nigger.

Even with the air-conditioning, he felt the sweat running down inside his shirt. So what should he do? Speed up or slow down? Fish or cut bait, he could hear his mama saying. She'd always said that. Fish or cut bait, son. You can't always be sitting on the bank, racked with indecision. She said that cute, his mama. Like she was French, through her nose. *In-de-ci-sion.* Mama, mama. What to do? He closed his eyes and saw her sweet face. Her pillowy chest. Laid his head on it, got lost in it for just a minute. Then snapped to.

Run, she'd whispered in his ear.

Run, Billy. Run for cover.

He threw the car into gear, gunned it.

Okay, lady. Sam was jerked back from her daydream to the here and now by an idiot in a car speeding too-close-for-comfort past her. She opened her eyes.

And there, lo and behold, right before her, was a telephone booth. Ma Bell was just waiting for this southern belle's dimes.

Out of the car, she listened to them drop. Boing. Boing. She flipped the pages of her book, back and forth. Who to call? Where? Maynard Dupree. Harry's home-away-from-home, the Esplanade Lounge. Harry's home number.

One potato.

Two potato.

She punched the buttons.

Harry wasn't home, but he had an answering machine.

"Hi, Harry? It's Sam. Listen, about yesterday. I'm real sorry—"

Thirty

"She say she need anything?" Joey asked Lavert.

"Some mozzarella. I already got it." Lavert was talking through the window that separated the back and the front of the white stretch limousine.

"At the Central?"

"Right. I got her some noodles and some tomato paste too. Kind comes in a tube."

"What you mean?" Frankie Zito was in the back with Joey, filing his daily report. "Paste don't come in no tube."

"Just like toothpaste." Lavert's head bobbed. "Use what you want, screw the top back on."

Frankie said to Joey, "Man knows more about being a wop than I do."

Joey laughed. "You hear that, Lavert?"

Lavert nodded his big head, keeping his eye on traffic as they turned onto Elysian Fields headed toward Joey's mama's house on Perlita out by the lake.

"Know more about wop *food,* anyway, huh, my man?"

"That's right." Lavert smiled, thinking about how he was gonna bring up the subject of Billy Jack real gentle, find out his last name, meanwhile not get Harry fitted for some cement house slippers, poking his nose where he shouldn't.

"You get Mama some cookies?" Joey asked.

"Sure did."

"Those almond ones she likes?"

"In the red can," said Lavert.

"I ever show you that trick with the cookie wrapper and a match?" Joey asked.

About a hundred times. "No," said Lavert. "What's that?"

"Remind me we get to Mama's house. We have our coffee, I'll show you."

"Good." Lavert smiled into the rearview mirror. Lots of teeth.

"So tell me, Frankie." Joey turned to the little man. "What you doing about that punk you telling me about? That fairy you got moving product?"

"Awh, Joyner ain't no fairy."

Bingo. That was the name Lavert had heard before. Joyner. Billy Jack Joyner.

"How you know? You seen him with the girls?"

"Come on, Joey. I seen him all the time, hanging out Mr. Kush's poolhall. He ain't no fag."

"Come on, Joey, my ass. You upsetting me, Frankie. I don't like talk. No kind of talk, you know what I mean?"

"I know."

"So? I want the talk should shut up."

"Right, boss."

"So? You take care of it."

"Right, boss."

"Lavert." Joey was tapping on the glass.

"Yes?"

"Pull over here. Frankie needs to get out."

"Whaaat?" Frankie's whine went off the chart. "Boss, we here in the middle of nig—we nowhere here. I don't need to go nowhere."

You couldn't see it unless you were looking in his eyes, but Lavert was smiling. They were at Elysian Fields around North Dorgenois, Law, Hope. White man in this neighborhood gonna shine. Gonna be a beacon. A light drawing no telling what kind of critters.

He pulled over smartly to the curb, handling the long car like it was a baby carriage. He got out and opened the door for Frankie, not even bothering to look him in the eye, just said, "Good day," closed the door, got back behind the wheel. Didn't look back.

He didn't need to. It was more fun *imagining* the little weasel darting this way and that. Hopping like a scared rabbit. Hoping a cab would come along. Knowing even if it did, it probably wouldn't stop.

"Now let's go see Mama." Joey leaned back. He lighted a cigar with the solid gold lighter his uncle Carlos had given him. The one with the notches. "Turn on my music, okay?"

"Okay, boss. You got it."

Lavert flipped on Joey's favorite tape—Sinatra singing "My Way."

The big white limo threaded its way northward, the neighborhood changing, past the Jewish cemeteries, turning left on Robert E. Lee. Just on the other side of the University of New Orleans campus, a few blocks away, was the huge flat surface of Pontchartrain. Lavert could smell the water, all the while shifting his mind forward and back between Harry's Billy Jack *Joyner* and that little bastard in the Pic'N'Pac.

Pic'N'Pac dude, G.T.'s dude, was right there. Lavert coulda picked him up with one hand, held him out wiggling like a cockroach. Be one down for Batman and Robin. One to go.

Except for that little peashooter.

A .38 bullet bounce around inside your head, it'll give you pause.

Had him, though.

"Lavert?"

"What?"

"You hear what I'm saying?"

"Nuh-unh. Sorry. Daydreaming, boss."

"I said, after we go see Mama, pick up Chéri, you drop us off, you run by that poolhall. Mr.—what Frankie say?"

"Mr. Kush's, boss."

"You know that place?"

"Sure do."

"Go take care that little faggot, whatsizname."

"Joyner." Lavert smiled to himself. Billy Jack Joyner. He had it.

An hour later, still the middle of the afternoon after a couple cups of coffee and a few jokes with Mama, Lavert was pulling past the guard at Audubon Place. Private, didn't *get* no more private than this, Uptown street off St. Charles right by Tulane.

White boy all dressed up in a silly suit coming out of the guardhouse, saying, "How ya'll doing, Mr. Cangiano?" Not pulling no Uptown AT, knowing attitude didn't get you nothing but sorry with the likes of Joey the Horse, who, anyway, had every right to visit the big old white people's house he'd bought here some time ago for Chéri.

And there was that lady now, running out on her front porch like she'd been sitting right there in the window waiting for Joey for a week.

"Would you look at that!" Joey said proudly, pulling the cigar out of his mouth. Like Chéri was a filly he'd been smart enough to invest in doing her stuff out at the track.

Unh-huh, Lavert said to himself. She was an eyeful okay. Bodacious ta-tas bouncing around in a bright yellow jersey like they were doing la cucaracha. That Chéri sure as hell knew which side her baguette was buttered on.

"Hi, honey!" Leaning in the door Lavert had opened for her. Big smooch. Fuck the neighbors.

"Where to, boss?"

"Where you want to go, sugah?"

"Ummmmm. Maybe I feel like snacking on some shrimp."

"Barbecued? Manale's, what you think?"

"Joey"—she gave it a giggle—"what would I do without you, baby, reading my mind?"

"Manale's, Lavert."

"Got it, sir." Hanging a left on St. Charles, headed back downtown toward Napoleon and the old Italian restaurant.

"You like those shrimp, Lavert?"

"The barbecued? Sure do."

"Good. You come on in with us. I'm awfully partial to 'em too. Maybe you scarf up that recipe?"

"Isn't it great what Lavert can do?" Chéri chimed in. "You 'member that time, Lavert, you drove us over to my daddy's, he made you that guinea hen gumbo?"

"Next week we had it on my table," Joey gloated.

"Was the andouille did the trick," said Lavert.

"When you gonna open your own restaurant?" asked Chéri.

"Now, darlin'. Don't you go putting ideas in my man's head."

As if Lavert didn't already have plenty.

"This way, Mr. Cangiano." The maître d' smiled, ushering the three of them past the waiting tourists in the bar and seating them at a corner table, Joey with his back to the wall. They ordered a pitcher of beer.

"Now, tell me, darlin'," said Joey. "What you been up to?"

"Nothing."

"Now I know you been doing *something*. You play tennis today?"

"Uh-huh." Chéri took a long pull on her beer, licking foam off her top lip like it was cream.

"Over at that club?"

"Uh-huh."

"You want me to get you a membership?"

"No, sweetie. That's okay. I go there with my friend Marietta anytime I want to."

"Uh-huh. You sure that's all right? No problem to get you in."

"Of course. Nobody ever bothers me and Miz Dupree."

"That's her last name? Dupree?"

Marietta Dupree. As in Maynard Dupree? Harry had said that name. Lavert filed it.

"You know Marietta, sugar. You met her last year, that dance I dragged you to."

"United Way," Joey grunted. "Bunch of stiffs."

"You're so bad." Her laugh was pearly. "And you met her stupid husband."

"Who?"

"Marietta's husband. That Maynard."

Lavert thought, uh-huh. Maynard Dupree, that was the one all right, a player in the tale Harry had told him. Now, how did that go? Maynard was an enemy of Church's, who was the dude who bought it on St. Charles, which was why the pretty Ms. Adams, Harry's dearheart—

"What?" Joey growled. "What about *that* Maynard?"

"Nothing, darlin'."

"Don't nothin' me. I heard how you said his name. What's this Maynard?"

"It's nothing. Really. I didn't mean a thing."

Chéri took out her compact and inspected her face, licking her little finger and smoothing her eyebrows. Joey reached over and lightly grasped her wrist between two meaty fingers.

"Don't shit me, Chéri."

"Oh, Joey. I don't want you to get upset about every silly man says silly things to me."

"Said *what*?"

The waiter who was delivering their shrimp jumped back as if he'd been shot. Which, taking a look at Joey the Horse Cangiano with his back to the wall, was exactly what he was afraid of.

"Put it there," Joey grumbled, grabbing up the bibs that came with the messy shrimp, tying one around his own neck to protect his silk shirt from the butter, patting another over Chéri's pretty chest. Lavert was on his own.

"You know how men are."

"Tell me what he said to you, Chéri."

"Oh, just the usual."

"Said he wanted to fuck you?"

"*Joey.* Shhhhh." Chéri did the embarrassed ingenue better than almost anyone Lavert had ever seen. "I'm sorry I said anything."

Joey cut dead eyes at Lavert. Eyes like ice-cold marbles. They always looked that way when he was serious, when the word in the front of his mind was *hurt*—as an imperative. "Add him to your list."

"*Joey.*"

"Hush, darlin'. It's done. Now let's suck up some shrimp. There's a good girl."

Thirty-one

Mr. Kush's Billiard Parlor and Café was a throwback to the twenties, left like an oxbow lake deserted by the Mississippi in the terribly chic neighborhood of Riverbend, where St. Charles ran into South Carrollton, and Uptown stopped short.

Kush's was hard by the corner of Plum and Dante—a more felicitous pairing Lavert couldn't imagine. He found a parking spot right in front, wheeling in his little old Fiat Spider with precision—a Tinkertoy after the limo which he'd dropped off along with Joey and Chéri back at the house on Governor Nicholls.

Full of shrimp and lust, they wouldn't be needing him for the rest of the evening.

Which gave him time for his own pursuits.

His and Joey's, he amended.

Never let it be said that Lavert wouldn't just as soon do a twofer if the opportunity were presented, and now that both Harry and Joey had asked for the head of Billy Jack Joyner, well, why not oblige?

Especially if he and Harry snagged G.T.'s little sucker along the way.

Keep going like this, he'd win six ways to Sunday.

G.T.—he sighed at the thought of her—being the prize.

Then Lavert stepped into the cool gloom of Kush's parlor, sporting his favorite soft khakis and an old cream-colored linen sport jacket over a blue workshirt, the shirt a throwback to his peapicking days up at 'Gola. He grinned in the mirror at the free man intended to stay that way. Mr. Entrepreneur-in-the-Making, Jr.

Overhead, fluorescent lights battled it out with curls of cigarette smoke. The crack of one brightly colored ball hitting another was the only sound—other than an occasional muttered *damn!*

Kush, actually Kush III, proprietor like his daddy and granddaddy before him, ran a tight ship and a clean hall. As high yellow as a man can be without turning white, he gave Lavert the welcoming nod.

" 'Doin'?"

"Fine. You?"

"Hanging. Wanna dog?"

Well, now, he'd already downed enough shrimp over at Manale's to satisfy your ordinary sixteen-year-old line-backer, but then, look at it carefully, the matter under consideration here was a Kush dog. The kosher frank grilled with unsalted butter. The roll crisped for just a sec. The chili, no beans, with hand-chopped meat, perfect seasoning. Two kinds of mustard: yellow French's, then a soup-çon of Zatarain's creole. Fresh coarse-chopped onions.

"Don't mind if I do."

"Dixie?"

"Please."

"Be a minute."

Around the big room sat twelve pool tables, mostly occupied by young men wearing tight jeans, some with cigarette packs rolled in their T-shirt sleeves, trying awfully hard to be cool. The billiard table, off to one side in an alcove of its own, made it a baker's dozen.

Prowling the billiard table were two white men in expensive suits. On a bench tableside, two old women perched like pigeons.

Lavert did a double take, then went back for thirds. He stopped Kush, strolling by, with a chin jerk. "That old black woman?"

"Aunt Ida. You know her?"

"G. T. Johnson's granny?"

Kush grinned. "I heard that voudou woman got her hooks in you."

"Says who?"

"Says the grapevine, son. You think them drums be still on you just 'cause you got all fancy, don't hardly come by no more? That don't stop them drums."

Now it was Lavert's turn to grin. What could he say? "And the little old white lady?"

"Ma Elise Lee."

Ahhhhh. It all fell into place. But what were they doing here?

"I tell you you ain't been coming 'round near often enough. Two little old ladies my chief billiards aficionados. Come in here nearly every afternoon."

"They play?"

"Clean your clock, you want to try 'em."

"You kidding."

"Ma Elise taught Ida. She say she learned in Europe. You know that's where all the good players come from."

Lavert and Kush watched for a minute as the two suits demonstrated a proper game, making ordinary pool look like the pedestrian occupation it was. Three balls—red, white, and yellow—rolling around on what looked like a pool table with no holes. Balls with no home.

The task was to tap the white cue ball into either the red or yellow ball, which must then touch at least three cushions before striking the third ball. The proper sequence of hits results in a point, or billiard. Fifty billiards, you're in the money.

The two little ladies leaned forward, their heads close together as they studied the older man's technique. Oooh, Ida whispered. Shhhhh, warned Ma Elise, who was feeling *so* much better, Ida'd got her out of the house away from her Zoe troubles.

"You know a short white boy named Billy Jack Joyner?" Lavert turned to Kush while picking up his chili dog, watching it almost disappear in his big hand, thinking he should have ordered two. Still could.

"Unh-huh. You know him too."

"Nunh-uh." Chewing. God, that was good! "I don't."

"Well, you ought to. Would if you come around more often."

"Jesus, Kush. You sounding like a woman pining for love."

Kush leaned over from his barstool, tweaked Lavert's cheek. "Thass right. 'Cause I be loving you."

"Get out of here." Lavert and Kush had no more than six weeks before been chasing some skirts in a club out the edge of Desire. But no more. Now that he'd taken a vow to win the hand of the fair G.T. No way. "You mean he comes around?"

"I mean you just missed him, dude."

"What?"

"Five minutes ago. Little sucker was in here hitting up one of my customers. Reckon one of his customers too." Kush nodded his head over toward the billiard table.

"Who's that?"

"Docs. Playing hooky from surgery over at Oschner, hear them talk. Hell, blood or billiards, guess I know which one I'd rather do."

"He was right here?"

"You record broken, son? Ain't that what I just said?"

"Shit."

"Don't be so down in the mouth. You come back tomorrow, he probably be here again. Do a lot of visiting with my high rollers."

And then there was hubbub of noise from the billiard table, one man clapping the other on the back.

"What you think, Ma Elise?" the loser said to the old woman.

"You didn't need to play defense, that last shot," she answered. "You supposed to make it."

"*Now* you tell me," the man laughed. Good-spirited. Lavert liked men like that. Looked like they enjoyed all the games of life. Would enjoy eating. Kind of men he'd be proud to serve in his restaurant. *Lavert's.* Wished he had a card index of all the people he'd met like that in this town. Send them invitations to his opening. That was the ticket. Send all the fancy Uptown dudes invites, come in and taste the fine spread, classy way to do it, G.T. at the door in a long dress, wearing a nice welcoming smile—not too much though.

"Game stretches our mind," the man was saying.

He was right. Lavert knew. He played it himself. Billiards encompassed infinite possibilities—like life.

He looked down at the tops of the heads of the two little old ladies who'd toddled over, stopped now, idling.

"You that Lavert Washington?" Aunt Ida asked.

He stood up. Tipped an imaginary cap. Always paid to be polite to the ladies, especially old ladies. Besides, his mama had raised no ignorant, bad-mannered fool. "I am." He gave her his big warm smile. "What can I do for you?"

"I know your mama," Ida said.

"Yes, ma'am."

"She knows me too."

"Yes, ma'am."

"Well, don't believe everything you hear."

"No, ma'am."

"Now, excuse us. Me and Ma Elise here's gonna get on home. Catch us a ride on the streetcar."

"I'd be proud to drive you."

"Humph. That's what my great-grandbaby said. You know G.T.?"

"Yes, ma'am, I sure do."

"Oh, that's right."

Had G.T. *said* something about him? Lavert's heart pounded in his chest like a bass drum gone nuts.

"Well, don't stand there, boy, looking like a fool. You gonna give us a ride, come on with you."

Four blocks away, G.T. was running some questions around in her head. She was wondering why Teri had made tracks out of Ida's house. Wondering how long it would take her to show up to home next door, then start all over again, that bastard Jimbo pounding her face on the floor. Wondering how twisted their little boy's gonna be. Doctor King. Indeed! All the Kings she knew were black. Couple of them, toddlers, named Martin Luther, but Doctor??? Crazy white-folks business.

She was also wondering about Lavert. Actually she found herself doing that a lot.

And she was wondering about Samantha. What could she do for her? She'd said she'd help, but she hadn't done a thing. She ought to give Sam a call. Ought to talk with Ida. She needed to stop being so *re*active. Get on the stick, girl, do something about Zoe too. She didn't know what was wrong with her, what had possessed her mind. (Big man hadn't even touched her, she'd already been hoodooed.) Well, first thing she ought to do was get together with the altar sisters. Do some transformations. Get on the case.

And stop being late. She glanced at her watch. Ida was gonna kill her.

She'd promised she'd pick them up. She'd *insisted* on it, knowing full well the old ladies would be okay on the streetcar.

Well, probably.

On the other hand, people were getting shot by drug dealers every day. Bystanders, sitting on their stoops, walking out their doors holding their children's hands, were suddenly blown away.

Never mind a poolhall.

She glanced back up.

Wait a minute.

Was that who she thought it was, driving right past her in that Town Car.

It *was* that little son of a bitch!

She'd stake her life on it.

G.T. did a U-ey in the middle of Dante.

The little sucker stared at her in his rearview mirror for a long moment, then floored it.

G.T. hit the siren. That was against the rules, off duty, but what the hell were rules for?

Thirty-two

Harry had gotten Sam's message, called her back, and made a date to meet her in the Pelican on Magazine. She'd wanted to see the place where he'd followed Chéri that afternoon of Mardi Gras eve—where he'd overheard the conversation between Jimbo and Maynard.

He was waiting for her at the bar now, whistling what he had of "I Thought I Knew How Angels Flew" under his breath. And there she was. God, she was beautiful.

"What's that tune?" she asked. Harry looked like a cool drink on a summer afternoon. It seemed years since she'd seen him.

"A song I've been working on."

"How's it going?"

"Great."

"Great."

"Listen, I'm really s—" Their mouths formed the words simultaneously. Then they laughed. Together. Again.

Sam looked somewhere to the side of his left ear. "You're looking pretty good."

"You always do."

She stared down at the toes of her shoes, feeling the blush rise up her neck, feeling like first grade. "So, who do I have to see to get a drink around here?"

"Lookin' at him, darlin'." Calvin popped up from behind the bar like a Jack-in-the-box. "What's your pleasure?"

"Perrier."

"No fancy water."

"Club soda. Slice of lemon. Splash of bitters."

So. She slid a little sideways look at Harry. Jeans. Old navy blazer. Loafers. Gray shirt the same color as his eyes. Did he just wink at her, or was that her imagination? "How're things?"

"Good. I've taken in a partner."

"At the office, you mean?"

Harry laughed. "No, I can't imagine my friend Lavert working for Uncle Tench."

"Is your Lavert a huge black man?"

"You know Lavert? Oh, I forgot, you met him with G.T. He told me that."

"Really?"

"We go way back."

"So what's he doing for you?"

"We decided to throw in together finding Billy Jack and G.T.'s little dude."

"What's his interest?"

"G.T."

"I see. Any luck?"

"We're meeting later for a nightcap to compare notes. We started only last night."

And it was only yesterday afternoon that he'd walked out on her at the Royal O. Why did it seem like *years* ago?

"Lots been happening," she said.

He wasn't sure he wanted to know about it. Was she going to beat him over the head with whatever she'd been up to? "Wanta tell me about it?"

Sure. The visit with Sister Nadine, Zoe and the french-fried rat—*bastard!* spat Harry—her little chats with Jimbo and Miss Cissy.

"Damn! You make me feel like I've been standing still. Though"—laying it out casually—"I did hop over to St. Martinville earlier today, met with Madeline Villère."

"You did! Really!" The *without me* was implicit.

"Now, as I remember—"

"Okay. Okay. It's just that Hoke, my managing editor, has been calling threatening to cut out my gizzard if I don't get back to work—"

"Which puts you on slo-mo."

"Exactly. So I was thinking I've never seen Cajun country, it would be a good opportunity—"

"It's not going anywhere," Harry said. "One day I'd be happy to drive you."

What was she *talking* about? This wasn't a vacation. Two minutes with Harry again and she was losing track of what was *important*. "So what'd you find out from her? What was she like? What'd she say?"

"Said it was high time you came to visit." He delivered the line to his beer.

"Harry."

"Okay."

Then he told her. She listened without interrupting for ten minutes, a major exercise in self-control. Finally, she breathed, Holy Toledo.

"My sentiments exactly. All that obsession with fat women—enough to make Jane Fonda commit suicide, don't you think? *And* that means Sister Nadine's a member of their club. You think Church's death could be about her? Maynard finally got tired of losing out with the ladies, offed him? Or hired Jimbo?"

"Jesus, I don't know. But what a couple of good-for-nothing losers."

"You're right there. At least Madeline's happy now. And the good news is she wants to get involved with Zoe."

"Absolutely great."

"I told her you'd call her."

"Why, Harry, that was awfully nice of you."

"Way my mama raised me. Can't help it." He tapped his glass on the bar in lieu of patting Sam. "Calvin, my good man, another round."

Calvin was Johnny-on-the-spot, as if he'd been waiting. Which he had been.

"You know," he said, wiping down the bar with a damp rag even though it didn't need it, "I couldn't help overhearing."

"Yep," said Harry. "Isn't that what bartenders do for a living?"

"Yeah, well, you know, some of what you've been saying, I've thought a lot about that afternoon you were in here before, you remember, that conversation the afternoon before old Church Lee died?"

"Yes?" Sam gave him her most encouraging smile.

"Well, you know how it is when folks get to drinking, fooling around. Say things they don't mean."

"So you don't think Maynard meant what he said about killing Church?" said Sam.

"Well, as I remember it, wasn't Maynard said that in the first place. That was Jimbo."

"You sure?" asked Harry.

"Well, hell, what difference would it make? I mean, they was just teasing. Talking big drunk talk. Hell, you believed a tenth of what you hear in here, you'd be on the phone to the police all the time. Couldn't ever make no money."

"And there was never any *further* conversation about it that you know of?"

"Sure not in here. And both Jimbo and Maynard Dupree come in time to time."

"Together?" asked Sam.

"Well. Let me think about that for a minute."

Sam watched the rag making circles. The old mahogany bar glowed.

"Nope." Calvin shook his head. "I'm sure they've not. They're not really friends, you know. May run into each other here, there, somewheres else in their drinking rounds, but"—he waggled a hand—"you know, different worlds."

Oh, well. Sam gave Harry a look. Certainly didn't hurt to ask.

"Sort of like that young guy came in here with Church one night last fall. Yep, that was the same kind of thing. Different worlds."

"What young man?" Sam jumped in.

Calvin went right on. "Of course Church Lee was no snob. 'Specially when it came to drinking partners."

"Could I buy you a drink?" Harry offered Calvin. "Maybe you could remember something about that young man?"

"Well, that's right kindly of you. Don't mind if I do." He poured himself two fingers of Glenlivet. Sam watched the lights bounce off the top of his balding head as he leaned forward, tipped the glass back. "Now"—wiping his mouth—"this was, as I said, sometime back in the fall. Pretty late one night. It was still warm. You know how we don't have but one season here in N'Awlins, summer with a couple days of cool—"

Sam choked down the impulse to rush him.

"—anyway, the reason I mention that is Church was sweating like a pig." He gestured down his chest, under his armpits. "Right through a good suit."

"That's *some* sweating," said Harry.

"Well, that's what I said too. Church said he'd been running a race."

"A race?" Sam echoed, trying to keep the rising hope out of her voice. A bell was ringing in the back of her mind.

"Yeah. Said he'd been chasing this young man he had with him. Then they both laughed. Like it was a big joke."

Sam grasped Harry's arm. The night Church was mugged. The story Zoe had told her. He'd bought the mugger a drink?

"Was it around eleven, eleven-thirty? Did Church say he'd been to a party?" Of course, that could describe many of Church's evenings—but then, this one had ended differently.

Calvin squinted. "Something like that. They came in, sat down there"—he pointed—"at the end of the bar. Stayed for about an hour. Discussing something serious, it looked like. Kind of peculiar."

"Because of the young man?" asked Sam.

"Yeah. Like I said, the dude, well, he wasn't, well, he wasn't Uptown, that was for sure. And if he'd been chasing Church, it didn't make sense—"

Sam had been holding her breath. "What'd he look like?"

"Little bitty guy. Not a whole lot over five feet tall. Runty. Blond hair."

SAM: "The guy at the airport!"

HARRY: "Billy Jack!"

And then they said the words over again a few times.

"Billy Jack!"

"The guy at the airport!"

"The little guy at the airport!"

"Billy Jack!"

"*Is* Billy Jack!"

Finally the light had dawned. Was it possible, the little guy at the airport and Billy Jack were the same?

"It's not only possible, it seems probable, doesn't it, now that you think about it?" Harry said.

It did. It was.

Sam threw up her hands. "Now what?"

Thirty-three

Lavert had picked the Napoleon House for the rendezvous with Harry, thinking the spot would retain some of G.T.'s vibes. That was earlier—long before he'd heard from the lady herself. Now *he* was vibrating.

By the time Harry walked in, Lavert couldn't wait. He wanted to grab and tackle him.

"Man, you won't believe what's happened!"

"Mine's better." Harry's grin came over his face like dawn.

"Don't give me that Bogart shit. I'm telling you I got the goods. I know the dude's name."

"Whose?"

"Billy Jack Joyner's, asshole!"

"Joyner? Oh, yeah? I'm telling you mine's better "

"*And* I saw the little airport dude. I ran right smack into him this afternoon holding up that Pic'N'Pac out on Coliseum with a peashooter."

"You don't say. Did you get his name?"

With that, Lavert got mad. "Man, what the fuck's wrong with you? You think I said, excuse me, sir, I'm taking a survey, could I have your name right here on the dotted line? You getting me steamed, man."

"Unh-huh. Draw me a Dixie, please," he said to the bartender.

"Zack, I'm about to bite a piece out of you. Guess you don't care now Chéri's got Joey pissed off at your Maynard Dupree, Joey wants me to do him. *And* your Joyner. Guess you don't care I just missed the Joyner dude at Kush's a little while ago. Then G.T. calls me. Says *she* passed the other little dude—the one who jumped out of the ambulance that day on the way from the airport—when she's going to pick up her granny. Old lady hangs out there at Kush's. G.T. chased him, but he was too slick, got away from her."

"Anything strike you funny about that?"

"About what? That we're closing in on both these guys, we know Dupree's in deep shit, been on the case only twenty-four hours."

"About the fact that Joyner walks out of Kush's, then not too far away G.T. passes the little dude she picked up at the airport? Same time? Same place? Same station?"

"You pissing me off, Zack. Talking to me like I'm stupid. I ain't stupid, man."

"Nope. But you're not seeing what's right in front of your face. I didn't either for a while."

Lavert drained the last of his beer, then reached over and polished off Harry's. He narrowed his eyes, exhaling hard through his nose like a winded prizefighter.

Then he got it.

"One dude! We looking for one dude!" Lavert was jumping around now. "And we know the little motherfucker's name! Couldn't be too hard to find out where he lives." Doing a little victory dance, boogying behind the barstools. "And *I* know where he hangs!"

"You always were my main man." Harry signaled for a celebratory round. Cuke-cool dude, smiling.

Thirty-four

Maynard was home relaxing in the tub. Or, at least, he was trying.

He could hardly think, his head hurt him so bad, not to mention the burning in his stomach, the flibberty-jibbities throughout his whole entire body, chills running up and down in little spasms.

Face it, man, he said, staring down at his fat stomach floating like a desert island in the tub of hot water. You've lost it. Bad.

Kids running up and down the stairs, Easter week, cowboy boots, goddamn cap pistols.

Pow! Pow! Pow!

The boots reminded him of Jimbo.

He closed his eyes and moaned.

That fucking Jimbo, holding the best tailor in New Orleans out the window. You could bet your sweet patootie he'd seen the last of Herbert. *That* was for damned straight. The man had made his clothes since he was in school.

"Daddy! Daddy!" Maynard, Jr., came bursting in the door.

"What the hell you think this is, son, Grand Central Station?"

The boy stopped, cap gun drawn. "What?" The finger of his other hand was creeping up toward his nose.

"*What* what, son?"

"What's Grand Central Station?"

"I pay eight thousand fucking dollars a year, more than it cost me at the University of Virginia, to keep you in private school, and you don't know what Grand Central Station is?"

"Ma! Ma!" the boy wailed, wheeling out of the room.

Great. Just what he needed. Marietta coming in here, giving him one of her holier-than-thou you're-such-a-terrible-father lectures.

He reached up, dried his hands on the thick white towel, plucked a cigar from the glass shelf. Clipped the end of it with his gold knife.

Flicked his gold lighter. Was there anything as satisfying as gold? Lit the cigar—ah, God bless those little Cuban bastards.

Then he leaned back and tried to pull himself together.

But he came all unraveled again—queasy like he had a bellyful of grease. What the fuck was he going to do?

After Jimbo'd left his office day before yesterday, he'd called a car for Herbert, sent Sally Jean home squalling when what he'd wanted to do was smack her, sat alone in his office for a long time—long past dark. Wondering where it'd all gone wrong.

Hearing his father calling him a pantywaist. Goddamn pantywaist, son. Should've killed Church right out. Always told you that. Sperm run out, weak when it got to you, always said that to your mama. That and her letting your curls stay so long, you wuz a kid, made you think like a girl. Think you *wuz* a girl. Still do.

God, how he hated the old bastard!

When Maynard was barely a pup his dad had said, That Church Lee, Davenport Lee's son, is twice the man of you.

That's why he went after Peggy Patrick, that fat little girl he and Church had first fought over as boys—to prove the old man wrong.

Now look what it had come to. He may or may not have killed Church. Jesus, he couldn't remember. May or may not have hired Jimbo to do it for him. Oh, God.

And now Jimbo was really leaning on him. Taking his money was one thing. Hanging his tailor out the window another. *Now* there was this mothering lawn-chair business, Jimbo strong-arming him into getting him on TV. Calling in celebrities! Was there no end? No end to his suffering? Oh, Jesus.

They were gonna laugh him out of Comus. Laugh him out of the Pickwick. Laugh him out of the Club. His name linked with this cockamamy scheme and this redneck.

Never again would he get to ride on the big horse in the parade. Never again would he be captain of Comus.

But wait a minute.

Maynard sat up.

What the fuck was he worried about?

This was New Orleans, the only town with a sense of humor in the whole United States.

He'd just laugh it off. They would too.

He reached for the towel again.

He'd make the most of it!

Hell! Maynard was getting excited now, he'd make himself a kind of eccentric hero, producer of the wildest stunt since Mardi Gras, if this goddamn lawn-chair sucker flew.

See. It was only a matter of attitude.

What the hell had he been pissing and moaning about? Maynard reached for the wall phone. He could *do* this! Never let it be said Maynard Dupree wasn't wired, didn't have the juice. Could he get Jimbo King and his Flying Lawn Chair on TV? You bet your sweet ass he could! Knew just the sweet patootie could do it for him too.

"Maynard."

He slammed down the phone and rolled an eye at Marietta, who was standing in the doorway with her hands on her hips.

"Yes, darlin'?"

"Don't you darlin' me, you son of a bitch. What'd you say to Junior?"

"I merely reminded him that he might take better advantage, given the cost, of his schooling."

"Humph," she snorted.

Maynard wondered what had happened to all those fine manners the young Marietta had learned in finishing school.

"I bet that's what you said. You gonna stay in here till you turn into a prune?"

"Why, Marietta darlin'. I didn't know you cared about my poor old body anymore."

"Well, you got that right."

"Now, sugah."

Marietta closed the lid of the toilet. She sat down, pulling one tan leg up, inspecting a scab on her knee where she'd fallen on the court. Playing with Chéri. A little chill ran down her spine. That Chéri—she'd told Marietta what she'd said to Joey about Maynard. Marietta cast a cold eye over to her pudding of a husband. They used to murder Caesars in their tubs, wasn't that right? Marietta's notion of history was a little shaky, but she knew she was on the right track here with the Italians. Caesars were Italians, right? And so was Joey. Mob Italian. And Chéri had made sure Joey was pissed as hell at Maynard.

Chéri'd said it was like putting in an order. It was only a matter of time now till she'd be free of this fat bastard.

In the meantime—"I hear you got yourself a new boyfriend," she said.

Maynard damply tongued his stinking cigar to one side of his mouth. "What?"

"You gone deaf, honey?"

"I don't know what you're talking about, May-retta." He waved his arm and his cigar. "Get on out of here. Leave me alone."

"I bet you wouldn't say that to Jimbo." She slid it in like a dagger.

Maynard thought his heart had stopped. Suddenly the bathwater felt like ice. "Jimbo who?"

"Now, darlin'. Don't be coy with me. I hear you been keeping steady company with that old boy. I think it's kind of cute. I always knew you hung out long enough you'd figure it was boys you liked anyway."

Maynard stood, the water pouring off him, splashing out of the tub onto the tiles. "Out! Get out of here, you bitch!" He was waving his arms.

"Okay, *darlin'.*" Staring pointedly at his little thing flopping. "You don't have to shout. I'm going." Sashaying out with a twitch to her cute butt. She knew it still was—cute, that is. Chéri told her so every chance she got. "But I'd be careful, playing around with trash like that, hon, I was you." She slammed the door behind her.

God damn her to hell! His cigar was all wet. Maynard jerked it out of his mouth and threw it on the floor.

Then he caught sight of himself in the floor-length mirror on the inside of the door. He was the spit and image of a sounding whale.

Jesus! Where had all the good part gone?

I'm making progress, Lavert had said to Joey the Horse this morning. Joey was a little hung over. He'd asked Lavert to whiz him up a couple of raw eggs, some fresh ground pepper, splash of grappa, touch of Fernet Branca, throw it in the blender.

Joey didn't want to hear about progress. Joey wanted to hear about history. Things done. Accounts closed.

But hell, Lavert thought. He himself wuddn't gonna *kill* anybody. He never had. Couldn't see any reason to start now, especially since he could feel himself so close to his restaurant, Lavert's. G.T. smiling at the door, all in gold. He'd decided her dress would be gold. Not cloth of gold, but gold the color of a bloody moon. With her complexion, it'd be something.

So what he had to do was: he figured Billy Jack Joyner was gonna be a piece of cake. Little dude was already in a shitload of trouble. Dealing. Holding up Pic'N'Pacs. Hitting on big-time doctoring dudes right in broad daylight, or practically, at Kush's. Wuddn't no way little dude wuddn't gonna do his ownself in. All Lavert might have to do is figure out a way help him along. He'd talk to Harry about it.

Mr. Dupree was a whole other ball game.

Harry saying he figured him to be their numero uno suspect doing Church Lee. Some crazy story about fat white women. Lavert shook his head. Go figure.

All he knew—following the fat boy now in his big old car, Lavert in his Spider—was Maynard Dupree couldn't drive worth shit. He kept cutting people off like he owned the road. Rich white men, no class, acted like that. He looked like he was in some kind of tizzy. Lavert had followed him from his house; now where was he going? Dupree stopped, parked in a towaway right in front of one of those fancy florists, and came out carrying a big bouquet. Was he, just like Joey suspected, calling on Miss Chéri? Nope, no Audubon Place for this man. He was going right downtown. Now he'd crossed Canal, so he wuddn't going to his office. Turned right onto North Rampart, taking Lavert back toward Esplanade, past Governor Nicholls, making a big circle tour this morning. Too bad they didn't have some tourists in tow. Lavert could give 'em a nice talk, explaining it all to 'em, your Quarter, your Garden District, your Quarter.

Now Fat Boy was pulling over like he was gonna park.

Lavert pulled right in beside him. Right tight.

Fat Boy looking up. Startled. Red in the face. Can't open his door.

Lavert, top down on the Spider, leaning over.

"Mr. Dupree," he said, knowing the effect he always had on strangers. Biggest motherfucking nigger they'd ever seen. "Mr. Dupree. I got a message for you."

Maynard made a strangling sound. Kind of like gargling. Funny thing, Lavert thought, about lawyers. You get 'em scared enough, they inarticulate as hell. All of sudden, like everybody else, they got a frog in their throat, a load in their drawers.

"Friend of mine said you ought to stay away from Miss Chéri."

"I—I—I don't know what you're talking about," Maynard managed, snapping his little eyes open and shut a whole lot. Sounding kind of like Minnie Mouse.

"Now, there's no point in lying. Just stay away from the lady, everything's gonna be all right." Lavert let two beats pass. "Prob'ly."

"Wha-what do you mean? What lady?"

"Well, you gonna have to pay for what you done already, but after that"—Lavert turned one huge hand palm-up, gave him the big super-reassuring grin—"well, then with what you got left, you cool."

"What I got left? What do you mean, what I got left?"

Now Lavert gave him the slow wink, icing on the cake. "Be seein' you."

Thirty-five

●

If there was one thing Billy Jack couldn't stand, it was people getting too close. That made him feel claustrophobic.

He'd been that way ever since he was a little kid, had seen this movie down at the Rialto Theater. He'd told Clyde Wayne, his next-door neighbor, he didn't wanta see it. He hated scary pictures. But more than that, he hated Clyde Wayne calling him a sissy, so he'd gone.

He'd been sorry ever since.

What happened in that picture was there was this woman who was terrified she was gonna be buried alive. She thought about it all the time, so she planned for it.

What she did was she spent a whole bunch of money having her tomb built in the cemetery on the family place, an above-ground tomb like these in New Orleans. She had it wired with a phone and one of those little TV cameras and a monitor, so she could see into her house from the tomb, could call them on the phone in case she *did* get buried alive. And vice versa, they could see and call her, that is.

So the movie goes on, lots of creepy castles and chains dragging around, bats, all that usual spooky stuff, and sure enough, eventually, the woman dies.

But it's cool, see, because she's really dead.

But, hold it, don't go out for more popcorn, because, the way they do to fool you in the movies, whoops, she's not.

The next thing you know, a whole bunch of years have passed, and they're showing you inside this satin coffin and the woman wakes up.

But it's okay, right? It's cool.

Her hair has grown—it does, you know, after you're gone—all the way down to her feet.

Her nails are so long they've curved all the way over to her palms. It's creepy as hell when she opens her hands, those claws looking like some kind of giant bird. She opens her mouth to scream, and her teeth are all scraggly, like little stumps.

But it's cool. You say, don't scream, lady. Just pick up the phone that's right there inside the coffin.

And just like she hears you, she does.

Then the phone rings and rings and rings and rings, and you get this really sick feeling, which you knew you would, after all, this is a horror movie. Then the picture shows you what the closed circuit TV is seeing in the house: nothing. Absolutely nothing. Everybody inside is done long dead and gone, because lots and lots of years have passed, and the big old house has been abandoned for a real long time. Curtains are hanging all in tatters, rats playing around on what's left of the sofa.

That lady was calling into an empty house. She woke up in her tomb just like she knew she'd do, took every precaution in the world, and still ain't nobody home. The last scene, she's trying to claw her way out of that satin coffin with those fingernails all curved down to her palms.

Well. Ever since that, Billy Jack had been scared to death of being squeezed in.

He had nightmares about it for years. His mama would come in and jerk him up out of a bed where he was sitting bolt upright in his jammies, sound asleep, yelling bloody murder at the top of his lungs.

He couldn't stand being in little spaces like elevators or having people coming too close to him, eating up his space. His air.

He liked to have gone crazy when he was in LTI, the reform school, their locking him in the hole, in solitary. That one time they did—it was that Dr. Frisbee's fault. He'd jumped on the man because he was saying the way Billy Jack felt about his mom was *weird*.

Coming up with his plan to pay Frisbee back was the only thing kept him together in the hole. He dreamed about it every night till he got out. Then it was easy as pie. He just kept following Frisbee until late one afternoon the man was driving the LTI station wagon over to the little town of Grambling, where they had the college with the nigger football players. Frisbee was going to pick up some poor little nigger kid they was putting in LTI. The nigger kid was in the station wagon when Billy Jack passed them. Billy Jack put on his flashers, pulled over like he was in trouble.

Frisbee might be a Jew, but he was still a southern gentleman, so he got out to help. Billy Jack was counting on that. Frisbee's eyes got big when he realized who it was was in trouble, not Billy Jack, was *him*, but by that time the tire iron was already coming down.

When they found Frisbee in the middle of I-20 that night, the paper said he'd already been run over so many times he was flat—just another piece of roadkill. The little nigger who was with him was still cuffed to the door handle. Billy Jack would have let him go, but he didn't have time to be messing around, had to git.

But that little nigger was a good little nigger. He never said a word to anybody about what went down. Billy Jack had kept track of that through some buddies still in LTI—where they went on ahead and took the little nigger when they'd finished grilling him about Frisbee. Nigger didn't say squat to anybody white, about that or anything else, the whole time he was in. Didn't say a blessed word for three years.

That was the kind of nigger you could like—the kind that understood about respect.

Not like that big jigaboo was on his tail, crowding him. Son of a bitch busting into the Pic'N'Pac like that. Damn! Just when he needed the score.

And who the fuck was this other dude asking questions about him? Dude wearing a beat-up old raincoat, said his friend at Patrissy's. Two people squeezing his elbow room.

Not to mention there was that woman he'd seen at Zoe's, the one he'd followed over to where he'd got rousted by the cop. The woman DEA agent was gonna be moving in on him, too, any second. He was sure of it. Just like he was sure Zoe'd sicced the DEA on him.

Zoe, that little bitch. Some girls never learned. No matter how many times you told 'em and you told 'em: just keep your mouth shut, just do business. The message just didn't get through. Sent her that fried rat, you'd think that'd do it. Wouldn't you?

But, oh, no. Not these girls, fancy Uptown girls, girls bought jewels every day from Mr. Adler. Girls born with his silver safety pins for their little diapers.

Zoe had actually *told* him that—he couldn't remember how it came up—she'd never worn Pampers in her life. Only the genuine cloth article, some poor woman having to wash 'em 'stead of tossing 'em out, good enough for her precious little butt.

He'd asked his mama about that. She'd laughed, said, son, I had more things on my mind than that when I was raising you.

He loved thinking about when he was her little baby, safe inside her. Then got to cuddle up to her beautiful breast and suck on her.

He remembered her singing hymns while she nursed him. He'd told her that. She'd laughed and said, son, how could you remember? But he remembered. He remembered, all right. After all, he'd still been sucking on her sugar tit when he was five. Almost six. Almost right up until he went off to school.

Mama said, now that wasn't true. Said they were never that poor, even if it was cheaper to nurse him than to feed him. But it *was* true. He knew it was. After all, he was there. He knew what he knew.

Right now he knew there was a whole lot of people getting way too close to him. And he knew that he had to forget about them for a little bit, because what he *had* to do was put together the money to get his mama's diamond necklace. And he also knew that right here on Prytania, which is where he was driving, he was gonna stop at Zoe's house, where she wasn't staying no more, and kill two birds with one stone.

Bird one: He was gonna rob the hell out of her house, fence the stuff, and take the money to Adler's.

Bird two: He was gonna make sure Zoe knew *he* did it, be another warning to her—back off with the fucking DEA lady.

Now here he was. He pulled right up in front of Zoe's house, where she used to live before she moved over to her grandmama's. She'd told him her daddy died. Likely story. But maybe he had. Billy Jack had never asked her any more about it.

Her daddy couldn't of been all that old—must of been some kind of cancer. Well, he couldn't go soft thinking about that now, feeling sorry for her like she was some kind of orphan. Though she was, didn't have a mother either. At least not he'd ever heard of.

But that didn't make no never mind. Business was business, and this little twat had been messing in his.

Turning him in to the DEA. Probably they were on *her* tail was why she did it. But that didn't make a bit of difference.

Billy Jack was around to the back of her house now.

Just like he thought, there were little decals on all of the windows said the house was guarded by this protection service. Like they was wired up directly to the police station.

Rich people would all have you think that. Didn't matter, they go right off, leave a first floor back window unlatched.

Billy Jack crawled through. He was so little, was no problem a-tall. He found himself in some kind of sitting room. He brushed himself off. Then he stopped dead still.

Everywhere he looked, the furniture was draped with sheets. Chairs, sofas, other big lumps he couldn't make out. A piano maybe? Thing looked like an elephant. But mostly what the place looked like was his nightmare from the horror movie.

Billy Jack froze. He could hardly breathe. With one hand he scrabbled at his neck, loosening his collar suddenly grown too small.

Fuck! Fucking heebie-jeebies!

He sat right down in the middle of the floor and put his head between his knees.

He felt like he did that day out at the airport when Joey's great big nigger came charging at him, got too close, then he heard all those gunshots. He'd felt sick to his stomach—just like he did now. Why was Joey's nigger coming after him then, anyway? And why was he after him now? What did it mean? Did it have anything to do with Joey, or was it just some weird coincidence?

He had to breathe through his mouth.

That's what he had to remember to do.

Breathe through his mouth.

Think good thoughts.

Think of his mama holding him close, singing "Amazing Grace" in his ear. That was his favorite lullaby when he was a little kid.

There now.

There now.

All better.

Billy Jack slowly opened his eyes and raised his head. He focused and, pro that he was, zeroed right in on a bunch of old silver picture frames somebody had dumped into a cardboard box and left on the floor next to the thing that looked like a piano under its sheet. Like they'd been packing, got interrupted, or thought better of it. They were good, expensive silver frames.

He picked up one and looked at the little imprint on the back. He'd learned to do that. Tiffany & Co., it said.

Great! Silver was silver. Gold was gold. Everything didn't have to be fucking Rolexes.

Billy Jack dropped the frame onto the floor, picture side up.

Then the faces jumped up at him.

Son of a bitch!

Goddamn son of a bitch!

There was Zoe when she was a little girl, standing on what looked like a front porch, lifting the skirt of a little white dress. She had great big eyes and cute little legs. She wasn't nearly so skinny then, was curtsying, sort of, playing around the way kids do, smiling like a sunbeam into the face of a man. Shit! *Look* at that man.

Billy Jack grabbed up more frames from the box. There! Look there! And there again! That one looked like it was taken just last year. The man had never told Billy Jack he was Zoe's dad. But then, the man had never told him his name either.

No names. That was part of their deal. He'd do the man like the man asked him to, man wouldn't narc on him to his mama, wouldn't even breathe his mama's blessed name.

Thirty-six

G.T. was in high dudgeon, sprinkling Ma Elise's front parlor with Flying Devil powder, verbena oil, and Saint-John's-wort, whispering imprecations under her breath.

"Girl, come and sit down," Aunt Ida fussed at her. "Watching you's got me plum wore out." Right after a too-big lunch, she and Sam and Kitty and Zoe and Ma Elise were spread across the sofas and chairs like a pack of dead cats.

"Coffee," said G.T. "You all need coffee." She disappeared for a minute, then reappeared with the big carafe. "Now." Pointing at Sam. "You called this Good Friday meeting. What you got?"

"I've got a mess. I've got all kinds of possibilities, but I don't know what to make of anything. What I need is help." And then Sam began dealing out the players one at a time as if they were cards in a jumbled hand. First was the blind man, Cole Leander.

"You think we ought to believe him," she asked Kitty, "when he says all's forgiven and forgotten? You don't think this is his way, dropping the suit, of his covering up something else? His conversion to the Lord notwithstanding?"

"*I* don't know." Kitty shook her head.

Sam turned to Ma Elise. "You've known him forever. What do you think?"

"Cole always was a big bag of wind. Actually, men like that, I always felt kind of sorry for them. I'd say we could count him out."

"Praise the Lord," Kitty piped up from her chaise. "I just don't think I have the strength to deal with that malpractice business."

"Which brings me to the question of Church's finances," said Sam. And then she recounted all that Cissy had said, trying to soft-pedal the role of Zoe's debut and Carnival expenses.

But none of it was lost on Church's daughter. "Oh, my God," the young girl moaned, her eyes dark holes in her too-pale face. "My God,

my God. I never suspected any of that. I bet he was worried to death."
Then she bit her lip. "And God knows I could have helped him."

"What do you mean?" Ma Elise asked.

"There was never any need for Daddy to worry about money. Just
like I've been telling you there's no need for us to pursue the insurance.
I said I'd be okay." She took a deep breath, polling their faces. "Don't
you understand what I'm saying? I'm rolling in cash. Don't you know
anything about drug dealers?"

Sam nodded, go on.

"Especially drug dealers with investment portfolios who take great
pleasure, as I do, in watching the numbers grow. Totting up all those
zeroes."

"And what are the numbers, darling?" Ma Elise asked the question
as if she were inquiring what Zoe would like for supper.

"About six million. Give or take a couple hundred thou each day
depending on the market."

"Sweet baby Jesus," said Ida.

"Holy shit," said Kitty. "Church would have been awfully proud of
you."

"Do you really think so?" Zoe's grin was unnerving. Sam had seen
corpses with prettier rictus. "Think he would have been pleased knowing how his little girl made her fortune?"

Ma Elise moved over closer to Zoe on the sofa, put her thin old arms
around her, gave her a big hug. "Shhh," she whispered. "Hush."

Sam shot Ma Elise a questioning look. Should she stop the questions
here for a bit? The old lady snuggled Zoe closer and nodded to Sam to
go on.

G.T. beat her to it. "The cops done anything more tracing that Buick?"

"You mean Blackstone and Shea, our brave men in blue?" Sam
shrugged. "I checked this morning. They're both out of town. I figure
either they've hit the jackpot, lying low with their info till they negotiate with their info till they negotiate with the highest bidder, or they've
gone fishing."

"Looks of them, I'd say the latter," said G.T. "How 'bout you?"

"I don't think they have zip," Sam concurred. Then, "Now, G.T.,
did you know your friend Lavert Washington is working this case?"

"Whose friend?"

"Too quick, girl," her great-grandmother snapped. "I saw that big
old boy yesterday over to Kush's. Your name came up, he like to
fainted. You know, I think he might be okay, even though his mama

been talking trash about us for years. He's certainly a gentleman. Gave us a ride home, didn't he, Ma Elise?''

"He sure did."

"He didn't tell me that," said G.T.

"Ah-ha!" said Ida. "Tell you when?"

"I called him yesterday to tell him I saw that little white boy, the one who jumped out of my ambulance that time coming from the airport. Saw him I was coming to pick you all up."

"Why's Lavert care?" asked Ida.

G.T. flushed. "He seemed to want to help me find him."

"Uh-huh. Uh-huh."

"Hush with your uh-huhing, old woman."

"Uh-huh. Smoke there's fire's all I know."

Sam couldn't wait to tell G.T. "Do you know who that is?"

"Who?"

"That boy from the airport?"

"Who?"

"Billy Jack Joyner."

"What?" Zoe sat up.

"That's right," Sam turned to her. "*Your* Billy Jack, last name Joyner, the same person G.T.'s been looking for—the one who jumped out of her ambulance, left her with a handful of paperwork."

"What on earth?" Zoe said.

"What do you mean, *her* Billy Jack Joyner?" Kitty asked.

"My supplier," said Zoe. "Where I got my coke."

"Oh." Kitty slumped back.

"And you know what?" Sam continued. "Harry and I discovered that your dad and Billy Jack had a drink together in the Pelican back several months ago."

"What?" Zoe cried. "Daddy and Billy Jack? I can't believe that."

Sam described the scenario as told to her by Calvin, the Pelican's barkeep, of Church and Billy Jack in the Pelican. "Doesn't it sound like that night you were telling me about? The night you said Church was mugged?"

"It *does*. But it doesn't make any sense. Why would he go for a drink with somebody who'd attacked him? And why on earth would Billy Jack mug *him* in the first place? And then why would Daddy come home and not mention *that* part?"

They all shook their heads.

"It must have been something else. *Somebody* else," said Kitty. "That doesn't sound like Church."

"Not even at his drunkest?" Sam asked, thinking of some stunts she'd pulled on the booze she wished she *didn't* remember.

"I can't imagine," said Ma Elise.

"Who told you all this anyway? Where'd you hear this story?" asked Ida. "And what does it mean?"

"What I want to know is how Maynard Dupree fits into all this? Did he have something to do with Billy Jack mugging Church?" Sam looked at them all in turn as if any or all of them had the answers.

"What do you mean, Maynard Dupree? What on earth are you talking about?" asked Ma Elise.

So then Sam told the story once again of Harry and Chéri and Maynard and Jimbo in the Pelican the night before Mardi Gras.

"Oh, Lord," said Ma Elise with a look on her face like she tasted something bad. "Maynard Dupree."

"Yes," said Sam, turning to her. "Maynard Dupree. You ladies weren't very helpful, you know, holding out about Maynard."

Kitty and Ma Elise exchanged a look. Then Ma Elise's eyes slid over to Ida's.

"Don't look at me," the old woman snapped. "I told you years ago you're doing the wrong thing there. I told you and I told you and you wouldn't listen."

"What?" Zoe asked. Zoe searched all their faces. "What? What?"

"Now," Ida said, her black eyes darting at Ma Elise, "you gonna tell her now?"

"What?" Zoe again.

"Oh, darlin'," said Ma Elise. "My little darlin' girl."

And then it all came tumbling out, the sad and sordid tale of Church and Maynard and their rivalry over Madeline, how they'd both used her, why she'd run away. Ma Elise and Kitty and Ida told the story together, each taking turns. "No!" Zoe cried again and again. "No! No! No!"

"But they both loved you so," said Ma Elise. "Both your mama and your daddy. Everything else was just—"

"Just their own madness," Kitty offered. "Your daddy's and Maynard Dupree's. Fueled by Maynard's awful daddy and our mother and father's boozing—and well, it goes on and on, doesn't it, our obsessiveness with history and family, our skeletons, our—"

"But it was *my* family," cried Zoe. "*My* life."

"And it still is," Sam said softly.

"What do you mean?" Zoe, who'd leapt to her feet, whirled, her curls wild and loose about her head. "They're both gone."

"Kitty and Ma Elise are still here. And Ida. And your mother wants to come back. Not here"—Sam gestured around the room—"but to you. To see you. To get to know you."

"She does, does she! Oh, really? How *nice* for her!" Zoe's arms flailed back and forth, and her mouth worked. She was on the edge of hysteria. "She wants to come back and see what she can pick from my daddy's bones?"

"Zoe!" Kitty cried, grabbing for but missing Zoe's arm as the girl wheeled past.

"Leave me alone. You all leave me alone! I *hate* you—" Zoe screamed and raced from the room.

Ma Elise rose to her full height. "I'll go see to her."

"Ma Elise—" Kitty started.

"No. Sit down. It was my decision to keep these secrets all these years. And I see now that probably I was wrong. So I'll take the responsibility for setting it to rights, as much as I can. Starting this minute." And she followed in Zoe's footsteps, out and up the stairs.

"Oh, my God." Kitty collapsed back into her chaise. She closed her eyes. "Aren't we Lees just bad Tennessee Williams? Lord, Lord, Lord."

G.T. shook her head. "Yep. Well, we're all something, aren't we? Families—"

Ida nodded. "I'm not going to say I told her so."

"But you did tell her. And you told me," Kitty said. "I don't know why we didn't listen to you, why we didn't know there'd be hell to pay one way or the other. Poor Zoe. Oh, God, we've made such a mess of Zoe."

"Whole family's stubborn," said Ida. "Always has been. Streaks like that go in families." She paused, stared off at nothing they could see. "It does make you wonder, don't it, what that Billy Jack got from his mama."

"What do you mean?" Sam asked. "His mama?"

"It gives you pause, don't it?"

"What, Maw Maw?" asked G.T. "What you talking about?"

"Billy Jack's mama."

"Who *is* Billy Jack's mama? What you saying?"

"Joyner. Billy Jack Joyner?"

"Yes, Maw Maw."

"Well, nobody ever told me that scrawny white boy you been talking about's name before."

"And now that they have?" G.T. was barely holding her impatience with her great-grandmother under control. "So what? So what about his mama?"

"Well, don't it make you wonder how a sweet angel like that could raise such a troubled boy?"

"*Who?*" G.T. and Sam and Kitty chorused.

"Sister Nadine. Sister Nadine Joyner. Now that you told me who Billy Jack is, don't you see the family resemblance? That's got to be her son. I'd bet money on it."

"Sister Nadine *Joyner?*" Sam cried. Her last name had never been mentioned before. And Sam had never asked. She leaned her forehead against her fists, banging her head softly.

Billy Jack—Zoe's supplier, who, it looked like, had mugged Church and then gone with him for a drink at the Pelican, who'd put on that show at the airport, who'd done God knows what else—was Sister Nadine's son? Sister Nadine, who was Church's lover. *Probably* Maynard Dupree's, too, if things were running true to form. Sure. Oh yeah. Uh-huh. Why not? Throw one more stone in the soup, one more mess of shrimp in the gumbo pot. It was too bad she didn't still drink. Disaster like this just cried out for a snort.

Nope, nope, she'd learned to look at it the other way. There was nothing so bad that a drink wouldn't make it worse. And this was bad.

Give her your basic garden-variety homicide any day. She still didn't even know whether Church had been killed with malice here or this was your basic hit-and-run.

This was terrible.

This was nuts.

Now, from across the room, she felt G.T.'s gaze on her and she looked up. G.T.'s golden eyes were ablaze, trained on hers as if she were willing Sam to see what she saw. And she was saying, " 'Member how short I said that guy was driving the Buick that night, Sam? How he could barely see over the wheel? You know, that Billy Jack Joyner is an awful tiny little dude."

Thirty-seven

"I still think their oyster po'boys are far superior," said Marietta.

"And that's why this is a free country." Chéri was taking a big bite out of her own French loaf loaded with shrimp.

They were sitting at the bar in D.J.'s, one of two or three big brawling family seafood places in Bucktown, right out on the south edge of the lake.

"Sometimes I think you could eat shrimp six times a day," said Marietta.

"Well, you know, sugah, you think that, and you'd be right on the money." Chéri ticked items off on her long fingers tipped with a bright orange manicure. "Yesterday I had Manale's shrimp barbecued, for dinner I was at the Bon Ton had the remoulade, lunch today I had me a big shrimp salad I made myself to my house."

"Erasers."

"I beg your pardon." Chéri's eyes got real big though she knew exactly what Marietta was talking about. They'd had this conversation more than once.

"Shrimp these days taste like rubber erasers. They've gone and bred the flavor right out of 'em," Marietta said.

"And you're telling me oysters are different."

"I am."

"Honey, you ain't got a drop of Cajun blood in you. What do you know?"

"I know I'm about to be one of the happiest widows in the state of Louisiana. *That's* what I know."

"Shhhhhh. What are you—"

"Oh, darlin' "—Marietta winking at the big man to her left who was working on his sixth Dixie, but talking to Chéri—"don't you even know when I'm joking?"

Suddenly Chéri perked up. "Would you look at that?" she said, pointing past Marietta's shoulder.

"What?"

"Is that Paul?" Pointing at a hugely fat man getting up from a table covered with what looked like the wreckage from a Tulane football banquet.

"Prudhomme? Honey, what would he be doing eating somebody else's cooking? I swear to God, I think you've lost your senses. Besides, that man idn't big enough to be Paul. And where's his cane?"

"In the movie," said the tattooed man around a gargle of Dixie.

"What?" Chéri batted her eyes.

"He played Paul in the movie."

"What movie?" Now Chéri gave him a little cleavage. She couldn't help herself, would flirt with anything that was warm and could crawl.

"*The Big Easy*. You see that movie?"

"That's right!" said Marietta with a snap of her fingers. Then waggling them in Chéri's face. "That's the man played the chef in Tipitina's. *Looks* like Paul. But anybody could see it *ain't* Paul."

"Well, fuck me very much," said Chéri, who didn't like to be wrong.

"Well, ma'am, I'd be happy—" grinned the tattooed man with the Dixie.

"Not you, honey." Chéri took back her cleavage, giving him her shoulder instead, then slid her eyes to the TV that was always on up behind the bar. "And who you think *that* looks like, sugah, you so smart?"

"Who?" Marietta was trying to figure out if she was mad at Chéri or not, flirting with that old boy when she ought to be flirting with her.

"You think that man talking on the TV looks like the man you married to? Your about-to-be-dearly-departed Maynard?"

"Lord, would you look at that!"

Sure enough, there on a cable station was Sister Nadine in a long silver robe, her blond hair damp and streaming down around her shoulders, shaking that tambourine, singing and shouting those songs. And there beside her, red-faced and sweating through last year's seersucker suit, was Maynard.

"I'll tell you what," Maynard was saying, his eyes sliding back and forth like he wasn't quite sure which camera was rolling, but going on ahead anyway with his volume turned full up, "you're gonna see the show of the century you come out to Lake Shore Park tomorrow at one P.M. sharp."

Marietta stared at Chéri. Her lover stared back. The air between them was a blaze of blue. Then Chéri waved her orange fingertips in an easterly direction.

"Right over there, May-retta," she said. And she was right. Lake Shore was about a half mile away.

"Shhhhhhh."

MAYNARD: "Now, I know you've seen Mardi Gras. And you've seen the Superdome. And lots of you have been to *New* York and farther. Lots of you've seen the wonders of the world."

CHÉRI: "And some of you have seen England, France, and little girls' underpants."

Marietta slapped her on the arm. "Would you hush!"

"But you ain't seen nothing till you have seen Jimbo King and his Fabulous Flying Lawn Chair. Brought to you by Dupree Productions."

"The *what?*" said both women close up in each other's faces.

Then Marietta started laughing.

"Hush. Now *you* hush," said Chéri.

But Marietta couldn't.

"What you are going to see if you come, and I hope you all *do* come out to Lake Shore tomorrow, is something you've never seen before. The mayor's going to be there. The governor's gonna be there. Representative David Duke is going to be there."

"Owwww. Owwww," Marietta howled. "Is he going to wear his designer bedsheets?"

"Quiet down, lady," said the man who was now intrigued by Nadine and Maynard. "George, cut up the volume on that thing."

"There is no telling who else might fly in for the event from Washington." Maynard giving it the big wink, lowering his voice to his idea of real sexy.

Marietta howled. "Would you listen to that? Chéri, honey, I think he's been watching too much Jimmy Swaggart." Noticing at the same time how easy it was for a fat boy like Maynard, get a little worry, little bad times on him, look all raggedy-assed.

"Lady! Would you hush!" The tattooed man was definitely pushed.

"You all really ought to come." Sister Nadine was throwing in her two cents now. "Sister Nadine's gonna be there. It's gonna be something. Day before Easter, man rising into the sky on a blast of hot air."

"You can say that again," cried Marietta. "Jesus Christ and Jimbo King. Can you believe it, Chéri?"

"Gonna fly out over the lake, over the Gulf, why, once he gets over the Gulf Stream, there's no telling where this boy's gonna stop." Maynard was holding one arm up in the air toward the heavens.

Marietta for sure couldn't stop. Kicking her feet against the bar. Pounding her little hands. Her breath coming short.

"May-retta, honey, are you all right? Is your asthma—?"

"I can't help—I can't—oh, God, get me out of here. I've wet my pants."

"May-retta!"

Thirty-eight

●

"I wish my daddy could have lived to see this."

Jimbo was standing in the middle of his living room in front of the supercolossal TV he'd bought himself last week with Maynard's hush money. Talking to himself, watching Maynard Dupree, attorney-at-law, man-about-town, bon vivant, and generally speaking a pillar of New Orleans society and the bi'nis community talking about him, *Jimbo King*, like he was something. Like he wasn't a redneck. Nor your white trash. Like he was free, white, and twenty-one.

Though he wasn't so sure about this Dupree Productions.

He hoped Maynard didn't think he was gonna take a piece of *his* action when the movie and the TV people came 'round, wanting to move him to Hollywood.

Nuh-uh. No way, son.

Jimbo wishing he'd had a picture taken of himself, Maynard could of been showing it to the folks.

Wait a minute! Why didn't Maynard take *him* along? Put *him* on the TV this evening with Sister Nadine?

Jimbo stepped over a few feet so he could check himself out in the mirror—the one with the seashell frame he and Teri had brought back from their honeymoon in Tarpon Springs. Full face. Gave himself a big grin. Good teeth. His mama had always said that was the one thing she was grateful to her daddy for, he'd passed along his teeth. Now Jimbo had 'em too. They wouldn't even need to cap 'em when he went for his screen tests.

Swiveled his head. Profile. He had a good strong chin.

He always hated that, when guys turned sideways, you could see they had wimpy chins.

His was like Michael Douglas's. Michael Douglas in *Fatal Attraction.* *That* was a chin.

He stepped back from the mirror. Sucked in his gut. Not that there was much. He was still hanging in there.

Hoped Maynard didn't think he was gonna steal from him.

What the hell? The phone was ringing, Hollywood already trying to find him. He wondered if he ought to get his number unlisted. People gonna start bothering him, trying to sell him cars, boats, condominiums.

He picked up the phone. Nothing. Then he realized it was the doorbell.

He threw the door open with his best smile.

"Hi, Jimbo."

It was Teri!

You could have knocked him over.

"Honey!" Jimbo opening his arms wide. "Come on in."

"I saw them talking about you on the TV."

He grinned. "That was something, huh? I bet you never thought you'd see that." And then he found himself giving her a big hug. And she felt good. What a *surprise!* that feeling.

"Where's Doctor?" he asked, suddenly really wanting to know. "Where's my baby?"

"He's right here." She reached back out the door and brought in the little boy.

"You left him on the *porch?*"

"Just for a minute." She looked up at him with tears in her eyes. "I didn't know if you'd let us in."

"Let you in? Let you in? Somebody could have *stole* him!" Then with the suddenness with which people get swept up with ol' time religion, with the fervor of the Lord's sending a clear message, Jimbo got it. Loud and clear.

This was the Lord's way of telling him, now hadn't Teri been praying for him all this time, he knew she had, and it was a sign that his Big Moment, or Pre-Big Moment, came on Sister Nadine's show—that blessed angel, Teri used to call her—Teri's favorite show. It was a sign. A divine convergence, what they called it, like when hot air and cold air and moisture and all that other shit comes together out in the Gulf, out where he used to work on the rigs, thought he was going to make his fortune, grunting, sweating, but no way, José, *this* was it.

And Teri, his blessed angel wife, and their little angel baby, had made it possible. And, praise the Lord, here they were again. His own little family.

"You been putting your hands on the TV?" he asked her, but knowing the answer in his heart. "Watching the show live in the afternoons?"

"Uh-huh."

"Bless you, Jesus!"

Teri gave him a funny look, like she wasn't sure she was hearing what she was hearing. Then she said, "That Mr. Dupree made you sound like you were really something, didn't he?" looking at him the way she used to from under her eyelashes. When she wanted to do it. Then running one finger under her gold necklace kind of nervouslike, like on the other hand she still wasn't sure she ought to be here. Wasn't sure he wouldn't hurt her.

He wuddn't ever going to hurt her again. He was as sure of that as he'd been of anything in his life. Jimbo fell to his knees.

Teri grabbed hold of him. "Honey! What on earth—you having some kind of fit? Here, let me—"

"No way, sugarplum." He had his arms around her knees now, her chubby knees he loved so much. He couldn't imagine that he'd ever felt any different.

It was the miracle of Sister Nadine, hands on the TV, just like Teri had always said.

"No way, baby. This ain't no fit. This is the power of the love of the Lord."

"Oh. Oh. Oh. My goodness." Teri reached into her bag, pulled out her little Hallmark datebook, started fanning herself with it, she felt that faint.

Doctor, sitting on the floor, was just staring at them. He always was the best angel baby.

"I just don't know how we're ever going to thank Sister Nadine and that Mr. Dupree," Teri said.

"Well, I do."

And he did. For now, like it came to him in a flash, Jimbo saw that if he wanted this flying lawn chair thing to come together, now that it had been given the blessing of Sister Nadine, which was just like it being blessed by the Lord, well, he was going to have to mend the error of his ways.

He was going to have to get Maynard Dupree on the phone right this very minute and tell him that he'd been shucking and jiving him all this time.

Let Maynard know not a blessed thing had happened.

Maynard hadn't had nothing to do with what went down with that Church Lee. At least, not as far as Jimbo knew. And for sure, Maynard hadn't hired him to do nothing, not like he'd led Maynard to believe.

Far as he knew, Maynard had gone straight home, drunk as a skunk that evening. Just like he had.

Drunk as a skunk and probably did lots of things he'd be ashamed of, especially with this new lease on life the Lord had given him, but he sure as hell hadn't been anywhere near the vicinity of St. Charles and pore old Church Lee.

He reached for the phone.

"What you doing, honey?" Teri said, still kind of nervous in her voice.

"Making amends, sugar. Making amends is the best way I know in the world to buy yourself some insurance."

"Insurance? Life insurance?"

"Happiness insurance, sugar. We about to buy ourselves a happiness guarantee."

"Held up the Pic'N'Pac on Coliseum? Why do you think he did that?"

"Sam, we're not dealing here with a rocket scientist," Harry said. "You know what I mean?"

"Well, you want to hear one that'll match that? Are you sitting down?"

"Lay it on me."

"You're not going to believe whose son I think he is."

"Mother Teresa's."

"Very funny, Zack. Though—"

"Possibility?"

"No. That just made me realize why I never asked her last name."

"Whose?"

"Sister Nadine's."

"I'm not following you, Sam. Want to run that by me again?"

"I never asked her last name because with people like that you don't. Sister Nadine. Mother Teresa. Madonna. Cher."

"That's an interesting assortment. But what's Sister Nadine got to do with T & A or the price of rice?"

"Ida says she's Billy Jack's mother."

Two beats, then, "You're kidding me."

"G.T. and I are going to go over and see Nadine right now, talk to her about it. Maybe get a bead on where Billy Jack is and what he's been doing with his spare time. Especially with what you're telling me about seeing Maynard with her on TV. I can't believe that. Maynard and Jimbo and this flying lawn chair thing? Is this making any sense, Harry? Or is this just the way you all do things in New Orleans? Our number-one boy Maynard, we've never even talked with him yet, and now he's hooked up with Sister Nadine, who's the mother of Billy Jack —could you check that out and call me right back—and *furthermore,* G.T. came up with something I can't get out of my mind. You know I told you she made a point of how the guy driving the Buick was so short? And we *know* how short Billy Jack is. We *know* he's crazy. Stone cokehead, I'm sure. I bet he's got a record, you check that too. Or shall I do that? *Know* he knew Church. At least well enough to have a drink with him in the Pelican." Suddenly Sam realized there was no one on the other end of the line. She was talking to herself. "Harry? Harry?"

Thirty-nine

"I went back over to Patrissy's and leaned on Billy Jack's friend, the maître d'. Our boy's at the Andrew Jackson Hotel, 919 Royal," said Harry.

"Do you feel stupid, or what?" said Lavert. "Right in the goddamn neighborhood the whole time. Why didn't we lean on that guy earlier?"

"Forget about it. Just get there pronto. Meet you in front."

Sam and G.T. and Arkadelphia were all piled up together in the front seat of the ambulance.

"You gonna get us in so much trouble, G.T."

"Ark, I wish you would shut up."

The fat man was shaking his head, which made Sam, who was sitting on his lap, feel like she was resting atop a tidal wave.

"You can't just be running around town in this vehicle like it was your own," Arkadelphia said.

"Why not?" argued G.T.

"What if we get a legit call while we headed on this personal business of yours—with the sireen going? It ain't good."

"What if I told you we might be going to pick up a potential murderer?" G.T. countered.

Arkadelphia laughed, squashing Sam up against the dash. "And why would that be different from any other run? Half the folks we pick up been slashing and burning one another like they're working cane."

"What if I told you he was Sister Nadine's son?"

Sam could feel the disbelief rising up like gas from deep down inside the fat man.

"Harumph. Humph. I'd say you done lost your mind."

"Is Nadine your personal savior?"

"Don't be sacrilegious, G.T. You know that's the Lord's role. Sister Nadine is just his agent."

Like Otis Dew? But Sam knew better than to bring that up. "Like an angel?" she asked instead.

"That too."

Then, though she couldn't see it, she could feel Arkadelphia's mouth shut into a prim line.

"What if I told you we were going over to Sister Nadine's tabernacle?" G.T. kept pushing.

"I've been there before."

"What if I told you we were going to visit with her personally?"

Beneath Sam, Arkadelphia stopped breathing. She counted to ten, then pinched him.

"Could I get her autograph?" he squeaked.

"Hell, yes," G.T. roared, firing up the siren. "Just like those pictures of Jesus Christ with his John Hancock that radio station sends you from Laredo, Texas, you give 'em enough cash."

Arkadelphia reached for the microphone. Said into it, "Blue Oldsmobile, blocking our way up there, would you kindly move your ass, please, and thank you."

"They on their way up," Clothilde, the day manager at the Andrew Jackson, whispered into the phone.

Then she grinned at the vanishing backs of the two men. They looked kind of like those guys in *Lethal Weapon*. Except in this case, the big black one was cuter. (Her mama would drop dead if she knew Clothilde thought things like that—like she hadn't spent her whole life fighting that damned busing.) But Clothilde herself had always fancied *big* men and tried to be open-minded about their coloring. And this one was awfully big. Hmmmmmm. So maybe she hadn't been so smart—she could hear their feet running down the hall upstairs, but it would be too late, Billy Jack would have already disappeared out the back—hadn't been so smart calling him.

But that was their deal, hers and Billy Jack's. And he kept her in a lot of toot for holding up her end of the bargain, which she had just done. Which meant they were even.

So. When the two cop types came back downstairs, maybe she'd tell them where Billy Jack went.

Wuddn't but one place that little ninny ran when he was scared. She'd seen it happen more than once.

Straight home to his sugar tit.

Maynard was sitting upstairs in Nadine's special kitchen, where all the pies and cakes for the TV show were baked. He took another bite. Holy Jesus! There was nothing in the world could beat Nadine's black walnut cake for sweet and delicious.

Except Nadine herself.

She was downstairs in the tabernacle's auditorium, rehearsing with the choir for the Easter service. She had come home after that promo for Dupree Productions, the flying-lawn-chair business, jumped in the shower, jumped out, given her hair a shake, him a quick kiss, said, Have yourself a snack, baby, you looking kind of peaked. Which he was, he just didn't have her energy. But then, she didn't have *his* sins on her mind either, didn't have that Jimbo breathing down her neck. And now that big buck, whoever he was, warning him about Miss Chéri. Miss Chéri, indeed! Marietta's friend, not his. The same Chéri had been in the Pelican that night, when he'd said whatever he'd said had started this whole mess? Jesus.

"Excuse me, Mr. Dupree."

Maynard looked up. It was Dana or Dian or Dion, or whatever that girl's name was, was Nadine's assistant.

"Did you receive your messages, Mr. Dupree?"

She was always so cool she gave Maynard the creeps. "What messages?"

"Your secretary's been trying to reach you all day." As if it were *his* fault.

"Oh yeah?" Maynard's head reared up. Sally Jean never called around unless it was urgent. She especially wouldn't call him here. "What'd she say?"

Dana pulled a little notebook out of her pocket. "Mr. King has to speak with you immediately."

Oh, God. What now? That bastard Jimbo was never happy.

"Is that it?"

She looked down at the little notebook again. "Mr. King came by the office. She told him you're here and he's on his way over. She said a Mr. Washington had called too. She said he said you'd know him from the spider."

"The spider?"

"I'm merely reporting what she said, Mr. Dupree. I didn't ask her what variety." She gazed off into the middle distance as if she were privately amused. She always looked that way. Then offered, "Black widow, perhaps?" She gave him a whisper of a grin as if she'd said something terribly amusing.

Black widow, indeed.

Black.

Oh, Jesus. Black as in that humongous black person in the little car. That little Fiat. Little Fiat Spider. Mr. Black Person—Washington she'd said he called himself—in the Spider. Oh, shit.

That was it. That was absolutely-rooting-tooting-finally-the-last-straw *it.* That was all he needed, Mr. Black Person Washington following him, calling his office on top of Jimbo King barging in here. Never could tell what *that* peckerwood might do. Might tell Nadine all about Church Lee, ruin his chances with her.

And here he'd just decided that he was going to marry Nadine, had decided it while he was sitting eating her black walnut cake.

It was the only fitting thing to do, sort of a recompense for Church and all their bad blood and, truth be told, all the pain that business had caused other people. Why, everybody thought men were so tough, but he could still remember the look on Madeline's face that terrible day she'd run up on him and Church yelling about her out in front of the Pickwick. And Zoe. Poor Zoe. He'd felt heartsick about that little girl ever since. It was one of the things that made him so mean. Made him drink. Made him sometimes want to hurt people. Round and round went that little snotwad of shame about his selfishness, pinging off the walls of his brain. But now, *now,* because of Nadine, he'd seen the error of his ways. He had to. It was all closing in on him. He'd give Marietta her divorce, he knew she wanted it, wouldn't even put up a fight, wouldn't drag her through the mud like she thought he would, just give her and the kids their share, like an upstanding gentleman. He wondered if he'd ever see the boys again. Oh, God. Well, there was nothing for it but Do It Right. Then hope for the best. Dear Jesus, he was so sorry. He hoped some of Nadine's grace would rub off on him.

"Thanks," he said to the back of the retreating Dana, who'd been standing there drinking her cup of coffee and studying him. "Thanks a lot for the messages."

"You're welcome." Then she gave him a funny look.

Well, he never had been very nice to her. He'd try now. "How's the rehearsal going?"

She shrugged. "Fine. Everything's always fine when Nadine's doing it. Right on target." And then she made a little gun with her hand like she was pointing it at a bull's-eye. Her idea of a friendly gesture. Pulled the trigger. Pow.

And she was gone.

Alone, he felt the pit of his stomach rise up again. The black walnut cake felt like a load of lead.

What was he going to do if Jimbo came over? Why wasn't Jimbo satisfied with the flying-lawn-chair TV publicity? The man was always wanting more and more. And what the hell was it now with the big spade? What was this crap about Chéri?

Then he saw Dana pulling that little trigger in her hand. That was it! Being sorry for the error of his ways was one thing, *but* there was no need to roll over and play dead.

So Maynard did his fat-boy boogie, out of the kitchen, down the hall to Nadine's private suite. He reached into the drawer of the bedside table, where she kept the .38 he'd given her. He'd taken her out in the woods and taught her how to use it. He'd said, sweet baby, you keep this. You never know. No way a gorgeous woman like you can ever be too safe.

He'd *wave* that .38 at Jimbo, that's what he'd do, scare the shit out of him. Let him know he couldn't push Maynard Dupree around anymore. Neither him nor that Mr. Black Person Washington.

Billy Jack said to himself: Run down the back steps of the Andrew Jackson. Now up the back steps of Mama's place.

Nobody would ever look for him here.

Those bastards. The nerve. Coming to his rooms like that.

Besides. He'd gotten it early—her surprise. He could feel the diamonds in the cross burning a hole through his pocket right above his heart, almost causing him a pain. On Good Friday. That was fitting, wasn't it? Fitting time to give the cross to her too. No need to wait till day after tomorrow, Easter Sunday.

Lavert and Harry were plastered up against the wall of Beulah Land Tabernacle, trying to figure out their best shot, when G.T. drove up, her siren blaring full blast.

"What the hell!" Harry waved his arms. "Turn that goddamned thing off."

Arkadelphia lumbered out of the ambulance, brushing Sam off his lap as if she were a Kleenex he'd discarded and forgotten. "You could show a little more respect at the door to the Lord's house," he sniffed at Harry.

"Sorry," said G.T., speaking to no one in particular but giving the eye to Lavert.

Whose heart jumped like a startled deer. He wanted to run over and grab her up and tell her all about Lavert's and the dress she was going to wear and the food he was going to cook and the good times they were going to have forever and forever amen when he was brought back to the here and now by Harry and Sam. Standing in one another's faces.

Sam screaming: *"You* are supposed to be down at records checking out Billy Jack. I told you *I'd* talk to Nadine."

"Oh yeah? Well, what about talking to her little boy instead? We went by his rooms, he skipped. Headed over here."

"And what do you think we're going to find out, all of us barging in there like a SWAT team?" Sam flailed in Lavert's direction, ended up punching Harry in the chest.

"Hey!" Harry wanted to grab that arm and pull her close. Or throw her to the ground, *then* pull her close. A little wrestling would do this woman a world of good. "I guess you want to run this show too."

"You bet your ass."

He was right. She did. There were some times she just couldn't be a team player.

Harry threw both hands in the air. "Then take it, lady. It's all yours. We're out of here." He jerked his head at Lavert. "Come on, man."

Giving General Taylor a long, melting look, Batman followed his Robin.

Billy Jack stood behind the closed door up behind the baptismal. From the other side he could hear the choir singing "Are You Washed in the Blood of the Lamb?"

When first he'd thought of giving the cross to Mama, the picture in his mind was it would be private—just the two of them somewhere quiet. At lunch, maybe. But now that he was here, and there were all those people in there—well, why not? Wouldn't it be even better to make a *thing* of it? A presentation? A ceremony? Maybe he should have gotten her a crown—then it could be a coronation.

Well, but he hadn't. And he was here now. He closed his eyes and took a couple of deep breaths, trying to steady himself.

Now, here was his plan. He'd slide through the door, then he'd be way up in front of the auditorium and above all of them. It was like he'd be the centerpiece. And then—he hoped the big lights were on because they'd light him up and the diamonds would sparkle like sunshine— he'd hold the cross over his head. Or, maybe he'd hold it out in front of his face.

He tried it a couple of times, this way and that, practicing variations.

Arkadelphia and G.T. and Sam were still outside, standing by the ambulance.

"Arkadelphia, you stay out here," said Sam.

"No way. You told me I could get her autograph."

"Stay outside and watch for Billy Jack."

"I don't even know what he looks like."

"You most certainly do," said G.T. "He's the little blond dude who jumped out of the ambulance that day out at the airport and left us with all that paperwork they're still hocking us about."

"Oh. And what do I do if I see him?"

"Sit down hard on the siren."

Maynard, the gun tucked into his gut where it hurt, was sitting up- stairs in the balcony. He thought, now, if he was Jimbo, what would he do? Would he walk in the front door like an ordinary white man? Then Maynard remembered Jimbo in the cemetery, wiggling an empty boot, then jumping him, wrestling him to the ground. Naaaah. No way that bastard would just march in, then strut up to Nadine and say his piece, queer his deal with Nadine, get it over. He'd do something sneaky. Like what? Maynard stared at the choir while he was thinking, scanning their faces. But wait a minute! Who was that? It was Jimbo! He'd stake his life on it! Jimbo had sneaked into the choir and was waiting for him right there in the alto section. He could see him clear as day. That snake!

Sam whispered to G.T. as they slipped into a pew, "We'll sit right here and wait for her to finish." Up in the front of the huge auditorium, Nadine's back was to them, her long blond hair streaming. She was leading the choir herself.

"Okay," said G.T., "if that's what you think."

"You have a better plan?"

"I don't know. I don't like it in here," said the New Age voudou priestess. She sniffed the air. "There's something rotten in here. It stinks."

"*I* don't smell any—"

Billy Jack was in position now. In the middle of everything, but above it all. All he had to do was push the button, and the blue velvet curtain would open. All eyes would rise up, and there he'd be—right behind the baptismal tank. He and the diamond cross would be dazzling.

"Hey, Mama, Mama, here's your precious son with your Easter present," he'd sing.

"The odor of sanctity, maybe?" whispered Sam.

G.T. gave her a look. "More rotten than that. What are you going to say to this woman anyway?"

"Just you wait."

Then the singing stopped. The choir seemed to be taking a break.

Sam stood, started up the aisle toward the front. It was a long walk. "Sister Nadine," she called. "Sister Nadine."

Nadine turned, hands on her wide hips.

Behind and above the choir loft, beneath a huge cross hanging on the front wall, a curtain slowly slid open to reveal the baptismal tank sunk flush into a niche in the wall like a giant aquarium.

On a narrow walkway behind the tank stood Billy Jack.

"Hey, Mama. Mama."

Nadine pulled her eyes away from Sam and turned back. For a second she was blinded by the glitter of something bright.

Harry and Lavert had crept up beside Billy Jack on the walkway. "Fly!" barked Harry from a crouch.

Lavert flew. He grabbed little Billy Jack, lifted him way up, then, holding him by the shoulders, dunked him into the cool baptismal water.

From the auditorium below you could see through the glass on the front side Billy Jack churning his little arms and legs, his blond hair waving like seaweed. Lavert held him under for a slow count of five, then dragged him up, sputtering. The diamond cross drifted slowly to the bottom.

Maynard had run down the balcony stairs, out the front door, and around the side of the auditorium. As he opened the side door, he realized the choir had stopped singing. He raced down hallways, turning right, turning left, to the door of the choir loft. He had to hurry before Jimbo got away!

"Leave my baby alone!" cried Nadine. "You're going to drown him! Help! Help! Lord Jesus, somebody help me!"

Sam thought she was going to have a heart attack. Men! Always cops and robbers, cowboys and Indians, jumping into the fray, guns, bazookas—"Look at that!" she turned and yelled at G.T. "Would you look at that? Harry says he's leaving and now—"

Billy Jack stared up into the huge black face pressed right down on his, the face of death.

"Talk, motherfucker," the face said.

"What? What?" he stuttered, then realized it wasn't Mr. Death, it was Joey the Horse's man—though maybe they were one and the same. But what did he want? Oh, hell, why pretend? He knew, all right. He'd known down in his gut since that terrible day at the airport when Joey had sicced the jig on him. Joey knew he was opening other territories, dealing with the spics, getting himself squeezed by the DEA. But it was all Frankie Zito's fault. Frankie wouldn't ever let him near Joey. Wouldn't let him tell Joey how he *really* was a made guy. He bet if he ever had gotten close to Joey he could straighten all this mess out. Joey'd be glad to let him be one of *them.* Now it was too late. Now he was going to die. He knew he was going to die. Billy Jack's mind raced.

"It's confession time," said Lavert in his very baddest voice.

Joey's man was right, thought Billy Jack. Absolutely right. It *was* time to confess, right here on the edge of a watery grave.

But where to start?

And then he was drowning again.

* * *

"Let him go! Let him go! Let him go!" Nadine was screaming. The choir was screaming. Sam was screaming.

G.T., on the other hand, thought Lavert was doing a right nice job. She liked men who took charge. Forget all that dicking-around shit.

"Why'd you run away?" Lavert asked.

"When?" sputtered Billy Jack.

"At the airport that day?"

"I—I—I was afraid."

"Afraid of who?"

"Afraid of you. Afraid of Joey."

Lavert laughed. "And now you know you were right to be."

Maynard felt like he'd stepped into the middle of a bad dream. And in the dream was that Mr. Black Person Washington, who'd been driving the Spider, who'd warned him off Chéri. Now he was drowning Nadine's son in the baptismal tank. What the hell?

"How do I get up there?" Sam was standing right up on top of Nadine now, screaming in her ear, pointing at Lavert and Billy Jack. And Harry. That goddamn Harry.

"I'm going to kill you!" she shouted up at him.

Billy Jack gasped like a tired fish. He was dying. He knew he was dying. Maybe he was already on the other side. But, no, he could still see his mama. She was standing down there, so pretty, with—why was *she* here? That curly-headed woman he'd seen with Zoe?

Now somebody else was yelling in his ear. "How did you know Church Lee? We know you mugged him. Why did you kill him?"

Who was *that?* Billy Jack could hardly see. Man standing beside Joey's man—with lots of curly hair, wearing a raincoat. Was it raining? It was awfully wet, he knew that.

Jimbo's ears perked up at Harry's question. Church Lee? Church Lee! He could tell them plenty about what happened to Church Lee. Or, rather, what hadn't. Now, where the hell was Maynard? And what the hell was going on here? It looked like one of those crazy art films. That little blond guy popping up and out of the water in the baptising tank like one of them little ducks. And Maynard nowhere to be seen. But he didn't think Maynard's old secretary would lie to him. She'd said he was here, so he was here. Now all Jimbo had to do to tell him the good news was to find him.

Sam was up in the baptismal, up in their faces. "Lavert, let go of him."

"Why, yes, ma'am," he said, "I'd be happy to." Giving her his best grin—like an egg-sucking dog pretending he was innocent. Knowing all the while from the way he was thrashing around that Billy Jack couldn't swim.

"Maynard, I know you're in here." Jimbo was yelling from where he was now, hanging out over the balcony railing. Saying, " 'Scuse me, ma'am," to Nadine, who swiveled her head up at him like he was another piece of fresh hell. Trying again—"Maynard Dupree, come out wherever you are, I've got something mighty important to tell you. Yo! Maynard Dupree!"

Lavert was holding Billy Jack up by the hair of his head. "I do believe I saved his life," he said.

"Try it," Harry said to Sam.

"You've lost your mind," Sam spat out.

"Go ahead. Ask him the big question. I think his pump's primed now."

What the hell? She leaned over to the miserable little bastard. "Tell us about Church Lee."

"Where? When?" Billy Jack sputtered. His lips were a little blue.

"At the Pelican."

"We were just having a drink."

"After you tried to mug him?"

Billy Jack attempted a nod.

Lavert growled, "Speak, boy. Speak."

"Yes!"

"What were you talking about?"

"Nothing."

"What do you mean nothing?"

"Nothing."

"Dunk him again," Harry said.

"No!" Sam cried, but too late.

"Talking about killing him! Killing Church Lee!" The words spurted out of Billy Jack when he could breathe again.

Sam looked at Harry. Harry looked at Sam. He gave her a wink, said, "Method's a little crude, but works like a charm, seems to me."

Maynard was determined to kill Jimbo. Where was that son of a bitch? He looked up at the balcony, where his voice had come from. Was he up there the whole time? He couldn't have been. He *knew* he saw him in the choir loft. But now Jimbo was *up there* shouting his name right out like that in the temple of his beloved Nadine. Come to show him up. Come to ruin his scene. After all he'd done for him. Given him money. Set him up with his crazy flying lawn chair.

Maynard clenched the .38 in his right hand. Maybe what he ought to do was jump up and save Nadine's son from Mr. Black Person Washington. *That* would set him up with her. No, first things first. Now it was Maynard Dupree versus Jimbo King—to the death. He wasn't going to screw up like he had with Church Lee all those years ago, the duel under the live oaks at dawn. He'd learned his lesson. He'd get it over with. Now. Clean.

"What do you mean—killing him?" Sam wanted Billy Jack to be more specific.

"He said he wanted to die. Said he was broke. It was all over. But he wanted his family to collect on his insurance."

"So why didn't he just die?" Harry growled. "Your story's not making sense, little man."

"I don't know, I don't know! I didn't even know who he was then!" Billy Jack screamed.

Harry rolled his eyes at Sam. "So what was the plan?"

"He told me about what time he'd drive home that night from the hotel. What route he'd take. I didn't want to use my car, so he got me that old Buick with no tags."

Sam raised her eyes to Harry's, then back to Billy Jack. "Where'd he get the car?"

"I don't know!"

Lavert shook him.

Then: "Off some old lady. Said she was dead. Said she was a patient. Said he'd never registered it again, so it couldn't be traced."

"And then?" Harry was impatient to cut to the chase.

"He told me to follow him from the hotel. Somewhere along the way he'd stop, and I'd do him."

"So you did," said Sam.

"Yes! I did it! I had to!" Tears rolled down Billy Jack's face, mixing with the baptismal water.

"Why?" asked Sam.

"Because he knew who *I* was. I didn't know who *he* was. But he knew who *I* was. And he said he'd tell my mama I mugged him. It was an accident I mugged *him*. But Mama'd be mad at me again."

Sam's shoulders slumped. Billy Jack's mama. Nadine. Church's girlfriend. Nadine. Maynard's girlfriend. Nadine. It was shades of the feud between the two men over Madeline Villère all over again. Except this time Church lost and here was Billy Jack.

Church, who was bust and wanted his daughter, rich as Croesus, to collect on his insurance, set up his daughter's supplier, the son of *his* girlfriend, to kill him. Dear God!

"Jesus!" said Lavert, and dropped Billy Jack into the holy water.

"You didn't do it, Maynard!" shouted Jimbo, leaning way out over the balcony now. "Can you hear me? I made it all up. You didn't kill Church Lee! I didn't kill him either. I don't know who killed him."

"You son of a bitch!" screamed Maynard from the choir loft.

"Maynard!" Nadine cried, whirling. *"You* killed Church?"

Maynard took his best shot at Jimbo, but he was out of practice. The bullet ricocheted dead smack into the middle of the glass front of the baptismal tank—which exploded.

Torrents of water gushed down into the choir loft—along with Billy Jack, who landed atop Maynard Dupree, knocking them both cold.

"Billy Jack! Maynard! Billy Jack! Oh, Jesus!" Nadine wailed as she raced up to her two men, only to slip and fall in the tide.

"He didn't do it!" Jimbo yelled from up in the balcony. "He didn't!"

"Who didn't?" Sam screamed back, wanting to make sure he wasn't talking about Billy Jack.

"Maynard Dupree! I just made him think he'd put me up to killing

Church. He couldn't remember because he was so drunk. Neither of us did nothing!''

Sam wasn't so sure about *that*, and she turned to tell Harry, but both he and Lavert had somehow (had they flown?) gotten themselves down in the snarl of water and glass and bodies that was Maynard Dupree and Billy Jack.

Harry was gently slapping Billy Jack, whose right arm was crooked at a very peculiar angle. Lavert was applying the same technique, though not so gently, to Maynard Dupree.

Arkadelphia, who'd gotten tired of waiting out in the ambulance, bustled up the aisle with the white pebble-grain Bible, his name inscribed on the cover in gold leaf, that his grandmother had given him on the day he was baptized. He carried it in his ambulance kit in case of emergency. "Sister Nadine," he called. "Sister Nadine, I am such a fan of yours. Could I trouble you to autogr—"

"Get *away* from me!" screamed Sister Nadine.

"Well, I never!" Arkadelphia puffed up.

"Never mind," said G.T., rising from where she'd hit the deck between two pews as soon as she'd seen Maynard's .38. She patted Ark on the arm. "Never mind. That little bastard's *ours*, bubba. After the police come and do what they're gonna do, we're taking Billy Jack Joyner into hospital lockup in *our* ambulance, and I want you in the back sitting on him, get *him* to autograph your Bible as well as that paperwork we got outstanding from *last* time we picked him up. You know what I mean?"

Forty

Sam propped up on an elbow, smiled her pretty smile, and said, "Play it again, Harry."

So he did.

It went like this:

I thought I knew how angels flew
Till you stepped off the plane
Toting all my dreams
In a carryon. Your smile
The end to all my pain.

I'd dreamed so long and prayed so strong
That love would come my way
But Friday eve till Monday morn
Were terrible nights and days

So I went out to the air-o-port
Down the long ramp
Laid my head on the tarmac
Said, Big plane, squash me flat,
I ain't going back, ain't going back
To that old misery, no way, Jack.
And there you were
Sashaying off that plane.

Saying: What you doing's wild, child
Making up new rules, fool
Gonna give your curls a whirl
'Neath this insane plane.

Come fly with me,
Don't die on me,
Streak the sky with me,
My love.

Who could resist a deal like this?
I jumped up on your wings.
Said fly me high
Oh my oh my oh my oh my
Waited my whole life
Who knew it could be so easy?

Oh, I thought I knew how angels flew
Till you stepped off the plane. . . .

"I like it a lot. It's come a long way," she said.

He rolled over, traced a finger across her breasts, naked under the sheet in his big brass bed, the one he'd run out and bought after the first time he'd heard Dylan sing "Lay, Lady, Lay." Hoping somebody like Sam would come and sprawl herself across it.

There you go, he said to himself now. Nothing like the power of positive thinking.

"Glad you like it." He grinned.

Sam looked around. On his bedside table sat a jumble of dishes and spoons. She remembered something about stopping at the all-night A&P on the way here last night for chocolate ice cream. In case of an emergency, Harry had said. Her lacy underwear made a small pile on a rattan chaise. She remembered that part better than the ice cream. Harry had undressed her *very* slowly. Folded things *very* carefully—at least up to a certain point. Your mama did a nice job on you—she remembered saying that. It was the last thing she said for a while you could quote in a family newspaper.

"Not bad for a kid," she said now.

"What?"

"I said for a kid you do pretty good work."

"Not bad yourself for an old broad." He reached over and grabbed a handful of her, his mouth on hers. Showed her he hadn't forgotten how quickly they found what they were looking for last night, the sweet fit.

After rerunning a few moves she wouldn't mind getting real used to, she said, "I didn't plan this."

"Well, I'm glad I did."

She punched him. "Scheming all along to get me here?" As if the thought had never crossed *her* mind.

"No, now that you put it that way. I kept thinking it would be upstairs at the Royal O. Or maybe a room at the Maison de Ville."

"Yeah. Uh-huh."

"You think I'm kidding?"

Sam leaned back against a pile of pillows and stretched long and lazy. Feeling like she did today, she'd happily listen to any kind of nonsense. "Give it to me from the top."

He strummed the chorus of her song on his guitar, saying, "Well, first I was going to take you to lunch at Galatoire's."

"Not bad. And what were we going to eat?"

"Oysters, for starters."

"Then—"

"Shrimp remoulade."

"And—?"

"And then a bunch of other stuff, and after coffee I was going to waltz you into one of those hotels."

Sam laughed. "I love it. Did you have some sort of line in mind—'That was good grub; now let's go make love'?"

"I never quite worked it out that far till last night."

He reached over and gave her a big snuggle. She gave him one back. And then there was some other sweet silliness. Finally, he said, "Well, it worked, didn't it?"

"What worked?"

"We ended up here, didn't we, after the cops came, G.T. and Lavert threw Billy Jack in G.T.'s ambulance, drove him to the hospital lockup—"

"Boy, Ark was mad as hell Lavert pushed him out, so *he* could go with G.T., wasn't he?"

"Ark'll get over it. Then they booked Maynard—"

"You think that'll stick? Attempted murder?"

"Uptown lawyer against a redneck unemployed pipehandler? Are you kidding? No way. Bet Maynard's already home having lunch."

"You don't think he's out at the lake?"

"Now, why would he be there?"

"I thought he was the promoter behind Jimbo's flying lawn chair."

"Well, he is, or was, but I don't expect what with one thing and another he's going to—on the other hand, you know, I bet you're right. What time is it?"

Sam felt around under the bed, came up with her watch. "Could this be right? One o'clock? I've got to call the airlines."

"Do *what?*"

"Call about a flight. I've got to get home. Gotta get back to work at that damned paper."

Harry switched on the TV behind him. "Not today."

"I'm afraid so."

"But it's the weekend." He was reaching for any straw in the wind. "Jesus!"

"That's right. Jesus, Easter, Easter Parade. We do all that this time of year."

"No, no, look at that! I can't believe it."

Harry turned around. No, he couldn't believe she'd go home just like that. They'd only gotten started. He stared blankly at the picture on the TV screen. Then slowly the images began to make sense. Or not.

That looked like Maynard Dupree in a white linen suit with a pale blue shirt and a gold watch chain, every inch the southern politician, yelling "Up, up and awaaaay!"

Up stepped a woman, a redhead, could that be Chéri? It was Chéri in a tight white dress, or what there was of it was tight and white. She was cutting the last tether with a pair of silver scissors, and off flew Jimbo in his green and white striped lawn chair. The gray weather balloons bobbed like crazy. Jimbo let loose a rebel yell. The lawn chair soared out over the lake, headed out to the Gulf and the wild blue yonder.

"Who's that?" Sam asked, putting her finger on the screen.

"Holy shit, that's Joey! The one with his arm around Chéri?"

"And those little kids?"

"Must be Maynard's. Yep, that's Maynard's wife, all right."

"Is that fat blonde with the screaming baby who I think it is?"

Harry squinted at the screen. "You bet. That's old Teri. Just one big happy family. Good God!"

Sam had seen enough. She stood, slipped on Harry's shirt, stepped out onto the balcony, and inspected the cloudless blue sky. "It's a beautiful day. A great day for flying." Then she turned. "Too bad about the Lees, though, isn't it? No happy endings for them."

Harry threw an arm around her waist. "I think Madeline will get in touch with Zoe. Things'll get better."

"I hope so."

"Don't you think you ought to stick around for at least a couple more days? Say good-bye to all of them? To Ma Elise? Stay at least through the weekend?"

"Go to Easter services at Sister Nadine's?" She gave him a kiss on the cheek. "Think she'll preach, her son in jail?"

"Prob'ly. Boy's gonna need a lot of praying. And you could hang out a little longer with Kitty. Roll some eggs around the lawn."

Sam rumpled his curls, gave him a little push back through the balcony door, back toward the bed.

He gave her a wink, punched on a Preservation Hall tape. Allan Jaffe's tuba burped "Saints."

He took her hands, pressed them to his chest. He had lots of curls there too.

"After a while we can go on over to Galatoire's, grab some late lunch," he said. "Maybe see if Lavert and G.T. want to join us.

"Thought lunch was supposed to be *before*."

"Darlin', don't you know *order* don't make no never mind, not about some things. Not when you're having a good time." He was waltzing her toward the bed, whistling the opening bars of "Lay, Lady, Lay."